Man from Mt. Vernon

MAN FROM MT. VERNON

Burke Boyce

HARPER & BROTHERS   NEW YORK

TO MY DAUGHTER

Susan

FOR HER GIFT OF UNDERSTANDING

Contents

Acknowledgments

My deep thanks go to Miss Helen Eldridge, Librarian, and the staff of the City Library, Newburgh, New York, for their ready kindness in making research material available to me:

To Mrs. Thomas Smidt and the Misses Bertha and Marie Smidt for their patient audience and encouragement:

To Mr. Edward Trevorah for his ever-amiable support:

And chiefest to my editor, Elizabeth Lawrence, for the combining of patience, support, and ultimate wisdom that I have needed.

B. B.

Vail's Gate, N. Y.
1960

Man from Mt. Vernon

I

April, 1775

Job says there's no such thing as Earth's becoming
An easier place for man to save his soul in.
Except as a hard place to save his soul in,
A trial ground where he can try himself
And find out whether he is any good,
It would be meaningless. . . .

Robert Frost
A Masque of Reason

He had been in the saddle since predawn at four o'clock, riding through limpid gray and the sun's slow lifting, making the rounds of the fields on the home plantation, and the field hands and fishing wharf and sorting sheds, the young tobacco plants that stitched parallels in the long acres between fence rows, and the small, jaunty, sprouted wheat, seeing for himself the work in hand and what was likely to get done that day.

The rounds were completed now, hours of reining at alternate trot and walk, and he turned the head of his chestnut mare toward the house. The sun was well above the horizon, sugary over the Tidewater miles, a blob of honey, and a bountiful soundlessness ran on and on.

The mare tossed her nose, playing at the bit, well knowing the custom of this daily ride.

He patted her neck. "There, there, Betsy, have your canter." It would be canter, not gallop. He prized his horses too much to gallop them unless needful. The spurs he wore on his big boots were seldom used.

Slackening reins, he set himself practicedly for the mare's rollick, gather and swing.

At that moment he caught sight of the poacher. The man was crouched on the near side of a rail fence, down a little slope toward the Dogue Run, the fence at his back and a weave of honeysuckle vines at either side of him. The man knew he'd been seen. He was gripping a fowling piece.

A pressure of knees, a curt word, a tightening of leather, brought Betsy to a halt, dancing.

In the next moment he saw Jack.

The young fellow, afoot, out for an idle after-breakfast ramble probably, stood something to the right of the poacher and partway down the slope, hesitating, obviously trying to decide between ordering the man off the place and the menace of the fowling piece and the poacher's snarl. The pair of them were checked, each on his spot, frozen as in a tableau, and desperateness spoke from one and irresolution from the other.

Jack was his stepson—Jack Custis, turning twenty. Jack would be unarmed, of course. So was he himself. To carry weapons on secure lands had for half a century been an absurdity. But one of his giant rages took hold of him. He felt it flaming up. Poaching was plain thievery. There were laws against it. This man was a sneak, a burglar of game, a petty killer caught and daring to threaten Jack.

Betsy mare spun at his touch and he pricked spur for once, lengthening her to a rushing gallop down the slope. Her hoofs drummed like quick heartbeats, guided and steadied by his balanced sureness that made the force of his body one with hers. Together they arrowed down at the poacher. The man faced them in a paralysis of disbelief, raising his gun, lowering it again, and crouching deeper. The stubbled chin dropped, the mouth gaping.

Betsy swept him past Jack. He heard the shout. "Papa! He'll shoot you!" He kept headlong on.

Now he was at the poacher. He swerved to the side of him, pulling Betsy to her haunches. In the blur of his rage he had a glimpse of ugliness, made more ugly by a fumbling terror, a too late franticness of thumb to find and cock the gun's hammer. Then his arm swooped, and his hand took the man by the slack of the shirt front like the plucking of a weed and hoisted him off the ground; instinctively, without gritting or strain, for hand and arm could heave a folded camp tent two militiamen would have had to struggle with. Another spur to Betsy, a surge to the fence, and the poacher was heaved and went sprawling over. He dropped like a lithe Indian from Betsy's back and vaulted over after him.

The man had scrambled to his feet and run a few paces, and turned, and in a suddenness was straddle-legged, the fowling piece at his shoulder, hammer at cock. Instead of disbelief now, his face read murder.

Behind him, Jack's lungs emptied in a hoarse yell of sound. He scarcely heard it.

He lunged forward.

The trigger jerked, hammer and flint plummeted to the firing pan. The pan powder flared in a bloom of smoke. The aim was point-blank, a yard away. Trivial, in his wild fury. The man, not the gun, was his object. He didn't slacken.

The gun's charge failed. Damp from morning fogs, or hastily tamped. No shot came. Only a croak and curse from the poacher.

The lunge took him rough against the man. He knocked aside the half-clubbed stock with a swipe of his left arm, and sent his right fingers to a throat. His left fist smashed at jaw and cheek, his foot shot out in the frontiersman's wrestling trick that cuts an opponent's legs from under him. The gun thudded to the ground, and the man. The gun lay where it fell. The man tottered upright. His face was a soggy, pummeled bruise, and he grunted with pain. He made off, fast as he could, along the creek's muddy shallows, lurching and splashing water.

Jack was at the other side of the fence, wide-eyed.

"Papa—" he said, and could seem to find nothing else to say, so that the morning became suddenly more still.

He rolled himself back over the fence and the scent of the first honeysuckle blooms roiled around him and in his yet-unquenched fire of anger he somehow resented the stillness. It was as though he were being looked upon by nature—looked upon, and tested, and perhaps found savage and wanting.

He took Betsy's reins from her neck and looped them on the saddle— he never rode curb—and drew a breath that was more like a shiver for the raw anger that had eaten him. Yet the anger, as always with him, had been a kind of cleansing, a purification by fire. It burned away the tensions built up inside him.

Heavily, doggedly, he realized that he must now offer some excuse for his outburst; some excuse to the stepson who had been witness to it. Some excuse for his madness in a fight and his enormous temper. How could he tell Jack of the years gone by that had made him what he was? Of the years that had anvilled his temper to razor edge, leading slovenly, drunken soldiers on the Virginia frontier and seeing the brain-spattered answer, the corpses and roasted flesh, of Indian raids? He had made an effort to tell Jack. But Jack, as young men will, merely took him facilely as someone from the older generation. Jack had not walked Indian trails.

The morning was so peaceful that he couldn't think, with clarity, of anger. Nor explain it.

He said stiffly, "Well, Jack, what would *you* have done?"

"I'm not certain, Papa."

There was an odd look in Jack's eyes—as if the fury, only half abated, might turn on him. But there was thankfulness, too, and a glimmer, very slight, of adulation. The stepfather had done what Jack had been fearful of doing; but the stepfather had been mounted, the best horseman in the colonies and superbly strong. The look pinpointed and then burst crawling out from its center.

Jack had heard his—well, to be frank—his preachments to their guests last night. One of his preachments had been that the man who lost his temper was on the weaker side. Now he had lost his temper. And Jack was fitting words to actions. On the one hand he heard his stepfather temperate; on the other he saw him raw, fighting. With the cold nose of youth he was smelling out inconsistencies.

"If you'll keep your head against a king, why lose it to a ratty poacher?" the look said. Yet it also said that Jack had been afraid for him.

This had all passed between them within a short space of time. Both had a shaken feeling.

He gathered Betsy's reins in his hand. As the older, it was for him to make the first move.

"We'll get back to the house, Jack. Perch yourself behind."

He flung leg over the saddle again, boosted Jack to a sprangle just ahead of Betsy's rump, and they started off at a plopping amble. He felt the warmth of Jack's chest, now and then, against his spine and shoulders while they rode. It was an intimate and caressing feeling. He had hopes for his stepson. Had always had hopes for him.

He made a mental note, as they wound along the wagon path toward the house, to set a better guard against poaching on his property.

He swam in the river that day, toward noon.

The river could best be described as a gentle and even immensity.

He breasted out of it with a final kick. With one hand he mopped water from his face, with the other he clamped on the dock's stringpiece. The hands were large and strong. Shaking drops from his hair he clung for a breath. His hair was brown, the tint of an autumn forest, and hung to the base of his neck in wet strands that glinted ruddy in the sunlight.

The lift from river to dock was effortless, a sliding body in a seal-like twist that rushed cascading water from him, from lean torso and muscled thighs. He splashed with his feet, in a last playfulness as swimmers do, and then stood.

He'd swum in a pair of white cotton drawers that plastered revealingly to him now, skin color coming through soaked cloth, and he stretched to his height, skin tickling with the bite of the river in late April, and droplets shining down his height. The road they had to travel from the crown of his head to his soles was six foot three.

He luxuriated in a deep breath. Winter was gone, and he could swim again. A happier cleaning than from a bedroom basin. He'd swum so in the river for fifteen years.

"Bishop."

"Yes, sir?"

"Enough for today."

"Indeed, sir."

The wrinkled man, who was like an aged hickory ramrod, had a cloak for him. He folded himself in it.

The day was warm, nearing hot, and the river smelled of shore and tide. Its name, Potomac, was an Indian one, meaning River of Swans. But the swans were gone now, slaughtered by gunfire as civilization had spread. There were, instead, the boats of his fishery fleet—he'd seen them ready to set out that morning—gossamered in the mile from shore to shore and skewering down stakes for seines for the herring run. The run was due presently and he hoped it would be heavy, a haul to fetch a fat price. He wanted that fatness, for he was short of cash.

Not that the want was new. He had it with him most of the time. His cash—when he got it—came from payments of British shipmasters, sailing in British vessels from British ports. There had been a time when he traded everywhere, but that was forbidden now, and his credits went to London agents and were inked on London books. The credit, such as it was, was strangling, though his lands and fisheries were productive. He had tried his best; tobacco; wheat—the finest, he thought, in the colony of Virginia for flour—and herrings, barreled and shipped. But there was still the pinch of money. The pinch of law.

It was a pain in the belly of the colonies this last decade, and had caused vomit.

He set his face for his house and climbed the path.

"Bishop?"

"Sir?"

"Tomorrow morning at four. Tell Cully. Betsy mare."

"Yes, sir."

He strode up the rise.

In a hundred yards or so, the path leveled to a broad tree-set lawn, rounded but fairly flat.

He walked across the lawn. A man sat on the columned terrace of the house.

"Your indulgence, Major," he said, and went indoors.

Two guests were on the terrace when he stepped out again. The major and the major's wife. Their chairs were at the far end, behind the line of slender white columns. Bishop was talking to them. The old man turned as he came up, and gave him a half-guilty look.

"I think they know the story, Bishop," he said, and watched the old soldier's sheepishness, and the militant back fading past the house corner.

"Thank you for pleasanting him," he said, sitting down. He had put on dark blue coat and breeches, white waistcoat and white stockings. His shoe buckles were plain, his hair powdered and tied in a queue. "Bishop takes to anyone who was with Braddock."

"Yes. We had the march all over again," the major said.

The major's wife nodded. Bishop, her face announced, had taken liberties with female sensibilities.

The major didn't seem to notice. Possibly he was used to her face. "The stench of gunnery and the troops falling like logs, and the Indian yells," he said. "Especially the yells. Then Braddock with his death wound, and Bishop cradling him on the ground in that damned woods road, and Braddock telling Bishop to take service with you, that you'd care for him. Oh, Bishop is imaginative. We had it all."

"Including the bloodishness of that ambush," the major's wife said.

"Braddock was not ambushed, ma'am," he said. "We met the French head-on on the path to Duquesne, and killed one of their officers with our first volley. But the other officer split his men and Indians down our sides, and it became forest warfare, not European. We were a ripe carrot inside the tines of a fork. General Braddock had never met that kind of fighting. He was not ambushed, but pinned. And a man did what he could. Bishop stayed with his general, and has never forgotten."

"Who could forget?" the major said. "And your covering of the rear guard on the retreats."

The major fetched a sigh, ingratiating, out of the past. In Braddock's march against the French in the western lands he had led an independent company. Had fought well. Had done other fighting for his king— well, too—in the West Indies. Now retired on half pay, he had married a widow with money, as the colonel had, and had bought lands near the colonel's brother, beyond the Blue Ridge. He was a fatherly-looking man, full-faced, wearing spectacles. His name was Horatio Gates.

"Who could forget?" he repeated, when no one filled the pause. "Time passes. Twice ten years since then. We are slaves to age, sir."

"It's nature," his wife said. "No one grows youthful."

"If I'd joined you in your river swim just now," Gates said, "I'd have taken an ague. But you're younger than I by four years. I'm forty-six."

"Horatio, my dear, don't talk yourself into senility before your time," his wife said. "The colonel has been a frontiersman; he's used to being tipped into rivers. You stay out of them."

"Yes, my dear."

There was another pause: prickly, as when men are conscious of being slippered by a woman.

Mrs. Gates broke the silence. "When do you leave for Philadelphia, Colonel?"

"In a few days, ma'am."

"You'll put in a word for Horatio?"

"He's already promised us," Gates said. "Excuse me, my dear"—and he went on before she could interrupt—"What do you foresee for this, Colonel, now that you've made your speech to the Burgesses?"

There was a hint of envy; but only a hint.

"It wasn't a speech, Major. A statement of fact. I'm not a speecher. I leave that to Henry."

"To say that you'd raise a thousand men, subsist them at your own expense, and march them to the relief of Boston—that's a speech, sir. The best ever made this side the water."

"I felt it was needed."

"Damned better than Patrick Henry's liberty-or-death bit. Damned bombast. Though it could stir a mob."

"Henry's an orator."

"He's handled a musket?"

"Not that I know."

"We'll need more than orators, sir."

"For what?"

"For our independency."

"Oh, independency. Major, no one in his right mind is thinking of independency." He smiled, a smile that widened the pinkish, slightly pockmarked cheeks. "I hold for the new petition to the king."

"And if that fails—?"

"Then we may have to take steps. But I trust not."

They were talking politics. As they'd talked the night before. As everyone, now, in the colonies, was talking politics. Politics, and how much the colonies would endure, and where the end would be. For ten years, now, the king's ministry in London had treated the colonies as a money tree, something to be shaken for the profit to be got. The ministry was, in a cold approximation of the facts, logical. There had been the French and Indian War, a beating back of French infilterings and grabbings of the Ohio valley and the pioneer lands. The colonists were stronger for this war on the French, stronger for the spatter of shot and the red drip of scalp twenty years since. Washington had fought in that war. And

Gates. And now the ministry thought the colonies should pay for the war, since it had protected them. But the payments had been laid on in a crudeness and the colonies had not taken them kindly. Successions of royal acts had been passed, and hooted and resisted, then repealed. Other acts had followed, wisely or unwisely. The matter was growing to a chip-on-the-shoulder between king and colonists.

"Look, for example, to Boston port," Gates said. "Sealed up, garrisoned, cut off from trade as punishment for that tea dumping in the harbor—which was a mere protest against London's monopoly. It's a grim situation."

"It is," Washington said, and wished heartily that it were not. He wished, at the same time, that he could have been spared the Gateses' coming to Mt. Vernon. He had sufficient to trouble him as it was, being a delegate to the Congress again.

Mrs. Gates spread her fan with a definitive motion and said, "In such a case, Colonel Washington will not be blind to your record, Horatio." She was a woman with straight, thick eyebrows and a rather mannish cast of face. She skittered her fan a little more than was necessary in the slight but soothing breeze. She said, "The only officer among us who has led troops by royal commission. If there comes more disagreement between the king and Boston."

"Well, New York has refused the tea too, my dear," Gates said. He said, "You also forget Charles Lee."

"Lee?"

"He's led royal troops," he said.

"H'mph," she said.

"He has, my dear. And stands for our cause now."

"He's hardly a gentleman."

"Does it require gentlemen, love, to show a rebuke to the ministry?"

"H'mph," she said again.

Washington caught the twinging note. If matters came to a head, Mrs. Gates would want her husband in the forefront.

"I think General Lee is sincere," he said.

"Do you?" Mrs. Gates said, and turned a look on him. Whether the look was genuine or not he couldn't say. "Very well, we'll dismiss General Lee."

Gates produced a fluctuating cough. "I don't know Lee, myself. I've not met him." He peered toward the breadth of the Potomac and left his sentence rather in the air.

There was a kind of significance in his silence, and when he roused himself it was to say, "I'd supposed you would be more fiery, Colonel, after your speech. Unless you mean to compromise."

"That hangs on who would do the compromising," Washington said. "It takes a shrewd mind. I remember an Indian powwow once—" and he broke off, seeing the Gateses' eyes go blank. "Well, remembrances are cheap coin. I won't load you with them. But compromise is better than bullets."

"Will the Congress compromise?"

"I can't say, Major. It will probably send another petition for redress of grievances. That's one of the reasons for its being."

"Petition, Colonel? Yet you'd lead armed men toward Boston. And you've been reviewing the militia companies hereabouts."

"To show the ministry we stand in defense. We have our rights as Englishmen."

"You forget the Boston massacre," Mrs. Gates said. "That was no mere show."

"The massacre—if you wish to call it that," Washington said, "was Samuel Adams' child. A poor sentry badgered and forced into firing, and then riot. Our own colonial lawyers defended the soldiers at the trial and got them acquitted. No, Sam Adams can whip up the Boston mobs, but he can hardly incite the whole colonies."

He spoke confidently, wanting to feel confidence. On such a day as this it took an effort of his mind to think of mobs and garrisons.

He crossed his legs and pushed further back in his chair, trying to hint by his shift of position that he preferred not to have the dinner spoiled by military talk.

The south wind streamed over the lawn. The grasses were tender, and his trees were bursting at their branch tips. The river below and away fused to dull beauty, darkening to ancient copper on the mile-off opposite shore. He could feel the wind along his cheeks; see a glimpse of woodlot starred with dogwood and redbud; could enjoy, beside him, the solid walls of his house, hear the unhurrying slap of hammers pounding at the improvements he had set, bedrooms for space, for hospitality, and for his step-grandchildren when they would be born. Things to be a satisfaction to him, and a practicality. He'd put his heart to it for years, since marrying Martha and bringing her here with her two children. Had read maps and plans, talked with architects, talked with farmers, testing manures and trying out new methods, experimenting with crops and fields, laying shingles himself when his carpenters failed him, and building Mt. Vernon for his own. It was his sanctuary, his holy place. He asked nothing more than to live here, and love here, and die here.

If he turned his head he could see Belvoir, the home of George and Sally Fairfax. The Fairfaxes had been his dearest friends. Had welcomed him, had him at their home when he was a stripling, a sprouting adolescent of sixteen. Sally Fairfax had smiled at him, encouraged him, written to him in the letter-fashion of the day when he was officering foul-mouthed troops on the western borders. But the Fairfaxes were gone now, like the graceful swans of the river. They had sailed for England, to an inheritance.

Belvoir still stood, though, on the mild bluff beyond the Dogue Run.

"On the frontier and with the Indians," he said, "a steady firmness counts for much. The king is not entitled to put his hand into my pocket unless that pocket has a voice in the Parliament. The king will recognize that. He will see the firmness."

"Oh, it goes back to the Braddock time," Gates said, melancholy. The king is squeezing that cost out of us. Well, as I've said—my name, my small services—if there should be an eruption—"

Dinner must be ready. Washington was hungry. He said, as a finale, "Bring your name yourself, sir. The Congress would welcome you at Philadelphia."

Gates's face drooped. He looked to his wife. "As to that," he said, "coming to Philadelphia, I rather fear—"

Mrs. Gates's voice edged through. "You see, Colonel, Horatio isn't a Congress delegate. He must depend on those who have that honor."

Gates reddened behind his spectacles, and Washington wasn't sure how to answer. Mrs. Gates might have been using flattery, but her tone seemed acid.

He was glad that Martha came out to the portico just then.

"Dinner's when you wish it, George," she said. "Nellie has just driven in."

He rose to his feet and kissed her and offered her his chair. She was small, becoming a little plumpish now, bustling and efficient. She operated the domestic side of Mt. Vernon without a flaw. He'd never regretted stopping to rest himself, once, at her Virginia home, White House, when she was the young Widow Custis, meeting her there for the first time and lingering on for supper and through hours afterward; never regretted having brought her as his bride to the plantation he owned from the will of his half brother Lawrence and from buying, eventually, Lawrence's wife's share. Martha had joyed him from the beginning with her cloudless smile and milky skin, her silk-brown hair and the mystery of a widowhood for a man overripe for marriage in his late twenties. Sometimes, in his barer moments, he wished she were not so damnably concerned with everything that needed doing in their household. Yet if she had not been concerned the household would not have gone so beautifully.

"Yes, Patsy," he said. "We'll give Nellie time to catch breath."

"She stayed at their home to oversee the spring cleaning," she said.

She stepped back from him. She had the knack of taking in a situation at a glance, and she laid the glance on the Gateses. Saw how the major was flushed, and his wife large in her chair, a female spider jealous of her egg. "Mrs. Gates," she said, purposely chirruping, "you'll adore our Nellie."

"A Maryland girl, I've heard," Mrs. Gates said.

"And a sweet one. She's a Calvert."

"A who?"

"That's a Maryland name. Jacky met her in Baltimore—on his way to the college in New York. And then he left the college to marry her. They'll be here in an instant."

"I've also heard about leaving the college," Mrs. Gates said. "We do get some bits of talk beyond the Ridge. We're not quite cut from the social world."

They smiled at each other.

Washington and Gates said nothing. Gates was cautious and Washington put on a host's mannered look. They were not eager to man the bark of talk through the reefs of feminine shoals.

"Jack must be a truly privileged boy," Mrs. Gates said.

"He is," Martha said—adding in a voice of satin—"to get Nellie."

"My dear, I've no doubt."

"We had our—" Martha darted a glance at her husband—"our discussions about the marriage. But we agreed. Jack wanted it."

"Every nineteen-year-old wants something," Mrs. Gates said in pulpit tones. "It usually includes a pairing."

"Jacky will be twenty now," Martha said, her voice like smooth molasses. Then, because this might seem an illogical retort, she said, "I give him his way, I know. He's the one child I have left. He's my world."

"Your world," Mrs. Gates said. She rather drew out the words. Her eyebrows lifted, and she let her eyes move to Washington—resting them on Martha's second husband merely long enough to make a questioning point. "Ah, yes, your world," she said.

Martha didn't give her the satisfaction of pretending that she hadn't seen. "Except for my dear George, of course," she added.

"Of course."

With that, Mrs. Gates achieved a curt weighing between the enigmatic and the sympathetic. She had spoken sympathy the afternoon before, when she and the major had reached Mt. Vernon, and she thought that was all that was necessary. Martha Washington had lost a daughter recently, in a tragic way; a girl of sixteen, carried off by a fit of epilepsy that had brought death within minutes. But loss was loss. If Mr. Custis' widow was still suffering from the blow, Mrs. Gates also had her own woes—or so she felt.

Voices came from the hall. The dinner would be soon.

As if afraid she had gone somewhat too far, Mrs. Gates said, "The colonel's so good to speak for Horatio. Not that we want to be importunate."

"My dear," Gates said protestingly, "you make me sound mercenary." And he put in a phrase, which he obviously liked, "My heart's in the cause."

"It's your due, Horatio," she told him.

Then Jacky and Nellie were with them on the portico, and brought the change of mood that young people carry where they go, like a scattering fountain whose drops fall on the olders around the rim, who still remember, and catch what they can of the bubbling elixir.

Everyone was cordial.

Major Gates congratulated Jack on his marriage and kissed Nellie, and Mrs. Gates turned gracious. "A pretty girl—so pretty. Mrs. Washington, you never told me. Nellie Custis, child, you quite take my heart."

It was the Virginia manner of doing things, the plantation manner. The manner of sociability, and informality, and a hospitable home.

The afternoon, the drowsy haze, the long-slanting sunlight were peaceful.

With a polite, murmurous ripple of voices they went in to dinner.

The *Maryland* Gazette

Over the roast, rare-done, and the glasses of wine, Washington listened to the table conversation. He was alert to turn it if Major Gates headed toward the brambles of politics. For although they all talked politics, Jack would laugh, and the Gateses' feelings would be riled. Jack laughed at a good many things other people took seriously. Jack was of the new generation, facing a breakup of his world, the loss of solidity, the folly and puling greed of his elders that would have their effect on him, emotional and physical.

Yet history, the ink-set pages of man, went on inexorably.

Jack would have to compromise, as all men had to.

Washington looked at his stepson, sitting beside Mrs. Gates. He had looked often enough before.

Well, every new age had to carve its pattern. He'd carved his own. And his mother had shipped him off to a half brother after his father had died, when he was eleven, because the pattern of his way was so iron against hers, even then. They had never been able to come to the grips of sentiment, he and his mother. He didn't know why.

Jack was neither rebel nor conformist. He was the most difficult of all, a mocker. But watching him at the table, Washington admitted at least that Jack had a gift for charm. It was a charm that even Mrs. Gates, making efforts to be pleasant, could not dampen. But he didn't know how Jack's growing would end. Didn't know if Jack stood for the youth sprouting in the colonies, if there would or would not be a breed of strength and expanding for the years ahead.

Opposite Jack, beside Major Gates, he saw Nellie. She was certainly pretty. Well born, well raised, her voice soft as Maryland and her smile reminding him of sunlight on a bay. A lovely and animated girl. Perhaps she would pierce through Jack's happy surface and guide him to something purposeful. Again, he didn't know.

Mrs. Gates's voice came sharp. "Oh, no, tomorrow morning. We must leave in the morning. We can't impose on you. You've so many visitors."

He heard Martha's protest, genuine but with a fringing of relief. He said, "Mrs. Gates, we like visitors. We're Virginians. Last week—or was it the week before, Patsy?—we dined alone for the first time in months." He met Martha's eyes, fixed on him from the bottom of the table. "A rare experience, I might say. Quite memorable."

Martha flushed, and Mrs. Gates said, "Tomorrow. In the morning."

"George," Martha said, "the Gateses will think we don't want guests."

"They know better than that," he said.

Mrs. Gates let the comment drop.

"Colonel," Gates said, "has General Lee been here?"

He stiffened slightly, hesitating. The redoubtable Charles Lee was a saturnine warrior from Europe's battlefields who had come to the colonies and written biting pamphlets against the king's ministry. Lee had descended on Mt. Vernon for the same reason as Gates: would Colonel Washington forward him with the Congress?

There was no point in evading, Washington thought. "Yes, he was here," he said, and added, for entertainment, "with his dogs. He had them into the dining room with him and threw them choice bits from the table. Patsy never turned a hair, though." He laughed. The laugh was full and wide-throated, deeper than his voice.

"Dogs?" Mrs. Gates said. "I'd have put them out."

"The performance was so comical," Martha said, "I just let them stay."

"You have more forbearance than I have."

"No, but I see the absurd side of things sometimes. It must be my Dandridge sense of humor."

Jacky leaned toward Mrs. Gates and said in a loud whisper, "Humor runs in her family, Mrs. Gates. Like a wooden leg. Mama thinks a bespanieled general is funnier than a bespangled one."

Mrs. Gates was surprised into a metallic titter. Martha drew her lips to a smile and beamed fondly at her son. "You see? The trait."

"Oh, but, Mama," Nellie said, "Jacky hasn't a wooden leg. I *know*."

They all laughed then. Nellie's sally was fair enough. And dinner had been good.

Washington passed the wine decanter around and began to crack almonds in his fingers.

Gates held his wineglass to the light, peering at the dark ruby color it reflected. "I suppose General Lee is willing to have his name considered by the Congress," he said. He said it mildly, and followed it with a tentative sip at his glass, which he put down with fussy care on an exact spot. "He's anxious for a military command, I suppose."

"Anxious! He's greedy for it," Mrs. Gates said.

"My dear—" he said.

"I told you he'd come fawning to the colonel," she said.

"My dear," he said, "the Congress may well prefer General Lee to me. I shall accept the least post with which it honors me." There was an undertone of deprecation, a hint of the long-suffering and unappreciated man.

Washington groaned inwardly. He'd hoped to avert this. He'd hoped the story of Lee's dogs would distract Gates's mind from Lee. He'd told the story purposely. But Gates wouldn't be put off.

"Oh, we've gone mostly to wheat," Martha was saying. "George finds that too much tobacco is a drain on the soil."

And Mrs. Gates was saying, "We're trying fruit. Something about the mild winds inland, and the rainfall," and Major Gates was nodding.

Smooth, so far.

He saw Jack's face—good looking, with straight bridge of nose that promised character one day, clear eyes widely set, neat, quick shape to lips and chin, an air of fun and indolence and assurance of getting what he wanted. He saw in his mind the contrast between him and Jack. At Jack's age he'd already been three years a surveyor on the frontier of the Ohio lands, a gun to give him food and a forest wilderness for roof. Jack had every comfort. At Jack's age he'd been working and eating and sleeping in a woodsman's deerhide shirt and leggings. Jack liked fashionable clothes (as his mother did) and wore them. At Jack's age he'd already been refused by two girls. Jack had a wife to satisfy the bedded nights. At Jack's age he'd been a poor relation, earning his way. Jack was secure in a home of his own and the rich estate he would get on his twenty-first birthday. Studying Jack, puzzling over him.

"I'm sure there will be esteem for you both," Washington said, "in the Congress," trying to be generous and impartial together. The choice of military leaders for the colonies wasn't his affair, and he dreaded arguing it now. He had not stomach for rivalries. From the corner of his eye he glimpsed Jacky's face. Jack was readying for some slap at the Congress and the military stir.

He glimpsed also, in time, the shape of Billy Lee in the doorway. Billy was his best Negro; shared the duty of body servant to him with the wizened veteran Bishop. The jet-black face was apologetic but important.

"Billy?" He signed Jack to keep still.

"Maryland *Gazette*, suh. For you. By express rider."

"Express?"

"Yas'uh. Rider went right on. Wouldn't stop to refresh."

"Let me have it."

He took the news sheet and unfolded it. The *Gazette* had been keeping him in touch with political doings in the general area of northern Virginia and Maryland, but it had never come to him by express rider before. As his eye took in the heavy-lettered heading and ran down the first column, he understood why it had been galloped to him now. The column was a report from Massachusetts. Some place called Watertown. He didn't recognize the name; but the other names, Lexington and Concord, were the key to the piece. Men had been killed there, in both those villages, Massachusetts militiamen and king's soldiers, in a foray from the garrison at Boston to confiscate colonial powder. Shots and a volley at Lexington, a skirmish at Concord, and the countryside up in arms and the king's troops dog-heeled back to Boston. The *Gazette* was racing the news to the southern colonies.

He read the whole item aloud, to a hushed room. He did not intend to be dramatic, but his voice overruled him. Finished, he dropped the news sheet beside the bowl of almonds.

No one moved. They were statues around the table.

No one spoke, until at last Martha said, "Oh, George," and this was a whispering sound.

Mrs. Gates was the first to get her breath.

"There!" she said shrilly. "I knew it!"

The words were sharp, almost gratified. Washington stared at her. She looked preening rather than horror-struck. He saw, as clarity gleams in a lightning flash, that she was expecting her major to be raised high by the whistle of these bullets in the north.

"Patience has given way," Gates said, blinking.

"It has," he said.

"New England fireworks," Jack said, sputtering.

"Jacky, that's no proper talk," Nellie said.

"All the country in for a merry day."

"Behave," she said.

"I am. They're who want to play."

"Jack, hush," his mother said.

He slid her a fleet, innocent look. He shrugged.

Gates had picked up the news sheet and peered at it through his spectacles. "It doesn't say which side opened first."

"The militia were marched against. They were on the defensive," Washington said.

"Yes, yes, clearly defending," Gates said.

"That will be a point for Dr. Franklin and our agents to make to the London ministry," Washington said.

"A somewhat blunted point by now," Gates said with a shake of his head.

"George, dear," Martha said, questioning, "the paper doesn't tell us. What were the militia trying to defend at Lexington?"

"The village green," Jack said irreverently.

"There were powder and provisions at Concord," Washington said. "Eight miles away."

"Just the distance for a musket shot," Jack drawled.

Nellie pinched his leg under the table and he subsided.

"They could have done as we're doing with the Williamsburg powder," Gates said.

"Perhaps," Washington said. Gates was referring to the Virginia colonists' powder collected in the magazine at Williamsburg. Governor Dunmore, suddenly and at night, had slipped the powder away under marine guard to a warship in the river. The town had poured into the streets and threatened to storm the governor's palace. But, as the phrase had it, cooler heads had prevailed. Dickerings with the governor were still going on for the return of the powder, but there had been no violence. That the colonial arsenals were claimed to be merely for civilian police purposes was a subterfuge recognized by everyone. "We can't say, Major. We weren't there."

"Adams and Hancock were there," Gates said, rustling the news sheet. "We know they've been out in the Massachusetts towns promoting the notion of an army. And if any man would trigger a wild militia musket or two, that would be Sam Adams. Not to remind you that Hancock is under conviction for smuggling and has fines to pay. Respectable fines, as we see them, but fines. They'd be reason enough to upset an apple cart."

"Oh, my heaven," Mrs. Gates said snappishly, "stop poking and puttering. It was bound to happen some way, Horatio. Just accept it."

"What Mrs. Gates means, Major," Martha said, not quite sure what Mrs. Gates meant, "is that to women the bloodshed and sorrow come closer than the question of who is to blame."

"I mean what I say," Mrs. Gates said. "It was bound to happen, and the men in the Congress can be glad they have Horatio."

"They can," Washington seconded.

A small lapse followed.

Nellie touched her napkin to her lips once or twice. "What do *you* make of it, Papa?" she said. Her little disarming gesture, the slight stress of the pronoun, brought the conversation back to its right emphasis without seeming to be rude. "How do you judge?"

"I'm too far away for judging," he said.

"But what will be done now?"

"We'll stand by Massachusetts, Nellie. I can't see but what we'll have to."

"With guns?"

"They may not need to be fired. I hope not."

"Oh, Papa, why be so solemn?" Jack said. "Don't frighten Nellie."

"I'd be sorry to, Jack."

"Some militia pop off a few muskets. Good Lord!"

"The king's troops have been fired on, Jack."

"And how far away? How far is Massachusetts?"

"A good many hundred miles."

"Then the devil with 'em." Jacky eased forward in his chair and reached for the almonds. "You're too pessimistic, Papa."

"Not at all," he said, and was conscious of the Gateses' eyes on him. "Lexington may have given His Majesty a lesson. A gathering of the colonies in arms will bring him something to ponder. It will be a matter of proof to him that we are united and determined. And no one need get into a passion about it."

"Passion?" Jack said idly.

"Passion," he said. "Things go best on a level keel, Jack."

Jack put on a sly grin. It was a mischievous reference between him and his father to what had happened with the poacher that morning.

"Level, Papa?"

Martha had been watching her husband's face. She saw the twitch of jaw muscles, the danger signal.

"Jacky," she said authoritatively, "that's enough."

"I was speaking politically," Washington said. But Jack had turned away and was making a remark to Mrs. Gates.

The dinner was done, and they rose from the table.

Washington apologized, and stayed for a few moments in his chair while the others went into the drawing room.

He was thinking, putting his fingers to the almonds and splitting them, and slipping them by habit between his teeth: thinking of Lexington and Concord, and what they might mean; thinking more forcefully of Jack, and of Jack's splaying, adolescent state of mind.

Here was a crisis between king and colonies which was certainly serious. Yet Jack had slid it off like water from a duck. Jack had no soberness, no goal. Jack had laughed at the oncoming cloud. That could be expected, he supposed, from someone young. Yet Jack's callowness, brashness, his devil-with-it attitude disturbed him. He couldn't quite find how to meet it.

He had tried to be a good father. Had loved Jack, put him in the way of a sound education, taken him into companionship on hunting rides and the workings of the plantations, shared the Williamsburg holidays with him, man and growing man, at the races and the theaters and at cards. Yet somewhere, more and more lately, there had risen the barrier between them. He seemed unable to reach Jack. Seemed to have shaped in sand and written in water. And it couldn't all be laid to Martha, for her spoiling of the boy. A part of the fault must be his. But how? He was at a loss to say.

It was not so much that Jack didn't see eye to eye with him as that Jack didn't see anything beyond his own concept of the sport of life.

He got up, eventually, and went into the living room, to Martha and the others. Before leaving the table, though, he picked up the gazette from Maryland and folded it slowly into his pocket.

There was much to be thought of.

Below the lawn at his doorstep the Potomac swept, ever placid in its tidal ebb and flow, encompassing his quiescent past and the hoped-for even tenor of his future.

Martha sat at the breakfast table, crisp and wifely, sorting out the linen napkins House Alice handed to her. House Alice was a deft, energetic Negress, with a strong classic nose and a quick eye, who had the "House" to her name to distinguish her from the other Alice, who worked in the fields. She turned the napkins over, one by one, and Martha set them down in two piles.

"These will do for rags—these will do a little longer for table, Alice."

"Yes'm."

"Linen wears out so."

"Ain't it truth."

"And the ships slow from England."

"Yes'm. But we can make do. Cotton stuff, if you have to have it. The folks can weave cotton for you."

"Yes, I know. . . . Take these—cut the frayed edges and hem them. We can talk of cotton later on. I like linen. . . . Jacky dear, how is your breakfast?"

Jack, eating, said, "Fine, Mama," between bites. He had pork and eggs and spoon bread and honey and jams, hominy grits and fish roe. He was Master Jacky, and the Mt. Vernon kitchen knew his tastes. When he and Nellie visited, there was no question among the cooks; they'd known

Jack from childhood, and they gave him what he liked best. He did not have to ask for it, it was there.

So, too, was his mother's smile.

She said, "Is it what you want, Jacky?" and he said, "Yes, Mama," and settled himself for what was to come, for he knew it would come by the warning of her eyes. Her eyes were always distressful when she felt she had to bring him to any accounting.

He went on with his breakfast, keeping an outward unconcern that the burden of the initiative was with her. There was no reason for him to start the matter going. He didn't feel in the wrong.

"Is Nellie still in bed?" she said.

"Yes, Mama."

"We'll send up a tray."

"No—she'll be down. She said to tell you."

His mother counted the piled napkins again, busying herself with them with a preoccupation that didn't deceive him.

"The Gateses left early," she said. "I asked them to stay over and go to the church services at Pohick with us tomorrow, but they felt they must get back." She said, "Your father's riding the fields."

"I could guess that."

"He has such joy out of riding. You know, dear, he's considered the finest horseman in the colonies."

"I can guess that, too. I've been told so often."

"Yes," she said absently. "Yes, of course." She had come to the bottom of the pile and the napkins were a shield for her no longer and she moved them a bit away and came to the nub at last.

"I think you've disappointed your father, Jacky."

He managed to look surprised over a mouthful of spoon bread and said, "How?"

"By your attitude, dear. Yesterday. You rather made a jest of the Lexington news."

"And Concord."

"Well, they're the same."

"Not to me, Mama. Lexington was a cook's brew. Mixed and ready. You heard what Gates said about Sam Adams."

"Major Gates, Jacky."

"Major Gates."

"That's right, dear."

"And Mrs. Gates is Majoress. Yes, Mama. I'll have to remember."

"There isn't any such title as that," Martha said, correcting, "for an officer's wife." But the corners of her mouth crinkled.

"Don't tell *her* that," said Jack.

He swallowed, disposing of the spoon bread. "Majoress," he repeated. "But you heard the major. Somebody put a tinder to some thinshanks' mind at Lexington. Thinshanks lolls around for four hours, waiting for the king's troops and smoldering to a slow ember, and when he sees 'em —crack!—and there you are, kindled. Then by Concord time the brew's boiling, and smells for a jollification. Whoop boys and dip in."

"Please, Jacky. People died there."

"They die in horse races, too, or fox hunting, or in duels. Or by falling off roofs at parades. Maybe the New Englanders have their own kind of sport—like street gangs and playing Indians at tea parties. I can't stop 'em, so I say the devil with 'em."

She saw that he wasn't angry, any more than he had been last night. He wasn't soured. His clear, lackadaisical brown eyes were half joking and completely indifferent. The searching conscience or the particular conviction were not for Jacky, who was dedicated chiefly to his idea of fun, and clothes, and fast horses—the sport to be continual and the clothes to be the newest. He kept his way through life secure in himself and in her, and in the fact that he'd always gotten whatever he wanted.

"The devil with 'em," he said again.

"Your father thinks it's deeper than that," she said. She thought of mentioning his language, but then thought better of it. Reproof never sat well with Jacky, and she wanted to keep him amenable, as far as she could. "This Lexington matter may affect all of us."

Jack speared the last piece of roe on his plate and forked it into his mouth. "Now, Mama—" he said, and chewed, savoring the roe, and put on the pseudoserious, philosophical look which he knew always impressed her because she dotingly saw wisdom in it. "Now, Mama, when Papa was out on the frontier before he married you, fighting Indian raids, was Maryland affected? No. Maryland sent out an officer who tried to outrank him, and Papa had to ride to royal army headquarters at Boston to settle the thing. You've told me. And was Pennsylvania affected? No. They left Papa to fight and rot and maybe be killed, because he came from Virginia and they were other colonies. They didn't care. Are they going to care now? No reason to. So why should *we* care?"

"But there *is* a reason, dear," she said. Her hand fluttered over the piles of napkins. How could she tell him that the chief reason, for her, was the man she had married as her second husband? "Your father feels there is. Those other things were long ago."

"Oh, feels," said Jack. But he was uncomfortable, a little set back because his mother, for once, hadn't wilted under his wise look. "I can feel, too. And I don't feel the same way Papa does."

This brought a break in their talk. On Jack's part it was a kind of need for assertion of himself. On hers, it was a gathering of forces.

He shot a glance at her over the table. He was remembering the year before, when she was seeing his stepfather and the other Virginia delegates off to the first Congress, and how she had stood in the Mt. Vernon hall, in the dawn, with the travel lanterns like fireflies by the coaches, with Patrick Henry and Mr. Lee and other Virginians around them, and had kissed his stepfather stanchly and had looked at the others and said, "Stand firm, boys. I know George will."

He said, "These congresses and committees and pompousness. These gloomy looks because somebody pulled a musket trigger. I think they're silly." He helped himself to more spoon bread, grinned, and said, "And if that be an attitude, make the most of it."

"I'll do nothing of the sort, you know perfectly well," she said bluntly.

"Then why are you scolding me?"

"Because you chose a very rude moment to express yourself. The Gateses were our guests, and very much in earnest."

The spoon bread lay pleasant to his tongue and taste. He cudded it from side to side between his cheeks. His eyes lit with their lazy twinkle. "Gates is such a granny," he said. "Major Gates, Mama. And the majoress is socked for war."

Martha smiled a little.

Jack knew the smile. They always came around to it when he and his mother had arguments. He pushed his advantage.

"You didn't like her either, Mama."

"I didn't like her shrillness, if that's what you mean."

"She had the face of somebody wagering on a horse. The major's her horse. I couldn't resist."

His mother couldn't decide whether to sigh or to chuckle. She elected to sigh. It put her in a better light, and saved some of her defenses. But it was a small sigh, for she never was really able to quarrel with Jacky, and he had all the tricks of getting around her.

"If your father is to be in politics," she said, "you'll have to watch your tongue, dear."

Jacky's answer was typical of him. At least she thought so. "Why does he have to be in politics?" he said.

"Because it's expected," she said. And she sat a little straighter, very straight in fact, and her voice had a commanding tone that might have made Mrs. Gates wonder. "Your father is a landowner. I shouldn't think, at this time in your life, I'd have to tell you."

"Member of the Virginia House of Burgesses for many years," Jack said carelessly. "Not elected on his first running. The second running, barrels of rum to the county voters, and he was washed in. Is that politics? You know, Mama, I've been thinking it might be fun. I'm a landowner."

"People don't go into politics for fun," she said stiffly.

"No," he said, "only into congresses."

"Jacky, that will quite do." She stood up with an abrupt pushing back of her chair. "I've tried to let you know how your father feels. How I feel. You've not been part of the colonies these past ten years. You've been busy merely growing. There is a heavy, heavy threat over us today, and an angry answer to that threat, and it's bigger than your jestings or Mrs. Gates's face. This has been going on for ten years, Jacky. Who knows, who can say, what will come of that fight at Lexington? Or of the new Congress? You push it all aside and shrug at it, and you are the one who should be saying, 'Mama, Papa, you can depend on me.' I don't know how this is going to end, Jacky. I don't know how it will."

She broke from the table and made blindly for the dining-room door. Jacky went after her, his normally easy-go-lucky body startlingly active.

He caught her by the shoulders and pulled her around.

"Mama!" he said. "Mama, don't talk like that!"

He kissed her.

"I love you!" he said.

She clung to him, and her eyes were wet and she shivered, and she patted his hair and his cheeks, and said, "I know you do, Jacky dear. I know."

His left hand stroked the blades of her shoulders, and he said, "I suppose it's the same as when I wanted to get married, isn't it? You and me against Papa?"

But she put her lips to his cheek and her palm to the gentle spot at the back of his neck, and said, "No—no, dear, not quite the same." She worked herself free from his emotion, and smiled, and turned, and left him under the glass-sided lamp in the front hall.

He heard Nellie's voice at the top of the staircase as she started down for breakfast.

"Jacky—" she said, "Jacky—?"

Her voice came brightly.

The pastel scent of earliest morning still hung in the air.

Yet he knew he must cut short his ride. His kinsman Lund Washington, settled in at Mt. Vernon, would be a good manager in his absence, would operate the business of the plantation, the seeding and harvesting and selling and buying and all the complexities and setbacks that stemmed from making a living from the soil. And Lund, now, would have the pink-hushed dawns, and dewed grasses in the sunrise, and the baying of his foxhound pack over the fields and across the bottoms of the wooded runs (for he wanted his pack exercised in his absence), and the elixir of wide air and the bold splash of a new day's color, perfect blue sky against the rust-red of Virginia furrows. And he would be in Philadelphia, leaving soon now, too soon, to sit on chairs and benches in city rooms, and hear committees and speeches and resolutions and long debates. Well, they wouldn't be too long, or so he hoped. Six weeks, he thought, six weeks at the most. The first Congress had adjourned in about that time.

He didn't look forward to being cramped into committee rooms in a city. He had small relish for it. Only his sense that now or never the colonies must assert themselves to the London ministry made him undertake it. He was active by nature, had been so all his life. His strength lay in action. Pubescent, he had romped with the bigger girls at school, and been caned for it. He had breasted the western lands, surveying first with George Fairfax over the Fairfax domain, then trecking warnings to the French who were filtering in on lands Virginia thought were hers, then fighting and surrendering in a rain-drowned little fort beyond the mountains, a fort he called Necessity. Then, disgusted with Virginia's lassitude and the hem-hawings of the royal governor, throwing away his officership.

He rather smiled, wryly, at that memory. That had been the first of seven times that he had resigned from military command. Pride, he knew now. A bulldog pride in him. A bleak jaw grip toward which he had been bent, as the twig is bent, since childhood.

Then Braddock had come out from England, to take Fort Duquesne from the French, on the triangle where the Allegheny and the Monongahela rivers married to make the great Ohio. And he had wanted to go on that march, but was only a civilian, and he'd relied on his friend Tom Gage, a royal lieutenant colonel, to get him placed as an aide to Braddock. Tom had done it, and he'd been sick and feverish on the hacking, slogging march through the wilderness, but on the last days he'd reached the front, a pillow on his saddle to ease his flesh-shrunk buttocks, and Braddock had crossed the river in the finest display he'd ever seen, and started the last ten miles, with axmen and scouts, toward the already beaten fort. And out of nowhere, out of a Frenchman's desperation and forlorn genius, had come the blunt meeting in the narrow, gash-hacked woods trail, and the Indians splitting down the sides, and two horses shot under him and four bullets through his coat. That he and Tom Gage had scraped together a rear guard for the retreat had been more instinct than skill. That the fame of him had spread to Europe, that chancellories had taken note of him, was so much nonsense. King George still offered him no royal commission as an officer, Virginia's governor still fuddled and wheedled about men and money to protect the frontier. A few months of that and he had resigned, and married Martha. Military life had not called to him since. Not for fifteen years. Until now.

It was odd, and yet it was not odd, that he should be retracing these things in his mind this morning. The Gateses' visit, the news from Lexington and Concord, had set him to reminiscence.

Tom Gage was his old friend. He'd seen Tom, dined with him at a party not so long ago, in New York City, when he'd gone with Jack to enter him at the King's College there. Tom was basically good-natured and good-hearted. The two of them, at Boston, if it came to that, could renew old friendship and find a way of bringing this stupidity to an end.

But was it a stupidity? He wasn't so sure.

On the one hand, as he worked it toughly in his mind, was an island, overrun many times by conquerors and therefore pegged to the stretch of authority, in spite of Charles I on the scaffold, and Cromwell, who was authority itself. On the other hand were the colonies, who had been conquered by no one but had themselves conquered. The parts of the puzzle did not fit. The stupidity was not so much on the colonies' side.

He wished he could decide things. He had been sloppily educated, never sent to English schools as his half brothers had been. He was tongue-tied, couldn't trade phrase for phrase, smoothly, with better-trained men. A retired colonel of colonial militia—that was all he was—with fifteen years of farming life behind him. And, he knew in a burst of instinct, with happiness and comfort around him.

"All right, Betsy. Home."

The poacher was not there this time, down the slope.

III

"A Member of This Congress"

The June weather in Philadelphia was hot, and the swarms of flies were a nuisance. They buzzed and pestered around the Congress members gathered in the meeting hall. Washington slapped at the flies and tried to give his attention to Mr. Adams of Massachusetts. Not Sam Adams, the Boston rouser, but John. Washington had heard Sam, too, declaiming from the floor and at work in committee. A downright radical, skilled at pulling the strings of the public mind, but too wild and heady for the dangerous times. He preferred John. John Adams had a certain fussiness, a certain ego, and occasionally a sorrowful complainingness, but he was unquestionably one of the ablest of the delegates. His sharp legal mind could match any in the hall, and the force of his intellect was obvious.

The nasal New England voice cut through the heat and the desultory hum of the flies. Something must be done, Adams was orating, to bolster the New England militiamen camped about Boston. Twenty thousand of them had trudged in after Lexington and Concord, ready to free Boston port once for all. But Massachusetts and the northeast colonies could not carry the whole burden. They must not be allowed to. With no support from the other colonies, the men would be disheartened. Supplies would grow short. The encampments would dissolve, the men would leave.

Washington opened the red facings of his Virginia uniform coat to give his body more air, and twisted on his chair seat. The seat got hard during the speeches. He had listened to many, the past six weeks.

He'd come up from Mt. Vernon with the Virginia delegates, pausing at Baltimore to review the militia companies there. He would have liked to spend some time with the Calverts, Nellie's mother and father, but

Baltimore had laid out a formal banquet for the Virginians, and his personal wishes had to be set aside. He'd found time to tell the Calverts, though, that Nellie was well and happy, and sent her love. He'd thought that Nellie's mother, for the few moments he spoke with her, was wondering if there were any signs of a grandchild. But he had not broached the subject. He knew nothing about it. Jack never talked to him about sexual matters. That would have embarrassed them both. He assumed Jack would beget children. But could also assume, even after fifteen years of marriage, that he could do the same; and the feeling of a competition with his stepson, a competition of virility and of prowess, as to whether he or Jacky would have offspring first, rather sealed his lips to Mrs. Calvert. He was doing his best in the bed, God knew. His nights with Martha were full and satisfying. But for fifteen years Martha had not seeded. It rode as a kind of scorn to him, a kind of mocking, that he was lack in reproducing himself.

The New England troops, Adams was saying, ringed Boston. But nothing had happened for two months now. Evidence was required. Evidence that the colonies stood back of them . . .

In the heat and the pester of the flies, Washington's mind drifted. He thought of the night before today, last night. He knew many of the Philadelphia families, naturally, since coming to the first Congress a year ago; and last night he'd spent the evening at the Shippens', a merchant clan, high in the city's society, and excellent company. There had been the daughter, Peggy—vivacious, laughing, and truly beautiful, a fascinating catch for someone—and her friend Rebecca Franks, beautiful in the same way but with the more gliding appeal, the richer and darker Jewish cast. Both girls were belles in the city, ruled a kingdom of romance and gallants.

He'd seen in them, startlingly, the quick sap of the young, and had an instinct that one or the other of these girls might tread on history—though which, he couldn't fathom, nor did he try to.

The politics were mixed, like the company. The Shippens were inclined to hold with the king, though Mr. Shippen's brother, a doctor with a wide practice and much reputation, stood for the colonies.

There had been banterings back and forth, lightsome things, as though nothing could ever really come to a conclusion between king and colonists, as though such a conclusion was unthought of.

Peggy Shippen had been teasing, and arrogant in a flagrant, girlish way.

Becky Franks had been quiet, and her brother David had been worshipful, as wanting to get into the war. The Franks family seemed neutral. There was another family, Tilghman, who were for the king. At least the elders of the family. The young son had seemed for the patriot side. (And that was the horror of this whole doing, that it was splitting families from families, and friends from friends, and sons from fathers.) The unscrambling of all this lay ahead, under a veiled future.

A vague future. As vague and disputatious as Peggy Shippen's laugh, or Rebecca Franks's soft murmur or her brother David's male cough.

He'd bounced both girls on his knees on his occasional trips to Philadelphia, and had slapped Franks in an avuncular way often enough on his bottom, so that now he should have felt free to talk of armies and commands and liberties and properties. But somehow he could not do so. Not with the Shippens. The house, by implication, by attitude, was a Tory house. No supporting of the Congress, no least motion of defying the king at Boston, nothing but pleasant teas and suave dinners to the named persons who came to Philadelphia from the other colonies. Not outside the limit of the patriot law, but not too closely bridled to it either.

Yet the food had been past cavil, and the talk good, and Mr. Shippen's brother, the doctor, was clearly patriot.

They had talked lightly of this and that, and then of Ticonderoga. That name, now, lay beneath the surface of all thoughts.

It was a strategic fort in the north, guarding the passage of the northern lakes above the Hudson. Its walls and its garrison straddled the passage between Lake Champlain and Lake George, on the border of New York and Vermont. It stood at a watershed. Northward, toward Canada, there was easy going for troops in bateaux, either against Canada or from it. Southward, a short march would reach the headwaters of the Hudson, beyond Lake George. The two lakes made a pulsing jugular between the heart and head of the colonies. They also made a water route for invasion, Ticonderoga standing guard.

Everyone had heard of Ti. It had come to fame in the former wars against the French and Indians. Ghostly names clung about it—Abercromby, Montcalm, Lord Jeffrey Amherst—the bloodcurdle of bayonet and clubbed musket. Of tomahawk and war whoop. For a generation it had blocked, even though fallen, a knifing down the Hudson to slit the colonies apart. The French had tried that, and failed. The Marquis de Montcalm had slaughtered Abercromby's men there, white lilies of France against St. George's banner; but had drawn back to Canada, cowed by the very wilderness and by the triumph-shouting legions under Lord Amherst.

Ti had always, in the memory of this generation, been a touch-and-go. Regiments from Europe, from England, had never been at their best in this tangled forest region. The regiments knew proper deployment, correct aligning, the comfortable, common thud of aim and fire. But they did not know the wilderness that lapped the lakes—the woods, the streams, the great maze of twilight and fallen trees and moss and rocks and curling brooks and rocks and dead branches and holes where a man could snap an ankle. They did not know huckleberry bush nor ironwood shrub. They did not know the American continent.

Now, out of nowhere, an Ethan Allen and a Benedict Arnold had pushed in on Ticonderoga and captured it for the Continental Congress. And any calmness, any talk of diplomacy, was lost thereby. For here was the sword point, here the lunge that showed King George the duel was real. Without sanction of the Congress, without knowledge or approval of any of the people, Allen and Arnold had set the powder train afire. The flames were up now, and the consequences must be faced.

A gesture. An egotism. A piece of bravado.

But still a fact whose consequences must be faced.

A fly crawled on Washington's ear. He slapped at it, but it got away.

The State House reeked with heat and the sweated smell of the crowded congressmen.

Washington was serving on a committee for finance, and one for ammunition, and another for planning defenses for New York City. But John Adams was not talking about any of these. Adams was talking about the army—twenty thousand men were enough to be called an army—squatted belligerent outside Boston. This army had been there for two months now. It must have evidence that the colonies backed it.

He agreed with Adams, that short round man haranguing on the floor for all he was worth. He loosened his stock to give his neck a touch of air, and told himself he mustn't think of social diversions, or of how the grafts on his cherry trees might be doing. He'd made the grafts himself that spring. But he must listen to Adams.

". . . Evidence, heartening evidence, that there will be support for New England and the Boston siege. Without such support, the whole cause of honest freedom, of liberty and property, will fall!"

Washington approved that phrase, liberty and property. He had heard it often in the Virginia House. It said what he felt. Without liberty and property where was a man's future? or peace? or life?

Adams kept on. . . . The army at Boston waited for encouragement. And the best, the strongest, the most telling encouragement would be for all the colonies to adopt that army and put it under command of a man who would represent the Congress and the continent.

"I admit," said Adams, hoarse from his talking by now, "that this might not be the proper time to nominate a general, and the choice of any individual will be a question of the greatest difficulty. But the choice should be made, for the good of the colonies. . . . A general to take full command of our American Army . . . And for my part I have one person in mind, and one only."

This was more than speech; this was blunt proposal. Washington agreed again. The army around Boston called for an appointed head, in the name of all the colonies. That would bring out and declare the needed unity. He looked at John Hancock, in the president's chair. Hancock was beaming. Eagerness for the appointment was on Hancock's face, and the expectancy of it. But the New England shipper, rich from rum and the smuggling trade, had no military accolades, and Washington couldn't think that Adams meant Hancock. Besides, to turn the army over to a New Englander would alienate the Southern delegates. Washington guessed that Adams would nominate, hoped he would nominate, Charles Lee or Horatio Gates. He'd spoken strongly for Gates when it came to military action.

Adams continued, not a man for oratorical suspense. The commander he was thinking of, the proper commander for the colonial army, to be called now the Continental Army, Congress willing, was sitting among them. A man whose proven ability, whose independent fortune, whose long experience in leadership on the frontier . . .

Hancock's face slowly began to take on a mottled crimson. Adams looked at him, did not stop.

". . . a gentleman from Virginia, known to all, a member of this Congress . . ."

His eyes went toward Washington, in the last row at the rear of the room. And there was a little sibilance of sound as the delegates turned, their heavy coat cuffs moving.

Eyes followed Adams', fixing on the tall Virginian.

And Washington, strangled, searching for cover, swung from his seat and dove for the door of the nearby library.

He pulled the door shut after him and blundered to the library table, leaning there.

A flood of shyness tossed him. He felt like a schoolboy on recitation day, tongue-tied in the middle of the platform and forgetting his piece. He detested this shyness he couldn't control, like his outbursts of temper, this public shyness that engulfed him since he had come of marrying age and two girls had refused him because he was big and gawky and hadn't the manners or advantage of an English schooling such as his half brother Lawrence had had, and was a poor relation without money and dependent on his western surveying and the connections of friends. That had cut deep. The cut bled anew in the library room with the whole Congress beyond the door.

He fumbled for his handkerchief and swabbed his forehead.

He didn't want the command, hadn't sought it, had tried to avoid it in a sort of panic as rumors went around that it might be offered him. Oh, yes, he'd been wearing his old militia uniform at the Congress, his blue coat with the red facings, but the uniform had only been his way of stating that politics seemed to be failing and the impasse would have to be ended by direct action. He'd not foreseen anything like this. It was one thing to pledge himself to lead a thousand men to relieve Boston. It was much another to have the command of twenty thousand thrust upon him.

He felt himself totally inadequate for such command.

On the other side of the shut door Adams' voice kept on, muffled. He judged the New Englander, with the lawyer's sagacity in the give-and-take of balance and compromise, would not press for an immediate vote. He would have, possibly, a day or two of grace. A day or two to save himself. A day or two to plead to the delegates that he was not the man.

Yet the thing seemed forejudged, inescapable. The arguments, the mounting sentiment, all pointed toward him. His friends surrounded him at the City Tavern, talkative and urgent over their dinner. He could see they felt they had logic and necessity on their side. He tried to sort out his own reluctance from the tangle of what they said.

"More knowledge of military doings than anyone on our committees."

"Practical judgment, soundly trained."

"Most battle-tried of our colonial officers."

"And who else is there?"

"Gates," he said desperately. He took more wine. It had ceased to have a taste in his mouth.

"Too old."

"Gates hasn't your reputation through the colonies. Or in Europe."

"Then Charles Lee," he said.

"Too high-handed. The people wouldn't accept him."

"The New Englanders," he said, "will resent a commander from outside."

"The rest of us would resent a New Englander. Leave New England to Adams. He'll bring the delegates around."

Washington looked around the rectangle of faces and waistcoats and wineglasses framing the table, and his heart sank. They would be too strong for him.

Charles Lee clinched the matter the next day. On the way along the street to his committee meeting he met Lee walking with his dogs, and as the spaniels tangled around the general's skinny legs, Lee stopped him and shook his hand and said his election was sure. "Schuyler and the New Yorkers are for you, Johnson and the Marylanders. For God's sake, you mustn't say no."

"I don't think I'm equal to it," Washington said.

"But, by God, you're the only man the colonies will follow," Lee said, "at the present." He took snuff, inhaled it accurately in each nostril, and let the drippings fall on his neckcloth. He was an abnormally thin man, angular, with a long bony face and a long bony nose. He put his snuff-box up with a flourish. "The eternal Devil damn me if we don't get seventy thousand under arms. We'll chase Gage out of Boston like a damned whipped cur."

Remembering his old enlistment problems along the frontier, Washington felt inclined to doubt the seventy thousand. Lee had been spreading this figure broadside through Philadelphia and among the delegates. Lee was slovenly, foul-mouthed, acidly sharp with his tongue, and famous for bitter pamphlets against the ministry in England. But he had a great repute. He'd served with the British Army, lost his career by criticizing the War Office, been a general on the King of Poland's staff. And he talked and acted like a military genius. Washington was glad to have him with the colonists. His guidance and skill would be valuable.

"Not to mention," Lee said, "that you're one of the rich men of our leaders."

"What has wealth to do with command?" Washington said, and then was a trifle uneasy under Lee's sophisticated smile, for the thought had never crossed his mind before.

"Oh God damme, Colonel, it's primitive as pricks. You'll fight all the harder because you've so much more at stake. This Philadelphia weather's foul, isn't it?"

Then Lee was gone, parading down the street.

Washington started on for his committee meeting. He went toward the State House, skirting close to the buildings, avoiding carts and drays and carriages, horsemen and marching militia companies and farmers with wagons of produce. People on the street made way for him. Some raised their hats and said, "Good morning, sir." Some merely goggled.

This surprised and mystified him. Of course he was tall. Of course he was wearing a uniform. But tallness and a uniform didn't make necessarily for show in the streets. Of course he had friends in Philadelphia. But these peering, doffing folk weren't his friends. He didn't even know them. Was it possible his name had been spreading out?

He walked slowly, thinking of what Lee had said. The colonies would feel more secure in him because his gamble would be so great. That was Lee's cutting way of putting it, and for a brief moment it flicked him on his pride—as though he were bonded, and a good surety risk. But he could see the practical side of it, too. He'd always been able to see the practical side of things. He did have more at stake; he did have much more to lose than many of them. The looks from the people who passed and stared showed him that, as the looks at the dinner had showed him last night, without setting the tune to words as Lee had. As he walked, mulling over those words, there came a single insistent thought. He had stood forward with the other leaders, he had been willing to share the burdens. If he refused the greatest burden now, if he shied from the responsibility, he with his wealth and his future waged on the game, what could he expect from the general run of the countrymen like these around him now, tradesmen and farmers and mechanics and hungry apprentices? Could he suppose they would make the sacrifices, rally into the field, and shatter their ways of life while he kept snugly in his own? Would that be his ultimate stance before them, that he counted his own well-being first? That his doubts and fears of himself, his craving for wife and home and lands had rotted him and turned him backslider? He continued to pace ahead, the passing figures going by him, unseen shapes. And pacing, pondering, fighting within himself, he faced at last what was required of him. He knew it with the hard knowledge of realization. For the sake of his honor and his self-respect he couldn't possibly refuse.

So it was done.

The unanimous vote, the formal appointment by the Congress, his formal acceptance. He told them he would serve without pay, asking only his public expenses; he wanted it so.

Then the dinner afterward, when the first toast was "To the Commander in Chief of the American armies," and the guests rose to their feet and drank the toast standing, and a following wave of silence swept the tavern room like a wave rolling dark over a wide and chartless ocean.

Later, his torment of heart poured out to Patrick Henry. "Remember what I tell you, Mr. Henry: from the day I enter upon my command of the American armies, I date my fall and the ruin of my reputation." And his gratitude that Henry pretended not to see the tears in his eyes.

Later still, when he could bring himself to it, the long letter to Martha at Mt. Vernon. "My dearest—" The quill hesitating, bearing tenderly on the lines, its shadow from the candle flame thick across his wrist. The letter that must somehow be written, saying he would not be coming home until autumn.

No, certainly not until autumn.

For that same week the two words "Bunker Hill" knifed down out of the north.

They escorted him from Philadelphia with a band, and militia officers, and members of the Congress in carriages, and a smart detachment of the Philadelphia Light Horse; and when after a while the music and the carriages turned back he rode on, the Light Horse with him as an honor guard to New York City, a drizzling rain pearling his cloak, and his face set to the first of the pulled miles that lay between him and Cambridge in Massachusetts, where the words had come from: "Bunker Hill."

Charles Lee rode beside him, the hawk-beak nose pendantent by water beads and the skinny shoulders hunched. Lee was on his military tune; it was his chief topic. His other was women.

"God damme, all that sweat and guts to fortify a hill and then lose the place. An addle-headed business. Why did they entrench if they couldn't hold?"

"To get there before Gage," Washington said.

"They're still before Gage. Before him, right in front of him, sitting on their arses around Boston. Hell's flames, sieges aren't handled that way. You press, you press, you press. You don't run in on the enemy and run out of ammunition. Who's this General Ward? Can't he count his supplies?"

"A Massachusetts man," Washington said. "He was a colonel of militia in the old wars."

"Oh," Lee said. "Ah, indeed." He didn't elaborate, but Washington could guess the rest: a New England militia colonel could have as much claim to be commander in chief for America as a Virginia one. But that the Congress had decided otherwise was not Washington's fault. He could only hope Artemas Ward, major general by Congress appointment, would accept him.

He said, "At least he's kept a force together."

Lee snorted. "Sounds like a churchwarden to me. By God, we'll put 'em straight when we get there, the bastards."

Washington shot him a look. He'd been wondering how the most advertised military expert in the country would take to being passed over himself for the command and appointed merely as a senior major general. The Congress had settled that, as it had with Ward, giving Lee what due it could in the tug and haul to make its nominations sit well with the different colonies. But Lee seemed satisfied, and Washington was glad. He would need Lee. He would need him very much. It didn't trouble him at the moment that Lee apparently thought so too.

Lee talked. "Food'll be no worry for us. Christ's name. It's summer, the country men can cart it in. Troops? Give promise of fighting, and troops will flock. Lucky for us Burgoyne was picked to reinforce Gage. I know Johnny Burgoyne from my service in England. I can write him in my personal hand. Johnny's a whoring gentleman, he may see things our way. We must try everything, we must press, press. How many men can we expect to find under arms?"

"I don't know," Washington said.

"And powder. Well, powder will be short, but the Congress has ordered more."

"If the Congress can make payment."

"Payment, pooh! Our powder merchants are patriots or they're not. Let the sons of bitches give. Then as for cannon—Damn this rain. Can't use my snuff." He blew his nose windily.

"The New England delegates spoke of cannon around Boston," Washington said, "but I've had no exact figures. No returns of any sort. The only cannon I'm sure of are those at Ticonderoga."

"Ti! A screwed wilderness from Boston, and the fort in ruins."

"General Schuyler will see to storing the cannon safe," Washington said.

Schuyler rode on his other side. Philip Schuyler, newly commissioned a major general, like Lee. A New Yorker from above Albany, very rich, owner of large landholdings and a small squadron of his own on the Hudson; reserved, formal, elegant in dress and speech; but with a clear mark of quality that Washington could understand. The two men were much alike, outwardly. Washington could have wished that Schuyler were going on to Cambridge. But Schuyler's post would be Albany.

"Damme!" Lee said. "Is nothing sure? Nothing but a few farting cannon at Ti?"

"Sixty cannon," Schuyler said coolly, "and one thing more. Our provincials at Boston have stood up to enemy fire. Isn't that enough for the time?"

Lee looked morose.

Schuyler said at once, politely, "But I agree we don't know much about them as soldiers."

"And damned less about the men who'll officer 'em," Lee said. "Do you know Putnam?"

"Only by hearsay." Schuyler meant Israel Putnam, said to be an indomitable old fighter, stanch at Bunker Hill, and a major general now by vote of the Congress as appeasement to the small-farmer class. "Have you met him, sir?" He turned to Washington.

"No." Washington shook his head. "No, except for you gentlemen, and Generals Gates and Sullivan, I've never met any of my officers."

This was true, but coming as it did on that rain-sodden road, and at that time, the statement had a certain grim baldness.

"Damme, we're in for a scuffling," Lee said. "Sitting a runaway horse in a blind fog."

Washington rode ahead in silence. He was beginning to wonder a little at Lee's shifts of mood, confident one minute, pessimistic the next. Yet Lee was right, as he seemed usually to be. And Washington had recommended him to the Congress, as he had recommended Gates. These were the two he relied on.

The Congress had given him Gates for his adjutant general. He would have Gates's help at Cambridge. He would have Lee's. And those two young men riding at his horse's flank, Joseph Reed and Thomas Mifflin, he would have them in his official family, the headquarters personnel that ate at the commander's table; Philadelphians both, well educated, well established, who had offered to go with him as military secretary and aide. He had dined at both their homes during the Congress sessions. He liked them both.

"Reed," he said.

A short splatter of hoofs. "Yes, Your Excellency?"

"Tell the captain of the Light Horse I'd like to quicken pace."

More hoofs, and a trotting tempo, and the jangle of bridles behind him. Yes, these four: Gates and Lee, Reed and Mifflin. He mentally added Sullivan, John Sullivan, a delegate from New Hampshire to the two congresses, this year and last, and newly made a brigadier. Sullivan would be an acquaintance, at least. He would be in Cambridge, too, probably with the sputter of zeal and energy he'd showed at the congresses. Aside from these men, Cambridge would be a place of strange faces and strange names; unfamiliar, unknown, and yawningly far from Mt. Vernon.

But in the damp plop of horses' shoes against mud, and the slow-unrolling, monotone scenery of the Jersey flatlands, he could not afford worry. He had other things on his mind: where muskets would come from, and money; shoes and wagons and bread and uniforms; discipline and battle tactics, and the courage to stand in the open against the king's regulars; enlistments, volunteers, a defense, and an army born out of anger and resolutions. And what sort of reception he would have at New York. He'd heard the city was largely Tory, and indifferent.

It turned out otherwise. When on a clear, warm June Sunday afternoon he sat in the ferry from Hoboken and looked at the New York shore drawing near across the Hudson he could see the crowd massed together to cheer him. They swarmed along the shoreline; the city's nine volunteer companies, merchants, mechanics, men and women and children, waving, yelling, huzzahing. The clamor rolled toward him over the water.

The jubilation and pride and sheer open-throated exuberance swept aside the memory of the soggy ride through the Jerseys.

"By God, sir," Reed grinned chokingly, "this beats anything. It's better than Philadelphia."

Washington grinned back at him.

Lee let out a startled curse and began to preen himself. Schuyler's handsomely chiseled face showed excitement.

And as the boat scraped alongside Mr. Lispenard's dock, Washington stepped to the land and stood bareheaded in answer to the shouts, and saw the people there and looked in their faces, and the tingle of a strange, deep, wordless emotion ran vibrant down his spine.

IV

Powder for Thirty-eight Shots

He wasn't back at Mt. Vernon by the autumn. Instead, in December, Martha was with him in Cambridge. He'd written and asked her to come, though he didn't think she would come because winter was so near. But she had. She brought Jack and Nellie with her, and Mrs. Gates.

It was a joy to him to have her by him again, in the large, square-built house whose view sloped flatly to the Charles River. The house belonged to Loyalists, who had left it and retreated into Boston, and it had rooms enough for his family and his personal staff, and he had moved into it as being less of an embarrassment than his first quarters in the home of Harvard College's president, Dr. Langdon.

He took her in his arms in the bedroom that was to be theirs, and she returned his desire with a warmth and deliciousness of her own.

"It's been so long, George."

"Seven months. Oh, my love, Patsy."

She said, "I'm glad I'm here. I've been lonely."

"I've been afraid for you," he said. "I've wanted you, God knows. And I've been afraid for you. The Potomac's an open road for the king's ships."

"Oh, that . . ." She laughed a little, and tossed her bonnet on the bed, and signed to Billy Lee to unpack her travel trunks and put her things in the clothes cupboards. "With ten minutes' warning, George, I can be on my way to friends inland. I did spend one night away, when some small vessels came nosing up the river. But I was back the next day. Don't worry about me."

"I don't, now," he said.

"Then it's all right," she said, as if that settled things. She loosened her travel cape. "Billy, I'll be changing my dress." She said it without prissiness. Billy had been a part of the family so long.

"Yes'm," he said, and went out.

"Will this last all winter, George?" she said. The gesture of her hands was a woman's one. It included the house, the army camp at Cambridge, the lines thin in barricades around Boston, and the city and its garrison and the far-off ministry in England. "I thought that once the king had proof we mean what we say—" She let the sentence dangle as though there were no need to finish it.

"I thought so, too," he said. "I may have been wrong." He began to walk to and fro in the room, slowly, twisting his fingers together behind the tails of his uniform coat. His commander's sash was tight across his chest, his boots thick against the floor. "I may have been wrong in a great deal, Patsy."

She had unfastened her dress, and stepped from it, and from her petticoats, and went to the journeying trunks she had fetched with her, and got others, and started to put them on. "But that's not for the moment," she said.

"No . . . Jack looks well. And Nellie."

"They're dear children," she said. "I don't know if they'll be happy here, but they rode with me for company." She went toward him, her flounced pantalettes making a starchy whisper. "George, do you know —people are calling me Lady Washington!"

He laughed at that. "You'll have to get used to it, Patsy. They're calling me Your Excellency." And he added, "I don't think General Lee likes it."

"General Lee has no privilege to like or dislike it," she said, as she held her underskirts and dress. "He's under your orders, isn't he? But do you like it?"

"Not especially. But it's a tribute to the position. Patsy," he said, "we're snared by this position. What do we do?"

Martha had the intuitiveness of her sex, and two marriages. Something was gnawing at this great giant. Things weren't going as he'd planned. She could feel it. The December afternoon was drizzly, and from somewhere outside came the sound of a drum, beating the rhythm for marching men.

She put on the petticoats while he paced, and went up to him and stopped his pacing with her circled arms.

"George, we do what we think is fit."

"Fit?" He broke away from her rudely, more rudely than he had ever done in their years at Mt. Vernon. "How do we know what's fit? How do we know where the end of this will be?"

"What is the end?" she said.

"That," he said. He swung an arm toward the window and the drum sound. "The Connecticut regiments are marching home. No pay, no future for them. I'll be poorer by four thousand troops tomorrow. And I can't stop them."

"Oh, George," she said. And said, "Dear, I can't pretend to know anything about military doings. Maybe these men *have* to go home. It's winter, you know."

"I know," he said.

"We have planted," she said thoughtfully, as she stepped into her finer dress, "what I would call a wild seed. No one knows how it will grow, George. Had you heard that Philadelphia wanted to give me a ball?"

"No."

"Well, the city did want to. But some of the newspapers objected, and Philadelphia people are mostly on the king's side, you know, and Miss Shippen and her family—you wrote me about them, about Peggy Shippen, and I dined with them—advised me against it. So I gave it up, and said I wanted no ball. But it's a wild seed, dear. I doubt very much whether the whole of the colonies are with us."

She said this with a kind of retreat, a kind of apology, a kind of salve to the hurt she was inflicting on him. But he took it as she had known from the first he would take it; had been certain he would.

"I've set my path. I can't do anything else but stand by it."

"Yes, George. But the king's path?" Unless she had known him so well she would not have put that question.

"There's been the Congress petition to the king, for relaxing of anger. There's been a petition to him from the Lord Mayor and Aldermen and Livery of London. But no word over here. And the king's troops have been shaken by Bunker Hill and don't durst stir out, and ours are so short of powder that we don't durst attack. A stalemate, and no one can see the outcome. I'd write to Tom Gage, but Tom has been replaced by another general. We just sit and watch, Patsy."

She had her dress on by now, her social dress. It was, as all her dresses were, in the latest mode. She glided up to him and kissed him.

"I'll hope you will keep on," she said.

"On?" he said. "Being at a standstill isn't 'keeping on.' We're here to free Boston, and we can't."

He spoke bitterly, for the gloom of the northern December lay on him, and the talk he had just been having with Charles Lee.

The talk had been disheartened by the feeble drizzle outside, and by Lee's obscenities. Lee had stood with his back to the fire, feeding snuff to his nose and warming his scambly legs, after their ride around the lines on the latest alert. There were alerts nearly every day, when the Cambridge camp thought the king's regiments would be pouring out of Boston at last, to be met by a few bullets and clubbed muskets and spontoons and flung stones, but nothing had ever come of that.

"Connecticuters," Lee said. "Slab-arsed whoremongers. Scurvy lot. Fiend take 'em."

Washington agreed. The Connecticuters' enlistment had ended, and six regiments were leaving camp.

"Bitch-bred whelps. And their muskets going with 'em. Damme." Lee sneezed as the snuff took effect—a total explosion of sound.

"But the muskets are their own."

"What of it? Commandeer 'em. Where'll we find more?"

"The muskets our privateers have been capturing."

"Privateers, privateers. By God, it's a farce, having to supply ourselves from enemy shipping. Is that a campaign?"

Washington couldn't say whether Lee's blast was genuine or whether it questioned his wisdom. He hadn't Lee's trained view on these things, had to give his judgments as he saw them. The Connecticuters owned the muskets they'd brought to the camp, and he thought they were entitled to keep them. Perhaps because he knew better than Lee the meaning of muskets in farm homes. He had seen such homes long and long on his western ridings. They needed muskets to eke out their meat supply, and for lessening the rabbits and skunks and raccoons and woodchucks and deer that marauded their crops.

Lee said, calmer and very dry-voiced, "Scabrous monstrosity. Everything awry, nothing right. Bastions ninny-placed, fortifications a pile of rot. Why did they dig in on Bunker Hill in the first place? If Tom Gage hadn't been so puling stupid he could have squeezed 'em off from the rear. Blundering Tom . . . I was told we had artillery. I haven't a gun or gunner worth a God damn. And the camps? Captains shaving private soldiers. Good Christ! Why? So the soldiers will vote for 'em. Hell's balls, they *elect* their officers! Diddle-daddle. And you know the powder count."

Washington knew. When he had reached Cambridge he'd been told —it had taken some days to get the report—that there was only enough powder in the camps to provide each soldier with three rounds of cartridges. And he had sat for an hour, saying nothing, stunned . . . Now they had powder for thirty-eight shots apiece. And no more in sight.

"If I'd known the truth beforehand," Lee said, "I'd never have taken this fornicating commission, so help me Belial."

Washington stared from the window toward the Cambridge camps, which he couldn't see, but from which, in the gray of the afternoon against the grayed clouds, rose a small mist of desultory fires and smoldering chunks of wood, a signal of winter tightening down, a call for huts and warm clothes to replace the hit-or-miss tents of old sails and the homespun shirts and breeches of summer. His fingers stroked absently on the windowpane. He had, somehow, to keep the project afloat.

He had, somehow, to make the London ministry listen and retract. "We can't hold the Connecticuters by force," he said. "We did last week, but not again. But the militia are coming in."

Lee could take snuff more disdainfully than any man Washington had known. "The Long Faces. Piss on the lot of 'em. They're coming in because some misbegotten idiot in the king's navy set Falmouth on fire with his ship's guns. They'll buzz like hornets, and back to the nest as fast. They'll not stay, not in this damned climate. God spare me, my backside's hot." He skittered across the room and folded himself into a chair.

Washington turned from the window. This man, this Lee, he thought, was a hard one to fathom. For all his foul mouth, some of his perceptions were keen. His military perceptions, Washington amended in his mind; Lee's other perceptions were chiefly devoted to women and obscenity. He thought that this was the Lee who had talked in terms of seventy thousand men in the Continental Army, who sputtered in the war councils of two hundred thousand rounds of ammunition before they could dare an attack on Boston; yet who had conjured up, in a single night, a hand-scrabbled earthworks at a weak defense spot on Plowed Hill, had done it by oaths, and military acumen, and a talent for command. He thought of the recent visit of a committee of investigation from the Congress, Dr. Franklin and two others, and the letter that had been the result of it: the Congress would be pleased to hear of some attempt by the army. An army that threatened to fall bare in the winter like leaves from trees. This was an irony. And he couldn't tell the people of the colonies, nor even the Congress, how weak he was in force, for then the troops of Boston would fall on him, and rout the camps, and finish the game. And this was a double irony, and gross. But it was what he lived with every day, what he tossed and lay awake with every night.

Lee was watching him cursorily, eyes half-lidded. He supposed Lee was expecting an answer ready-cut, a commander's answer. He had none. Lee, he imagined, would have had one, if Lee had been in his place, the commander in chief, His Excellency. Lee's look seemed to say so. . . . Where were they? Oh, yes, Lee's backside was hot, and Lee had been belittling the militia.

"They're all we have, General. Until the colonies send us more enlistments."

He realized it wasn't a brilliant statement, the words of a battle genius that could draw something out of nothing. And he saw Lee's eloquent shrug. Lee was capable of eloquence, silent as well as vocal. "Well," and his cutting voice turned now to silk, as silk can cut when drawn in certain fashion across flesh, "Billy Howe's in Boston instead of Gage —got the post, most likely, because his father was a king's bastard. Royalty looks to its own. Power spreads itself. But we may be lucky. He may be a blunderer, like Tom Gage. Or maybe he'll be bed happy or a drunkard."

"He was brave in the fight at Bunker Hill."

"Umph. Bravery's one thing, command's a damned other. Which may save our belly buttons. We could win or lose this case on Billy Howe's night habits."

"We don't know Howe," Washington said. He tried not to let disapproval show in his voice. Like most passionate men, except the rakes like Lee, he was modest.

"Freedom gained by a sheet fight," Lee said. "Howe between the sheets and us between the guns," and he broke into a laughing cackle and slapped his sides like a scarecrow.

It was then that Billy Lee, knuckles rapping excitement at the door, had said that Martha's coach was in the road outside.

Washington had run out immediately. The black Billy was beside him, ahead of him, bounding down and giving an arm to Martha, and to Nellie, and bobbing his head to Jacky, and then an arm again to Mrs. Gates.

Washington, hurrying on the path from the front door of the house, heard Lee's acid voice behind his ear.

"Good God, the female Gates. That demoness."

Martha met his headquarters family and some of his generals the next night. The drawing room was crowded, and full of talk and formality and the glintings from uniform buttons and the shine of silks and brocades under candlelight. James Warren was there, president of the Massachusetts legislature, and his wife Mercy, a briskly intelligent and sensible woman, and a few Cambridge social couples. Many of the Cambridge society people had taken refuge in Boston; but James Warren's brother had died in the fight at Bunker Hill.

Washington watched Martha maneuver the evening easily, and was delighted with how she did it—all these people, most of them new faces to her. Her training as a Virginia hostess had been thorough. She had the art of graciousness. She didn't flinch, even when General Putnam, looking and acting like a rumpled bear, had grabbed her hand in a callous paw while being introduced: "Mitheth Wathington, it'th a thertain honor, ma'am," and had waited with a defensive truculence to see if she would smile or change expression.

The Gateses came, as was to have been expected. Mrs. Gates in a gown of green bombazine, heavily flounced, with a necklace of green stones to match; and she prodded her general from group to group around the room with the reckoning intensity of a child guiding a toy sailboat down a brook. Charles Lee was absent. Nested in his own headquarters, he said he preferred the company of his dogs to that of humans. Washington was rather relieved. Lee was an enigma, an unpredictable explosive, with a prickliness that could turn friends to enemies.

Washington needed friends. This gesture, this upfling against London and the ministry, seemed to have developed into an attrition and a lazy, cannon-shot slackness. His troops were tired of the dragging months in camp. They would be dropping away from him, like the Connecticuters. He couldn't tell how many of them would stay on through the winter. Most of their enlistments would end with the end of the year. He couldn't tell if replacements would come in to him or not. He had to look to friends in the trades and in political office who could talk to governors and persuade colonial assemblies to call for more men if he were to keep his muster rolls full. In such a case, he felt no insult that the dart-tongued Lee stayed at home with his dogs.

The evening went off well, he thought. Jack was on his good behavior; Nellie looked fetching and made an animated second to Martha's bubbling spirits. He walked about, nodding here, speaking there, and saw with satisfaction that the generals and the New Englanders would accept his family, as they had accepted him.

He caught snatches of talk.

Mrs. Gates was saying, "An important post, yes. But Horatio really should be given the opportunity to use his talents as a field commander. He was signaled out for special mention by the king once, you know—"

And Mrs. Warren, "Oh, the men diving from the bridge—and the Cambridge ladies. It was *too* funny, Mrs. Washington—"

And General Greene, "The riot in the camps. Marbleheaders against Morgan's riflemen. The Marbleheaders hadn't seen hunting shirts before, thought the fringes were womanish. There was a brawling. Must have been a thousand in it. I rode out with His Excellency. The Marblehead colonel—Glover's his name—couldn't stop it, came a-sweat to headquarters. His Excellency took a six-foot fence, horseback, and left the saddle and knocked two of the roughest heads together. That finished 'em. It was a smashing business. Some very nice wine afterward—"

Washington spoke to General Ward. The general's health was bad, it seemed, and he might have to resign. Washington wondered if it were health or the general's unhappiness with his rank. A third of the officers the Congress had appointed were in the same state. They all wanted the highest positions. They were more jealous than fishwives. Except for geography and the tug of politics, Ward might have been in Washington's place. Washington tried to be as tactful as he could. Ward's attitude toward him was correct and unbending.

But aside from this, the affair was successful.

With the last guest gone, they dropped into the drawing-room chairs to relax a little, and Jack sprawled and Nellie wriggled her feet halfway from her slippers and said, "They don't study for fresh air up here. I wish they did."

"They can't," Jack said. "They'd freeze."

"Well, I wish they did," she said.

"Loosen something," Martha said. "Jacky, help her."

"Oh, no," she said. "Jacky tickles." She got up and stood with her back to Martha, and Martha's fingers worked for a moment, and Nellie gave a relieved sigh and sat down again.

"Your Papa won't mind," Martha said.

"Your Papa's going to do the same," Washington said. He unfastened a button or two of his waistcoat and was thankful to Nellie. He'd been having only five hours' sleep a night, what with the immensity of writing that piled on him—orders, letters, reports—his aides couldn't compass it all. A small unbuttoning was a luxury.

He said, "What do you think of them?"

Martha pursed her lips and looked at Jack, and Jack looked at Nellie. Nellie looked at her slipper tip and then raised frank eyes. "I liked General Greene," she said.

"He limps," Jack said. "And he's bald. He was wearing a wig. I saw it."

"That doesn't make him a worse officer," Nellie said.

"A limp," Jack said.

"Does it, Papa?" Nellie said.

"The Rhode Islanders said so," he said. "When they began forming companies they wouldn't have him for a captain. He enlisted as a private. They found they'd been wrong. I'm glad you like him, Nellie. His camp is the best in the army."

Jack shrugged, and changed the subject. "What I liked was Mrs. Warren telling about the men swimming in the river. Pulling their clothes off to the skin, baby-bare, and standing up and diving from the bridge rails, and the Cambridge females shocked in their carriages. Mama heard her. Mrs. Warren laughed."

Washington's mouth twitched. "So did I. But we can't afford to offend the females, Jack. You'll learn that, in time. I gave orders. By the bye, I was in the Rappahannock once, and two town women stole my clothes from the bank, and I . . . Well, never mind," he said, for he had caught Martha's eye.

"No, never mind," Martha said. Jack and Nellie had giggled, and her George was grinning. She made another change of subject. "Stay to the important things, George. I don't think Mrs. Gates is too fond of you."

"I'm not too fond of Mrs. Gates," he said. "Is anyone?"

"That's not to the point," Martha said. She had put on her serious manner, which could be as strong as his, and she said, "I think she wants General Gates to shine more."

"Gates is a fine adjutant general. He's a plodding man, thorough, at home with facts and figures. He's best off where he is, and so are we."

"But Mrs. Gates isn't content to have him where he is," she said. "George, did you see her tonight?"

"She was being very social."

"She was being political. She was doing her best with these New England people. You should keep alert about the Gateses."

"Very well," he said, and poured a last glass of wine for himself and Jack. Martha and Nellie had left off their wine some hours ago. He felt in too good a humor to be ruffled by Horatio Gates or his wife. He said, as one does who reviews an evening in his thoughts, "You were excellent with General Putnam, Patsy."

"Putnam," Jack said languidly. The warmth of the room had crept over him. "A farmer with a lisp and a powder horn."

"Excellent, Patsy," he repeated, ignoring Jack. "Putnam is thin-triggered about himself. I should have warned you."

"I have *some* sense of manners, George," she said.

The shortness of her tone showed the strain she had been under, doing her duty to ingratiate herself as the commander in chief's wife.

They respected her feelings for a moment.

"There weren't any young people," Nellie said. She lifted her head and smiled and said, "Not that Jacky and I ought truly to care."

"No, there weren't," Washington said. "You and Jack won't find the headquarters amusing, Nellie. We can't give entertainments as we did in Virginia. But you can always go back to Virginia."

"Oh, no," Martha said. "I want Jack near me." She stopped, and added quickly, "And you too, Nellie dear, naturally."

"Of course, if you need us, Mama," Nellie said.

"Oh, yes, dear," Martha said.

But she had her eyes for Jack. Jack twisted smugly.

"Certain, Mama," he said. And he said in the deeper voice he'd adopted since he'd been married, "But, Papa, it's still a frolic. What'll you gain by it? Soldiers that swim bare-bottomed in the river—'scuse me, Mama—"

"Swam," Washington said.

"Oh, certain. Swam. This is December. Now they pick up the cannon balls from Boston and sell 'em for iron."

"Jacky, how do you know?" Martha said.

"I rode out to the forts today."

"Jacky!" his mother said.

"I had to pass the time somehow," he said.

"You're not to go to the forts, Jack," Washington said. "There's danger, and you don't belong to the army. You will please stay away."

"But it was sport to see the balls land. They roll, and the Yankees scramble for 'em while they're still hot," Jack said. "What's the harm in that?"

Washington was about to answer with some sharpness and words about the foolishness of youth when a memory wrenched at him. In his own youth, so distant now, he'd penned a letter from his first wilderness fight to his brother. He'd said something to the effect that he'd heard bullets whistle and there was something charming in the sound. His brother had read the letter to friends, a copy of it had traveled to England and been printed, and been seen by King George II. And the king had observed, maturely, having been in battles himself, "He would not say so if he had been used to hear many." He was scarcely, he felt, in a position to read a lecture to Jack. It all amounted to the same complexity: he couldn't censure Jack no matter how much he felt censure called for; there was the record of his own young days.

Jack had twisted again, half mocking, half in earnest. "The Gateses' boy has the best of it. He stays home. Not dragged to a battle front and then told he can't go near it. That takes the spark out. It's only a frolic, Papa."

"No," Washington said, and knew that twenty years ago that would have been a lie. He wasn't sure that it still wasn't one, though the five hours' sleep a night weighed in the balance.

"Officers," Jack said. "A limper, a lisper, and a sick Puritan. What's the Congress given you? Except for Sullivan—"

"You talked with Sullivan?"

"Yes, he's full of ginger. Except for him, one other. That beefy fellow from Massachusetts. Lincoln?"

"Yes." Washington leaned over, and freed his foot from its shoe as Nellie had done. "I rate him next to Greene."

"I wouldn't know ratings," Jack said. "Not as you draw 'em up, Papa. But do your other generals have to be doctors' cases?"

Washington downed a rather large swallow of his wine. Jack irritated him. Possibly Jack intended that. Jack had not had a very good evening. Now, under his mother's wing, he was working off his boredom. A painful concept slowly began forming itself in Washington's mind. He was committed to a slash against his king, to win a compromise. But he was, too, committed to a slash against his family, that part of his family who was his wife's son by another husband, and who, for all his beardless age, could come between him and Martha. He wished he knew where Martha stood, and sent his eyes to her and saw her eyes on Jack, and thought he knew. Then he grew angry. The whole nonsense was ridiculous and implausible. The colonies had made him their military commander. There was more to that than Jack or Martha felt.

"Speaking of doctors' cases, Jack," he said, and the bite in his voice was heavy, "you should see Major Knox. Fat as a lump of butter, and with a maimed left hand."

"Oh, capital," Jack drawled. "Is that the best the Congress can give you?"

"It's the best I can find," he said shortly.

Nellie said, "Papa, there's so much against you, isn't there?"

But Jack said, "Cripples, cripples. Give up, Papa, and enjoy your life."

"You shush," Nellie said.

Jack said, "One more for the doctors. Isn't anybody healthy but us?"

"Jacky, you've had enough to drink," Martha said. "Go to bed, dear." And she said to her husband, "Major Knox? I don't remember he was here tonight."

"He's miled in winter," Washington said, "fetching guns taken at Ticonderoga."

Martha met his look, catching the subtle change in his voice and knowing what it meant. "Can he bring the guns, George?" The question proved her concern for him, a concern he treasured. If he were in trouble, Martha would be at his side. Though, if Jack were in worse trouble . . . He shucked off the thought.

"If he can," he said, "we'll have Boston."

He got up and put his glass on the table and carefully buttoned his waistcoat. He gave a wink of eyelid to Nellie for her half-shod feet. "Jack, while you're here, stay back from our lines. We have cannonading every day, and Nellie's to keep you in hand. I'm glad the New Englanders like you all. Now go to sleep."

"But, Papa," Jack said, and got up with the lazy, springing confidence of youth, and faced his stepfather with the blandness that was youth's, too. "You said you'd free Boston yourself."

The blood came slowly to Washington's cheeks. "It depends on whether Knox can fetch the guns over mountains and snows," he said. "Things aren't as I'd thought."

"Oh, then, what the devil?" Jack said.

He hadn't expected that Martha would know anything about Benedict Arnold, nor that she would talk of him. But she did know, and she did talk, waiting until a few days later to do it.

They were together in their room, after supper, the candles lit and the world dark outside. Martha was loosening her clothing, and Billy Lee had brought in the bed warmer with its long handle and cargo of hot coals. Washington dropped off his uniform coat, unfastened his breeches.

Martha waited until Billy Lee had slipped out and then said, "There's a man I'm curious about, George. A Colonel Arnold. Is he about? I've not seen him."

"How would you know of Arnold?" he said.

"Oh, quite simple, dear. In Philadelphia. From Peggy Shippen. We had the news of Ticonderoga there, you know. And Miss Shippen seemed interested in the colonel. She asked me to write her if I met him in Cambridge. But I haven't met him."

"He's not here," Washington said.

"Then where?" she said.

"Beating up toward Canada," he said.

"Oh?"

It was a measure of their trust in each other that she didn't ask any further, and that he told the story as fully as he could remember, stripping off his clothes like the shucks of an ear of corn, and going between times to the bed to see that the warmer would cover the spots where they would lie.

"Arnold came to me last September," he said, and told her the story:

The countryside around Cambridge was russet and gold with early autumn and tinseled with small ponds, and the siege of Boston was at a standstill, when Reed announced a caller.

"Mr. Arnold is waiting on you, sir." Reed was scrupulous about titles. Arnold had resigned his Massachusetts commission, was no longer an officer.

"I'll see him."

And so Arnold had come in, a stocky, swarthy man under middle age, with gray-green eyes that flickered like firelight. Washington had let him stand while he went over the summary of the man in his mind: Ticonderoga, a proven instinct for attack; a violence of action and a personal pride; a knack for getting things done. Clearly a fighter.

There was a slight bow, a smile, a quick hand smoothing dark hair in place, and a brusque meeting of looks.

"Sit down, sir. You've left the Massachusetts service."

"I have."

"Your reasons?"

"Meddling boobery."

"Sound enough reasons."

Washington could sympathize. He'd resigned from the Virginia militia out of sheer frustration. He could understand Arnold.

"We'd opened the whole of Champlain," Arnold said. "I could have spun up into Canada. But the damned politicians, the interferers, the hogs in uniform swilling for command. They smothered me with their dirty slops. I left 'em."

Washington didn't smile. Arnold had certainly opened Champlain, from the head to the foot. He'd not been content with the capture of Ti, but had stormed north to seize the small fort at the lake's outlet, the gateway to Canada. Here was a battling man.

He also knew that Massachusetts had been pinching pennies and had accused Arnold of not accounting for expense moneys. But he didn't want to be drawn into that argument. It was none of his.

"Many officers wouldn't have tried your push up Champlain," he said.

"Many officers are old grannies," Arnold said. "Or young ones. Men will go anywhere if spirit's put in 'em."

"Yes," Washington said. "Though I haven't had experience of that in this Boston siege."

Arnold nodded curtly and let Washington make the next remark.

"You spoke of spinning into Canada, sir."

"It's the logical thing. Soon and hard. The ministry troops are weak, there. Any fool would see we ought to have Canada before the ministry can reinforce and make a drive down the lakes. But the damned New England pettifoggers put a leash on me."

Washington tried to view him clearly, this Mr. Arnold, already controversial. A blunt person, outspoken. Possibly not easy to get along with. But the times, as he saw them, were not suited for easy men.

He said, "You know Canada?"

"Traded there. At Quebec."

"You're familiar with the city?"

"Ought to be, by God."

"Suppose we could get you to Canada again?" Washington asked, and watched.

Arnold's face took fire. It had the look of a mountain lion. "With troops?"

"Troops."

And he had laid out the prospect for Arnold—the Congress setting to attack the feeble garrisons in Canada and hoping to bring the Canadians in to join the colonies.

"General Montgomery, under Schuyler's command," he said, "will aim for Montreal. My own strategy is for a second drive through Maine, toward Quebec. Montgomery would swing down from Montreal to join it."

"A double nip," Arnold said. "Yes, by God!"

He had an impetuousness that made the room tingle.

"The Kennebec route, Mr. Arnold. I've been over it on the map. Is that possible?"

"Anything's possible."

"M'mm. How will winter treat you?"

"We'll beat it," Arnold said.

"I won't be able to supply you," Washington said.

"We'll supply ourselves," Arnold said. "There's a way through everything."

"Then the Kennebec?" Washington said.

"Yes, sir," Arnold said.

Arnold's gray eyes were true, and full of a kind of exultancy. Washington congratulated himself. The ex-officer in front of him had shone in action with as sure a grasp of strategy and an instinct for daring tactics as anyone in the colonies. He said, "I would welcome you, Mr. Arnold, as leader of this wing of attack. Your record in the northern field qualifies you. Will you accept a commission from me?"

"How soon?"

Washington rose and went to the door. Arnold jumped up. Washington said, "Reed? General Gates, please, if he can spare me a moment."

The spectacled, passive face of Horatio Gates loomed in the hallway. He must have guessed that something might be afoot; he and Washington had been pondering a commander for the Kennebec push.

"Come in," Washington said. "General Gates, Colonel Benedict Arnold of the Continental Army."

The two shook hands.

"The colonel," Washington said, "has agreed to take a force through Maine. He will need men, equipment, and what stores he can carry with him. This must be done as soon as possible. Will you set it in motion, General? I'll have Reed draw up covering orders tonight."

There was preliminary talk, broad and sketchy, and Gates and Arnold left. Washington sat again at his paper-piled desk and followed them out of the room with his eyes. He saw Arnold's short, stocky, tight-knit body, and his fist pounding into a tough palm, driving home to Gates the urgency for speed, and more speed, to get the expedition furnished and under way.

"He is a man," Washington thought, "after my own kind."

The sun was setting, low behind the Charles River. He looked at it momentarily, at the cool radiance of an early fall sunset and the river winding flatly in the fading light.

"It was like a great copper snake," he told Martha.

V

The King's Answer and Knox's Guns

"Well," Jack said, "the hunt is now up, as the saying goes."

He came unexpectedly into the upstairs sitting room of the Vassall house. The rooms on the ground floor below were given over to headquarters offices, and formal callers, and the dinners the staff and varying officers of the day ate with the family. Upstairs, the Washingtons had at least a sort of privacy, and Martha and Nellie spent much of their time there, especially since the winter weather made outdoor excursions a cold and questionable pleasure.

A small fire apologized in the fireplace. Jack's mother was crocheting fringe for a mobcap, and Nellie had a piece of sewing on her knees. Most of the Cambridge ladies did sewing, and it was made into bundles and distributed through the camps, where it disappeared like water drops in a thirsty desert; there were too many summer-clothed farmers in the camps to be warmed by a few needles. The pierce of a January sun put a haze of pale charcoal through the room's western-facing windows. Martha and Nellie had been speaking of Mt. Vernon, and Martha had been wondering if House Alice had taken pains to store the plum jam properly and if Lund was pushing the carpenters along and had done anything about the old kitchen well, and had just said, "Your father keeps asking about Mt. Vernon; it's a wrench to him not to be there," when she saw Jack.

"Whatever's the matter?" she said.

Jack's cheeks were slapped to color by the day's raw flail. He cradled a fair-sized black cannon ball in the crook of his elbow.

"A present for you, Nell," he said, and went over and bumped the thing to the floor at her feet.

"For mercy's sake," Nellie said. "Jacky, what are you up to?"

"Nothing," he said cryptically. "Bringing news. Papa will bring it, too, but I'm ahead of him."

His mother stopped her crocheting, adding a quick lock stitch so she would know where she had left off. "What *is* that, Jacky?" she said. She knew what it was; she only wanted to know why it was there, in her room.

"Gift from the king," he said, and grinned and looked pleased with himself. "I wrestled it from a Hampshireman in our earthworks. He didn't need it, he'd have swapped it to a sutler for drink. I thought we ought to have a memento of today. For our parlor in Virginia. King's compliments."

"Fiddledeedee," she said shortly, for something about Jacky's look and behavior upset her. She said, "Your father told you not to go to the lines."

"Lines, Mama?" His face had innocence, and mischief, and another feeling she couldn't quite, at the spur of that moment, define. It was a rawer sense than she had seen in him before, a shock. "There aren't any lines," he said. "Mama, there wasn't a man—oh, the Hampshireman, but he was scavenging—there wasn't a man for hundreds of yards along the works. Only the British union flag on a pole."

"Your father has forbidden you," she said.

"But you can trace the balls coming; you dodge 'em," he said. "It's a sport. I've got to have *something* to do."

Martha bristled. Her nerves were tired. Keeping her fun-fed son within bounds this winter had not been easy. She loved him. But she knew his indulgences, his immaturities, his assumption of his personal wishes and personal triumphs. She rather regretted the knowledge in her cooler moods.

"Having plucked this object," she said, "from your Hampshireman, what do you propose for it?"

"Give it to Nell," he said. "We can use it for cracking walnuts on our hearth."

"That ugly thing?"

"Mama, it's a symbol."

"Never mind."

"They taught us about symbols at the college. In New York." He twined his fingers at his coattails, behind his back, and looked so much like his real father that Martha unconsciously put a hand above her bosom, to her neck, her own fingers taut. "Symbols are for things people want and dream about and can't get. Like the First Crusade. *Deus vult.* All the other Crusades, and what good are we doing? So here's a cannon ball from the king. Because the king's going to war with us. We're a parcel of rebels. We'll submit, or he'll trample us down." He halted, and stared at his feet, and nudged the cannon ball with a toe. It stirred sluggishly. "Souvenir of the occasion," he said.

Martha had stood. Nellie made no sound.

"Jacky, you've been at some tavern," Martha said. "Gentlemen don't frequent taverns in the morning."

"Who's a gentleman?" he said. "Not me. Not you, Mama. Was a paper read this morning in the camps. The king's speech to Parliament. Answer to the Congress petition. We're all to graciously knuckle under and be nice colonies. If we don't, we're barbarians and will be beat. That's you and me."

Nellie said, "Jacky—" and pushed herself from her chair and put an arm around him. And Martha said, "The Congress petition?"

"Door's closed," Jack said. "Papa and his reasonableness. No reasonableness any more. The king's decided." He grinned. "So I've brought you the cannon ball," he said. "Symbol," he said, and looked for a chair and sat down.

Mrs. Gates occasionally dropped in, and although Martha wished she wouldn't, Horatio's lady sipped tea and devoted herself to what Nellie called polite venom. There was no way of avoiding her, for her husband was third in command and she took full advantage of her position. Martha was by now sure that Mrs. Gates would press that advantage, but she had no proof, nothing she could tell her husband. She had tried to warn him but he had laughed her away, and she was racked by the problem of how to make him understand. He was too honest-minded for his own good. Since the king's rejection of the Congress petition, everyone knew it would be final war, not merely a flaring-up to relieve Boston, and jockeyings and maneuvers for power and place were inevitable. Human nature was what it was. Martha, astute, realized that there are few disinterested and wholly dedicated people. The most things a man does he does for his own gain. And the gain is chiefly short-sighted. It is also selfish. So Martha had to face the selfishness of Mrs. Gates.

She faced it over teacups and Mrs. Gates's smile, which had a curl of triumph at its edges, and the bleating of January winds against the corners of the Vassall house. And she was thankful that Mercy Warren was there, and Nellie.

Mrs. Gates had arrived importantly, as she usually did. She was wearing brown today, a brown silk relieved by a ring of crystals at her faintly wrinkled throat and crystal droppings from her ears. Martha was in a gray-purple, Mrs. Warren in blue. Nellie had chosen crimson, a choice that Mrs. Gates's eyes, the eyes of a wealthy and dominant woman of Virginia, had flashed to Martha as not being quite in the humble manner of the youngers. Martha's eyes had flashed back quite as strongly. Nellie, her eyes said, could dress as she liked.

Tea was poured, not too well. Martha, used to slave service in Virginia, found the New England household help a little past her ordering or her ken. She did the best she could. The Northerners, of course, didn't have many slaves. But then the Northerners, also of course, didn't have plantations, or cotton or tobacco, or the need for spreaded labor in the fields. George, she knew, rather abhorred slavery. He made no difference of color against color. He'd listened to a poem recited by a Negro girl at his headquarters a few months ago. But to turn the Negroes out on the world to fend for themselves would be tragedy in their present state. The poor blacks would have no surety, and no experience at earning a living. It would be like freeing sheep into a forest of wolves. . . . What was Mrs. Gates saying?

"I assume you all know. But it *is* a disaster. There's no other word."

Nellie lifted her chin. "We could call it an accidental disaster, Mrs. Gates."

Martha glowed inwardly at the girl. Nellie had the knack, and the spirit, for recognizing insinuations and cutting past them to the truth.

"Disaster all the same," Mrs. Gates said, and busied herself with her tea. "Accident or not."

"But beyond human planning," Mrs. Warren said sociably.

"And not irretrievable," Martha said. "Colonel Arnold is still alive. The general counts heavily on that."

"It's as may be," Mrs. Gates said. She put her teacup in its saucer, rigidly, and said, "To send a mere thousand men through the forests of a Maine winter, ordered to attack the strongest city in Canada—well, my dear, what could one expect?"

"Victory, possibly," Mercy Warren said sweetly.

"General Montgomery was there," Nellie said.

Mrs. Gates smiled with the pity she used for lesser adversaries. "So he was, Nellie," she said. "And now he's dead."

There followed a cutoff in the talk. Nellie looked at her teacup, Martha stirred her spoon mechanically, and Mrs. Warren pinned down a sputtering. There was, to be frank, no gainsaying Mrs. Gates. Montgomery was a corpse on the narrow path approaches to Quebec, Arnold was hit by enemy fire and his troops orphaned and shivering in the Canadian wilds. That Montgomery had been riddled through, as a kind of chimeric trigger-chance, by a drunken sentry whose alcohol flamed him to fire a last shot, was not the question. The question was that the Canada exploration had failed.

"General Washington set Arnold on that track through Maine," Mrs. Gates said. "Starvation, pain, and hardships that would sap any will to fight when they *did* get to Quebec. But I've no doubt he knew what he was doing."

"That was before I came to Cambridge," Martha said. She added, "And the general must take the decisions."

"Oh, surely," Mrs. Gates said, "and the responsibility."

The silence shook.

Nellie said, after a lapse, "So the Canadian project is lost, Mrs. Gates. Have you any other in mind?"

Martha laughed inside herself. Nellie was not precisely a lesser adversary. She could match Mrs. Gates.

"Not entirely lost," Mrs. Gates said, and looked tellingly at the three of them. "But it wants reinforcing. Horatio says General Schuyler, who has the over-all direction at Albany, is heavily ill, and we have no reinforcements we can spare from here. Therefore—what?"

She continued her look.

"I can't answer," Martha said.

"Someone will have to take firm command in the north," Mrs. Gates said.

Nellie burst out. She was normally an easygoing and lightsome girl, but she writhed under Mrs. Gates's obvious smugness. "Papa couldn't dream of replacing General Schuyler!" she said.

Mrs. Gates raised placating eyebrows. "But he will," she said.

They dropped the topic there, by unspoken mutual consent. The afternoon at tea was supposed to be a social one. If Mrs. Gates had paid her call in order to criticize and to unsheath vindictive remarks, Martha and Nellie and Mrs. Warren had had too much practice in gentility to oblige her. Nellie had faced up to her, but was not by temperament nor training nor way of life hardened to stand too long against Mrs. Gates's acidity. Nellie had been softly brought up. Martha, as the general's wife, knew she must curb her tongue lest she do him harm. Mercy Warren moved familiarly among the ins and outs of Massachusetts politics, but in broader regions she was out of her sphere.

They replenished their teacups and left the field to Mrs. Gates. They spoke of dinners proposed, and what could be done for the soldiers shivering under sail-canvas tents in mid-January, and how the firewood had been cut for miles around the Cambridge camps and little more in sight. And Mrs. Gates rose to go.

"So nice, my dear."

"So nice," Martha said. "Again, certainly—any time."

She watched Billy Lee escort Mrs. Gates down the path in front of the house toward where a carriage waited, and said to Mercy Warren, "I wish I knew what she's up to."

Mrs. Warren was getting into her cloak. "General Gates," she said, "is up to making friends with the New England politicians. I can tell you that much. Hover over your husband, dear. Hover like a mother hen."

Then she was gone, too. And Martha, alone in the entrance hall with Nellie, was turning a troubled face to her daughter-in-law and was saying, "But Nellie, your poor father has to be allowed *some* mistakes, doesn't he? There isn't a man in the world can be perfect. . . ."

He knew he'd made a mistake. A heavy error in judgment, military judgment. He'd funneled Arnold through Maine in winter and lost rugged and valuable men. Whether or not Quebec could have been captured, whether or not Montgomery's death had been an obscene twist of fate, he had lost men, needlessly, sprawled grotesque in the northern woods where the snows and the ice-chipped waters covered them. His first strategic move had been a murder of half the force sent out. He knew there were arguments against him, and headshakings in the Congress. He knew, himself, that he was none too sure of himself. He hadn't relieved Boston, he hadn't brought Canada in to the colonists' side. He had simply sat outside Boston, unable to move because he had no powder and no guns, and triggered a march to Canada that had ended in a shambles. The Congress could take some of the blame. But naturally the Congress wouldn't. He was the commander in chief. It was his duty to advise or restrain. He hadn't done either.

The Canadian fiasco bit deep into his mind as he stood up to talk to his war council. The people of the colonies wanted action from him. But the action would have to be successful. One more failure, like that at Quebec, would be disastrous.

These were whirling thoughts, obscure and shot through with instinct. The instinct of self-preservation. The instinct of a farmer longing for Mt. Vernon, where Lund was capping off the old kitchen well and busying the carpenters on the new wing. The wrench, here, was between what he wanted to be and what he wanted to do. The wrench was between the two parts of his nature. Was he a Virginia planter or was he the military leader of the colonies, with war lowering at him?

He looked slowly around the council room, and knew. He saw Greene, Gates, Sullivan, Putnam, Lincoln, and Thomas. He saw, almost as though it were a gypsy's tracings of a palm, a resurgence of hope and of individual force, a force that rose and closed around him and could prop him against swirling politic-managed authority and the skeleton rattlings of bureaucrats. He must play the leader, let the farmer go. He was committed to it. These men would sustain him.

But he had a problem to submit, and they were watching him.

He wished he had Charles Lee with him. Lee was in New York, though, suffering from gout and laying plans to defend the city—his own idea and one that dazzled the Congress, John Adams especially. Washington would have liked to see Lee in the northern command, feeling as he did that Canada was so important, but Lee wanted to take Greene and Sullivan with him and Washington refused to split the two generals away from the main army at Cambridge. The matter was still in the balance.

So he was without his best lieutenant. Sullivan had enthusiasm, Greene was untried. Gates sat unobtrusive in a corner, his spectacles off, blinking amiably.

"I've been to Framingham," Washington said, and thought his voice sounded too high-pitched, insistent, and cleared his throat and dropped his tone lower. "Harry Knox has done the incredible. He's brought fifty-two cannon, nine big mortars, and five cohorns from Ticonderoga. We've just about enough powder to serve them."

A stir in the room, an applauding murmur of voices. Things were not entirely in the gloom. Thus far, thus good.

He felt behind him for his chair, and hinged himself into it. He felt his proposal would be better put in an aura of informality.

"I've also been to Lechmere Point. I went there today. The ice is frozen solid across the channel. All the way to Boston. We have a bridge."

He swept his eyes around the half circle of generals. They were mute.

He said, "Bunker Hill has been taken from us, and is so strong it can't be recaptured. But we could assault Boston across the ice. Now."

He sat back in his chair, as giving them leave to speak what they felt. They hesitated, shifting uneasily in their own chairs.

"Sir." This was from Greene. "Sir, what are our forces?"

"Above seven thousand militia, above eight thousand Continentals," he said. He'd memorized the figures a quarter of an hour before.

"The assault wouldn't use Knox's cannon, sir," Sullivan said. "No time. The weather may not hold."

General Thomas said, without implication of criticism but also without belief, "Are you proposing to advance on Boston across bare ice with nothing more than musketry, sir?"

"I am."

Perhaps it was desperation that had brought him to this. Perhaps it was desperation that led him to read approval in the council's questions. Thomas seemed to be doubting. But that was the function of Thomases, if he remembered rightly.

"The Boston defense," he said, "cannot count on more than five thousand foot. We would be above three to their one."

"The one being entrenched and palisadoed," Greene threw in.

Washington didn't rebuke him.

"But unsuspecting, Greene. And unready. After all, how did Arnold and Allen take Ti?"

"It's rather a different proposition," Greene said. "Ti was a fortress, a defensive spot. It had no choice of movement. It had to sit where it was."

"So does Boston," he said. "Unless—" and he stressed the word and stressed the look he gave them—"unless General Howe marches out against us. Why doesn't he? He could scatter us."

There were answers to that.

"Howe isn't a fool."

"He hasn't enough transport for a campaign."

"What would he get by it? He'd be hounded back."

"You can't strike into New England without rousing the militia."

"Exactly," Washington said. He'd been waiting for this last argument. "But Howe may be reinforced before he strikes. In that case, he *could* sally out. He could lay the countryside waste. I'd like to attack him now, over the ice. Will you give me your votes?"

They came in, one by one, quite frank, and recorded by his aides. When they had all been tallied, he was crushed. His generals, unanimously, were against him.

"Thank you, gentlemen. That will be all."

His generals against him. The country against him. His judgment doubted everywhere. His leadership.

He walked slowly from his office and toward the stairs that would take him to Martha. This was February. It would soon be spring now.

He heard voices—whose, he didn't know—"A slaughter, wouldn't you think?"

"More than certainly."

"Across the ice. Pure folly."

"He's being driven by circumstance, of course. Can't dawdle here forever."

"Oh, yes, yes . . . But can you smell out a flaw, sir? A weakness in military sense?"

"You have a word there, sir, perhaps."

He didn't try to see who the talkers were, but went upstairs to Martha, his boots heavy on the treads.

With all his generals vetoing his straining recklessness, his dependence was entirely on Knox. His whole chance of taking Boston lay with the fat major. He forced himself to patience, and called Knox to headquarters.

He said, "Dorchester Heights, Knox. Cannon mounted there would control the city."

Knox nodded. He'd studied Muller and Vauban, and the science of artillery. "They would."

"I've not fortified the Heights before, for we couldn't defend them. Howe may have been afraid for the same reason. But now your cannon would give us superior weight. You agree?"

"It's the best use we could make of 'em, Your Excellency."

"Can you do it?"

Thick-bellied, worn dead from slogging and bullocking and warping metal monsters along impassable December trails and through three hundred miles of blizzard and thaw and high-tumbled peaks between Ti and Framingham, Knox said that he could.

It needed more weeks to fetch the guns to Cambridge. But once they were there, Knox did it in a night. With men, and wagons, and backs and shoulders, and tugging ropes, and volunteers from Dorchester, and spades and picks and tied bundles of straw piled into breastworks.

The guns, planted, turned the score on Howe and made Boston untenable.

Howe took to his ships, he and the Boston Tories, and his sails dimmed on the horizon.

Washington assigned General Putnam to lead the advance into the open city, and read a message that came from General Sullivan, closing in on Charlestown. Sullivan reminded him, with a Celtic flash of triumph, that the day was March 17, St. Patrick's Day.

V I

"Our Lives, Our Fortunes"

It seemed natural to be in Philadelphia again—natural and very pleasant, at the end of May. They had nice accommodations, he and Martha, Nellie and Jack, and there would be his old friends, the Shippens and the Frankses and the others, and his sessions with the Congress. Yet he felt an incertitude—a kind of shamefacedness, the self-doubting that had gripped him when the Congress had nominated him to command the army.

He'd come down from New England as the conqueror of Boston; had come first to New York and then on to Philadelphia, carrying new honors. A vote of gratitude from the Massachusetts legislature, an honorary degree from Harvard College, praise and a memorial medal from the Congress. Yet he was not the conqueror of Boston. He could see months of motionlessness at Cambridge, hobbled by lack of everything he needed for taking the offensive. The conqueror of Boston was Knox. Knox with his cannon dragged painfully from Ti. He knew, from the public view, from the view of the army he commanded, the praise would have to be his. But it was a wormy knowledge gnawing at his self-respect. He told himself that he would have to learn, as he had never learned as militia colonel on the frontier, to curb his tongue.

He led the army. They wanted to believe in him. The Congress had chosen him for the people and put him at their head. He had been raised on a pedestal, like a statue. He could give credit and due recognition, but he couldn't say flatly the truth, "It wasn't I, it was Knox." For if he faltered in the statue's pose the whole structure might crack, leaving rubble. He was forced to endure, with his own inner iron, the gales of the times. There was no tolerance in the casting for gusty exactitudes.

The image had been molded and set up. A hero, a rallying point. In the people's eyes and in the common cause the image had to be preserved.

As to his being a hero he was a little vague, not being too sure what a hero was. His hit-or-miss schooling as a boy had only given him names of which he could make small concept at age fourteen. Solon, Pericles, the Gracchi. Other names. But that was beyond the matter. He was pushed to the front of the stage and must play his part. As he'd often seen players of parts at Williamsburg. In the theater.

Did it boil down, then, to playing a part? Or did it boil down to sincerity? To the mere honest task of leading soldiers against the king? And he decided, yes, the last was right. For in the first, he was already finding there was a cankerous lack of sincerity in many men. The parts they played were parts for their own gain.

His quandary, he was finding, was not all a matter of bullets and battles. It was also a matter of persons and politics. He shrank from understanding this, but knew within himself that he would have to meet it in time.

This sort of thinking drained him. The sessions with the Congress left him tired, debating on means and measures and the officers to implement them. He was worried about the safety of New York. He was certain Howe would strike at the city. He was heartsick at the sodden mess in Canada—too few men, too little food, a slowly wasting sore too many miles away. General Thomas was up there, to try to bring a shape to things. But the smallpox was rampant there. . . .

It took an effort to tune himself to the gaiety of the Shippens' drawing room. He'd rather not have gone out for social evenings. But the Shippens were good friends, and he knew that sociability was expected of him. And Peggy Shippen was a sweet chit. Her spirits bubbled out like clear spring water.

"Dear General, what sport to see you again. But I shall be a good girl and treat you with great awe."

"Me? With awe?" He saw she was bantering.

"Oh, can you ask? The laurels you wear."

He laughed, and pretended to look startled, and charily passed the palms of his hands along his temples. He lowered the palms in front of him and spread the fingers, empty.

"Don't deny it," she said. "I vow I'm almost afraid to talk to you."

"My pretty Peggy. A crushing fate."

"Isn't it."

"Never may it fall on me."

"But it must."

"Too cruel. How can I prevent?"

"Lend me a store of courage," she said.

"Gallantly, if you'll repay the loan."

"With interest." Her eyes twinkled.

"How?" he said.

"I shall take my borrowed courage," she said archly, "to observe that I am put out with you for shooing Colonel Arnold northward."

"Ah." He appeared to ponder. "And where should I have shooed him? You use an inelegant word for a colonel, by the way."

"Southward," she said. "Where Philadelphia is."

"The colonel thrives on opposition," he said with mock gravity. "He might have found too little of it to the southward."

She gave a quick humorous giggle. "Colonel Arnold? Too little opposition? From me? Oh, sir, what are you saying?"

She spoke loudly on purpose. The others in the room heard her, and there were smiles all around.

"Peggy is enamored of the mysterious Arnold," Dr. Shippen said, jesting in the tone of a nonsense meant for nothing. "Has spread it all through Philadelphia, the baggage."

"Oh, Papa. Baggage? What's safer than to be enamored of a beau I've never set eyes on and who is miles apart from me?" Peggy tittered. "It's a girl's best way to keep her chastity. Besides, if you must know truly, I'll confess. It's the general here who is my dear." She pressed Washington's arm daintily, and raised tiptoe and kissed his cheek. "He's my knight and I shall never desert him," she said.

Then she shifted her mood and turned quickly serious, showing that she had been only amusing herself, that this was all a game to her. "How is Mrs. Washington?"

"Quite well," he said, conscious now that she meant him to speak to the company. "This is her thirteenth day and she has few pustules. A good sign, Doctor?" He turned his eyes to Dr. Shippen.

"Very good," the doctor said.

"You really asked her to take inoculation?" Mrs. Shippen said. "Isn't it dangerous?" She sat by the open window, her back to the tight starlit street and the red brick of the city's houses, chatting with Mrs. Gates. She gave her tone a polite incredulity.

"Not as dangerous as the smallpox itself," he said. "Mrs. Washington has been exposed to it by living near the troops in Cambridge and New York, and there may be other encampments ahead of us. Inoculation is the best for her. And for them."

"The brave, sweet soul," Mrs. Gates murmured. The implication was that of martyrdom for Martha.

"*I* should never dare it," Mrs. Shippen said. "Nor be asked," and she plunged a look at her husband.

"You'd be wise to, sister," Dr. Shippen said.

"Oh, you doctors," she said.

Mrs. Gates said, "General Gates *does* apologize for not being here, Your Excellency. But his engagement to dine with Mr. John Adams tonight—" She had said that earlier in the evening, but seemed to relish repeating it. Washington noted that she was calling her husband "General Gates" now, rather than "Horatio." Which was natural, he supposed. The Congress had made Gates a major general, and it was probable Gates would be given a separate command, removing him from his duties at headquarters. "So we're both bereft, aren't we? Give my respects to Mrs. Washington. I shall certainly call when her condition will allow."

Washington bowed slightly. He didn't want to become embroiled with Mrs. Gates. If he'd known she would be at the Shippens' he wouldn't have come at all. But Mrs. Gates was everywhere in Philadelphia that May. As the wife of the newest major general, and a moneyed woman, doors were opened to her. She had a sharp tongue, and a sharper social sense that could not be casually dismissed as snobbery, and she was a fountainhead of gossip and of politics.

"Mr. Adams has been most kind," she said. "General Gates has had such friendly letters from him. For of course the general *does* work hard."

"He's been my best right-hand man, ma'am," Washington said.

Mrs. Gates drew a silence around her, and smiled, and did not reply. It was as though to have been a right-hand man was somehow beneath dignity. Embarrassment riffled, like the forebreath of a squall on a mirroring lake.

Peggy used soothing tactics. She was alert and sensitive as a young doe. She said, "And that darling Nellie, General. Is she well?"

"In good health," he said.

"When does she expect?"

"In August, I believe."

"So soon? Gracious, how will you feel to be a step-grandfather?"

"Older," he said wryly, and enjoyed the room's laughter.

"Though of course," Mrs. Gates said, "it's not the same, my dear General, as though it were a grandchild of your blood. It needn't age you. It doesn't age you for any of *us*."

He pivoted toward her, bluntly. "You mean, ma'am, that it's no doing of mine."

"Well—" she said, and simpered. "Well, one could hardly call it a doing. It's of a piece with nature, isn't it?"

He went red to the roots of his hair and wished he could control the redness. Mrs. Gates had flicked him on the raw. On his inability to have children who would provide grandchildren of his own. He felt his immense size as a kind of caricature in the room, a kind of impotent plaster colossus for men to stare at. And women, too. Yet he knew. . . . There had been the bed nights with Martha. . . .

He said, "Certainly a piece of nature. And Jacky's wife is a loved part of it."

"Indeed she is," Mrs. Gates said. "I recall those charming evenings in Cambridge." She had gathered the room's attention to herself now, and she made the most of it. "We may be going back there soon," she said.

"To Cambridge, ma'am?"

"To Boston. General Gates is being assigned to command there."

This was the first news Washington had had that he might lose Gates altogether. He was speechless for a moment, fighting pride and resentment and a feeling of being utterly alone. If the Congress saw fit to transfer his two most experienced generals, Lee and Gates, to the far corners of the colonies without consulting him or even telling him of the moves, how could he hope to bring the war to a success? It seemed that in defying the king it was to be every man for himself—particularly the men in high positions. The loss of Gates as his adjutant was bad; the loss of Gates from his councils was worse.

But the Shippens were expecting him to say something, he saw. He saw Mrs. Gates was looking smug.

He walked to the nearest chair and sat down, the tall movement of his body flickering in the candle flames of the chandelier as he strode under them.

"I'd hoped General Gates would share the defense of New York with me," he said.

The peopled room could read his dismay. He had no art of varnishing the canvas of his thoughts.

"Will Howe come for New York, sir?" The question was from David Franks. As an admirer of Peggy's, though a rather forlorn one, he was a privileged visitor.

"I think he will. It's General Lee's opinion. And mine."

"And mine, sir. The largest city in the colonies would be a prize."

"More than that," Dr. Shippen said. "Howe in New York could control the lower Hudson and block the best roads to New England."

"Oh, dear," Peggy said. "In that case I should never see my gallant colonel."

"In that case," Franks said, "I pray that Howe takes the city." He thought twice and said quickly, "Forgive me, Your Excellency. The joke's in poor taste."

"I should think so," Mrs. Gates said with acerbity.

"Your duty there, sir—" Franks said, and flushed.

"No one expects a man bewitched by a smile and two lovely eyes to be a model of taste," Washington said. "You don't need forgiveness, Mr. Franks. You need sympathy." He grinned, and Franks grinned with him.

"Not to add," Mrs. Gates said in a voice that cut with finality, "that Howe could come for Boston just as well as New York."

Washington nodded. He preferred not to argue.

"With the royal navy behind him Howe could come for any city on the coast. And win it." Dr. Shippen made the statement a dogmatic fact.

"Not to add," Mrs. Gates said again, "that General Gates says one guess is as good as the next. Why New York? Why not Boston? Is there a person here who can be sure what Howe will do?"

"The Congress wants New York defended, ma'am," Franks said courteously.

"It is also sending General Gates to Boston," Mrs. Gates said. "And I, for one, declare it a wise move. For many reasons." She tightened her lips in significance and did not enlarge upon the reasons. Her face, the straightness of her shoulders, hinted the reasons might be guessed by anyone not too bedazzled by laurels.

It was an unamiable evening for all of them but Mrs. Gates. She thoroughly enjoyed it.

Washington had called Jack to the room he used as an office. The room was at the front of the inn where the family were staying in Philadelphia while Martha convalesced from her inoculation, and sounds and smells of the street outside wove half-muffled through the partly raised sash: the intermittent squeal of cart axles, plodding hoofs, farm boots scuffing on brick sidewalks, hawkers' cries, and now and then a whiff of manure or West Indian molasses or casks of rum; with the fainter but definable drift of tarred rope and oakum from the Delaware wharves. The aide on duty had admitted Jack and then left.

Since Jack seldom studied his own mind, he never studied others'. He moved from day to day cheerfully blind to the signs to be read in a face, to the telltale deepening of a line or the sag of a mouth corner, and was by habit as indifferent to these as he had been to his college books. For the most part they told him nothing because he didn't trouble to read them. But today he thought his father wore a look of strain. It was not a physical strain. He'd known his stepfather tired before, after hard riding around the farms, and it was not like that. It seemed to be from the inside, a tenseness, a worriment about the future and the unknown. He'd seen the same on the faces of slaves brought ashore to the plantation for the first time.

Though he was waiting impatiently for tomorrow, he kept his manner quiet, rather reserved. This would be the last he would be talking with his stepfather, who would be responsible for protecting New York, until the question of holding the city for the colonies was settled in one shape or another. Either Sir William Howe could capture the city, or his stepfather could defend it. That is, if Howe attacked the city at all. It was not certain yet. Howe might land troops at any point he chose along the Atlantic coast. He had sailed from Halifax with warships and transports, and vanished into the spaces of the sea. Jack had learned these things as common knowledge around Philadelphia.

Washington nodded him to a chair, and he sat down.

His stepfather switched his own chair around from the slant-top desk at which he had been working. There was a single fold of paper beside him on the desk's open writing shelf, and a small sheaf of paper currency, stacked neatly and tied with a ribbon, and the knot sealed with a wax seal. He let his left hand rest on it while he turned, tapping it gently with his fingers for a few seconds before he spoke.

"Excited, Jacky?"

"Lord, yes, Papa." Jack grinned his infectious grin. "Who wouldn't be?" he said.

"No one in your place." A quirk of Washington's mouth showed the grin was irresistible, pressured though a man might be. "It's good to see you happy."

"It's good to *be* that way."

"This has been long for you. You and Nellie. But it's meant much to your mother and me, having you near us."

"We'll be near again, Papa. When you're back in Virginia."

"Old times, eh?"

"And new ones. We'll bring the baby to visit."

"Your mother will adore that."

"So will you, Papa."

"Why, yes." Washington was startled and pleased at the acumen behind Jack's playfulness. It cut home, to the heart of his feelings. "Yes, so I will," he said. "This aged step-grandfather."

"Oh, come now, Papa."

There was a kind of merriment, now, on them both, an easiness. Washington leaned, patted Jack's knee. The motion was clumsy, but genuine. Jack accepted it for that. For its genuineness. For its memories of the ridings with his father in the dawn, and the plays and the gaming tables at Williamsburg, and the trip to New York to the King's College there, with the stop for the night at Baltimore. Especially the stop at Baltimore . . .

"You've made everything ready," Washington said.

"Oh, yes."

"And a sturdy coach."

"I've seen it. At the liveryman's. It's well sprung. Should ride without jolting."

"A solid coach, and steady horses. Those are the main points, Jacky."

"Yes, sir."

"You leave in the morning?"

"Yes, Papa. Early."

"An early start is best, always." The long legs crossed themselves, silver shoe buckles biting morsels from the windowed light. "There may be some items Nellie will want with her in the coach while you travel."

"I know."

"Have you arranged for them?"

"Oh, Papa. Why fret? Billy Lee's doing the packing."

From the easiness of a moment before, Jack felt himself restive. This sort of catechism made him a schoolboy, as if he couldn't handle a trip from Philadelphia to Virginia. Yet he had to admit he'd handled few such trips by himself, and that Nellie's pregnancy made this a fragile one. His stepfather was merely anxious.

"We'll manage finely, Papa," he said, his tone less edged.

Washington caught the tone, and smiled. He enjoyed his friendship with Jack, even enjoyed the ebullience and carelessness and irreverent witticisms of his stepson, for these had been denied him when he'd been young himself and growing up in a harder time and more sinewy life than Jack would ever know. In Jack, although the thought was not a conscious one, buried far in the sands of the present and remaining only as an unmarked hummock of the past, beyond his power of search or archaeology, he lived again, vicariously, the youth that should have been his.

He said, as one traveler to another, "There'll be no need for hurry. Don't go breakneck, Jacky. You've an itch to get home, I know." He smiled with a wry lugubriousness. "So have I, by the same token." And the smile turned to a confession, lying mutual and naked and intimate between them. "I'll think the best day of my life when I get home. But your trip, Jacky—make it slowly, for Nellie's sake."

"We'll crawl. Papa, Nellie's precious to me."

"Nellie. Of course, Nellie. And the baby. Be careful of it."

"You think I wouldn't?"

"Oh no, no." Washington brushed this aside. He drew a slow breath and looked down at his crossed knees.

He hesitated a moment, and said, "What I think is this, Jack. You're going to be a father. You have a chance to be one. Don't take any risk of throwing that away. For you're coming to the uttermost riches of a man's life."

He let the breath trail from his lungs, and put his eyes direct on Jack's.

"You will guess what I am trying to say. Possibly I am talking for myself. Forgive me."

Surprise made Jack blink. His father's words, the sudden gravity, the lifting of a curtain that opened a whole new scene to him put a sudden knot at his throat. He had never seen before, never guessed, that his father had a wound in his longing, in his pride, in his affection, that could not be cured. Only now, now that he himself was to be a father, was this revealed to him. He felt a terrible shyness. He felt he was seeing his father stripped. And he wondered at the seeing. And a swift, impulsive sympathy rushed through him, brushing the wings of pity.

"Papa, I wish you were coming with us."

His father shook his head. Strongly, as though shaking the drops of the Potomac from him after a swim, the drops of a great tidal flow in which there was no wharfage for him unless he made one.

"I wish it, too," he said, "but I can't, Jacky. Your mother will come when she is well, though." Then, as if there had been too much of seriousness, his voice went jocular. "That is, if I can keep her from joining forces with me at New York."

"But Mama oughtn't to go there."

Washington cocked an eyebrow. "Suppose you tell her that, Jacky."

Whereon they both laughed. As married men, together, knowing the ancient force of wives.

"She'll be for home, though, before the guns begin," Washington said. "I promise you, Jack."

"Guns," said Jack. He said, "At New York, Papa?"

"There's no saying. I think so."

"Always the same. Guns or no guns. How or where or why? Good God, what for?"

"For the Congress. The Congress wants New York held."

"That's Lee's notion. I heard that in Cambridge."

"Mine too, Jack."

" 'Hold New York,' Lee said. And where is he now? Off to the Carolinas, being chief man. He likes that."

"He's defending Charleston. There's an attack pushed there."

"But he's not with you. Neither is Gates. Papa, I catch the talk at headquarters. They say you can't hold New York. Rivers on two sides and a bay in front. Enough to float the whole king's fleet."

Washington made allowance for Jack's ignorance, for his emotional approach to something he was not muscled to grapple with, not trained. He said, "The Congress wants the city held."

"Oh, the Congress." Jack bit the word.

"I have my commission from the Congress. You're not a soldier, Jacky."

"Nor will be, Lord willing. Papa, they ought to let you go home."

With that, their talk came to an empty stop. Jack felt he had had his say. If there were any real concern in his argument over New York, it was too blanketed by his nature to be much roused. He only wanted things to be at Mt. Vernon as they had been before the fighting had started. Washington, for his part, saw no need for longer explainings that must end where they began.

The street sounds increased in the room as their voices stilled. Sounds of everyday living, the jostle and squawk and chattering procession of a normal, heedless time. To judge from the sounds, there might have been no war in the colonies at all.

Washington rose, and closed the window further. He came back to the desk and stood by it, by the sheet of paper and the currency notes.

"I'm sending Lund money for the new wing," he said. "If you'll take it for me, Jack."

"Certainly, Papa."

"Two hundred fifty pounds," Washington said. "I've written Lund."

"I'll give 'em to him."

"Thank you, Jack." He took a quill pen from its stand and dipped it in ink and laid it on the desk and moved the shaker of blotting sand closer and smoothed the paper. "This is the receipt."

Jack said, "The what?"

"The receipt."

"You mean—from me?"

"It's customary, Jack."

"You want a receipt from me, Papa?" Jack's expression was nonplused.

"Merely a statement that you have had the money."

"But we both know that."

"It's a large sum, Jack. It should be signed for."

Little sharp pricklings began to run upward along Jack's jaw from under his neckcloth. He frowned at the paper and the quill and stared at his father. "Don't you trust me, Papa?"

"That's quite beside the matter. You hardly need to ask."

"As if I was some stranger—"

"Not at all."

"As if I was making to cheat you."

"Jacky. Nonsense."

"It has the looks that way, doesn't it?"

Washington was mild. He said, "When you come into the management of your own monies, Jacky, you'll find that looks and business are different affairs. At least I hope you will. A receipt for money changing hands is simply good business. Receipts are a rule of mine." He paused, and rubbed his chin. "A receipt is simply a record," he said. "I wish all my generals kept them." He was thinking of Benedict Arnold, and Arnold's tangled accounts with Massachusetts, which had nearly cost the colonies the services of that brilliant fighter. He said, "Purely business, Jacky. I'm only following my rule."

The voice held mildness, but Jack thought he had never known his father so cold. There was an inflexibility in his father's figure, standing in front of him by the desk, that left him helpless. And being helpless, angered. The anger was rougher in him because of the intimacy that had gone before, the companionableness they had both been enjoying. The contrast sat harsh on Jack.

He said, "But I'm family, Papa, not business."

"The rule is the same, though."

"You could break a rule for your family, couldn't you?"

Washington considered his stepson slowly. The boy was plainly upset, hurt in his pride, and, perhaps worse, in his sentiment. Washington was not entirely aware of the sentimental hurt. The unawareness was one of his failings. He'd not been raised in a sentimental atmosphere.

He said, "No, Jack, I couldn't. A rule is a rule." He reached for the pen, held it toward his stepson. "Will you sign now? I must go to the Congress."

He came back from his meeting—it was a botched, political thing, getting a little this side of nowhere, loud words on supplies and where they would come from, and what colony had its quota of militia in the field and what had not, and where the pay could be got for the Continentals, and whether Gates or Schuyler should take the northern command at Albany, and how to make best use of the remnants of the Canadian expedition, which was falling back, trounced, to Ticonderoga, Arnold at its head. General Thomas had died of smallpox on the St. Lawrence. The northern route down the Hudson into the colonies lay bare to the king's troops, and the governor of Canada, Sir Guy Carleton, was a shrewd soldier, and New York at the Hudson's mouth, fattened like an oyster for swallowing by the ships and regulars and mercenaries of Sir William Howe. For there were mercenaries in the fight, now. King George was hiring German Hessians and Brunswickers to bring the colonies to their senses.

These things confronted him in the Congress. They called for a strength and a physical means of defense the colonies simply didn't have.

He came back to find Martha and Nellie and Jack in their small parlor room at the inn. He had an hour or so with his aides—letters, memoranda, reports—and then went to the parlor. It was low-ceilinged and stuffy. He was almost sorry he hadn't taken up the invitation to stay at Hancock's house while Martha recovered from the pox. But he hadn't wanted to expose Hancock to the disease.

As he entered the room he could feel the unfriendliness in it. Martha and Nellie scarcely looked up from their sewing. Martha was quilting, a great map of cotton stuff spreading away from her lap; Nellie was threading embroidery on a child's dress; Jack jogged a knee-crossed leg up and down and read the newest gazette.

"Well, my dears," Washington said.

He lowered himself into a comb-back chair. It had short arms that left his wrists dangling as he relaxed his elbows on the narrow wood. "Well, tomorrow is the departure."

Nellie looked up. She looked down again, at her sewing. "Yes, Papa."

"For Mt. Vernon," he said. "And then your own plantation. Jacky and I have been over the details. It should be a happy trip."

He was met by silence. Martha yanked a handful of quilt across her dress, and brushed at the wrinkles the quilt left. "It would be happier under other conditions, George."

"Oh?" he said. "What other conditions?"

"I think you know."

"I think I don't. What are you getting at?"

Here was, he understood, as by male instinct, the question of all husbands to all wives. The question that all wives waited for. But, being male, he couldn't avoid it. "What are you getting at, Martha?"

"You know," she said. It was also the prerogative of wives to repeat the phrase, not so much tentatively as with assurance, turning it like a probe into the weakness of a man, into where he had already been hit. And, with the turning, the subtle imagery of a beardless tad being paddled behind an outhouse—this is for your own good. "You know," Martha said.

Guilt—no, no, he wouldn't call it that—perception flooded in on Washington and brought his next question.

"Jack?" he said. "That receipt?"

"Yes," Martha said.

"But I made that clear to him. The thing's a money question."

"Money or not, you needn't have insulted him."

"By asking for a receipt?"

"Your own stepson," she said.

"Martha—there is such a thing as a transaction. A financial matter."

"That may be, George. From your view. You can scarcely expect it to be from mine."

"The view is commonly accepted, my dear."

"There is also such a thing as common kindness," Martha said, ignoring his remark.

"Where is kindness involved?" he said.

"It would be a kindness to show your kin you have faith in them."

"How?" he said.

Nellie looked up. The color had heightened in her cheeks. Her embroidery needle poised aslant in her hand in mid-air, nervously.

"Mama," she said, rather breathless, "I don't think Papa means—"

"You will leave this to me, please, dear," Martha said.

Nellie returned to her sewing.

"Jacky is my son, dear," Martha said.

Nellie bent her head, a little stiffly. She plunged the needle in and out of the embroidery with quick, sharp strokes.

Jack didn't interfere. He sat quiet, the old amused and teasing smirk on his face. His mother was coming to his rescue. She never failed him.

"How, Martha?" Washington repeated, as if there had been no interruption, "how should I show my kin?"

"By not treating them like persons in some counting house," she said. "You're too high-handed in your attitude to Jacky, George."

"Because I insist on good business habits?"

"Too high-handed," she said. And with the sudden pincering all-inclusiveness mothers are capable of, she added, "Except when you're being too soft with him."

"Which is it this time?" he said. She was forcing him to sarcasm, where she would have him at her mercy.

"I don't wish to argue," she said flatly, and left that burden to him.

He considered the burden, and side-stepped it gingerly. There was something ridiculous in this scene, he thought; yet there was something more, too, of heavier significance than a quarrel over a signature. It was the underground twisted current of emotions and possessiveness and stream of love that eddied and scoured sunless through the caves of their minds and that threatened now to burst to the surface. He tried mollification.

"I've always had faith in Jacky," he said.

Martha bent over her sewing, like Nellie. Like Nellie's, her needle moved faster.

"Even when he wanted to marry?" she said.

There. It was out. In spite of him, the stream had boiled itself into the open. Or perhaps because of him, his stubbornness about the receipt. The stream had boiled up once before, but he had hoped it had receded. That had been when Jacky married.

He cast about for an answer. "That had nothing to do with my faith in Jacky," he said. "I didn't think the moment was right for it. No more than that."

Martha came as near to a sniff as he had ever heard her. The break between them over Jack's marriage plainly still rankled. "Didn't think," she said.

A thread snapped. She made a gesture of disgust and pushed the half-finished quilt to the floor. "Didn't think. And dear Jacky in love," she said.

"Martha—not again, please," he said. "I didn't object to the marriage as such."

"You wrote that letter to Nellie's father."

"I wrote to say I felt Jack was too young."

Martha merely looked at him.

"He needed to go on with his education," he said.

"Education for what?" Jack cut in on them. The smirk had gone from his face, and his lips smiled uncertainly, like a climber pinned to a cliff but morally sure of handholds. "Papa, how would you have felt if somebody'd tried to stop you from marrying Mama?"

"I only asked a postponement, Jack. My letter to Mr. Calvert—"

"Was uncalled for, George," Martha said.

"Lord, Papa," Jack said, "it was your fault I met Nellie in the first place. You took me to the Calverts' that night we stayed in Baltimore, on the way to the college. Don't blame *me*," he said, "if you threw Nellie at me."

"Jacky!" Nellie said.

He blew her a kiss. "He did," he said. "If we'd not stopped at the Calverts' I'd never have known you."

"That's true, George," Martha said before Nellie could speak. "You introduced them to each other. And then you tried to step between them."

"We've been over this before, Martha."

"You won't take the consequences of what you do. You don't like consequences. If you didn't want Jacky to fall in love it was stupid to lead him to a pretty girl like Nellie in the first place."

"I said we've been over this before."

"Very well, George. And I said I won't argue. It stems back to that nasty receipt. You're doing the same to Jacky now as you wanted to do then—simply overriding him. You're right and the rest of the world is wrong."

"I wrote to Mr. Calvert honestly. I told him what I felt. Do you want me to play lies, Martha? Jack's in my charge. I'm responsible for doing the best I can for him. As to the receipt, I say that's essential. Jack has signed it. Let's have no more of this, please."

They felt the rise of his anger. Martha bristled herself. Nellie dropped needle and thread and put the tips of her fingers to her lips. But Jacky murmured, in a light, lazy drawl, "There speaks the autocrat. General —suh."

Washington lunged to his feet. He was fast, but Nellie was faster. She was on her feet before he was. Her body rocked, her arms were flung to the side as if to steady herself.

"Stop it!" she said. "Oh, stop it!" When they had looked at her in bewilderment her hysteria calmed, but the words she had to say came from her in a spate.

"Of course, Papa wrote to my father! Why shouldn't he? He's a right to his ideas, hasn't he? He only wanted the best for Jacky, the way he saw it. The letter didn't hurt my father. He didn't mind it. He understood what Papa here was aiming at. And it was a gentleman and dignity letter. You all shouldn't make such talk. You, Jacky, you just be thankful to Papa. You just remember it was him fetched the two of us together! Forget the silly receipt. Now you've set the baby kicking inside me and I'm going to be ill!"

She darted for the door, sobbing.

Jack followed her, dripping contrition as he went.

"Oh, mercy," Martha said. "Oh, mercy."

"There's such a thing," Washington said, "as going too far, Martha. Your fondness for Jacky is—"

"Absurd, George? No, I can't admit that." She smoothed calmly at her skirt and stood up also. "You know what Jacky is to me," she said. She added, in her housewifely tone, "That receipt, George. Will you let me have it? Or will you tear it up?"

They were face to face. His height loomed over her, but the spirit in her eyes was as strong as his.

"Will you, George?"

His jaws clamped. "No," he said.

She turned from him and left the room without a word.

It was his duty as commander in chief to have the declaration from the Congress, in early July, read to the troops.

He had them paraded, standing in serried ranks and attentive—or as attentive as it is possible for soldiers to be—and he sat his horse in the middle of their sight, and gulls from New York's harbor wheeled and floated above, and the smell of sea and barnacled pilings wafted over the parade grounds from east and west, and from the distance the lump of Staten Island crouched like a banshee, and the voice of the officer who was reading climbed throaty above a massed appearance of respectfulness.

"'When, in the Course of human events, it becomes necessary for one people to dissolve the political bands which have connected them with another, and to assume among the powers of the earth . . .'"

He paid attention that was nonattention. Martha had left for Mt. Vernon, cool still over their differences about Jack. And Sir William Howe was surely for New York. His frigates were nosing at the outer hook.

"'. . . For cutting off our Trade with all parts of the world. For imposing Taxes on us without our Consent. For depriving us in many cases of the benefits of Trial by Jury . . .'"

He hadn't known of this declaration, hadn't been consulted about it. He was only an officer—the commander, yes, but still an officer—subject to the dictates of the Congress. The declaration took him rather aback, as, he felt, it would take many others. It was a radical step, desperate.

"'We, therefore, the Representatives of the United States of America, in General Congress, Assembled . . .'"

He thought of Jack, rebellious as the Congress was. Not meaning rebellion, but somehow propelled toward it. He thought of Martha's doting on Jack. Of his own emptiness, his failure to get children. Was it his failure, or Martha's? Was it a frigidity in her, a tensing of love for her boy that kept her from conceiving other boys that would be his? He took off his hat, in the view of the soldiers, and wiped his forehead with his handkerchief. In any event, he must be more fatherly toward Jack. Less high-handed. And less soft. (Martha's words, and he knew their rightness.) He must find a middle way, a patience.

It seemed to him that everything called to him for patience.

"'. . . And for the support of this Declaration . . . we mutually pledge to each other our Lives, our Fortunes, and our sacred Honor.'"

H'mm . . . That would be Jefferson, who was beginning to show himself adept at the pen, as Henry was at oratory. And the declaration meant that bandied and avoided word, Independence. Probably it was inevitable, things being as they were. But he felt no great surge of excitement, only a dull settling into a weightier harness. For it was he who would have to make the independency good. The Congress could proclaim, but he must do the fighting.

Muskets rattled, and the troops filed off to the drum beat.

He rode off to his headquarters, slowly, signaling his aides to stay behind. The Congress, in its wisdom, had framed a United States and declared them free. He wondered, from the small acid experience he had had so far, whether the freedom would be strong enough, stable enough, mutual enough, to make it worth the while.

VII

Christmas Night, 1776

" 'By perseverance and fortitude we have the prospect of a glorious issue; by cowardice and submission, a sad choice of a variety of evils—a ravaged country—a depopulated city—habitations without safety, and slavery without hope. . . .' "

The words knifed chill and sharp and biting as the morning air among the thin ranks of men. Washington sat his horse, motionless, and watched the men. They stamped rag-wrapped feet on the ground to fight off numbness and frostbitten toes, and their looks told him nothing. But he thought they should hear what Tom Paine's lantern-lit quill had penned in their camp, thought they should know, from one of their own, the full weight and desperation of the crisis. Put in such trumpet language, the knowledge might stir them to keep their courage a little longer.

It was five months since they had listened to the other message, the independence declaration by the Congress. They had heard that in the heat of July, in New York City, by the banks of the Hudson. They were hearing Paine's words now in December winter, huddled forlorn, like a last hope, on the far side of the Delaware, the king's troops massing on the opposite shore and chafing to get at them. In those five months their looks had been drained of anything except blankness. They could give Washington no response from their eyes. But some of them slanted their muskets smarter.

He signaled an aide. "Convey my esteem to Private Paine. When he has more of his writings I should like to see them. Dismiss the regiments." Then to Knox, a great-coated bulk in the officer group behind him: "Will you ride with me, Colonel? I must make certain about the boats myself."

They reined to the left and moved off along the riverside, he and Knox, their horses hock-deep in melting slush under a heavy sky. Trees stood leaden against the sky, their limbs gauntly bare, and the river ran bloated, gray and sullen.

He scarcely noticed. If the scene was grim, his thoughts were grimmer. He was thinking of boats. Boats that would let his enemy cross the river and start the chase again.

His army, his life, the life of the country depended on his order that no boats were to be left on the other side of the Delaware.

This was a stopgap, only temporary. But everything since July had been stopgap, and retreat, and loss, and retreat again. The year that had begun so well at Boston was ending sick and diseased at the Delaware. He had been beaten on Long Island, whipped out of Manhattan. The king's bugles there had shrilled the "view halloo" at him as if he were a hunted fox run to earth; and he'd flown into one of his rages and still didn't remember how his aides had pulled him from the front of the battle and sure slaughter. But he did remember his hoarse croak, seeing the militia and Continentals streaming past him, running from bullets: "Good God, are these the men I'm to defend America with?" . . . A check to Howe's forces above Harlem Heights had been promising but slight, for Howe controlled the waters that flowed past New York and could outflank him at will. He'd been shouldered from White Plains, ferried his army to New Jersey, reinforced Fort Washington on the northern spur of Manhattan, inspected it, decided to hold it; and within twenty minutes, from a row-barge in the middle of the Hudson, had seen it captured, with thousands of men and precious guns and powder. From then on he had reeled backward through the Jerseys, Howe at his heels, running him to the Delaware. He had got his army over the Delaware, with the river between him and Howe, and was paused now in a kind of panting relief, safe for a moment perhaps, but not sure of the moments to come.

Behind him were confusion and fright. The Congress had piled all the responsibility, all the authority for the war, on him, and had scurried out of Philadelphia to a safer distance. In front of him was the Delaware, with Sir William Howe sitting confident in Trenton and scouring up and down for boats. The Continentals were a plucked remnant of a sorry half year's defeats. The only ray in the gloom was that Benedict Arnold, commanding singlehanded, had built a fleet of ships from raw timber on Lake Champlain, and had fought it to the last hulk and the last gun to beat back an invasion from Canada and win a winter of grace for the Hudson Valley, with a chance to strengthen that lifeline. But Lake Champlain was long miles from the Delaware. If the invasion had pushed to the Hudson, the war would have been ended. But if Howe pushed across the Delaware, it would be ended too.

The plans must be from day to day. There was no larger strategy any more, nothing left on which to base such strategy, much less carry it through.

Washington held his horse to a walk, using his spyglass. "That cove's empty, Knox."

"Colonel Humpton's work, sir. Not a skiff left other side for Howe to float on."

"We'll ride farther."

His lines stretched along the river for twenty-five miles. Howe might cross anywhere and he had to be ready to meet him. He and Knox found hasty breastworks, and soldiers with pick and shovel. The river crested yeasty at its shallows, and a white glaze thickened along its edges.

Knox said, "Howe could build rafts. He could pole across."

"Or march over on the ice if there's a freeze," Washington said.

The fat colonel had no answer for that. The picture was plain. He said, instead, "Is there anything more from General Lee, sir?"

"No," he grunted.

He didn't mean to be curt with Knox, who was predominantly a kindly man and whose geniality was as broad as his beam. But Lee had become a perplexity. The bony general had come back, full of success at Charleston, in time to rejoin the army around White Plains. He had lingered on in Westchester, at the head of five thousand men, proposing to do something against New York while Howe chased Washington southward. He'd done nothing, though, and had parried all suggestions and appeals to come to Washington's help. Washington felt that he and Lee together, with five thousand more men, might turn the scales. Lee, however, had taken his own time, and was only now moving casually down through the Jerseys in a westering parallel to Howe's rear posts.

"No, no other word. I don't know when to expect him."

"But General Gates will be coming, sir?"

The statement was more of a question, for Knox, too, was curious about Gates, like the whole headquarters. And again Washington couldn't be sure. He couldn't be sure of anything since the Long Island battle—even the simple necessary things like flour and shoes and clothing and blankets. He knew only that Gates had been sent out from Boston by the Congress to take command of the northern army when it straggled from Canada; and had had quarrels with General Schuyler, and was now reported to be leading some regiments to Washington's aid. But news of him had been few and far between. He seldom wrote reports to his chief.

"We must assume he'll be here in due season," Washington said.

That meant before the Delaware froze, or before Howe could build rafts. Howe had Hessians now, German troops hired by Lord North's ministry, and was promised reinforcements up to thirty thousand. Washington had less than a tenth of that number.

"Do you see any boats over there whatever, Colonel?"

"None, sir. I'd say we have every keel within forty miles."

"Then we have a breathing space, at least. We'll go back to headquarters."

They went back, and the sun slacked, and night fell; and Knox went to his cot and thought of his round and luscious Lucy, and Washington took up the letters on his desk. Letters from Lee, delaying, promising, saying that he knew what he was doing, and insinuating that major generals, operating at a distance, should be allowed their own judgments. His troops, he said, were in good condition.

And another letter. One from Lee to Reed. Washington had opened it, as a matter of business, Reed being absent in Philadelphia. But it was more than business.

The lines of it rose up at him: "I received your most obliging, flattering letter—lament with you that fatal indecision of mind which in war is a much greater disqualification than stupidity or even want of personal courage. Accident may put a decisive blunderer in the right, but eternal defeat and miscarriage must attend the man of best parts if cursed with indecision."

Indecision?

He dropped the letter as though it had fangs. Fangs and bite, and a serpent's poison.

He could read its begettings. His aide had written secretly to Lee, the secrecy of doubt. Lee had answered in stark criticism.

"Indecision," Lee said. The commander in chief, on whom everything hung, was indecisive.

He stood up, walked the room, sat down again.

He saw, from the outward look of things, that this would seem true. He'd not yet won an open battle. He'd squeezed the king out of Boston, but not since then had he yet defended a single post. He'd thrown men away—and supplies and guns and ammunition—to be battered beyond the Delaware with a herd of draggled ragamuffins.

Indecision . . . The word mocked him, as the powers loaded on him by the Congress mocked him, too. He had no force to which he could dictate, only emptiness and disillusion to work his authority on. His hounded retreat through the Jerseys had turned hundreds of Americans into Tories, ready to go over to the king. He'd counted on the Jersey militia to muster to him. They weren't mustering. As for Lee—if he took a dictator's voice there, that high-blown and flighty general might promptly resign.

Well, did it matter now? Ten days, he thought, would put an end to his army. Ten days at most. The game was pretty nearly up. He would write to Reed, explaining how he had come to see the letter, and with no mention of personal hurt; for personal hurt must be sloughed over in the cause of unity. But unity itself was very nearly a wraith, an insubstantial ghost. He could hardly trust his men to fight any more, and he wondered, knowing now the sneers behind his back, if they trusted him. He couldn't blame them, in his heart, if they didn't. Their Congress had declared them independent, and he had led their independency to nothing but rout and disgrace.

Because he would cling to every foothold, though, he began a letter to Putnam in Philadelphia, asking what Putnam could do in the way of rousing the militia in the city. Yet even as he wrote he remembered Sam Adams' opinion. It had been quoted to him. All the despondent opinions were quoted to him. "Nothing can exceed the lethargy that has seized the people," Sam Adams had said. And was probably correct, Adams knew the popular temper. In victory, the temper was enthusiastic. In doubt and uncertainty, torpid. He had only been able to offer doubt and uncertainty. The people, the country, were slack, spiritless, confused. They no longer greatly cared. Submission seemed inevitable, better than struggle, and safer. The shine of Boston had long since tarnished. His thought twisted and turned, trying to evade the final decay.

An aide knocked, came in.

"Yes?"

"A man asking to see you, sir. Honeyman, by name."

"Oh. Yes. Send him in."

The man entered. His dress was a cattle drover's. He had mediocre features, nothing prominent in eyes or nose or lips; a slouched body and an indeterminate air.

Washington scanned him. "From Trenton, Honeyman?"

"Yes, sir."

Washington put the letter to Putnam aside for the time, nodded to the aide to leave the room. Honeyman followed the aide with slitted eyes, and both he and Washington spoke low.

"You have a report, Honeyman?"

"I have, sir."

"We're alone."

"Yes, sir." The spy took a half step forward, his plain face wrinkling in a kind of exultancy. He said, "General Howe, sir."

"I know about Howe," Washington said.

"Yes, sir," Honeyman said. "But you don't know this, sir. Howe's drawing back into New York City, going to winter quarters."

"Howe? To New York?"

"Gospel, Your Excellency, and Lord Cornwallis trailing after him." He slapped his boot tops with his hat, shy in the presence of his general and employer. "And there's a troops' pay chest coming to New Brunswick, sir," he said.

Washington stiffened. He cleared his throat before he spoke. "Is that certain, Honeyman?"

"Certain as I stand."

"They might be pulling the wool over you."

"Over me, sir, John Honeyman? Sir, who'd go about to think I had ears for news? Or any place to take it to?"

The simplicity spread and sat so bland on the leathery cheeks that Washington laughed.

"No. No, they wouldn't reckon you intelligent, not from a view of you." He dropped his laughter. "There's a certain asset in hiding the light under a bushel, Honeyman, in spite of scripture. It leaves the enemies in the dark."

"Yes, sir."

"We should both remember that."

"Yes, sir."

"So Howe is gone."

"Clean away. Them sort fancy boys don't fight in winter, sir."

"It's against military practice. By God's grace we aren't practiced."

"No, sir."

"And who's at Trenton? They can't all have gone."

"No, sir. They's a garrison stationed, you might say. Hessians."

"How many?"

"Fourteen hundred or thereabout. To make a guess."

"Commanded by—?"

"Colonel Rall, sir."

The name hit. Washington harked back to a hill near White Plains. Rall and the Hessians had overpowered the hill, crumpling his right wing.

"Rall—ah. Tell me, is it safe for you in Trenton again?"

"I dunno, sir. They take me at value, 'course, a country lump selling beeves. But the Hessians are tightening, now. They've got the guard job, y'see."

"Very well. Stay out of Trenton."

"Yes, sir."

"Thank you. That's all."

"Good day, sir." Honeyman started for the door.

Washington halted him. "Honeyman?"

He faced about. "Sir?"

"Be cautious for yourself, Mr. Honeyman. You are valuable to the army."

"Yes, sir."

The door opened, shut with a click of latch. Then there was the aide again—Fitzpatrick, Harrison, Tilghman—he paid no mind, his aides were changing so often now. He ordered a council of his generals.

They clustered to him, and a chair groaned under Knox, and Greene eased his limping leg on a stool and pushed back his wig, and Sullivan scowled and fiddled with coat buttons, and they and the rest took attentive attitudes while he paced. He was too excited to sit down.

"Gentlemen, I am apprised that Howe has retired to New York. Lord Cornwallis is following him. They've left Trenton manned by less than two thousand Hessians. You will please submit your thoughts to me, gentlemen, for going over to the attack."

The generals stared at one another with almost unbelief. And in their eyes were the looks of men snatched at the final instant from the gallows.

For he meant to attack.

He needed money. The troops hadn't had money all year and wouldn't fight on promises tricky as the weather. He wrote to Robert Morris, his wealthy merchant friend in Philadelphia. Morris scraped up the money from somewhere; Washington suspected it was a personal loan from the Quaker John Martin. No matter, though. The money came in.

He wrote to Gates again. He wrote to Lee. He studied maps and watched, agonizingly, the Delaware ice.

There came an express rider. The rider brought shock. General Lee had been captured in bed, at a Jersey inn, fuddled with wine, and with nightgowned women raising hysterics. The capture was so easy as to be almost comic. It was done by a few dragoons.

He sent Sullivan to fetch Lee's troops to the camp, and they were not five thousand; a worn, despondent lot, feet swathed in slabs of beef hide.

Gates came on the same day as Sullivan. Gates's regiments, for Gates had called them so, amounted to six hundred.

He swallowed his disappointment—a habit he was growing used to. He was glad to see Gates, the affable smile, the fatherly face; and he wrung Gates's hand hard. With Gates at his side, things looked well again. His other officers were young, untrained in maneuvers and the tricksy co-operation of battle. Long Island had proved that.

"When you're rested, General, I must beg your advice. I've a hard assault in mind."

Gates's response was limp. It had the stagnancy of a tidewater pool at ebb. "My advice can be given now, sir. The army can't possibly be reorganized this side of the Susquehanna."

Susquehanna? That would be a retreat for another hundred miles. Washington was thinking of attack.

He said, "Susquehanna?"

"Obvious, General. The troops' enlistments end with the year. Mine won't re-enlist for more service. Lee's will be the same. So will yours. It's the Congress, sir."

Tired, tired, Washington thought. Yes, the Congress. That august body was playing politics with the army, and Gates was shrewd enough to know it. He wished he could be shrewd or subtle, or anything except merely stubborn. The Congress had decreed that the new army next year —if there was to be an army—would have officers appointed by commissioners from the states. This was logrolling, back-scratching, a scramble for votes to keep the congressmen in lush living at Philadelphia or wherever they scattered to. As dictator, he'd already decided to veto that foolishness.

"We'll change that face of things, Gates," he said.

"What face?"

Washington thrust away the Congress. "The Susquehanna," he said.

"Not in the few days left to you," Gates said.

"But with you here, General—?"

Gates's head waggled. The waggle bespoke sympathy rather too shallow, too easily evoked. "I've had a long march, sir, bringing my regiments to your support. I am worn. I must think of my health. I intend—oh, naturally with Your Excellency's permission—for Philadelphia. And there is personal business, besides."

Washington felt his cheeks tensing, his stomach a knob of cold. He forced a smile. "How long in Philadelphia, Gates?"

"Oh, not long, not long."

But the answer seemed evasive. Evasive as Gates himself, as he saluted formally and went out.

And then Washington was left to himself. Left to nagging questions that badgered and bit at him. Would Lee's jibes at him run through the army? Did Gates's open reluctance mean what he thought it meant? He couldn't believe that the man who had sat under his portico, asking him to use his influence with the Congress to promote that man, would desert him now. Desert him for personal, prideful reasons . . .

There were maps, of course, and Washington made use of them, big-fingered. "McConkey's Ferry, above Trenton. Nine miles. Get your troops there, Greene. And Sullivan. I'll be there. Opposite Trenton, General Ewing will cross with the militia. Cadwalader lower down, with his Pennsylvania troops . . . We'll march on Trenton from three sides. At dawn after Christmas day."

He heard the stiffness in his voice, and the stiffness meant he was determined. He heard Greene's questions, pointed, a trifle shaken.

"Your Excellency—perhaps we should consider a diversion instead? A foray against Rall's wagon lines, say. Or some feint to distract attention while we—while—do you seriously intend to make a crossing of the river, sir?"

"Don't you intend to, Greene?"

Greene swallowed, took off his wig, rubbed his bald head. Frowned in a startled way, as if a blunt probe were reaching at his spirit, measuring it to that of his commander. Then he smiled.

The smile was like a warm fire in Washington's heart.

There was no fire on Christmas afternoon. The weather was vile and Washington's nose was red. It always reddened in cold, being large and prominent, like his body. He pinched at it with thumb and knuckles and felt it tingle, and watched the men march by toward McConkey's Ferry. Knox would be at the ferry, obeying orders. "You've the lungs, Colonel. Shout 'em into the boats," he'd told Knox.

Nothing, he thought, could be worse for such a gamble than a day like this. Snow had fallen during the night, enough to cover the ground, and half his men would be marching through it barefoot. The wind was blustering in from the northeast, whipping mercilessly by at thread-bare coats and raveled breeches and the hunched backs that plodded past him. Yesterday the Delaware had been rough and fast flowing, but open; today the ice was driven loose from creeks upstream, and the river would be swirling with ugly floes. A weight of sky promised more snow to come. It was as dismal and raw and shelterless an afternoon as he could remember. The shabby columns were outlined in the midst of it like phantoms.

The whole prospect had a phantom quality. His plan was good. He had the boats, he had artillery, he had ammunition; what he lacked in men could be made up in suddenness, in surprise. But he also had word from Reed: ice was forming thick along the shores farther down the river, Putnam was dubious about fetching any troops from Philadelphia, the affair looked discouraging. He had word from Cadwalader, who was to cross below Trenton: the general warned of small numbers, and not to expect much. He had no word from Ewing, opposite Trenton. With the river icy and the night sure to be violent, it might be possible that neither of the other two prongs of the assault would get across to support him.

No indecision now, though; none. He would go on without the others if he had to. It seemed to him the night was in his favor; the wind and ice would hamper him, but the wild weather would keep Hessian patrols close to quarters and would help to cover his crossing.

He scrubbed at his nose again, signaled Billy for his horse, and mounted; nodded to his aides, and started the ride for the ferry. A local farmer rode beside him as his guide. He had been thorough about that—guides and scouts for the unmarked roads and deceptive, branching lanes in the pitch of night. Nothing must go wrong.

Lee was not with him, nor Gates nor Putnam. None of his major generals was there. The outcome, a few hours from now at Trenton, rested on him and him alone. The consciousness of this rode beside him more real than the guide.

He studied his men as his horse drew slowly along the line of trudgers. In the graying twilight their faces were indistinguishable, their heads bent and their necks tucked down into shoulders rounded against the pushing gusts. But here and there he could see a pair of legs cased in red flannel, and he smiled. Friendly ladies and gentlemen of Philadelphia had sent the army a few hundred discarded coats, some with flannel linings, and he had ordered the linings ripped out to use for breeches, and had written gracious thanks to the ladies and gentlemen for their collection of old clothes. He was glad part of his troops were warmer dressed. His own slaves at Mt. Vernon were better cared for than these fellows who had marched and fought and suffered for a year while their country sank into indifference.

The thought of Mt. Vernon stayed with him. They would be gathered there now, in the dining room in the peace of the late afternoon—Martha and Jacky and Nellie. Possibly his sister Betty and her husband Fielding Lewis, from their handsome brick home Kenmore, in Fredericksburg. There would be the baby, too. His step-grandchild. Jacky's daughter. He only knew her name, Elizabeth. Little else, except that she was healthy and was four months old now. Martha's letters gave him few details; they had been stilted and aloof, plainly showing that she was still put out with him for setting his foot down in the matter of that receipt from Jack. He understood it wasn't so much the receipt as the setting down his foot where Jack was concerned and refusing to budge. Abiding by the rules he believed in . . . He wondered who the baby looked like, Jack or Nellie? He wished he could see her, and hoped he wouldn't be awkward when he did. He'd had so little to do with babies.

Mt. Vernon. Its family, its life, the rolling spread of its lands. He felt its pull on him and felt the urge to talk, to smooth his mind.

He spoke to the farmer beside him. "What are your crops hereabouts?"

The man looked dumfounded. But he gawked, coughed, and made a go at it. "Oh—ah, most sorts, I guess. Hay, wheat, barley, the like. Pretty good stuff. Pasturage for herds."

"Truck gardens?"

"That's more the Jerseys. Sandy soil there. We do grains and cattle, mostly."

"Not many herds in Virginia. Tobacco and wheat."

"I hear. Tobacco's a one-cropper, though."

"Yes, runs the soil out. I've been adding to my wheat. What about corn here?"

"Oh—ah, corn too."

"It's like tobacco, it wants fertilizer."

"E-yah."

"How do you fertilize?"

"Well, us in Pennsylvany likes compost. Rotted stuff. Then we got manure, o' course—an' hog's guts when we slaughter, an' dead fish. Your dead fish is a good 'un. You slap your dead fish in a corn hill, you'll get ears."

"The Indians do that."

"So does Pennsylvany."

The man's reticence slid slowly away. They talked in the tacit fellowship of those who know the earth; talked of methods, and seasons, and yields per acre, and the slosh of men's feet was in their ears and the wind bannered the manes and tails of their horses. The talk brought to Washington the smell of long furrows above the Potomac; and an account of what this Pennsylvania soil could raise beyond, the soil of the western lands where he'd surveyed and fought. The lands were rich. Would produce. Wanted only a freedom from fear and the ploughshare of an owner. If in Pennsylvania, why not in the Ohio country? Why not farther, and farther, far as the Mississippi, which he'd never seen? But freedom was the keystone. He fell silent, thinking.

The farmer pointed, then "Yonder," he said. Faint glimmers in the dusk, faint shadows of comings and goings formed out of an eeriness. He gave an uncertain, half-military twitch to the woollen muffler wrapped around his head and ears, and clapped heels to the ribs of his gelding, and disappeared.

Washington went on and found Knox. The colonel was sweating in spite of the cold.

"It's moving slower than we reckoned, sir. This weather, and the damned ice."

"Can we get across by midnight?"

"I can't say, sir."

"Do what you can."

Washington went toward the riverbank, where the boats were loading. It was so like Long Island that he began to sweat, like Knox. Long Island, the East River, his men tumbling in a death of silence into boats manned by Glover's Marbleheaders, those New England fishermen. Tumbling as routed troops, saving their necks in a Godgiven fog that would cover their escape to Manhattan. But he knew the difference between that scene and this. He must grasp at the difference, wrench it, rudder it to his advantage. This was attack, now. Was not rout.

The river was ugly, of an ugliness born bastard from storm and thaw. He was not afraid of water. He'd been raised by the side of rivers. He'd said to Gates, when Gates sat petitioning on the Mt. Vernon portico, how he'd been pitched from a raft into the freezing Monongahela, and had swum out alive. But his troops weren't all river-hardened. They had stout boats, though. Durham boats that hauled iron ore from upper Jersey to Philadelphia. Forty feet long, sixty; eight feet wide; capable of fifteen tons. They could be poled from planking laid along the gunwales. Each end had a heavy steering sweep. They'd take the men over, more or less dry. There'd be confidence in the Marbleheaders. The men would remember the retreat from Long Island, as he did.

Then he saw the ice. It jammed against the shore, thick and jagged. Crunched against hulls, and creaked and ground and snapped in the current beyond, in the darkness. It was a lift and heave of whiteness, a fang of white, a claw; a wild shouldering, and a sucking, sickening lollop diving under the surface.

The imp dance of a frozen hell.

Wind cumbered the boats. They were monstrous to handle. The ice blocked them, clogging their sides. The Marbleheaders blistered the frost with curses. Profanity couldn't melt the ice.

Knox bawled. His voice was a trumpet. Men slithered and scrambled into the boats. Fell, bumped on each other, clawed for footing. A boat pushed off, another in its place, polemen wrestling wind and eddies.

Slow, too slow. He dragged out his watch and squinted at it.

He could scarcely see his watch. Night was coming down fast, and more lanterns flickered. They must all be across, he thought; they must all be across before dawn.

He arced from his saddle and walked away from the river. His nose was numb and he pinched it again, unconsciously, with the reflex of a frontiersman who had preserved that nose from the bite of trackless winters.

At a small distance, in a wide semicircle, troops were waiting to embark. He walked around their lines. They squatted in a frigid silence, blended in groups clustered against the wind. They slapped at chests, bellies, scrawny thighs, trying to keep them with the feeling of life. He had to be careful not to fall over hunkered shapes folded like stone images. They did not recognize him. He didn't care. Nor did they. They had been waiting here eternally. All about the semicircle faint white clouds of human breathing puffed and vapored. There was no word from anyone.

Horses neighed. Hoofs skittered at the riverside turf, and a rumble of gun carriages blanketed the wind for a moment. Knox, the cannon, the horses.

He looked at his watch again. Nine o'clock.

He walked up and down, up and down, between the squatted regiments and the brawl of the loading beaches.

The loading dragged. The regiments left, rising one by one from the powdered snow and making for the boats. But it was a painful rising. A haphazard loading. The grim semicircle didn't seem to lessen.

There was little noise. No yelling but for Knox's hoarse, barked shouts. He'd ordered complete silence. And tasted a kind of secondary triumph because the men were obeying him; moving mute, deathlike, crowded indistinguishable heaps piled on heaps, over and over constantly across sterns and gunwales.

They laid ramps, and the first of the guns went into the boats. They were eighteen to be loaded.

So it came to nine o'clock, and ten. And eleven.

"Will we do it by midnight, Knox?"

"No, sir."

"When, then?"

"God knows."

Besides the cannon, there were the horses. And a thousand men. They still shivered around lanterns on the Pennsylvania shore.

Shortly after eleven snow fell again. It was mixed with raw and driving sleet.

"Billy—"

"Yes, Gen'ral?" Billy was riddled with cold, like the rest. Washington felt sorry for him. But the dark face and the white-tooth flash of readiness didn't acknowledge self-pity. "Yes, suh?"

"My compliments to Colonel Knox, and I should like to cross when it is convenient."

They warped in a boat for him. It grated on the shore ice and a hundred men tumbled aboard. He and Knox sat at the stern.

The poles thrust and strained. The current circled them. Ice jabbed the bow, to swerve it downstream. The polemen clumped forward, stabbing at the river bottom, putting their muscles against wind and floes and the river's suck. White jagged pieces, thick and menacing, heaved above the port gunwale. Their weight tilted the thick boat. But it crawled on, sluggish.

The wind's squawl was high now, the cut of sleet was dagger-wise. The troops in the boat cowered still. They were sluggish, quiet with the quietude of fatalism. Washington, staring at them—as far as he could stare in that blackness—wondered how far fatalism would go; how far it could be led, or driven. How far the human frame, the human mind could endure.

The boat took a lurch.

"Ho, that's the secret," he said. "Shift your ass, Knox, and trim ship." It was a stark attempt.

But Knox turned eyes on him a minute, and then laughed. And laughs came from the frozen hulks in the boat. And he laughed, too. Knox's poundage couldn't affect the boat, but a good laugh could. And Knox wouldn't mind. The cackles from midships would make them all feel better. The story would go round, and they'd all be easier for it.

"Thank you, Colonel," he said.

He listened to more laughing. Knox's was as loud as any.

So he crossed the Delaware for the second time. And sat on an empty bee hive on the far bank, the enemy bank, and took stock.

It was past midnight. They'd need two or three hours more for the crossing. Trenton was nine miles away, and sunrise would come about seven in the morning. Small hope left of a night surprise, even of a dawn one. He could give up the attack and ferry his men back again, in daybreak and with the danger of Hessian bullets; or he could push on into an unknown. He sat pondering, judging, weighing his decision, while Greene came over, and Sullivan; Stephen and Mercer and St. Clair. New Hampshiremen, and Virginians, and Marylanders. The last guns. Last horses.

It took a further hour to jumble the troops into marching lines. Officers slapped them into place, jerry-built companies in a grove of hickory and black oaks.

Greene came up. "What orders, Your Excellency?"

"Shoulder firelocks."

The march began. Over roads that were coated with ice, treacherous. Men couldn't hurry, couldn't make time. But time was essential. The hour was four o'clock. Three more hours, and he'd be discovered. He had planned to have seven.

He egged the columns along. "Push on, boys, push on." They did their best, slithering, sliding, groping for a footing and holding to each other to keep upright. They covered four miles to a cross-roads village.

He let them rest here, for they were near to exhaustion. He ordered a snatch of breakfast from the three days' cooked rations they'd brought. Someone fetched him a beaker of rum from a farmhouse and he drank it without getting off his horse while he talked with Greene and Sullivan. His route was laid: Sullivan to take the crossroad skirting the river and come in at the bottom of the town; he and Greene, with Knox and most of the cannon, to follow their present road to the town's upper end. Trenton had about a hundred houses built along two parallel main streets. The two columns would act like the jaws of a nutcracker.

"Set your watches by mine, gentlemen, so that we hit as near together as possible. Whichever column meets the Hessian pickets first, push on without waiting to hear from the other. Get into Trenton before the enemy can form. Remember they'll be soggy from their Christmas."

He watched Sullivan move off, and Greene. Some of the men had fallen asleep where they had dropped, and had to be waked and propped to their feet. Then he followed Greene. There were between four and five miles to go.

A cold, angry, sleet-knifed dawn began little by little to lighten the countryside, the flat fields and the fence rows and the umbrella ribs of the trees. Washington's hands worked on the bridle reins. Hope of surprising the Hessians was lost, lost in the ice of the Delaware. But he went on. He strained for a sound of the enemy. The chief sound in his ears was the tattoo of sleet pellets rattling on his tricorne hat.

Then he saw that Greene had halted. The marching had stopped. A chill went through him more biting than the storm, and he spurred forward. A small company of men stood in a field by the roadside. "Americans . . . they're Americans. . . ." He heard the word along the ranks as he came up.

He reined toward the group. "Where is your commanding officer?"

"Here, sir. Captain Richard Anderson, Fifth Virginia, Stephen's Brigade."

"What are you doing here? Where have you been?"

"General Stephen sent us over yesterday, sir. Our orders were to make a scouting party and find the enemy's outposts but not to start a fight. We found 'em, and were pulling away when we ran into a Hessian sentry in the storm. We shot him so he wouldn't give the alarm, and were just now on our way back to the ferry."

"Shot? Shot?" He hardly felt how the hoarseness rasped to fury in his throat. "To tell the Hessians there are Americans this side the river!"

His eyes blazed around on his staff and generals. They looked cowed, panicky before him, like men facing an avalanche. He saw General Stephen, and burst out in a roar: "How dare you send a patrol across the river without asking or receiving authority! You, sir, may have ruined all my plans by putting them on their guard!"

General Stephen had no answer. He seemed to crumple.

The columns on the road were staring, listening. Washington was conscious of them and broke off rigidly, masking himself with a false calm.

He drew in a slow breath through his reddened, paining nose, and said to Anderson, as well as he could, "Your men must be tired after such hard service. You must march in the vanguard, where you won't suffer from the delays of the troops in the rear."

The march started again. He rode at the head of the columns now, with his aides and Greene, just behind the advance guards. He had no way of knowing if that Hessian shot dead had been a warning to Trenton, and he wanted to find out for himself.

It was eight o'clock when the guides told him they were about a mile from town. He halted the columns again to form them for the attack and to let Knox's guns be dragged toward the front. A rider galloped toward him across a field from the direction of the river.

"Your Excellency—"

"Well, sir?"

"General Sullivan is in position, sir. He's met no enemy. But his muskets are wet and useless for firing."

"Tell Sullivan to use the bayonet. Advance and charge."

It was firm in his heart to take Trenton.

"General Greene, put the men at the long trot."

A few scattered houses began to appear. A farmer was chopping wood in a dooryard. Guides said the enemy posts would be sighted any minute. Washington cantered over to the farmer.

"Can you tell me where the Hessian picket is?"

The man gaped, and let fall his ax.

"You needn't be frightened, it is General Washington asking."

A stupefaction on the face—a finger pointing. "Them. There at Howell's place."

And at almost the same minute, a wild, surging yell: *"Der Feind, der Feind! Heraus! Heraus!"*

The Hessian pickets, twenty or so, tumbled out of the house. Behind him, Washington's columns opened fire. The range was too long. They pushed in closer. When they were in range, the Hessians gave them a volley. Bullets whistled over Washington's head. His columns fired a second time, a third, and the Hessians scattered and fell back across the fields.

Washington shouted to Greene, "Make for the head of the town!" and waved the columns on. Visibility was poor, the footing still foul. He wanted to get to high ground where he could have a better view of how the battle went.

They were still at a trot when musketry rattled up from the river road. It was followed by a gun's boom. That would be Sullivan, with some of his muskets dry at least, already at the town. Washington felt something touch a release spring inside him.

The Hessians were massing to the defense. He could see them ahead of him, formed in the streets that were coming into sight now. He found the higher ground he needed, galloped to it, and stopped the long trot of the columns and ordered them into battle line.

"Give room for the artillery! Bring up the pieces!"

He knew from his maps there was a road on the left that led by back ways to Princeton, a road of escape.

"General Greene, deploy to cover the Princeton road."

Hessian volleys kept the Americans pinned at the head of the streets. A musket ball struck his horse's shoulder. The sorrel screamed and reared and pivoted in a circle. Washington dropped like an Indian from its back and the watchful Billy fetched another. His staff crowded around.

"Keep your places, gentlemen. Where are the guns?"

Musketry and cannon fire were growing heavier at the bottom of the town: Colonel Stark and the Hampshiremen, he thought. Stark was leading Sullivan's van. The jaws were closing.

The guns were ready now, Knox's guns. The artillerymen rammed the charges home, fed the muzzles, uncovered the touchholes they had protected all night. The first blast plunged down the street.

Greene had thrown a detachment leftward to the Princeton road, put his main forces at the streets' heads, and sent others around behind the houses, dodging forward through alleys and paths, flanking and firing.

The Hessians' discipline was good; they stood well under fire. Washington saw them wheel cannon into place, aimed at Greene's men. With their infantry and artillery in order he expected them to charge. He was bracing himself for the charge when Knox's guns roared first, and then Greene's men poured forward in an onslaught.

This carried the Americans to the center of the town. At the foot of the streets a deep, steep-banked creek, with a single bridge, cut off retreat in that direction. He didn't know what was happening there, but in the absence of any messenger he hoped Sullivan had been able to block the bridge. It seemed likely. The gunnery there was continuing, and from what he could see the Hessians were milling and running and trying to form again in the fields to his left. He ordered more battalions toward the escape road in their rear, and sent his reserves into the fight.

It seemed to him that he could make out a few white Hessian hand-kerchiefs fluttering from raised musket barrels.

The firing grew desultory. He rode deeper into the town to study his position. Halfway down King Street he met some Hessians. They were helping a bleeding officer into a church. The officer's side was ripped apart by bullets. He asked his name. It was Colonel Rall.

At the same time a young American major slewed toward him, riding gingerly on the slick road. He recognized James Wilkinson, Gates's aide. Wilkinson had brought him a letter yesterday afternoon at the ferry: a letter from Gates, saying that Gates unfortunately could not join him.

"Major?"

"From General Sullivan, Your Excellency. The general's compliments, and the last Hessian regiment has just grounded arms in surrender."

Washington felt an impulse for an unseemly yell. He governed himself in time and thrust out a hand. "This is a glorious day for our country, Major Wilkinson."

He hardly knew what to say or do. His staff gathered to him. He could make out Greene, riding from the fields where the bulk of the Hessians had herded; and Knox at the head of the street, on foot, laughing and talking with the New Yorkers' artillery captain, Hamilton, and slapping a fat fist on a still-smoking gun. He could make out American troops filtering in from the bottom of the street, Sullivan's men, their bayonets fixed. A wave of thankfulness went over him, of affection and respect for his soldiers. For the first time the American Army, small as it might be, had attacked in the open, without benefit of breastworks or defenses, had charged enemy guns and broken enemy ranks; for the first time in a year it had won victory; and this after a night when any soldier would have cried out to put his head under a blanket and curl in a shelter. He had seen the frozen ground red-stained from cracked and bleeding feet.

One of his new aides, Fitzgerald, came up and saluted.

"Report on prisoners, sir. The estimate is above eight hundred. Probably a score of the enemy killed, fourscore wounded."

Eight hundred prisoners. Not enough to make up for the losses on Long Island, the losses on Manhattan. But it would suffice, it certainly would suffice. And it would show the king's ministry that fight was not yet snuffed out in America. He would write to the Congress. For all his dictator's powers, they were his chiefs, the elected representatives of the people. The words shaped themselves in his mind: "I have the pleasure of congratulating you on the success of an enterprise. . . ."

His aide Tench Tilghman, the Pennsylvanian, could write that letter, later from headquarters. He turned to Fitzgerald. "Our losses, sir?"

"None killed, four wounded. Among the wounded, Captain William Washington and Lieutenant James Monroe."

Captain Washington was no kin of his. Lieutenant Monroe he knew of, for the lieutenant was from the Virginia county of his own birth. He was amazed and delighted that his men had got off so easily.

But sitting his horse in the middle of the Trenton street he knew, with a sinking of his heart, that one stroke had not cut the knot. There were enemy troops to the north, as near as Princeton. There were more enemy outposts to the east and south of him. His troops were small, the Delaware lay between him and supplies from Pennsylvania. The snow and sleet were getting worse and the temperature was dropping. He consulted his officers. They'd been busy stoving in hogsheads of rum to keep their men from getting drunk. He put his own conclusions to them.

They saw eye to eye with him. The army must recross the Delaware, let the victory stand as it was, and not chance anything more.

Greene put it for all of them, succinctly: "If the ice thickens in the river, but doesn't freeze hard enough to carry men and provisions, we'll be starved here. The Hessians' stores won't feed us for long."

"Order a march to the ferry," Washington said. And he said to Fitzgerald, "Select a group of the Hessian officers to dine with me at headquarters." And then he said, "I should like to pay my respects to Colonel Rall. He may be dying. Will you go with me, Greene?"

VIII

A Back Road to Princeton

The storm went on all day, gusty with sleet and the weather at near freezing.

They were without sleep, and empty in belly; worn, and dizzied by fumes of rum, forty hogsheads of it stove in by their captains and lieutenants to keep them from getting drunk; too many for Trenton village to feed if they stayed, too few to risk battle again if they marched farther.

So they pulled away from their victory and retraced the miles, and ferried their prizes over the river, the captured cannon and assorted loot and the almost thousand prisoners, and slithered back to their camp in Pennsylvania to roll up in any cover they could find, and by then it was the second morning since they had left.

Washington gave them tribute.

The first thing he did was to order a message for sending to the Congress. Tench Tilghman readied the draft of it—the dark, square-faced young fellow who'd been at the Shippens' in Philadelphia was on staff now, an aide—and Washington read the outline and asked for a final paragraph: "In justice to the officers and men, I must add that their behavior upon this occasion reflects the highest honor on them. . . ."

It was good to put his signature to that message. And he ordered that fieldpieces, arms, horses, everything taken at Trenton were to be valued and the money shared between officers and men.

The next thing, before sending the Hessians off to prison camps, he had some of the Hessian officers to dinner. His motive was politic. They had no part in the basic quarrel. England was as foreign to them as America, and perhaps a courteous treatment of them would show them America was more than a barbarous land to be tramped over for hire.

Perhaps they could be persuaded to change from the king's pay to the Congress'. There was nothing to be lost by hospitality, and there might be gain.

They were a tight-knit, virile lot, in perfect trim, red-cheeked and fair of skin, many of them striplings. They ate with voracious appetites. But they had more shudders for their river passage than curiosity about Americans. They used the French language, aping the custom of King Frederick of Prussia, and gestured, and rolled their eyes upward in an awe of memory. With Reed sitting by him to translate, Washington could catch the drift.

"That hell stream—*mon Dieu!*"

"To come ashore I must wade seventy paces through ice. You saw me, Albrecht."

"You. *Ce n'est rien,* your little wade. You did not observe me. I sunk up to here, to my chest nipples."

"I shall write my sweetheart. She won't believe."

"Who would?"

"For me, the ice pieces were alive."

"For me, as the fiend is alive."

"*Mort de ma vie,* Your Excellency, to go twice across that horror. Your men must have the nerves of giants."

Washington gave a cautious nod to the compliment, and was glad the Hessians had been too terrified to look closely at the exhausted, trembling, frazzled, half-dead files of his skinny regiments.

"On no other night, though," a lieutenant said, leaning forward two or three chairs away, "would you have taken us. On no other."

"True, Your Excellency. *C'est véritable.* But Christmas night—"

"And spitting snow."

"But certainly the snow."

"You wouldn't have taken us."

"It was Dechow's blame," someone said. "He commanded the patrol. Heavy guard and brace of cannon. Then once—just this once—he calls off the patrol for the damned weather."

"Rall was warned on Christmas Day."

"*Mes amis,* the colonel was getting drunk."

"Be silent, lieutenant. The colonel is dead."

The talk died also. There was an embarrassment of looks, as if in their wine the young officers had set their tongues too loose. Tarnished the shine of American pride.

Washington pretended not to notice. He was playing the host. He said, "I regret his death, gentlemen. He was far from home, as you are.

But I've asked the Pennsylvania Council to canton you and your troops in our German settlements in this state."

He was trusting to his notion that being in German-flavored surroundings would soften the Hessians.

But he saw no such thought in the faces around the table. The faces were ruddy with candlelight and wine. They were controlled, knowing themselves forfeits of war and disliking it, yet accepting the fate stolidly. They were not, however, of a softening breed.

Well, he thought, neither was he. He respected them.

Another notion came to him. Had they been studying him as he had been studying them? They'd never met the English king's commander: they might find something sympathetic in the Congress' one. He lifted his glass, tasted at it, and said to the young lieutenant—the name, he'd gathered from Reed, was Wiederholt—

"Lieutenant Wiederholt, now that you've seen me, what do you think of me?"

The Hessian's cheeks burned redder. He looked at his own wineglass, and then at the fireplace at the end of the room with its smoke-daubed mantel, and twirled the wineglass delicately on the table top; its base clinked slightly in a silence that was half-amused, half-vibrant, his hand unsteady.

"Your Excellency is courtly, but very reserved. I would put you down as elegant, sir. I would also put you down as having a sly expression."

"Sly?" Washington said, when Reed had done translating.

"Very quick, sir. Knowing."

And the lieutenant heard the suck in of breaths around him, and braced himself for a blast, but Washington threw back his head and laughed.

Well, the Hessian officers were adamant in their own code of honor, and the Hessian ranks were meek enough, and he entered the expense of the dinner in his financial accounts when he went to his desk afterward.

There was a letter from General Cadwalader. The militia brigadier hadn't been able to cross the Delaware the night of the Trenton fight —three hundred feet of ice blocking the shore, he said. But he had crossed since, and was in New Jersey, and raging to beat up any enemy detachment he could find. "Send part of your army," he wrote. "I'd be glad to hear from you before we set out."

Glad to hear from you. . . . It meant one thing. Cadwalader saw a chance, if the main army came over.

The main army was hobbled. Washington knew it, sure as he knew his finger knuckles around the feathers on the quill. Two nights without sleep, twice over the Delaware, gaunt for food and rest. Rest could be had, in a fashion; but food was scarce—bad weather, bad commissary. It would take several days to fill stomachs and rebuild strength. And after several days? . . . Enlistments ran out at the year's end. Today was December 27.

But Cadwalader said Trenton was left open. The nearest enemy in force was at Brunswick, where the royal pay chest was. Only an outpost was at Princeton, a little northward.

He dropped his pen.

"Tilghman."

"Sir?"

"Ask the generals to meet with me."

The generals backed him, their ears tuned to the knock of opportunity. There would be another tussle with the Delaware, another march to Trenton. The news was fair. Success warmed patriotism, and the militia seemed likely to join in, and the Light Horse troop of Philadelphia, and General Mifflin with reinforcements from the city. They could reckon on a heavier weight of troops than they'd beaten the Hessians with. Here was promise of a sharp follow-up, much better than letting the moment go by default.

Enlistments were the stumbling block. Immediate, imponderable. If most of the army scattered for home before the week was out, the rest were only a drained nag baffled.

He was very sober, speaking to his war council, and scowls and terseness said they were thinking the same as he.

"We must hold the men a little longer. By any means, gentlemen."

"What means? Gun point?" The words snapped. They were from Wayne. Anthony Wayne, a Pennsylvanian. Something of a dandy, and a cutter of swaths among the women, but with much of Benedict Arnold's fire in battle. Wayne's face was bold and full. His shoulders were aggressive.

"No, that failed at Cambridge. They won't be coerced."

"Nor have freedom unless they fight for it," Greene said.

"Without pay?" someone said. "Their families have to eat. Congress can't even beg the money."

"I think the only sure means is hard money," Washington said. He let the words sink in, and said, "I'll offer a bounty to any soldier who will stay with us for six weeks more."

"That might prod 'em," Knox said, and his voice had bitterness. Sullivan said, being a politician by nature and mindful of voters' pocket-books, "How much bounty, sir?"

"Pennsylvania is giving its militiamen an extra ten dollars for a winter's campaign. It's a high price, but we can't risk offering less. Nothing's forthcoming from the other states."

He paused for comments, and a colonel in a far corner of the room said, "God damme, I despise my countrymen! They hold their purse strings as if they'd damn the world rather than give to their army! I wish I could say I hadn't been born in America!"

No one answered that, and the muteness was ugly and disillusioned. They all knew how few of the people were taking any real hand in the war, how few really cared, how many put pleasure and profits above everything. How few, and how many, and liberty having to be bribed, a donkey with a carrot dangled to its nose.

General St. Clair had a question. He was a Scotsman. "Where would the bounty be comin' frae, sir?"

"The Congress must raise it," he said. "Or I will. Out of my personal estate."

There was no other way. Either the army would disband in four days or it would listen to the jingle of cash.

He said, "The present men in the lines have done fine service. They're not to be despised if they're homesick. Or despised if they take a bounty for serving longer than they agreed. I'll guarantee the bounty for them."

He didn't have a bounty, and the Congress didn't have it. But the Congress had given him authority and he was using the authority as he saw fit. The army had to be kept in the field. It was the only support of the revolution. Perhaps the dollars could be begged from Robert Morris again—sound dollars, not paper from the Congress' printing press. Failing that, he'd sell Mt. Vernon.

They came to the vote then, the situation not being one to be solved by talk, and the generals were unanimous for a return to Trenton, and he thanked them.

"The first day the troops are able, gentlemen, and with Providence keeping the river passable."

When they had gone he set himself again to his notes and reports, his letters and orders and administrative lists. He had aides, but they were always changing, for civilian life for family reasons or for field duty for military ones. There never seemed enough of them for the head-quarters work to be done.

As he stubbed his quill over the paper, writing cramped and small-spaced, for even paper was scarce with him, he wondered if he could hold the army together. He thought that the winning of the Trenton fight, or any fights to come, would not be as large a thing as his maintaining any army to fight at all.

They recrossed to Trenton. Of the three crossings they had made within a week, this was the worst. The weather was biting raw, the Delaware clogged thick with ice, and snow six inches deep on the ground. It took two days to get all his army over, with the baggage and wagons.

Trenton was empty. There was no sign of an enemy, and his spies could tell him very little. This worried him. General Cadwalader was on his right flank, reporting that the Hessians had evidently made a deep retreat. Other reports were uncertain. Howe seemed to be sending troops down from New York and Amboy, and to be fortifying Princeton, not too far to the north. Otherwise, blankness.

He chose a bivouac south of Trenton, behind the creek that cut past the bottom of the town, where his guns would be in good position. To the posts and garrisons through the Jerseys, at Morristown and Hackensack, he sent orders to make trouble and diversions; they might keep Howe from attacking him. He was matching Cadwalader's impulsiveness, taking advantage of the enemy's retirement, but he wasn't quite sure where he was going.

The immediate problem was his army. The calendar, inexorably, marked December 31. After that date, no more service, no more regiments, no more shouting lines, thinned and scrawny as they were, to throw against trained enemy battalions.

"Greene, will they stay? Sullivan, will they re-enlist? Will they take the bounty?"

Greene and Sullivan couldn't give him hope. He caught the glumness in their voices.

But he had one last thing he could do.

"Start up the drums," he said. "Put a New England regiment in line."

And he rode out to speak to them. He didn't like speeching, it went against his grain. But he couldn't let this army go home. He had to keep men in the field, weak, pathetic, hungry, barefoot as they might be. Without this rally point, liberty was gone.

He gave them his best arguments: how they had buffeted the enemy, how there was good chance to buffet again; how as veterans they were needed for the next few weeks. He promised the bounty, and as well as he knew how he asked them to stay.

When he had done he rode to one side, to his staff, and the men's officers took charge. "All who'll take the bounty and fight on for six more weeks, step forward!" The calls went up and down the line.

There was hesitation. That was to be looked for, naturally: men had to digest the startlement of the commander in chief acting as a recruiting sergeant. The hesitation prolonged. It grew to half a minute, a full minute. The wind blustered and the clouds scurried, and among his staff group a horse tossed its head. Washington fixed his eye on the paraded ranks. They did not move. They stood ankle-deep in the trampled snow, silent. No man of them stirred, no man stepped forward. The nightmare came clear to him that no man would. They were refusing him. They wanted done with this.

"Who'll step forward, who's for campaign?" The officers urging, a forlorn heartiness.

No one.

Time's space widened and sagged. It draped around him in a slow inanimate smother. The members of his staff did not look at him. They were shamed at being there, witnesses to his shame and sick at heart. They kept their stares on the ground, or the treed horizon, or their horses' ears. Anywhere but at the specter of his failure.

His senses saw the failure. His mind would not. The stake at gamble was too big. This regiment would give the cue for the rest of the army. It must be won over, here and now.

He reined his horse and rode to face the regiment again, to the center of the motionless line. In the profound silence he lifted his hat as a mark of his entreaty toward the men standing there, and his voice, which usually went higher when he was under stress, came low and throbbing. He hardly heard it as his.

"My brave fellows, you have done all I asked you to do, and more than could be expected. But your country is at stake, your wives, your houses, everything you hold dear. You have worn yourselves out with fatigue and hardships, but we do not know how to spare you. If you will stay only one month longer, you will give a service to liberty which you probably never could do under any other circumstances. The present is emphatically the crisis which is to decide our destiny."

The drums rolled when he stopped talking, and he saw men look at each other. Some of them whispered together. One man stepped out, then a few, then more. His earnestness, their consciences, or perhaps their own spirit, had started the contagion. By the time he thanked them and returned to his staff, only the invalids or the nearly naked stood to the line.

His officers surrounded him. They beamed and were jubilant.

"Call out the rest of the regiments," he said, "and offer the bounty."

"Shall we enroll the men who stay, sir?"

"No, sir. Men who volunteer in this fashion don't need enrollment to keep them to their duty." And his staff could look at him now, for there was no disgrace or failure written on him, only surety and the pulse of his heart.

He believed in councils of war, in consulting his officers, gauging and balancing their opinions, for he was not so unhumble that he could trust to himself entirely in everything. He was pleased to learn, the day after his plea to his troops, that the Congress had voted him even greater authority for the coming six months, giving him the naming of regimental and company officers, the reorganizing of the army in any way he saw suitable, the recruiting of more regiments, the setting of their pay, the scope for adding more artillery, light horse, and engineers; for calling militia from the states, and commandeering what supplies he would need at a price that he should decide. This was an immense scope. He knew it. He could be an absolute monarch if he wished, and no one to oppose him.

But in matters of strategy and tactics he preferred the voices of his generals. He had never assumed that his single decision would be always the right one; and the sense of being so much responsible lay always on him.

January was two days old, and his officers were with him in a dingy room around a single candle stuck in its own wax on a table. The room served as living room, dining room, and kitchen in a two-story frame shanty. General St. Clair was using it as a headquarters. Washington had called the meeting in this room because his own headquarters in Trenton was in enemy hands.

Sir William Howe could strike like a snake when he was prodded. The Trenton affair had prodded him. He had sent Lord Cornwallis down from New York at full speed, and that morning Cornwallis had hit out of Princeton at Trenton with five thousand men. All day long Washington had sent infantry and artillery forward, with orders to hold as long as they could, to play for time until nightfall. At four o'clock the troops had fallen back along the Trenton streets, firing from the corners of houses as they retreated, and then filed across the creek over its wooden bridge, while Washington sat in his saddle at the bridge's end to calm panic and assign his officers their new positions. Cornwallis had swarmed huge into Trenton. Washington had seen the early evening campfires beyond the creek as he rode to the war council in the shanty.

His generals were muddy and worn and drawn-faced. They understood, as he did, that they had only the creek and a few hours of night between them and Cornwallis. His Lordship would force battle in the morning, and he had enough force to annihilate them. The day's fighting had made that clear.

The candle spread a wan light, and in the inkiness outside American cannon barked spasmodically.

"Are you still firing, Knox?"

"Oh, we chuck over a few now and then. Keeps 'em from enjoying their new quarters too snugly."

Whatever the situation, Washington thought, Knox stayed cheerful and optimistic. He wished he could say the same for his other officers. Sullivan was scowling and rubbing his hands together, Greene looked wary and dismal, St. Clair was dour, Cadwalader scowling; his old friend, Hugh Mercer, who kept an apothecary shop near his mother's home in Fredericksburg, had a grim jut to his jaw. All these men, he said to himself, had left homes and hearths and good ways of life to assemble here on the banks of a creek at the outskirts of a scambling Jersey village on a January night—for what? For this?

He did not try to define the "this." They knew it without definition from him.

"Gentlemen, here is our question. Lord Cornwallis is in superior number. He will strike us tomorrow. What is our answer?"

A moment's pause. They knew the answer, but none wanted to shape it.

Then Sullivan said, as a kind of parrying, "If Cornwallis attacks tonight?"

From a little outside the candle's circle, Reed said, "I don't think he will. I've ridden along the creek. The water's high with the storms. He won't risk it."

"Besides," Greene put in dryly, "it's a military maxim that the stronger force shouldn't attack at night. Cornwallis believes in maxims. All European soldiers do."

He gave Washington a glance. It said that Greene wasn't opposed to non-comforming methods of warfare.

"But should we stand to battle here, gentlemen?"

"No . . . No . . . No . . . The space too cramped for movement, the river at our back . . . The ice . . ." The answers were definite.

"Retreat across the river? Or to the lower Jerseys?"

Sullivan said, "Cornwallis would have us before we'd got half over the river. Besides, the Durham boats are miles upstream."

Cadwalader said, "You'd get no support in the lower Jerseys, sir."

"Added that a retreat would blast the army apart," Greene said. "They stayed for the prospect of a fight."

Curt phrases. Clipped. The phrases of men led into a trap.

Washington said, "Should we make a fight of it, then?"

"That would blast us, too. Damn it, sir, we can't stand."

"Nor can't run, General. Backward, at any rate."

He looked around. What was in his mind was a dangerous movement, hard to execute: a movement direct from an enemy front to his flank and rear. It took speed and utter secrecy. But Indians could do it. He'd seen them.

"If we run sideward—" he said.

They didn't understand. They were silent.

Then came St. Clair's voice, with the burr the Scotsman had never sloughed off. "Yer right flank is free, sir. I've been a-horse there this day. Cornwallis hasna covered it. There's a road."

"Reed's told me," he said. "A woods road. It parallels the main one and runs to Princeton. I don't know its condition."

"But a road," Greene said.

"Yes, General. And a spy of General Cadwalader's says the Princeton garrison has been left weak."

"That's so," Cadwalader said.

"Cornwallis' greatest weight is against us now at Trenton. He has few troops in Princeton. Eighteen miles beyond Princeton is another small garrison at Brunswick, with seventy thousand pounds sterling for Cornwallis' payrolls. We might be able to reach Brunswick."

The idea was only half-formed for him, developed on the moment's spur as the day's battle to hold Trenton had gone against him. But in the pallid light of the candle he saw how his generals snatched at it. The tactic was a possible one if they could carry it off.

He heard Knox. "The road will be plain mud. Will it take guns?"

"I said I don't know, Knox."

He heard Greene. "The baggage? The wagons? We can't lug those along."

The rains in December had been heavy; and then the snow; and then, just lately, a deep thaw. A wood road would be impassable for wagons. He knew that. He said, "Send the baggage and wagons to Putnam in Philadelphia. For the guns, we'll drag 'em after us. We've no other course. Shall we risk it?"

They would.

"Very well, gentlemen. Fitzgerald, notify General Putnam to be ready to receive the baggage. Each officer will alert his regiments to march at midnight, without a sound. I warn you, without a sound. No yelp or musket shot. And the gun wheels muffled. I'll have your orders written. Thank you."

They streamed from the room. The candle burned on unsnuffed, its

flame eating downward through melted wax that congealed in a widening circle like white lava. They had forgotten it. So had he. He was
away from the door and into his saddle, a wraith in the embered glow
of Cornwallis' campfires scant yards away, beyond the creek.

With the first few lunges of his horse in answer to spurs he felt the
difference. He wondered if he were in his right mind, or in the midst
of a miracle. For instead of the slosh and suck of hoof fetlock-deep in
mud his ears and his body knew the hard, brittle crunch of a free trot.
The horse was not bogging down, nor laboring. It was dancing over a
solid surface.

Tilghman put the words for him. "Good God, sir, the ground's been
freezing these two hours. We'll have no mud."

"We're lucky, Tench, very lucky." It was all he could bring himself to
say. The freeze would save him—and save the plodding legs of his men.
Save, too, the miring of Knox's gun carriages. They would all move
faster, easier, for this freeze. He saw it as an act of Providence.

He saw his camp also, making his rounds, finding his way by the
tremble of fires and the shapes of men shaken awake to pack their flimsy
goods in the wagons, and by the wisps of shielded lanterns. The horses
squealed at being hitched, but horses always squealed; and Cornwallis'
horses would be squealing and stamping too, tethered out of doors on a
nasty night. Knox's cannoneers had found rags somewhere, and were
wrapping them around wheel rims. The companies were forming.

He wanted four hundred men to stay behind and make a show that
his army was still there. He picked a Virginian to command them.

"Colonel Scott, you will keep the fires blazing with fence rails all
night. You will work on the trenches guarding the bridge. You will
make as much noise and activity as you can. You will defend the bridge
until dawn. And then slip away."

"We'll do it, sir. Y'all can be sure, sir." And he turned and shouted.
"Boys, don't fire high. If any of 'em bastards puts their feet on the bridge,
shin 'em!"

It made Washington laugh, and the laugh did him good, like the laugh
in the Durham boats while he was crossing the Delaware to take
Trenton.

So, now.

They had fourteen miles to go. He started them at midnight, as he'd
said. There wasn't a word, a sound. His five thousand with their horses
and cannon slipped off to the right, crossed the creek on a farther bridge
which Cornwallis hadn't bothered to cover, and were swallowed by a
forest. The road had been freshly cut over, and the men stumbled on

the butts of tree stumps, and the gun carriages wrenched and tilted crazily, and men slept standing when the columns halted. They tripped and fell, the men, and got up or were pulled up, and went on marching. They moved all night in a grisly blackness, a misery, a something out of hell. They had been phantoms on the march to Trenton. They were walking corpses now, dead men monotonously living. He couldn't see, for the blackness, the bloodstains left by torn feet, but he knew they were there. He thought of Mt. Vernon, and shoved the thought from him shamedly. He thought of simple homes, and wives, and children; fat hogs and cattle, and fields that prospered under plow and scythe. These, also he shoved from him. There was enough pain, and homesickness, and fear that night without adding to it by imagination.

His aide Fitzgerald breasted up to him. "Fork of the road ahead, sir. And the sun's rising."

"Get Greene, Sullivan, Mercer. Halt the columns."

The map brought by Cadwalader's spy showed that at this fork a woodcutter's path went on to Princeton, and the road he was taking swerved left to meet the main road to Trenton at a bridge over a brook.

He had his plans, his orders were terse. Cornwallis would find him out when day broke, and would be pounding back from Trenton.

"Mercer, you and your men to cover the Trenton road. Break down the bridge over the creek. Sullivan, take your division by the wood-cutter's path and get to Princeton. Greene, your division stays here in reserve." It was the sort of attack he liked, and was recommended in the military books; an attack from different sides, like a pincers.

He watched Mercer move off with his men, then Sullivan.

The sun had nudged higher. After the blind night the daylight was brilliant, and cold, and tingling. Trees, roads, fences, fields wore a daz-zling crown of hoarfrost, a frigid, white, tiny-spired coating that turned the world into an incredibly lovely, incredibly frail and delicate fairy-land. Within the rim of the horizon everything was beautified, every-thing made wonderful in crystal adornment. The world stood like a snow princess, glacier-pale and virginal.

With the sun warmer in the sky this would degenerate into slop and collar-wetting drip. But for the moment it was beautiful.

Mercer's men were out of sight. So were Sullivan's. He asked Fitz-gerald, "Where are Cadwalader and Hitchcock?"

"Back on the forest road, sir, with the militia."

"Very good."

He was about to tell Greene to follow Sullivan and make a rush for Princeton when he saw men running—Mercer's men. They climbed a little hill, went down the other side, seeming to stampede through the fields toward Sullivan's troops. Behind them musketry snapped.

Something had gone wrong.

"Come along, gentlemen—"

What he found made him blanch. Mercer had met enemy troops on the Trenton road, and had fallen back and was trying to make a stand by an orchard fence. Mercer would have to have help from him. He heard Mercer's volley, the enemy volley, then silence.

"Why don't our troops fire again?" These were his aides, asking.

"They're riflemen." It took longer to reload a rifle. He listened until he heard Mercer's second volley.

Then he saw men scurrying for the rear, saw the head of Cadwalader's militia column coming up. The retreating and the advancing men tangled together in a confused, disorderly mass. Two fieldpieces began to boom beside Cadwalader's column. They held the enemy at the orchard fence.

Cadwalader galloped up. "Your Excellency, what orders?"

"Rally the men. Mercer has his guns in action."

He sensed the danger of rout—of his bone-dragged, scarecrow army snarled in its own columns as Braddock's army had been snarled on another forest road twenty years ago. For the moment he had only the militia to rely on. But behind them were Hitchcock's Continentals, tough soldiers who could fight.

"Get them in line! Put the broken squads to the rear, and form!"

Greene was with him, and Cadwalader. He saw the Continentals loping forward. "Stay with us, fellows, brave fellows! There's only a handful of the enemy, we'll have them soon!"

The militia stopped their milling, dressed into some kind of line. After all, they were out of range. They gaped at him as he spurred in among them.

He put himself at their head. "Hitchcock, take the right. Colonel Hand, cover the flank with your riflemen. We'll advance. Every man hold his fire until I order."

It might not have been by the book of usage, but it was action.

"Forward now!" he said.

There were redcoats at the orchard fence, a line of them. He led his men on until only thirty yards lay between him and the glinting enemy muskets. He drew rein.

"Halt. Fire!"

A blast from his troops. An answering one from the fence. He saw his aide Fitzgerald cover his face with his hat.

The smoke cleared. Fitzgerald leaned toward him. The aide's mouth was twisted. There were tears down his cheeks.

"Thank God, General! I couldn't bear to watch you being killed!"

It surprised Washington that anyone ever worried about his safety. He shook Fitzgerald's hand. "My dear Colonel, bring up the troops. The day is ours."

It was. He realized it with the kind of acuteness that was being forged in him on one anvil after another, one climax after the ones before. The day was theirs. And he sent Cadwalader's cannons forward, and extended his lines around and around, and waved his hat, and led a bareheaded charge.

"It's a fine fox chase, my boys!" At terrible, triumphant last he was answering those taunting bugles that had brayed the view halloo after him on Harlem Heights last summer.

Another of his aides, Moylan, was managing to keep up with him as he raced. "I'll take those fellows, Moylan! We'll have 'em prisoner!"

He heard Moylan pant. "But where are your troops, sir?"

He turned in his saddle, and looked. He and Moylan were alone. He had outgalloped everyone.

But it had been a smart battle. A smart ride. He swung onto the Trenton road, with the enemy broken and scuttering down it, and remembered the bridge. Mercer hadn't been able to destroy it. There was an American detachment on the road. He beckoned their officer.

"Your name, sir?"

"Varnum, sir. Massachusetts."

"Take a detail and break down that bridge."

"Are there enough men, sir?" A touch of the hat as a salute.

"Enough to be cut to pieces," he said, and pulled his horse's head toward Princeton.

There were hands to be shaken, officers to be praised. He met Hitchcock, who was pale and coughing with fever and had bulwarked the right wing. "My dear Colonel, thank your Rhode Islanders in my name for what they have done." Hitchcock's hand, Washington thought, had death in it. Death seemed to be with General Mercer, too. Washington had only a vague report of him. "Captured, they say, sir, with seven bayonet wounds. Not likely to live."

He abhorred the slaughter and the blood. He abhorred the barbaric pouring out of life. Mercer had been a good friend of his. When he came to a wounded redcoat on the ground, he stopped. "My good fellow, don't worry. You put up a good defense, and everything we can do will be done for you."

He had ridden fifty yards when he heard a scream of pain, and facing back, saw a battlefield ghoul, a lump of a man, yanking at the wounded soldier's coat. He rode at the man with drawn sword. "Damn you, get off! Get off! Moylan, set a guard over the soldier till he can be fetched safe."

He had no joy in triumph over human bodies. And he thought of Mercer.

He shook off the notion of this and rode on to Princeton. The reception he got from his generals dumfounded him. "Your Excellency, we thought you dead!" . . . "Or taken" . . . "Wounded" . . . "You expose yourself too much, sir!"

How could he tell them that when there was a battle in prospect something rose up inside him that wiped away, like a cloth at a window glass, any fear of bullets or capture or wounds? How could he tell them that since he was a boy on the frontier he'd been tuned to the quick music of bullets, and had never counted their final cost, the final piper to be paid? This wasn't bravery in him, nor any bragging. It was simply his nature, his way. He said, "Here I am, gentlemen, alive and whole."

And here was his problem, just as alive and just as whole. He held Princeton—oh, a regiment or two of the enemy had holed up in Nassau Hall, and some artillery, manned by Captain Hamilton, threw a few shots at them, and then they surrendered or ran off toward Brunswick. The fight by the Trenton road had sapped their enthusiasm.

But his scouts told him that Cornwallis was coming up fast, puffing and blowing from Trenton. And his eyes, and his generals, told him that his troops couldn't face another fight, another march, or the storming of another town. If he had had five hundred fresh men he could have gone on to Brunswick, and the stores and the payroll treasure there. But the troops were dead on their feet, used up, at the limit of endurance. He knew it, and knowing and understanding what he had done, and what he could have done more if he had had the strength, he gave orders to march out of Princeton, north, and turn left toward a village he had been told was strongly situated in the Jerseys: Morristown.

Cornwallis, he was sure, would go chasing on past to Brunswick.

I X

Ambition, Pride, Politics

Martha was overjoyed at the letters George sent her after Trenton and Princeton. The news of him had been desolate all autumn. The letters changed that. She read them avidly, and read the fulsome columns in the gazettes, and took the congratulations of her neighbor Mr. Mason of Gunston Hall, and of Patrick Henry, who'd given up military life to be governor of Virginia. She bundled all the praises together and carried them over to Jack's plantation. She kissed the baby Elizabeth, and exclaimed at how the mite had grown (as grandmothers are expected to exclaim), and sat with Jack and Nellie cozily after dinner.

"Your dear father is wearing laurels again," she said. "Have you seen the *Pennsylvania Journal?*"

They had not.

" 'Washington retreats like a general and acts like a hero,' " she quoted, proud of having memorized the sentences. " 'One age cannot do justice to his merit.' . . . Isn't that fine, Jacky?"

"Fine," Jack said.

"And Mr. Morris says he is the greatest man on earth." She preened herself, then sobered. "I wonder how he is doing for stockings," she said.

Nellie tittered. "Mama—stockings a worry? When there's a war?"

"They'll expect it of him," she said.

"They'll expect a lot more," Jack said.

Martha turned on him. "What more?"

"Oh, Mama—do we rise or fall on a darning needle?"

"But, Jacky—"

"Or a hole in the sock?"

Martha steadied herself. She made the back-straightening movement that always signified she would take charge of a situation. "Jacky, your father is a great man now. The first in the country. He shouldn't have holes in his stockings."

"As I gather it," Jack said, "there are more men with him who have holes in their trousers. At the backsides."

"Jacky, you will please not to be vulgar," she said.

Nellie said, coming tactfully between them, "Has Papa asked for you to be with him this winter?"

"No," Martha said. She said, "His letters have been full of military things."

"No word about stockings," Jack said.

"He wouldn't think of them," Martha said.

She wanted to go to Morristown. To go to this huge, slogging, praise-laden husband. But he had not asked her. And she would not go of her own accord. She still was ruffled by the break between them, about Jacky, when she had left New York City in July. Her written words to him, since, had been on the cool side.

He hadn't shown signs of caring. And she couldn't go to him on a pretext of stockings that needed mending. She was irritated that Jacky flaunted the stockings.

"Nor would you," she said.

"Oh, Mama—just to have you darn my stockings—"

"Fiddledeedee," she said.

This visit to her children wasn't turning out as she had thought it would. She felt vague and unhappy.

She said, "They put so much store by your father."

"And he mightn't live up to it?"

"Jacky—you know he can."

Nellie got up and thrust femininely at the fire with a poker, breaking flame-eaten chestnut cordwood into hot embers between the andirons. Chestnut was a good wood for winter; it burned longer and hotter than birch or aspen.

"Now that Papa has shown his mettle, it isn't so bad, is it?" she said. "Shouldn't we just leave it to him?"

"With holes in his stockings?" Jack said.

"Jacky," Martha said, "you're incorrigible." And felt maternal.

"Your dear father will be wanting me," she said.

"My dear father is a general," Jack said. And he looked at his mother, and abruptly there shot from his eyes, strangely maturely, the difference between a generalship and being a husband and stepfather.

Martha could not quite counter it.

"Yes, he's a general," she said. But added, not to be defeated by either son or husband, "But the commander, Jacky."

This time she could counter him. Still, rocking homeward in her Mt. Vernon coach, she felt that the trip to her children had left her rather swamped. They didn't seem to appreciate the seriousness of things. Stockings, of course, were only her wifely means of expressing it. She wished she could talk forensically about this Liberty, as Governor Henry did.

She was not prepared for Mrs. Gates's call. The call should have been, in the normal course of events, rather by way of accident, a stopping-by along the road, a pause for accepted hospitality, as all Virginians accepted hospitality and lavished it, a travel pause on the way from Philadelphia to the Gates plantation. But Mrs. Gates made it something different. Her arrival at Mt. Vernon to spend the night had the air of a visitation. Martha sensed it as she settled her guest in a bedroom in the new wing, and confirmed it from the swift instinct of House Alice as she gave her instructions for the kitchen—a soup, a fowl, a joint, vegetables, and dessert.

"Yes'm, Miz' Washington. Dinner for a general's lady."

"For a friend," Martha said, and weakly avoided the quick tingle in House Alice's eyes.

"Yes'm," House Alice said, but Martha knew, as she knew her slaves and her plantations, that the word would go to the kitchen that General Gates's wife was looking mighty cat-and-canary.

The servants at Mt. Vernon, being loyal, could recognize storm signals. They had their grapevines of tattle from the world beyond the plantation fences, and must, long since, have opinioned Mrs. Gates as a woman with a whiplash tongue and a thirst for high place. Her manner on this visit had certainly not been lost on House Alice. Guesses and rumors would be spreading from Alice, and likely from Mrs. Gates's coachman if the kitchen could get him talking, and every ear would be opened.

Sensing that something was in the wind, and thinking rather ruefully that House Alice was probably more aware of it than she, Martha dressed slowly, and went down the white-balustraded staircase with its midway landing and mahogany rail, slowly, to dinner.

Mrs. Gates had dropped her attitude of importance. She seemed to have shed it with her traveling clothes, and at the dinner made herself a pleasant and chatty table guest.

"Philadelphia is more crowded than ever. You'd not recognize it," she said. "Of course the Congress has moved back there now, after your dear husband's triumph, and they say it will be quite safe, at least for the winter."

Martha knew this already. George had written her that Howe would probably not stir during the cold months, and that he himself couldn't. So everything was frozen to an immobility.

"I've not been much in Philadelphia," she said.

"Oh, avoid it," Mrs. Gates said. "It's a veritable rabbit warren. Teeming. I had my best cloak splattered by a buttermilk cart, if you'll believe —and to cross a street from one shop to another means a disgusting scramble among carters' drays and bakers' wheelbarrows."

Martha remarked that she would not care for that.

"Still, in Philadelphia one does keep in touch with things," Mrs. Gates said.

"How are the Shippens?" Martha said.

"They entertain. They always have. They invite society in for evenings. The disaffected part," Mrs. Gates said. "Personally, I think the Shippens have Tory leanings."

"I've not seen such in them," Martha said. "I've only visited there once or twice, of course. But George is very fond of Peggy Shippen."

"As well he may be," Mrs. Gates said. "She's a consummate little actress where men are concerned."

"George has known her since she was a mere girl," Martha said.

"Oh, not that there's anything amiss. Acting for the men's benefit is a female prerogative—if the female wishes to stoop to it. My dear, this cherry bounce is excellent. And not that I'm saying Peggy Shippen is always acting. But I've had chances to observe her, and I think I can discriminate in the behaviors of our sex, and I do say that Miss Shippen can turn her acting off and on at will." Mrs. Gates gave a brittle, deprecatory laugh. "Well, I suppose all of us can, if it comes to that. . . . Yes, really superb cherry bounce."

"Mr. Lund Washington laid it in for us," Martha said. "He'll be glad you approve." Then, afraid this might be taken as smacking of faint sarcasm, she added, "He's so conscientious in everything to do with Mt. Vernon." Besides, she wanted to shift the talk. She didn't want to become involved in gossip about Peggy Shippen. She had the innate perspicuity to have realized, from the earliest days at Cambridge, that as the commander's wife she could no more afford to engage in personalities than the commander could. The realization put a restraint on her and kept her aloof, often, from the exchanges of confidential chitchat she would have enjoyed. It did the same, she knew, with George. But aloofness was the price they had to pay, if the stream of the war was not to be diverted into shallow rivulet factions.

Mrs. Gates accepted the shift. She was as astute as Martha. And more aggressive, and a quicker opportunist. She took the new topic and shaped it to her own purpose. She had been wanting to arrive at that, sweetly.

She said, "I wonder if you know how fortunate you are in having a man like Mr. Lund to look after the property while your husband is away."

"I certainly do," Martha said.

"I envy you," Mrs. Gates said. "We haven't any Mr. Lund. My son and I have to manage alone. He's a darling child—well, of course not quite a child any longer—though a mother always likes to think 'child,' doesn't she?—and he's a strong prop for me in holding our lands on a paying basis. Yet with General Gates to be in Albany this winter, it's hard."

"Oh? Will General Gates be in Albany?" Martha said. She'd barely said it when she bit her tongue and knew she had stepped into Mrs. Gates's trap. But she put on a composed smile and said to herself that the trap would have closed sooner or later. She only gave a quick glance to make sure House Alice was not in the dining room at the moment. House Alice never spoke when there were guests, unless spoken to, but from the glee on Mrs. Gates's face Martha couldn't be sure the provocation wouldn't be too great for House Alice. She said, "I hadn't heard."

"Oh, yes," Mrs. Gates said. "It's all over Philadelphia. Though I'm not surprised the news hasn't come to you yet, Mt. Vernon not being precisely the hub of events. General Gates is appointed supreme commander in the north. By the Congress."

Her inflection of the word "supreme" was taut as a bowstring stretched to the arrow.

Martha refused to flinch. In many ways, particularly in the way of courage, she was the equal of Mrs. Gates. She said, "My dear, I am so happy for you. My husband has always said that General Gates is one of his best."

"He'll be at Albany," Mrs. Gates said. "I understand from Philadelphia that it's a most strategic post. There seems to be a full invasion forming, to come down from Canada. In such a case, General Gates is to be there to put a stop to it."

"I'd thought General Schuyler had the post at Albany," Martha said, and again, to her chagrin, sensed the frailty of her statement even as she made it.

"No longer," Mrs. Gates said.

She made a deliberate, rather mannish swipe at lips with her napkin, and finished off her glass of cherry bounce. House Alice glided in silently, motioning to a young black lad in her wake who refilled the glass. Mrs. Gates ignored it.

"I shan't go to Albany, I'm afraid. I'm not situated to do so. Shall you be going to Morristown?"

"I've not decided," Martha said. The black lad approached her glass but she waved him away. She wanted a cool mind, the coolest she could know, to find if Mrs. Gates's arrow was aimed where she thought it was.

"No one will think the worse of you if you don't," Mrs. Gates said. "The place is well off the main track of things. A village in the Jersey countryside. There'll be no activity there, social or military."

"I don't pretend to engage in military activity," Martha said with some acerbity.

"Oh, naturally not. But General Washington does. Though settling for the winter so far from either Philadelphia or New York—well, he knows best, truly."

Martha could have slapped her. She smothered the impulse, not so much from good breeding as from pride. Mrs. Gates had let fly the arrow, but Martha would never let her see that it had hit. The target, as she had suspected, was George's competence as a general.

She simply said, very coolly, putting on a front she was far from feeling, "I hope you will relish the dessert, Mrs. Gates. Fruit from our trees, and a bowl of almonds." She couldn't resist putting a postscript. "I'm certain you will. It's the general's favorite."

The scene was duly reported in the kitchen, she knew. Going to her bed that night, after House Alice had applied, with stiffened back and a telling slap of movement, the warming pan to the sheets, she could sense the workings of nettlement and anger all through the folk at Mt. Vernon.

She had a letter, at last, from Morristown. It came, not from George, but from Tench Tilghman, and said the general was very sick. An attack of quinsy. There was doubt, even, if he would live.

She told Lund to get word to Jacky and Nellie by one of the men, and shrugging off the bumpings of her carriage along roads that were not tended as they used to be, set out for George's encampment the next day.

George met her himself, handing her from her carriage at the door of the Freeman Tavern in the mid-March slush of Morristown, and kissing her in front of his staff and the grinning sentry. He looked drawn, his usually hale cheeks were a poor color, but aside from that he seemed to have gotten back his immense health. She breathed a thankful prayer. And she remembered the formalities and smiled appreciatively at the staff officers, and Billy Lee took charge of her traveling trunk, and she and George went inside.

"How are my stables?" he said. "How are my horses?"

It was almost boyish, the way he put the question. Yet not so much boyish as with the depth of a man who was eating his heart out for his home, for the wideness of green fields that made his life.

"All well," she said. "All in fine condition, Lund says."

But when they were in their upstairs room she turned on him. "Couldn't you have asked first about little Elizabeth?" she said. "Are your horses the most important to you?"

"I'm sorry, Patsy," he said. "I'm not used to being a grandfather."

"She's a darling little thing," she said. "She'll have Nellie's eyes and Jacky's coloring. And George—you didn't even let me know you were ill."

"It came all of a moment," he said. "I had no warning. Suddenly I was bedridden and the doctors were cupping my head. I was certain I'd die."

"You could have had someone write me."

"Patsy, there was the army. If I'd died, someone had to take the army. When I could talk at all, it was with Nat Greene."

"Is the army more important to you than your family?" she said.

"I'd have left the army to Greene," he said.

"And left Jacky and Nellie and baby Elizabeth to whom?" she said. "Does the army stand higher with you than your kin?"

He sighed with the weariness of a convalescent. Martha was still unforgiving. She had come to him because he had been in danger of his life, but, coming, and seeing him recovered, would not forget the smoldering of emotions between them.

"You're jealous of the army, Patsy," he said. "That's not right."

"And you're jealous of Jacky," she said. "Is that right, either?"

He went to the clothes cupboard, which was a bulky Dutch *kas,* and took off his uniform coat and pulled out his dressing gown and put it on. He didn't want to answer Martha. He was not a sophist. But he could suspect that when two people threw jealousy at each other, both could be wrong. Jealousy, in its primal force, he regarded as a fear. Martha was, at base, afraid of the army. Was he afraid of Jack? Of Jack's pulling at Martha as the army pulled at him? Of a conflict, tight and devastating and pitilessly human, inside the broader conflict of war? He would like to evade those questions.

She took his silence for agreement, and fell into a silence of her own, satisfied not to argue since nothing could be really gained in any case. She had been irritated by his not asking at once about little Elizabeth, and the irritation had provoked her tongue. Another woman would have understood that—perhaps even another man. But George did not. He was sensitive himself and readily hurt, but he lacked certain refinements of sensitivity where others were concerned, particularly on the spur of the moment. She felt besides, half-consciously, that he had grown beyond the need for her support; his campaign at Trenton and Princeton had raised him to a fame she had never known for him before. He towered above any man in America.

In the silence they could hear the buzz of voices, troops lined up to be inoculated for the smallpox; and the lyric flutings of a few chickadees, and downy woodpeckers rattling at oak bark, and the clink of spades and mattocks laboring to build Fort Nonsense, which was of no use at all except to keep the regiments busy. Outside, limned against the sky, the buds of ash trees were a jet and shiny black, and among the laced tops of maples and birches spread an elusive, virginal, roseate tint, where tentative sweet sap painted the coming blush of spring.

Martha relented. She was not, with all said and done, a shrew like Mrs. Gates.

She said, "Next summer you can bring this to an end, George, and then come home. You'll have more men, what with the fame of Trenton, and the king's ministry will see it's hopeless."

"Men?" he said. "They're deserting every day."

She chilled at his voice. "Oh?" she said. "But why?"

"The itch," he said. "Lice. Sores. No food."

"You wrote that you had food."

"Yes, when I still had a quartermaster general. I haven't one now. Food's scarce, Patsy. And the men want none of this doing. Their officers cheat them out of clothes and pay. The hospitals are death houses, the commissary's a tangle. They want for home, as I do."

She looked for a chair, and sat down. "It had all sounded so fine," she said.

"It isn't."

He sat down, too, on a pine settle, the dressing gown falling wide to show his bony knees. "I miss Gates and Lee," he said. "I'm left to fight single-handed."

"Oh, now, George," she said. "You can get General Lee back, can't you?"

"When we capture an enemy major general to trade for him," he said. "It's not likely. But I had a letter from him."

"Oh?"

"He's living well in New York, now that they've decided not to hang him. He asked me to send him his dogs."

Martha repressed a giggle. She saw, from her husband's face, that he was doing the same.

"What did you answer?" she said.

"I told him his dogs are in Virginia."

"Well, I've never liked him," Martha said. "And speaking of Virginia, Mrs. Gates put in at Mt. Vernon. Did you know General Gates is to be at Albany?"

"Yes. I've had that from the Congress."

"I think that's a slap at you, George. Mrs. Gates made it very plain."

"It probably is."

"Won't you slap back?"

"No," he said. "The Congress employs me, Patsy. And through the Congress, the people. Mrs. Gates can smirk as she likes. If the people want Gates, they can have him."

"She made it a very obvious point that you're letting your army rust away in a country hamlet, while her husband has taken a crucial area under his command and will be full of action," she said. "I'm positive she's made the same point wherever she can. And loudly."

"Mrs. Gates doesn't know military matters. This army isn't strong enough to move on New York and challenge Howe. We must play the cat-and-mouse game with him. Here in Morristown Howe can't easily get at us, but I can keep an eye on him and be a thorn in his next plans —whether up the Hudson to Albany or down to Philadelphia. Let Mrs. Gates talk her country-hamlet talk," he said.

Martha slapped her hands together. Angry as she had been at her husband a few moments ago, she was angrier now. He seemed so un-seeing of what might be threatening him.

"You're blind, George!" she cried. "Don't you realize the Gateses want to topple you?"

She swung around and began to dress for dinner.

There was a knock at his office door.

"Come in," he said. He felt he had been saying that endlessly and endlessly all winter, like a parrot.

Colonel Hamilton entered. He was rather short, handsomely well knit, and exceptionally groomed. The Hamilton who had captained the New York guns at Trenton and pounded the last of the Hessians into sur-render in Nassau Hall at Princeton. Greene had been impressed with him and had suggested him for a staff position. The young colonel wrote well, spoke well, and thought with a cool clarity. Washington was al-ready finding his talents very useful.

"Major General Benedict Arnold, sir."

Washington leaped up, catching sight of the stocky figure behind Hamilton.

"General Arnold. Good God, but this is happy, sir!"

"Your Excellency—"

The two men locked hands. Hamilton withdrew.

"Sit down, sit down, General."

He'd not seen Arnold since the Canadian debacle except for one day, to send him to organize defense in Connecticut against enemy shipping raids along the coast. He was glad to see that Arnold looked well, recovered from his wound at Quebec.

"Your trip," he said. "An easy one?"

"Tolerable."

Arnold would have had to come from Connecticut across the Hudson at King's Ferry near Peekskill, skirting New York City, and then down along the snaking mountain valleys to Morristown. With Howe holding New York, the more direct route was blocked. Traffic between New England and the rest of America was confined to King's Ferry and to the ferry at New Windsor, a few miles above. A thin lifeline.

He said, "I've been waiting for you, General. We must have you in the field again soon."

"Thank you, sir."

"Either here, or in the north. We'll need strength in the north."

"We will," Arnold said flatly, and Washington agreed. General Burgoyne had reached Canada with a large army out of England and with an imposing mass of Hessians, and would make an invasion of the northern Hudson, down the lakes, and join powers with Howe from New York. There was no secret about it.

"I sit and watch," Washington said. "Merely watch. Howe might go for Philadelphia."

"Damned fool if he does," Arnold snapped. "Or he hasn't had his orders from London."

"We don't know what he's had. But Putnam is at Peekskill, with what I can spare him and the hope of the militia coming in. Sullivan has a division in the Hudson Highlands with orders to be alert. I think the push will be at the Hudson."

Arnold nodded, but the nod carried reservation. "In the Congress, sir," he said, "some might think you're too partial to the Hudson. They might think Philadelphia should be buttressed."

"Damn, General, if the Hudson is captured the war is lost. What's the value of a single city against having the country's throat cut?"

Arnold shrugged. The shrug held a gesture of warning. "The Congress is in Philadelphia," he said.

Washington ignored this. He said, "My wish, General, would be to offer you a command on the Hudson."

Arnold's face lit briefly, as though it were a justification and a balm to his cut pride. But his left hand sliced in a rough, negative gesture.

"I've some matters with the Congress first, sir. I'll take no command until they're settled."

Washington disregarded the gesture. He appreciated the whirlwind of energy and pride behind it.

"General," he said, "you've been very patient."

"Your letter," Arnold said. "Only because of that. I'd have resigned when the Congress appointed a batch of damned unfledged major generals over my head."

"But you didn't. Your letter in answer to me had a great dignity. I hoped you wouldn't resign. And the Congress has made up for its error, since." He looked with significance at Arnold's new epaulets.

"Oh yes, yes," Arnold said. "A major general for breaking up a raid on Danbury. Had nothing to do with wideness or a leader's prevision. The Congress tosses me promotion like a nut to an ape, and votes me a horse. I haven't got the horse yet. And I haven't got the seniority I had as a brigadier. I've been bumped upstairs to sit on a lower stool."

Washington put his look from the epaulets to the vivid eyes that burned out of Arnold's darkish skin. The look held there. He reminded himself that here, facing him, was the man who had made an incredible march through a Maine winter of wilderness; who would have helped storm Quebec but for a drunken sentry and weak-kneed panic. Arnold had hacked a woebegone flotilla from green timber on Lake Champlain, and fought it to a standstill until it was sunk under him, staving off the first invasion from Canada and possibly saving the war; a man who'd done everything required of him, and more.

He reminded himself, too, that this man made enemies by his outrightness, his free speaking, his impatience with compromise and weak counsel—and, above all this, his consuming scorn for expense accounts when fighting was to be done.

"General," he said, "I can only hope that for the need of the army and the country you will put yourself above questions of rank and seniority. Congress is a political body and does not always know these finer points."

Arnold's eyes, boring at his, flickered, even hesitated. It was as though they were somehow appealing, asking for help, for the rescue from the ugly pit into which a man might be driven to cast himself in the name of rectitude and his own worthiness. Then the hesitation, the intimacy were gone.

"I'll remember, Your Excellency."

"Thank you, General."

"But before I do—" this came blurtedly, confused—"do you think I'm honest?"

"Yes. Certainly."

"There are those who don't. Too many don't." The eyes were a cold fire now. "They whisper against me, and make charges. I want a settlement with the Congress, and an investigation of the charges. I'll have my name cleared before I'll fight again. Can you get me a hearing?"

Here was a stormy petrel. But like the petrel he could wing through the storms. "I'll give you a letter to the Congress, General."

And then Arnold startled him. For Arnold, who had been sitting on the other side of the desk, his legs crossed and alternately drumming on a thigh and beating time to his phrases with a polished boot, stood up and put his palm on the desk top and leaned over it.

"Will you give me one thing more, sir? Will you give me to hope that when these rats in the Congress start gnawing at you, you'll fight 'em as I'm doing?"

Washington did not answer. He could find no answer. He thought of asking Arnold what he meant, but he knew what Arnold meant. So far, none of his aides or generals had brought it out into the open. He sat silent, looking at Arnold.

"They're beginning already, sir. Munching at you. Small men fearful of a big one. I've had the reports in Connecticut. You call for an oath of allegiance by Americans, and a pip-squeak congressman screams 'Tyranny' and wants your knuckles rapped. John Adams says to beware of demigods, and that you're not his superior while he's on the floor of the Congress. You went up too high after Trenton and Princeton, and they'd like to pull you down. Don't let 'em."

Washington remained quiet. He could feel a flush, though, creeping up his skin from under his neckcloth. This is what Martha had said.

"You will have your letter to the Congress tomorrow, General," he said. "You are a judicious officer with great activity, enterprise, and perseverance."

Arnold's hand flung out to his. "And my deep respects to Madame Washington, sir."

"Mrs. Washington has returned to Mt. Vernon," Washington said. "She says she only hears the last gun of one campaign and the opening gun of the next."

He watched Arnold chuckle, humanly, with a kind of relief, and salute, and go out.

He was aware, those early summer days—had been aware of it for several months—that there was a hesitancy about him in the Congress. It welled from two sources. The first was that he had drawn such praise to himself after Trenton, and adulation he was painfully conscious of. The second was his sheer inability to do anything, to follow up the Trenton smash with another smash just as electric—as if he'd been one of Dr. Franklin's conveyers of the lightning from heaven.

On the one hand, John Adams and the political kind were suspicious of him. On the other hand were the amateur militarists.

With Martha gone, he pleasanted his afternoons by rides, once or twice a week, with his officers and their wives. He liked the company of women. Liked their smiles and transparent modesty, and the enjoyment of teasing them to the limit, verbally.

"Oh, General, please—"

"La, Your Excellency, I vow—"

Or, "If I take your meaning, sir, what's to become of my honor?"

He liked to flirt. He was remembering the Virginia girls who had refused him. He was tasting compensation now. But he never could quite bring himself to taste the compensation in a bed.

He played catch ball with his younger officers for exercise, and bandied jokes with Caleb Gibbs, a pure Yankee and captain of his body-guard.

"Colonel Hamilton's apologies, sir," Gibbs said one day, "and Johnny Burgoyne's on the march, and do we stop him with Gates? . . . As to say, sir, do we slam 'em shut, them gates?"

"That's not your best, Caleb."

"No, sir."

"Try again at dinner."

"Yes, sir. But you'll avow the name's tempting."

"I'm surprised at you, Caleb. You a New Englander. Tempting?"

"Oh, well, sir, we do yield to temptation on an' off. How'd we populate, else?"

"Not by off, Caleb. Not by off."

He put the captain's squawk behind him and went to his office. Hamilton was there, looking disturbed.

"The Congress wants you to decide, sir, between Generals Gates and Schuyler. I've the motion here."

He laid his riding whip on the table. He usually used the branch of an elm or ash. It happened to be ash today. "Decide, Colonel? On what? Can't the Congress make up its mind?"

"No, sir. The Congress leaves it to you."

He rubbed his chin and surveyed Hamilton thoughtfully. There had been a tug of war between Gates and Schuyler as to who was to be in charge at Albany. Each man had had the post twice. The question had become one of politics, New England against New York. The Congress, politically cowardly, was shying away from an answer. So the Congress had passed it to him. Must he be a politician as well as a warrior?

"I've heard you speak well of General Schuyler, sir," Hamilton was saying.

"I have an equal regard for General Gates."

"But with his actions, sir?" Hamilton had a young man's lofty look. "The scene in the Congress?"

Washington nodded, knowing the scene Hamilton referred to.

When, in one of its reversals of mind, the Congress had shunted Gates off at Albany and picked Schuyler, Gates had come roaring down to the floor of the Congress, and had shouted and ranted like a madman until his own faction had surrounded him and got him to retire. A childish, volatile exhibition, stuffed with menace to the general cause. Perhaps, Washington thought, Martha was right. But he had his rules and abided by them.

"The danger is personal," he said to Hamilton. "These are my senior generals. They're both my friends. I can't declare for one or the other; there'd be the cry of favoritism. That cry could split us. I can't let it go out."

"But the Congress has put the decision to you, sir." Hamilton was frigidly formal, knowing what he would have said in Washington's place.

"I'll ask to be excused, Colonel. I must stay impartial. I can't back either without giving offense. You must understand that my reasons go beyond partiality. To plump for Gates or Schuyler, one or the other, would be fatal. It would bring spites in the army, and the breaking up of our whole effort. I submit this to you, Colonel."

"Yes, sir."

Hamilton left then. Whether convinced or not, Washington did not know. He stood at the table, his fingers going unconscious among the papers on it, and asked himself if this country could ever sink its differences and come to the beginnings of freedom; or, in spite of politics, to the deserving of it.

He thought, too, that he was not as blind as Martha had accused him of being. He could see what Gates's acts were leading to, and he could crush Gates if he wished, now, before too late. It was simply that he was not as concerned with honors and pre-eminence as many other men. That had been drubbed out of him a quarter century past, on the Virginia frontier. The drubbing had brought him much. Perhaps even a recklessness for his own life.

X

Beset

"The enemy has gratified me," the boy said, "with a bullet."

He was clearly a boy. He was red-headed, and slim, and thrashed on his pillows in impatience at his bandaged leg and he was about the age of Jack. Jack had a wife and baby, and Nellie was expecting again. This boy also had a wife and baby. But similarity ended there. His wife could hardly be expecting, being beyond the Atlantic; and he was far more volatile than Jack. Ecstatic and irrepressible.

"I've written about it to my dear," he said. "Versailles will learn. A wound that I had by your side."

"Get well of it soon," Washington said. "The surgeons are to treat you as if you were my own."

He stared down at the bed and the rumpled pillows.

Time had passed for him. There had been Howe's sailing from New York and into Chesapeake Bay, and red-jacketed battalions outflanking him at Brandywine Creek, and failure at Germantown, in fog, where his troops had fired on each other and Judge Chew's stone house became an enemy fort and slowed his attack, and one of his generals was found drunk in a fence corner and another had fallen asleep in the saddle from sheer fatigue. Howe was snug in Philadelphia now, with the Congress fled and he himself still hanging on the outskirts, still in the shreds and the cold. There was a terrible gap between what he strove for and what he could say.

But something must be said.

"You will be cared for, Marquis."

"Oh, I make no doubt of that." The boy's face lighted. "No doubt while I'm near you."

Washington pondered, embarrassed. What had brought this French nobleman, stripling as he was, over here to fight for America?

Was it glory? . . . He'd known the tug of that. Adventure? . . . He'd known that, too. Was it possibly, just possibly, a dim-perceived spiritual something? The same dim-perceived something that drove his own will on? What was it? . . . Staring at the boy's quick, expressive face, Washington grasped for the finality. Freedom was the finality for him, ground like beef through a chopper but emerging meaty and sustaining and close-compacted. At least this might be so if the army could last. But the boy?

The youngster had a good many names. Gilbert du Motier, etc., etc., ending in Lafayette. Washington hadn't mastered them all. There'd been too many titled Frenchmen coming to America recently for him to cut through the elaborate mazes of their names. The American agents in Paris had been busy, capitalizing on France's war against England, and the colonies were aswim with Frenchmen looking for rank and the tassels of pride and the chance to spit out at King George. But this boy seemed more devoted than most. He seemed as if he sought a Grail, a peculiar, forceful essence that would be shining and holy. And he was so very young.

Washington could recollect their first official meeting. Could never forget it, as a matter of fact. The boy had equipped himself like a child turned loose among toys—uniforms, horses, pistols, all the trappings of warfare—and the Congress had appointed him a major general, though with an insulting coolness because the Congress was having a bellyful of these volunteer Frenchmen, and he had descended on Washington one day at the American camp with a dazzling brilliance.

Washington had been sinkingly conscious of the contrast to his own ill-equipped and almost shabby generals. But he used what tact he could. "It is somewhat awkward, Marquis, to show ourselves to an officer just come from the French Army."

Lafayette's response had been instant. "It is to learn and not to teach, sir, that I am here."

The boy had smuggled himself out of France against the orders of King Louis, and he made himself so modest and convivial and willing to learn that all the officers and all the army loved him. Washington admitted freely that he loved him, too. If he'd had a son, it might have been like this.

He shook his head, clearing dreams from his brain. "We should try some new stroke now," he said.

Knox was with him in the sickroom. He took a species of comfort from that great bulk, in the way Knox stood by him in all his decisions.

Whether this was military wisdom on Knox's part, or sheer loyalty, he was not able to fathom. He suspected a balancing of both.

"Against Howe?" Knox said. "Ten thousand?"

"We'll do it, General," Lafayette said.

Knox looked down at him and chuckled in his throat.

"We can, General," Lafayette said.

"Be patient, Marquis," Washington said.

"If I'd patience I'd still be at Versailles." The red hairs waggled on the pillows, the slim body inched itself higher. "I am not of patience. That I do not have. I have the slowness of my wound, and the need to walk again."

Here was not only a dedicated boy, but a firebrand, Washington thought. The still-adolescent marquis had not even felt the bullet in the flesh of his leg at the Brandywine. Someone had to tell him that blood was running from his boot top.

"I also lie here and have an anger for General Conway," Lafayette said.

"Oh?" Washington said.

"Conway?" Knox said.

Conway was an Irishman in the French service, had come over with the volunteer onsweep from France and been made a brigadier.

Knox said, "Anger?"

"*Mon Général*," Lafayette said, and twisted on the bed and flung out a hand toward Washington. "*Mon Général,* this dirty man has written to General Gates thirteen reasons why we lost at the Brandywine. I think he would spread it in public ears."

Washington said, "How?"

"The Congress has ears," Lafayette said.

"That's damned strange," Knox said.

"Having ears? No."

"Putting it to the Congress. You said he wrote to Gates."

"He will publish it everywhere." Lafayette broke into a nervousness of French, caught himself, wrinkled his nose apologetically, and returned to his bumpy English. He was picking up the use of it around the camp and the dinner table. "The letter is private, he says. But he shows it to me, so pleasant, so amiable. He wants it spread far, *entendu*. He will see it gets to the eyes of men in the Congress."

"Well, damme, we lost. So we lost. Who the devil wants reasons?"

Knox, in his loyalty, was discarding reasons. But there had been enough of them. New ground, not properly scouted; Howe's feint at the center of the American lines overestimated while his left circled away, past unguarded creek fords, to roll up the American right; a dismal lack of reports and army intelligence. Except for prodigies by Greene and Anthony Wayne, the American Army would have been chewed to garbage.

Washington was culpable. Howe had outsmarted him. But his mind was on other battles to come. He said, "Why did General Conway show you this letter, Marquis?"

"For my favor," Lafayette said frankly. "General Conway looks for the advancement in France, when this is over, and I am a friend of his patron at our court. He was so warm toward me, called himself my soldier." He shrugged in disgust. "He dropped words to me, *mon Général*. Words that whisper I should leave the country and make for France while he schemes here. *Enfin*, that things would swim better under a different command."

From Martha, from Arnold, now from Lafayette. There was opposition to him, criticism of him, and the opposition and criticism were making headway.

He braced himself. He had expected criticism. What had he told Patrick Henry, that night in Philadelphia that seemed so many ages gone? From the hour of his appointment as commander he dated the fall of his reputation. He had never asked, never wanted, acclaim. His moving wish had been to serve. He knew he was not for sputtering fireworks like Lee, nor for cautious administration like Gates; hardly knew, indeed, what he was for, rooted here by the bed of a beardless foreigner, with only his own bulldog stubbornness and the ponderous weight of Knox behind him.

He said, "I don't know General Conway well, Marquis. But I know your trust."

"It is for you, *mon Général*. Only for you."

He patted Lafayette's hand on the quilt and took Knox away. The huge general was making rumbling noises in his chest, not good-naturedly.

"Damme!" Knox said. "If anyone's pot shooting at you, behind your back—"

"We don't know for sure, Knox. I'd rather think not. Poor Sullivan is taking most of the blame for Brandywine."

"Sullivan's a martyr!" Knox could bellow to shake leaves on trees. "A tomfoolery damned Congressman trotting after him on the battlefield taking notes of his orders. Who could keep judgment in that fix? And a bastardly Frenchman wanting to lead the right wing and racing Sullivan to get there first. I saw, I saw. Farcical theater piece." He slammed his tricorne on his head, shaking his jowls and filling his great lungs massively. "Now there'll be another investigation by the Congress. Another court-martial for a general. Sullivan will have to answer to these pip-squeaks. But by God, if I don't think they're setting their sights on all of us."

Washington wanted to avoid an explosion. He had too many gun-powder personalities around him already.

"Whatever the Congress concludes about Sullivan," he said, "he'll stay in his command, Knox. I'll have my way, for once, about that."

"Yes, sir, I'll stand to it, help me, Almighty. If the Congress sits on its buttocks and cashiers generals, who'll win the war for 'em? And what was the little marquis hinting about? Have the pip-squeaks got you in their sights, too?"

"We'll let time work," Washington said.

Time already had, as Knox would know. In Knox's mind was the memory, the very recent memory, of another French general. His name had been du Coudray. He had come to headquarters panoplied in self-built glory and with sixteen minor officers in his train and had assumed he would be taking over the artillery command from Knox. He'd been a braggart and a show-off and a knout of argument in the army and the Congress both. Luckily he'd insisted on riding his horse onto the flat raft of the Schuylkill ferry instead of dismounting as anyone of sense would have done; and his horse had lunged off the ferry into the river, and he'd drowned. The Congress and the army were relieved, even John Adams, who had his own view of soldiers who didn't fit with Washington's. But it had been touch and go for a while and the aftermath rankled in Knox. He'd come close to being put under the orders of a spangled foreigner.

"We'll let time work," Washington said.

He was in a cold rage to do something, anything. Howe nestled in Philadelphia, but American forts on islands in the Delaware still peppered the river. He had the prescience that they would fall, unless Gates sent him help. Gates sent a token force, too small to tip a scale. The forts fell.

Everything crumbled.

A Congress committee came to him, polite but critical, with the air of men who sit in armchairs and steer events without the clash and agony of being in the forefront. He told the committee in plain words and plain seeing the shackles that tied him: not enough men, not enough clothes, not enough food, not enough enlistments of troops that would be wanted for a lengthening war. He thought the committee had caught his urgency—hoped it had caught it. He knew very few Congress members now. Most of those who had given him the chief command had gone home, out of public service, to mend their own fortunes and professions; leaving him on the field of battle. Very few of the new Congress members had even seen him. And sitting in armchairs and steering events was one thing; putting events to the proof was another—in ice and sleet, and mud, and summer's angry sun; with faulty cartridge boxes and no shoes, a trickle of food and less than a trickle of pay, and half the countryside sullen and the other half grasping, and courts-martial sprouting like mushrooms overnight, and five hundred lashes on a bare back for desertion.

But while Howe was in Philadelphia, Howe had to be watched. Maybe attacked again?

His generals, brought to council, said no.

He argued his best with the best of them, Greene, Knox, Sullivan, Wayne, but gave in at the end. They were right. They doubled back at him the facts he had thrown at the Congress committee. Not enough men or equipment or transport.

And he dismissed the generals, and his troops snored under such makeshift shelters as could be made for them, and he had a three-pronged choice. The first prong was capture and a rope's noose at his neck. The second was more retreat, into the west. The third was hanging on, a hoping, a tortured and slogging persistence. He preferred the last choice. But he wasn't sure if his officers would. Nor the country.

He was fogged, as he'd been at Germantown. He had so little to go on.

The word "beset" was overworked in the letters his aides drafted for him, to Governor Trumbull in Connecticut and Mr. Morris in Philadelphia and Mr. Laurens, the president of the Congress at York, poised like startled birds among the green-swept undulations and solid ridges of Pennsylvania.

"Beset" seemed almost to be his countersign.

Shortly he would have to go into winter quarters. He would have to hole up, like the fox the enemy called him.

But where? Not too near Howe, and yet not too far.

He thought of Wilmington, and listened to Greene, who pressed the idea. But there were difficulties there. Wilmington was full of Philadelphia refugees, and the Pennsylvania Council cried out to Congress that its own state ought to be protected. He could have wished there were no such things as Pennsylvanians; he'd had his wrestlings with them since he'd first ridden west as a Virginian. Yet, going over his maps, he found a place which would most likely satisfy everyone, except the army. It was defensible behind the Schuylkill River and the valley creek, a high triangle covered with woods that could be used for winter huts. Not so close to Philadelphia as to be surprised, not so far as to be out of any action Howe might make. Pennsylvania would be reassured.

It was politics—bowing to the civilians—to their convenience and comfort and their squeals to be secured or kept from having to break the even tenor of their ways, the smooth and gaining mercantilism of their lives. Well, the war must be some way seen through. He'd go to this spot on his maps. It would serve as well as any other. It would keep the Continentals alive. If they could get food. But food would be a problem anywhere he wintered. His commissary, Trumbull, son of the Connecticut governor, was sick. Would have to be replaced.

He was more than gloomy when he chose the spot. But it seemed all he could do.

There had been an ironworks along the creek, so it was known as the Valley Forge. He began to lay plans to winter there.

A kind of hopefulness ran in the news from the north. A large forage party, probing east from Burgoyne's army in midsummer, had been thrashed at Bennington. Men of the Hampshire Grants had done it, led by John Stark, who'd showed so well at Trenton and then resigned in disgust over the Congress' methods of appointing generals.

And, tailing that, a westward wedge of invasion, driving down the Mohawk Valley to meet Burgoyne at Albany, had been fought to a standstill by valley farmers under an unknown militia general named Herkimer. Herkimer had died of wounds after an indomitable day of blood and the howls of Burgoyne's Indian allies; and Benedict Arnold had swept out of Albany to finish the business, using the babbling of a half-wit farm boy to spread the word ahead that the Americans were coming like the leaves of Birnam Wood. Herkimer blocked the valley, and Arnold cleared it.

A kind of hopefulness. But over a month ago. Gates sent him very little notice of how things were progressing in the northern department. Burgoyne was still inching toward Albany and control of the Hudson.

He puzzled as to how he could prevent that. And knew he couldn't. He had so little to work with. He ordered Morgan and the riflemen to join Gates—they'd be quick and deadly at forest fighting—and tried to find some hopefulness in his own predicament. It was ugly. Except for Trenton and Princeton, he'd had two years of defeat. The country wanted something else of him; the Congress was for boldness, for flagrancy.

He felt like a street-corner beggar, seeking pity. Yet that was the last he wished. For it was his creed that seeking pity, which was the same as self-punishment, was a withdrawal from the real truths, a cringing denial of the depth and meaning of being alive, and human, and capable of ideas. So long as a man is alive, he thought, he wears his own certain magnificence. And if he dies in that magnificence—what then? All must die in any event, and the manner of the death is not important. Only the weakness or the courage of it.

One could die slowly, as he and his army were dying. Or swiftly. But every man who dies in weakness weakens humankind. By courage he builds another step on the ladder to—to what? The ultimate was huge and evaded him.

He was simply fighting a war. He could not lay out a pattern for humanity. That task was too great for any mortal mind, considering what he had found so many men to be. He could only trust to a Divine Providence, and to holding off Howe through the winter at the Valley Forge, and to coming to another summer when he might be able to march.

Able?

Not with his tatterdemalions. Not with his crow-pecked lot. He'd been able so far to hold them together as a token force, a visible buttress for the future, but they were dwindling every day, slipping away and away like dried sands from a child's castle on a sea beach. They had marched before, yea; and fought; and won. But now, too few, too weak, too drained of everything, what could he ask of them?

If it came to that, what could he ask of the Congress? and the people? More and more sacrifices. More and more money and men and an army's needs. Less greed and pleasure and more of that common sense Private Paine had written about. But the experience of the past two years didn't leave him very sanguine. His role of fox, he thought, was about played out. Even a fox must eat.

At this juncture he had word of Burgoyne again. Not from Gates but from New York's Governor Clinton. Burgoyne had reached his limit. He'd been scotched on left and right, at Bennington and Oriskany. His supply line from Canada stretched thin and lengthy, the American forests on the upper Hudson hemmed him like the palings of a fence. His troops had been mauled in fighting, the turkey-cock gobbling of Morgan's men and Arnold's slashing charges had cowed them. Burgoyne had broken off the fight and asked for terms.

The terms, Clinton wrote, would be surrender.

Washington saw only that word. Surrender.

That Gates had not reported this to him made no matter. He gave orders for a triumph day. Speeches, and extra rum, and fireworks. He put on the best jubilation he could, for the best American victory so far.

Gates's name blazed in the reflection of Saratoga. The Congress took him to its heart. He would keep command of his army, and have a gold medal and the Congress' thanks, and his young aide Wilkinson was promoted to brigadier because Gates wished it for bringing news of the surrender. And it was flickered about that Gates might even deserve more.

Martha had a different view. She served tea to Mr. George Mason at Mt. Vernon and gave her view succinctly, as she could do when roused.

"I just hope Mrs. Gates won't come to croak at me," she said. "Or maybe I hope she *will* come."

"I don't think she will," Mason said. He was a wealthy Virginian, a neighbor, a little aging now, but solicitous of Martha and Mt. Vernon while its master was away. He had served in two congresses and drafted the first Bill of Rights for the Virginia Burgesses. "Which might disappoint you, Mrs. Washington?" he said.

"Fiddledeedee," she said. And saw him look at her, and gave a small, social laugh. "Well, all right. Of course I'd like to tell her down."

"A rather large consignment, ma'am."

"Large? What's large about it? Who won that surrender, Mr. Mason? Arnold and Morgan, that's who. According to the gazettes. Her Horatio had nothing to do but sit and wait for the northern states to pour out men to him. After Janet McCrea was murdered he was sure to win."

Mason nodded, frowning over his teacup. Outside, the lawn was still a stubbled green. A cardinal flashed scarlet in the sun.

He said, "Janet McCrea. Betrothed to a Tory, murdered by Burgoyne's own Indians. A pathetic tale. But that can't be all of it."

"Of course not."

"But why?"

"Why? . . . Well, leaving out the hapless Miss McCrea—oh, Mr. Mason, wouldn't it be terrible to be in her place? Riding along roads you thought safe? And suddenly to have savages at you and see the tomahawk aimed for your skull?"

"Yes. A tragedy in ignorance."

"Ignorance?"

"Of Indians. Burgoyne is a European. Doesn't have the least conception of them. His standards are civilized. He expects others to be. When he expects at all."

He tasted at his tea, and wiped his mouth slowly with a napkin, and said, "But why, ma'am? Why Burgoyne's surrender?" He twitched a smile. "If you're going to face Mrs. Gates you'll have to have an answer."

"So many farmers came in," she said. "Why don't they come for George?"

Mason settled his cup carefully in the rim made for it in the saucer. He put the cup and saucer on the table. "General Gates has never been beaten," he said.

"I think that's insulting," Martha said promptly.

"Not at all. Your husband will be the first to say so. He's not been—shall we say—successful? Oh, I know the reply to that. He's been forced to fight in more or less open country, where the European tactics have better sway. Gates fought Burgoyne in virgin timberland and a few scrabbled farms, with men used to hunting among trees and shooting out the eyes of squirrels. But still, the general has not been successful."

"Then what am I to say to Mrs. Gates?" she said.

"Nothing. For she won't come here to croak. She'll be too busy pushing her husband's prospects with the Congress."

"Mr. Mason," she said. "Do you think she'd try?"

"She and her husband both," he said. "General Gates is the star in the firmament now. Why wouldn't they try?"

She put down her cup, too, and looked at him. She felt very weak but very defensive. She could stand off an onslaught of many Gateses. George would not be humiliated, or thrown down.

Oh, she had seen this, she had seen this coming.

"What to do? What to do, Mr. Mason?"

"Steadiness, and be resolute at his elbow. I hear from the Congress. The cabal is blossoming but it's gardened by spindly men."

"You don't think General Gates can overtop George?"

"No, I don't. But I think he'll make the effort."

"He'll simply have to be stopped."

Mr. Mason smiled. A slow, sympathetic smile that had futility in it.

"If he makes the effort," Martha said, "he may be successful there, too."

"I can't deny he may be. I can only tell you what I think."

Martha's expression said plainly that that wasn't enough. "I wish my poor husband had General Arnold beside him," she said. "General Arnold fights."

Mr. Mason's smile gave way to a shrug. Arnold had been wounded again at Saratoga, badly, and was in an Albany hospital. "General Arnold isn't popular with the Congress, Mrs. Washington. He takes a truculent attitude."

"As well he may."

Mr. Mason gave another shrug, not of impoliteness but of impotency to unravel all the twisted skeins of the war. He remarked that he must be riding back to his own plantation before dark. Martha accompanied him into the hall and to the west door. His servant and two horses were waiting there.

"Mr. Mason," she said suddenly, "how long would it take Jacky to become a member of the Congress?"

He turned, incredulous. "What? Who?"

"Jacky. My son."

"For the Congress?"

"Certainly."

Mr. Mason's aplomb, his correctness in social manners, were nearly shattered. He let out a startled exclamation before he could recover himself. The woman in front of him, the wife of the commander in chief, was like a dove with ruffled feathers. Every feather, every fiber of her, declaimed that if the Gateses wanted to make this a pecking match, the whole of the Washington family would be in it.

He struggled for the conciliatory note. "Jack's not known in the county," he said.

"But his stepfather is," she said. "And was a burgess besides. How soon can Jacky get to the Congress?"

Astute, legally minded, a long-time student of human failings, Mr. Mason refused the folly of arguing against an aroused woman's preposterousness. He said, "The best road is probably through the Burgesses. The Virginia House."

"Then shouldn't he go there?"

"It would be a start, ma'am," he said. "But the road would be long."

"But a start."

"Oh, yes. Though I caution you, before Jack ever gets to the Congress this backbiting at the general may be over."

"It could be over sooner," she said, "if the Gates faction realizes we're going to combat them."

"True. True enough."

He'd not estimated this combativeness in Mrs. Washington. She was wrong, of course, flying off on the only tangent she could lay hands on. Jack Custis in politics couldn't help his father. But the nettled lady in front of him, up to now so docile, so housewifely, and now so vigorous, must be assuaged.

"I'll be happy to give backing to Jack's candidacy," he said. And bowed, and went down the few steps to the gravel roadway, and left Martha to her worries.

She didn't worry for long. She was not a worrier. Gates had triumphed, and belittlement threatened George. The bare fact was, beat it through her mind as she could, like whipping the white of an egg to froth, was that Gates had soared high above George.

She scribbled off a note to Jacky that night, and sent it by a rider.

She would be glad to have him in the House of Burgesses. Glad to have him coming forward in politics as a buttress to her George, who was flung into the forecourt of jealousy and the target for every jack and cheap-shooter.

"Announce that you will stand for election to the Virginia House, dear Jacky," she said. She added her loving good wishes to Nellie for an easy confinement.

Then she made her travel schedule for the Valley Forge. Not that George was sick this time, but that he was in a dirty-handed battle and that she wanted to battle alongside him. For the first time since she had married him, he greatly, emotionally, needed her.

He seemed to be at the end of his tether.

Beset.

XI

Winter, 1777-78

She sat with General Greene's wife and the wives of other officers in a half-formal group around the fireplace in the small room, and listened to an odd noise that quavered distantly at the windows, and said, "What is that?"

It was a crow noise, made by human throats. It struck the window-panes with steady reverberation. "Caw," it said. "Caw, caw, caw."

"Perhaps there's some news in the camp," she said.

Kitty Greene raised hands from her lap in a soundless motion that took, from its soundlessness, a significance that women best understand.

"Hardly news," she said. "The cawing means 'no meat.'"

"Oh," Martha said. "Oh, mercy." She glanced about at the faces. Uneasy eyes and straight-lined lips met the dread that swam into her mind. The officers' ladies, it seemed, were amply familiar with the cawing. She said, "For the troops?"

"For the troops. Or anyone else."

Martha was newly arrived. This was her first gathering of females at the Valley Forge, the kind of unassuming and introductory *salon* etiquette expected of her, and she knew none of them very well. She could not even yet address Mrs. Greene as "Kitty," though she had the impulse to do so. General Greene's wife was several cuts above the others. Martha had already learned that Kitty Greene spoke French quite well. That would be a help in the social niceties with the Frenchmen of title who seemed to be so numerous in the camp. And she had polish and the graceful airs of a drawing room. But "Kitty" would be a little too intimate, now, according to Martha's standards.

So she said only, "It can't have been happening often."

"Once or twice before. General Greene says it's bound to worsen."

Martha fought down an audible sigh. She had always to remember that the luxury of sighing aloud in front of any but her family could be hurtful to George.

"The same quandary, then," she said.

"The same." Kitty Greene nodded. "Mr. Trumbull is ill—no fault of his, naturally."

"Oh, no."

"And General Mifflin is absent." She put a touch to the Mifflin name that was not lost on Martha.

"Absent?"

"Well, otherwise occupied. With the Congress chiefer than with the camp. We've not seen him."

The caw, caw, caw persisted.

Martha said, "Is there any sort of food?"

"Scarcely any. Unless you wish to plunge your hand into a barrel of rotting fish. I saw a sergeant do that yesterday, and I was like to vomit."

Surprisingly, she could say this with a ladylike quality. She stated it calmly, as a matter of fact.

"But what's to be done?" Martha said. There was a thinly piled tray of little flour biscuits beside her on a tiny circular table, and a crockery pot that held tea. She started the biscuits around and saw them go from hand to hand. "There must be something."

Martha felt shock. This seemed to her like a drubbed bowing to circumstance. But these women had been here longer than she had.

Pouring herself more tea, and raising her eyebrows at the group, the crockery pot poised, she said, "General Washington wrote me that the supply of food was good here."

"That was before we'd hutted," Kitty Greene said.

By now, Martha knew enough of camp life to know what hutting meant. She'd been through that at Cambridge and at Morristown. It meant getting the regiments out from under summer canvas and under winter logs. George had said in his letters, not so long since, that he wouldn't move into the Hewes house, with a roof over his head, until his Continentals had wooden burrows to sleep in. She was glad they had managed this before the weather turned too icy. But this lack of food, this starvation, staggered her.

She still remembered she must not show fright before these women, for their minds would mirror the fright and carry it back to their husbands. "But what causes this?" she said. "Who is responsible?"

"You could say Mr. Trumbull," Kitty Greene answered. "Or General Mifflin." Again that peculiar intonation, which Martha noted. "But that wouldn't be all. Americans won't sell to the army, Mrs. Washington. They hold supplies until the price will go higher. We're being starved by our own people. Not to say, of course, that the country hereabouts has been scoured to the bone."

One of Martha's characteristics was simplicity. She disliked being circuitous. She preferred to cut direct to the core of a matter and come to its essence. Every woman can do this, but some do it more habitually than others. She put the teapot back on its stand, and asked one more question, "Then how are we to live?"

There was a blank space, and one of the wives said, "My husband says that's in the hands of God."

The cawing became fainter, dying away as the men moved off on the shallow plateau behind the house.

"The officers will be quieting them," someone else said. "Promises, of course. There's nothing else to give them."

Everyone nodded. The talk picked up again.

"Promises won't hold them forever."

"Still, crow cawing is better than plain mutiny."

"The poor starvelings. They have to work off their misery. I'd do the same in their place. It's at least a salve to their consciences."

"Making a protest. Yes."

"If the protest doesn't get out of hand."

"The officers must see to that."

"Myself, I feel just as sorry for the officers. We've been five months without pay—"

"So have the men."

"Yes, my dear, but the men don't need to plead and cajole and explain and keep holding out hope, when hope may be as empty as a private's stomach. *There's* a task to sicken anyone. My husband is really ashamed to face his men."

A quickly muted gasp ran through the group. This was perhaps too outright, too bald and close to home for the commander's wife. They looked skancewise at Martha to see how she would take it.

Before Martha could frame an answer if one should seem called for, the farthest woman in the group spoke. She was the small, rather wiry sort, and her voice chirped. She said, "My husband *can't* face his men. Modesty confines him to our hut."

Bits of laughter twisted and spun nervously.

Martha didn't understand. Kitty Greene came to her aid.

"Oh, yes, Mrs. Washington, I've been neglectful about our more personal situation. To save you from embarrassment—if you enter a room and some officer should back up against the wall or plunge out of the room altogether, he is not being rude. He merely is hiding the holes in his breeches. There are some parts of a man's body we women are not supposed to see—unless we're married to the man."

Again Kitty Greene carried it off with a charming lightness, and the laughter became more relieved, and Martha joined it.

"To be sure," Kitty Greene said, "it's not a subject for laughing. And yet—well, with the officers, at any rate—"

"It certainly is not," a wife said. "A sentry with nothing but a blanket around him over his nakedness. I passed one today." She added primly, "Naturally I didn't look."

"No, you can't look," Kitty Greene said. "Oh, not because of privacy. We're all married, aren't we? We know how men are built. But because of suffering. One shouldn't gape at suffering one can't ease."

"But can we ease it?" Martha said.

Heads shook a negative. Clothing wasn't to be had—so far. Nor shoes. Nor more blankets. Nor anything in the way of protection against a winter. Nor against the eyes of the camp females.

"We'll just have to pretend we don't see," Kitty Greene said. And she said, circling the group with her eyes, "Are any of you ladies so weak as to faint from shock at seeing the color of skin?"

Martha was much taken by her, and by the other women at the reception. In all the frankness, the spreading open of lacks, and negligence, and inefficiencies, and blundering—and possibly worse—there had been no word, no intimation, of giving up. There had also been no word of General Gates. His name had not come up, and Martha was as well satisfied that it had not. That was something between her and George and the Gateses. She guessed that Kitty Greene would know something, but guessed also that Kitty Greene wouldn't reveal it. Could not be asked nor expected to reveal it. These women, sitting at tea and biscuits in the house at the Valley Forge, had their own problems as she had hers, and would not be driven—what was that word somebody had used?—well, well, forget it—coerced beyond the boundaries toward which they would go. She would get no help or direction for her campaign against the Gateses from this ladyish assembly.

They had fallen, now, to talking of whether Kosciusko planned another entrenchment, of whether Du Portail had sketched another redoubt.

"Shall we meet here," she said, "more or less regularly? With sewing? I've to do a pair of stockings for the general, but after that I'd be glad to work on anything the army can use. Would you care to join me?" She added, smiling toward the fireplace, "And the room is warm."

He was outworn when he came to dinner. That damned fiery Pole, Count Pulaski, was being difficult. A matter of cavalry. Of rank. In his judgment, Allan McLane was as worthy as Pulaski. Or Harry Lee, with his Light Horse. He had to settle these things—jealousies, ambitions. Always those. He had also to fight. After dinner he went to the bedroom.

It was frigid.

Billy Lee, warming pan in hand, hot ashes prisoned in flat brass, said, "Suh. The best I can, suh." And he knew Billy Lee's loyalty and acknowledged it the only way he could, by sitting down and jacking off his boots while Billy held the jack for him.

"Suh, since eve'ybody's so hungry—"

"Well—?"

"You could take from around here, suh. You know, live off the land."

"Commandeer. Snatch supplies. I know, Billy."

"No one will blame you, suh. We'll starve if you don't."

"Yes, very possibly. That's all, Billy."

And Billy went out and Martha came in. She'd undressed in another room. Her nightgown was thick and fell straight around her. She looked a furred and burrowing animal about to hibernate for the cold months ahead.

It had been only two days since her arrival from Mt. Vernon. Martha had been dutiful, as a wife, but he himself was still unsure after her long remoteness from him, her championing of Jack. Their nights had not been overly rapt.

He said, "The bed's been warmed, Patsy. Don't take a chill," and turned down an edge of the sheets for her.

"That isn't the needfulness now, George," she said. She stood very upright, very firm, though she was shivering. "The needfulness is for you, and what will become of you. Oh, George—" This was their first chance of being alone since the afternoon, the first chance she had had of crying out her mind to him; and her sudden forward movement made her flannel nightgown seem somehow frail and diaphanous. "Oh, George, the ladies—I had the whole from them. All this—this bottomless despair for you. Oh, my dear!"

She opened her arms, and he spread his in answer. The action was so natural, so uncontrived and impulsive, that there was no call for words. A direct and welling urge shucks off explainings. Martha went to him, shattering the last barrier between them, because he was so beat upon. And he took her because he snatched as a man in a whirlwind at the solace she could provide.

"George—my dearest—"

"My dearest Patsy."

He undressed swiftly.

Billy Lee had heated the bed to a deliciousness.

The next morning, dressing for breakfast, she was not so precipitate. She disregarded George's long shanks and his rather knobby knees while she hid her own plumpish thighs inside drawers and petticoat. Modestly, she averted her talk from what had happened between them the night before. Her George was a hungry and impetuous lover.

"The ladies were telling me," she said, "what the cawing meant yesterday. Can this camp be fed until spring, George?"

"I can't say, Patsy. Unless it can, the war is over."

"This is so much worse than Cambridge, or Morristown last year. Heaven knows last year was sorry enough."

"I've written to the governors of the nearest states, Patsy. They may be able to send me cattle. And we'll make raids on Howe's supply lines. And may have to seize food from the local farmers. Though I don't like that. It will be a last resort."

"It wouldn't endear you to the Pennsylvanians," she said.

"Certainly not." He pulled on his breeches. His stomach muscles were still flat and hard as a man in his twenties. "I can't endear myself to everyone. In fact, I think I'm endearing myself to no one. Had you heard the Congress has created a Board of War?"

"No," she said. "No, I hadn't."

"Gates is to be the president of it."

"Oh!"

She dropped her pomade jar with a little clatter among the few articles she used on the round, three-legged table that served her as a toilette. Her response was half exclamation, half the seal of suspicions confirmed.

"Gates?" she said.

"Yes. And Mifflin is on the board."

Mifflin. She remembered Kitty Greene's lingering intonation on that name yesterday. Mifflin, once her husband's aide, now a Pennsylvania general. A heavy drinker. But she knew little else about him.

George added information. "Mifflin thinks I should have held Philadelphia."

"I see," she said. "The way General Gates held at Saratoga."

"Yes."

He was being perfectly frank with her, perfectly open. In his situation anything but frankness was stupid. She had only a small grasp of military affairs, a rough harvest gleaned from headquarters dinners and what the winters at camp had taught her; but if they must go down, it was best they go down together, confiding in one another.

"Then," she said, "General Gates is raised above you."

"It would seem so."

"And General Mifflin doesn't like you."

"I'm afraid not."

"Oh, Mrs. Gates, Mrs. Gates," she said. "That dragon. I'll defy her to my dying day."

"Oh, Patsy, don't let's talk of dying," he said, and shrugged into his uniform coat and held out his arm. "Time enough for that when Howe can put a halter around my neck. And I don't think my neck is fitted for a noose."

She marveled, as she had marveled before at this giant: at the way he could take adversity and thrust it from him.

With this, they went down to breakfast.

Nellie had had her second baby by now. Jack wrote that it was another girl. They were going to name her Martha.

His letter gamboled a bit, after the fashion of new fathers—as well as Jack's own fashion:

> *She has blue eyes [he wrote] but Nellie says all babies have blue eyes at birth. I presume her to be right. How do women come to the knowledge of such things? They absorb them out of the air, it would seem, and spring them at husbands like traps. The child is a cute monkey. She has the customary fuzz of hair, which I think will be brownish when she grows, and the customary number of fingers, a most respectable set of lungs, and an incontinent wetness. Which is not to say, dear Mama, that we name her after you for those reasons. But because someday, when she has become dry, she will mingle in society and may be an honor to you. Tell Papa that Mr. Lund W. says his horses are in fettle, but that money is losing its value. He pays twice for nails what he would have paid last year, even though they are made in this country, and other costs are rising. As for the privateer Papa and I are sharing, she is not yet on the way but may soon be. And I have decided, Mama, to go by your advice and—*

"Oh!" Martha said, breaking off.

She had been reading the letter aloud to George, in the quick pleasure of having gotten it (the roads and the mails being so uncertain), without having scanned it beforehand.

"Oh!" she said.

"Oh?" he said. "What?"

They were dawdling by the fire in the downstairs parlor before going to bed, the gathering of officers and wives for songs and the passing of an evening having broken up.

"What next, Patsy?"

She had not intended to tell him. At least, not until the result might be fairly sure. She had a feeling that he also might have a feeling, and that it could cause complications.

But she had overrun herself, unwittingly. She folded the letter, put it in the bosom of her dress, which was a modish purple—for they had had Captain McLane to dinner that night, who clothed his troop in his own household table linen and made such brilliant raids on enemy supplies; and the Greenes, of course, and Knox; and the latest gift from the Congress, a General von Steuben, who spoke only German and alehouse French—and she said, "It's politics, my dear."

"Jacky writing of politics?"

His questions had the incomprehensibility of the masculine, her answer the dart of the feminine. "In your footsteps, George. Isn't it splendid?"

"What's splendid about it? And what politics?" Although he knew Martha, he couldn't keep himself from scrubbing his forehead with the back of his hand. A sure signal, he knew from previous bouts, of foreordained failure with her.

Martha saw the sign. She said, "Jacky is standing for the Virginia Burgesses. For the House. I'd not wanted to tell you, until he'd won."

"Why should he be a Burgess?" he said.

"He's the richest young man in Virginia. Can you think of any better reason?"

He could think of reasons why not. There were Jack's youthfulness and incompetence, his lack of any experience, and his brashness. Washington had found, through years, that a man could be stretched taut and pluckable as a violin string; that politics was a hassle—the hassle of who tuned the peg.

"I wouldn't want it for him, Patsy," he said.

"Not for him. For you," she said.

"Patsy, what could Jack possibly give me?"

"Another bulwark against Mrs. Gates."

"Patsy dear."

"His letter says he has support in the counties."

"Probably he may. But what then?"

"The Virginia House. The Congress."

"And Mrs. Gates—where is she?"

"Oh, George, you're too provoking!"

"A kin in the Congress wouldn't raise my banner by an inch, Patsy. But you've put Jack to this, my dear. I can't say I applaud it. . . . Oh, yes, for Jack himself. But not for me. That's impossible."

"Everything has always been impossible between you and Jacky," she said.

"You're wrong. You're biased, Patsy. Jack and I have hunted together, gambled together, theatered together—"

"Wenched together?"

"Stop that!"

Martha secretly admired the slap. She had been wrong; too brisk in this pro-and-con. She let the silence dissolve.

"But Jacky's going into politics," she said.

"And I don't approve. He's too young."

Martha had her last shot now. He'd practically put the lanyard in her hand. She tried not to show too much triumph, but triumph was in her.

"You said the same thing when you tried to keep him from marrying," she said.

And knew, agonizedly, for she had not wanted it like this, that the old wrestle over son and stepson was still dormant between them, put to rest by her coming to the Valley Forge and by his need of her, but perilously close to being awakened at the least touch.

He knew this as well as she did, and veered off.

"Let him make the try," he said. "It can't do any harm."

Martha rather shuddered at his indifference. "George," she said, "why can't you be as clever about Jacky as you were about General Conway? Why can't you see and know?"

He stiffened. "What's Jack to do with Conway?"

"Nothing, except—oh, except you found General Conway was criticizing you to General Gates, and sent the criticism back to General Conway, and he sent it to Gates, and Gates spluttered and sent his answer to you and to the Congress, and you asked why Gates didn't make the letters public if he was innocent, and Horatio spluttered again, and everybody laughed. It was all in the gazettes. We laughed, at Mt. Vernon. You were adroit, George."

"I have an odd distaste for being undermined," he said.

"Is Jacky undermining you?" she said.

"Lord, no," he said.

"Then let him try for the House, George. And there's one other point —this privateer. You and Jacky and another man—I haven't his name."

"It doesn't matter."

"No, but you're going shares. Is Jacky thinking of sailing on the ship?"

"Patsy, that's for seamen. Jack will stay on land."

"I'd want to make certain," she said. There was no disgrace in buying and fitting privateers—hulls, armed and fitted, that would prey on enemy shipping. The game was profitable and popular. No one saw anything criminal in it. But Martha wanted to make sure Jacky wouldn't take to high seas with cannon and cutlass. She had a horror of that.

George's reply mollified her somewhat. Jacky would stay on land. He belonged there, eminently, with Nellie and the two children—and with her. She rose from where she had been sitting, half facing the fire, and the purple dress, stitched as fine as the sewing women at Mt. Vernon had been able to do it, rustled and whispered.

"Since you say so, my dear," she said. And added, with a delicious lack of sequence, "Isn't it sweet that they're naming the baby after me?"

When he could, when weather and letter work and reports and consultations allowed, Washington got outdoors for something more cheerful and relaxing than inspections of the scrawny camp and played catch ball with his aides and younger officers. He was not yet fifty, still prided himself on muscles as vigorous as in his days of surveying the western lands and fighting in the French and Indian War. His main annoyance was his teeth, some of which were false, now, and were held by wires which needed recurrent tightening by pincers; but his body was still sound. He pitted it, for sport, against Tilghman and young Laurens and Hamilton and Harrison. They were all in their twenties, except Harrison, who was slightly above thirty and was called "Old Man" by the others. But Harrison could throw a ball, and so could Washington. The sport was exercise for him, and he craved exercise; his physique demanded it. Sitting for hours at a desk, cramped in a headquarters room, made his skin itch and tingle, and his lungs seemed to collapse.

He felt no loss of dignity in playing ball. He, his aides, the shouting officers who joined in were all penned in the same fold for the winter, and all needed exercise and a break in the routine. There was no disrespect in a ball that came stinging into his palm, or in the yelps that went up when he missed, his boot soles sliding in the snow, or the whooping if Laurens or Harrison gathered in a hard one from him. The players would be more than correct when they got back to the military business of the war. In the meantime they were letting off their energies, as he was. It was a mutual, unstated male assistance, one to the other.

It was a loud, happy, forgetful breaking off from the woes and worries that galloped over the Valley Forge, a tonic that speeded up the sluggishness in the blood and lifted weariness from the mind.

"Ham—you've missed!"

"Tench, throw here!"

"General, sir, to me! Ready!"

Stragglings of troops, off duty, meandered down from the plateau and cheered both sides.

"Eee-yah—clumsy! Pitch it, pitch it!"

"Laurens up!"

"Heave, Gen'ral! Heave!"

The winter was rather kindly to them. They had not much snow. But he knew that when he came in from outside his nose would be red as usual. Hamilton's nose was not red, as Ham saluted by his desk. But then, Ham's nose didn't protrude so.

A half hour since, they'd been playing ball. Hamilton was an aide now. Proving himself the most brilliant one.

"General Greene, sir. You asked for him."

"Oh, yes, thank you, Ham. I'll see him."

The limping general was ushered in. Hamilton left, and closed the door. Washington waved Greene to a chair.

He came direct to his goal. No sense in beating about the bush.

"Greene," he said, "will you be my commissary general?"

He blunted the blow as much as he could, by the almost pathetic tone of his voice. It hurt him to do this to his best officer. But the army was starving.

Greene made a motion as if to scrub his head, remembered his wig, and dropped his hand in a feigned casualness.

"Quartermaster, Your Excellency?"

"The army has to be provided for. I've thought, Greene. You're the best to do it."

"But I'm on active duty, General. I have my troops."

"When we come to fight, Greene, lead your troops. But furnish us between whiles. I don't ask you to give up your command. I ask you to supply us."

No other man in the country could have begged that sacrifice from Greene. He knew it. It meant wrangles with people who were supposed to be Americans and supposed to be fighting for their liberty, but were not; in details of bookkeeping that would be pawed over by the Congress; and the innate hostility of the Congress itself toward anyone who handled the public money. It meant tossing Greene into the arena of the political lions. But he had no one else. He had to save the army.

"Will you, Nat?"

Greene's eyes took on a sorriness, a changing.

"If I could have time, sir—to think."

"Take time, Nat. But we must have you."

"I wish it weren't so, sir."

"You know it is. We hang on you."

"Yes, General. Yes, as you say."

Greene walked out, after saluting, his wig a little askew.

Martha scraped up what food she could find from the headquarters table and the kitchen in Mistress Hewes's house and made the rounds of the soldiers' huts, and gave out the food where it seemed most called for.

She had Kitty Greene with her this morning. They climbed the path to the plateau where the huts were, and saw the regimental streets breaking away from them in rough geometric angles. The day was not too harsh. There was only a low, piercing wind that blew from the east with the damp and penetrating chill of the ocean; and a lowering gloominess of clouds; and the feeling of being pressed like inanimate grains in a millstone between frozen earth and imponderable sky. But at least there was little snow. A few inches of it. Just enough to have a sentry stand with bare feet in his hat while he tried to salute.

"I get so flustered," Martha said. "Their treating me like Lady Washington."

"It's only respect, Mrs. Washington," Kitty Greene said. "If it were a cringing or a fear it would be different."

"Oh, mercy," Martha said. "No one has to be afraid of me."

They walked by an intersection of two camp roads, where scant-clad Continentals had hitched themselves to a cart with grapevine traces and were lugging it over the ground.

"Those dear, ragged Continentals," she said.

"Most of the horses are dead of starvation," Kitty Greene said.

The slow, penetrating, unrelenting push of air from the east, from the sea, fribbled at their skirts. They turned up a slush-frozen street of the Maryland regiments. As far as they could see, the land was dour, like the sky, and rolled in a long ground swell to the horizon, naked and forbidding. At one spot, not too far beyond, the new German, von Steuben, was drilling troops. He had a musket in his hand and was shouting.

"Do officers handle muskets?" Martha said.

"Not our officers," Kitty Greene said. "But von Steuben does. And he swears in German and French. Asks his aides to interpret for him. That's probably his training squad there. His Excellency has put him in charge of training. The men revere him, I'm told."

"Oh," Martha said. There were many things George did not tell her.

"Came to the camp as a volunteer, like so many others," Kitty Greene said. "But then, like Lafayette, seems to have so many adoring him. . . . Oh, here are the huts. Shall we try this one?"

"We'll try all," Martha said. She trailed Kitty Greene into the first, which was bad enough, four scarecrows on straw, but none at the extreme of life. They ducked heads into the open again.

"By the way," said Martha, "where is the Marquis de Lafayette? The general hasn't told me. I've heard of him."

"Oh. The marquis? He's off to make an invasion of Canada. With General Conway."

"Canada? Conway?"

"The Board of War ordered it," Kitty Greene said, and picked up her skirts and sloshed her galoshes through the snow.

"The general hadn't told me." Martha fought to keep a balance between insouciance and a blindfolded wife. "You say, the Board of War?"

"Yes."

"Where—where Gates sits, does he not?"

"Where he sits."

"And orders this Canada invasion."

"It appears so."

"And it's under way?"

"Yes and no. It doesn't seem to be going too happily."

Martha looked away to where General von Steuben was giving a fierce demonstration in the use of a bayonet. The men so far had mostly used bayonets as roasting skewers around the campfires. She said, "A shortage of troops, perhaps."

"Oh, they have the whole northern army. Many of the Continental regiments that fought at Saratoga are still in the north."

A fresh whiff of wind tugged Martha's skirts. She clutched at them with her left hand. Her right held the basket of food. "But Mrs. Greene —give those Saratoga troops to my dear general and he might have enough, I should think, to fight General Howe again for Philadelphia. Why another expedition to Canada? We've only had disaster there."

"And will again, my husband says. So does General Arnold. His letter to General Washington on the subject was violent, according to Nathanael."

"Then why does General Gates order it?" said Martha. It was not so much a question as a wrench of angry pain that her George must bow under to a project that was none of his making but which he couldn't prevent.

"Possibly General Gates is swelling himself," Kitty Greene said.

"You feel so?"

"There are stories."

"I should like to hear them."

"Well, straws perhaps," Kitty said. "Straws in a breeze. But the breeze could turn to a gale. When the marquis—that's Lafayette—was appointed to this Canada campaign by the Board of War, he was invited to York in Pennsylvania, where the Congress is. General Gates is there, too."

"Oh, he *would* be," Martha said. "His wife would see to it that—" and stopped abruptly, remembering her position.

Kitty Greene gave her a wry smile and didn't pursue that topic.

"They tendered the boy marquis a dinner," Kitty went on, "and flattered him and fawned on him. Gates and Mifflin and Conway and the officers who've taken up with the cabal. They sat him on Gates's right, as guest of honor, and toasted him and Gates, and I suppose everything else under the sun, and then the marquis got to his feet and toasted General Washington, and all the faces there went pink, and some glasses went untouched. Lafayette was in a rage about it when he came back. And then General Morgan—Dan Morgan, the riflemen's general—brings a tale of how Gates whispered at him and insinuated a change of high command might be for the best, and how he said bluntly to Gates's teeth that he'd never serve under any commander of the army but General Washington. It was all over the camp. He made no secret of it." She broke into a partial giggle. "The backwoods general isn't the subtle sort."

Martha read fealty in Kitty's eyes. She could read fealty in the eyes of the starveling soldiers who slouched past her, gawking and touching their hands to their foreheads in a kind of reverence. A reverence not so much for herself, she was sure, but for her George. This army, here at the Valley Forge, would not be unfaithful to him. They were a strong tide. But another tide was creeping in, lapping at the underpinnings of the structure George was building with such agony.

She had a mind to turn back. To go back to her bedroom, and give up the struggle, and simply have a good cry.

"Here's the next hut," Kitty Greene said.

Kitty's poise steadied her. As George's wife she couldn't go back, any more than he could. They were both caught in the holocaust.

"Knock at the door, my dear," she said.

The knock was not answered. They fiddled with the whittled latch, pushed the door open, and went in.

The hut was at first too dark for good seeing. The glazed paper of its tiny window was sooted over with smoke from a fireplace whose chimney was too short. But Martha could make out that there was no table, no chair—only the four walls, chinked with mud, and a musket dim in a corner. The place smelled of human bodies, even in the cold of March;

as though it had never known air or sunshine, or any wafting of clean winds. Small wonder, she thought. The winds hereabouts, in midwinter, had not been of the wafting kind. But she was suddenly stifled, as if a foul-reeking cloth had been clamped to her nose.

Eventually she could make out the figures who inhabited this place. A man lay flat on his back, to one side of the ash-thick fireplace. A pale, feeble-embered glow came from the fireplace. A woman sat beside the man, squatting cross-legged.

The man lay on naked earth. He was naked, himself, to the knees. A hole-shotten shawl covered him from knees to chest. Obviously a woman's shawl. From his drop-jawed mouth came a series of stranglings and rattlings that gripped and twisted at Martha's stomach. She had never heard such sounds before. But she knew at once, sickened, as she was, what they portended. She faced death.

"Kitty—" she said, and thrust out her hand.

Kitty's hand was in hers, holding hard. "Yes," Kitty said.

The woman scrambled upright. "Oh, my God! Miz' Washington."

The man did not know what was going on around him. The throaty rattles continued.

"Miz' Washington."

Martha gestured, brokenly, toward the basket on her arm. "Food?" she said.

"No'm. He 'way past that. He's a sergeant," she said wildly, and, more wildly, "I'm his wife."

"Oh, my dear," Martha said. "My dear."

She heard Kitty Greene sob beside her. But this was not a time for sobbing. Sobbing was simply a weakness. She withdrew her hand from Kitty's, moving forward.

"Is there anything at all that I can do?" she said. "Anything?"

"Nothing, Miz' Washington, now." The woman was gaunt and hollow-eyed and the tendons of her neck and her thin chest stood out like weather-scoured roots. "Nothing except to pray," she said.

"Then we'll pray," Martha said.

She looked at Kitty Greene. The look was met, and the two women dropped to their knees.

XII

"Generals Gates and Mifflin Have Leave to Attend"

The first sap threads of March spun themselves into April tapestry.

Leaves of birches and willows and wild cherries flecked the woods with tiny emerald beauty, and the minuscule unfoldings of oak and red maple blazoned delicate stitchings of the colors they would wear in the autumn. The hickory buds, bursting, wore the shape and tints of tropical flowers. Soft, frail, ivory-toned hepaticas rose daintily on their stems like the dustings from a star, twinkling at roadsides and in the sheltering of stone fences. The evergreens—hemlock and yellow pine and white—were nubbled with furred and saucy tufts, and the ash trees wore pale topaz.

There were the sounds, too. From the bottom lands, where the red-wings cher-eed and the peepers set up a jangling like constant little sleigh bells in the night. And the parade ground, where robins hunted for worms and spoke like ungreased axle wheels; and from the dead limbs of trees where downy woodpeckers drilled themselves homes, and from the live trees where upside-down nuthatches squeaked liquidly and hunted insects. They were harbingers of other sounds to come: the blue-bird's trill, the catbird's endless and varying music, and the hard, sharp, insistent croak that said the flickers were mating.

Color, and sound.

And, added to them, the spring's smell.

A smell of warming earth, a nostalgic smell, known to those who are roamers or tillers of the land, and not entirely lost to those who dwell in cities; for even into the cities the smell of spring can permeate. At the Valley Forge it was the pungency of a distant skunk, digging for roots and surprised by dogs; it was the scent of vapor from thawing places; a hint of carpeting pine needles; the clearing deliciousness of a south wind.

Spring holds so many delights. Its recurrent promises should humble and dwarf and yet invigorate a man.

Washington, as a farmer, felt this, but was in no mood to realize it to full extent.

He had a sputtering Lafayette to deal with.

The Valley Forge winter had passed. Nat Greene had agreed to take over the quartermaster duty, and between his cool administration and Allan McLane's raids and the outright scooping up of food where it could be found, the camp was eating better. The Congress had named a colonel—Jeremiah Wadsworth—to head the commissary, and the colonel was doing more than well. Clothing was still scarce, but the summer was coming. Martha and the officers' wives patched and sewed and knitted where they could.

He sat at his desk and said to Lafayette, "Try to be tame to this, Marquis."

"I should call Gates to a duel!" Lafayette said in a boy's fury. "I cannot be tame to it. *Nom de Dieu,* to put me to an expedition with a great show of stir and then to make of me the butt of disgrace and jokes in America—in Versailles—in the whole world! Expedition, *parbleu?* Hah! An aborted monster! A madman's dream! I sit in Albany with my hands tied. I am left sitting so. I am told, 'My esteemed Marquis, you will get the things you require.' I do not get them. Axmen, wagoners, engineers, mortars, powder and shot—they do not appear. All is turvy-topsy. The regiments are not paid. I write to Gates for money. 'Yes, yes, esteemed Marquis, of a sureness you shall have it.' I do not get the money, which I learn goes elsewhere. It is a cheatery to me. I am pulling at a rope of sand, and General Conway is going out of his mind for the vexation. And then—pouf!—airy as you please, our loud expedition is ended and we are ordered to return. I know where I will return! I will return to France!"

Washington let the gale blow itself out.

When there came a breathless stop he said, "You had every right to expect support, Marquis."

"But no support at all. That Gates is a—is a—oh, *mort du diable!*" And Lafayette wound up in a flurry of French that could only have been profane.

Lafayette was justified, of course. The expedition for Canada had never got beyond Albany. Gates had bungled the venture, somehow. Gates and Mifflin and their Board of War.

"General Conway is handing in his resignation," Lafayette said.

"Which the Congress might very sensibly accept," Washington said.

He wouldn't shed tears over that. Conway had been overweening from the beginning, and arrogant. One of his pet questions to volunteer noblemen newly come from France to help officer the Continentals had been, "Did the Congress see you before it appointed you?"

"Yes," Washington said. "Very sensibly."

Lafayette was not in a state to appreciate dry sarcasm. He said, "I have my honor. I will not submit to being made a fool of."

"No one sees you as a fool, Marquis," Washington said. He'd not wanted to send this firebrand to Albany in the first place. He'd not approved of another thrust at Canada. But he had had to bow to the Board of War, set up by the Congress with men hostile to him in the majority.

"No, no," Lafayette said, "it is all over. Done with." He jumped up from his chair and started pacing the room. "I will not submit. *Enfin, c'est tout.*" He was a titled and polished aristocrat; he was a believer in liberty; he was a youngster seeking fame. The three skeins of his being, of what he was, and why, knotted and tugged in him.

Washington had come, by the thorny patch, to a certain insight. After his own abject surrender to the French, long since, in a rain-sodden fort he had called Necessity, in the western lands; after the Virginia frontier stockades, and the years of this present war he had painfully put behind him, he felt capable of seeing men as perhaps they did not see themselves.

He said, "What of me, Marquis?"

Lafayette clumped to an abrupt halt.

"You, *mon Général?*"

"The simple matter of it is," Washington said, "that I need you, Marquis."

Lafayette stood immobile.

"Pray don't go back to France, Marquis."

"Where else should I go?"

"Nowhere. Stay here." The immobility gave a sign of wavering, of chance. Washington said mollifyingly, "The Canada flurry was none of your making. All of us know you are not to blame. Versailles will know it, too. Dr. Franklin will see to that. I can't think your honor is involved."

"No?"

"No. You were pushed out on a rotting limb. Stay with us."

"I don't know. I don't know. These nasty whims and jealousies. These Gateses. These politics. Liberty seems to me a thing being devoured by its own worms."

Washington dropped his head in his hands. What could he say? What could he answer when Lafayette was throwing the truth at him?

He made the best reply he could.

"Come to dinner tonight, Marquis. We'll toast—in rum and water, no Madeira while the troops suffer so—we'll toast to our friends. One of the chiefest is you."

There were no jokes or any hint of failure for Lafayette at the camp —only sympathy and a warm show of liking. Washington was careful to see to that, though it didn't need much doing, what with the way the camp had taken the marquis to its heart before he'd been sent on his goose chase to Albany. The headquarters staff were plainly sorry for him, and, off duty, companionable; the general officers soothed him; and Dan Morgan blasphemed mightily about his treatment at Gates's hands. In such an atmosphere, Lafayette let his anger simmer down.

Martha accepted him at once. His manners, his gay talk, his young fire, and his courtliness appealed to her; and as a woman she was fascinated by the background of dazzle and luxury and European culture against which the marquis moved.

"To think, George," she said, "he's actually walked beside the fountains of Versailles. And listened to the best minds of France. And chatted with royal ministers and with the king. And carries it all so modestly."

"Modestly, I'd say, because he sees no reason to boast to us," Washington said. "He regards such things as natural. But he is attractively unaffected."

"I suppose that is the word for him," Martha said, though she was conscious, within herself, that she might have chosen some less pallid word for this boy who carried with him the spark and flare of the world's most resplendent court.

"Yes, unaffected," she said. "And truly sweet. As a female calls a man sweet, George, without any—any implications." She blushed, and hurried on. "Besides, he reveres you, and anyone who reveres you is someone I'm compelled to be fond of."

So Lafayette stayed on. And presently was riding with Washington two miles out along the road from the Valley Forge that led toward Philadelphia. Troops were lined along the route, the Continentals, and they looked smarter now, in the spring, for the training von Steuben had hammered into them, and the bands—such as they were—made music.

For General Lee was rejoining the army. Americans in Rhode Island had captured an enemy major general and Lee was being exchanged for him.

Martha had not been too enthusiastic about this. She'd said, as Billy Lee was adjusting the uniform coat and straightening the epaulets and giving the boots a final slick and brushing the tricorne, "George—are you sure you want General Lee back?"

"He's an astute general," he said. "My second in command."

"But his dogs—"

"Patsy dear, dogs have no concern for us in what we're aiming for."

"Oh, bother," she said.

"I'll have Lee here with me, if I can't have Gates. Dogs or no dogs."

"H'mph. Gates is nuzzling with the Congress at York."

"But Lee is exchanged," he said. "And on his way. I feel, Patsy—I know—that I should do him honor."

Then she had done a strange thing. A strange and sudden thing. She had stepped close to him and put her hands on his shoulders and looked up at him rather long, and the pupils of her eyes had dilated and dissolved, as the pupils of the eyes will do in shock, or passion, or a sharply uncovered truth. "I don't like him, George," she said.

He had taken her hands from his shoulders, gently, and now he was riding out with Lafayette and his generals and his staff to meet Lee.

He dismounted when he saw Lee, and shook his hand, and brought him back to headquarters between the double file of troops.

And when Lafayette said, jogging beside him, "*Mon Général,* he looks indeed like a man who might be surprised in an alehouse," he said, "A misfortune, Marquis. An unlucky chance."

There was a dinner for General Lee at the headquarters, and a band played music continually while they ate, and Washington was elated to have Lee with him again, and elated at other news. For the Congress had voted half pay for seven years after the war to all officers, and a bounty of eighty dollars to each soldier. It wasn't riches, but it was the only way to keep an army together. Patriotism, he was now certain, wasn't enough. A man's patriotism ran only so far as his pocket. So far as his family could eat.

They gave Lee a room behind the parlor, and set his baggage there, and waited breakfast for him the next morning. He put in a late appearance, pouch-eyed and slovenly and monosyllabic. Hamilton came privately to say, an hour afterward, that Lee had spent the night with some hussy, a sergeant's wife he'd brought with him and let into headquarters by the back door.

"It's certain, sir," Hamilton said. "It'll be common gossip within an hour."

"For God's sake, Ham," he said, "keep it from Mrs. Washington."

Hamilton shrugged. In a camp like this, keeping anything from anyone was an impossibility. The shrug suggested a sophisticate's tolerance. Washington saw the shrug, but didn't care to combat it.

"That's all, Ham."

"Yes, sir."

Whether Martha learned, he never knew. She said nothing. He loved her more for her silence.

But she was not silent about Jack. "George, dear," she said, cornering him the evening after Lee had come in, "Jacky wants to buy a house. What do you think?"

"Think? I can't give an opinion, Patsy. He has a house already."

"But this would be a different one." Difference being, of course, in the feminine idea, a perfectly apparent charm.

"Is that an argument for it?" he said.

"It's certainly not an argument against it."

Washington conceded. He didn't want to plunge into the cloudy waters of a mother's reasoning.

"Jacky and Nellie will live there eventually, after they've improved the place," Martha said. "A good deal of land goes with it. And they'll call it Arlington, after the old Custis estate. I think that would be touching and romantic."

"Jack hasn't written me about it yet."

"No, he asked me to tell you."

"I suppose he mentioned the location and the present owner."

"Naturally."

Knowing Jack, Washington could have raised a point or two about the "naturally," but he slid them over, merely looking impassive.

"It's a beautiful spot, Jacky says," Martha went on, already lyrical with plans and visions. "High above the Potomac, not far up from Alexandria, with a sweeping vista of the green flats on the other side of the river—the river is much narrower there, you remember—"

"Yes."

"—and owned by Mr. Alexander, who is willing to sell."

"Alexander? H'mm. Then Jack will need a little advice."

"Now don't go about to prevent him, George—please."

"I can't prevent. Jack's master of his inheritance now. But since I've managed the inheritance for a good many years while he was a minor I shouldn't like to see it nipped by Mr. Alexander. Money is getting touchy enough as it is. Alexander will be so afraid of doing himself out of a few dollars that if Jack offers him more than he ever expected to get for his land he'll still tack and yaw and try to get to the windward of Jack. I'll write."

"Oh, George, will you? You've such a clear head for business. And it *would* be lovely if Jacky and Nellie could have their Arlington."

He wrote the letter to Jack, and went out and tried to be patient with

Lee's carpings at what Lee saw in the camp, and with Lee's notions for reorganizing the army, notions that didn't match with his. He assumed Lee would send the notions to the Congress. Everyone sent notions to the Congress.

Captivity, he discovered, hadn't changed Lee. The scarecrow general was still witty, obscene, and stuffed with self-confidence. Washington gathered that the captivity had not been onerous. Lee had been allowed to go freely about New York City and among his friends of the royal officers, and had had altogether a sociable time of it. But he brought back a bagful of rumors and table talk that might be turned to good account.

"Howe hasn't attacked you," he said. "Not surprised. Sir Billy's snug as a flea in Philadelphia. Has a Mrs. Loring as a bedfellow, pays off her husband with a commissary appointment for prisoners. Why should he bare his shanks to a winter campaign? God damn, the luscious Venus ought to have a medal from the Congress. She's American, too. Ain't it odd that Loring rhymes with whoring? Oh, Jesus, there've been verses."

He cackled, and plugged snuff into his nose, holding a forefinger at attention under the skinny beak, waiting for the sneeze.

"The officers of His Gracious Majesty," he said, talking past the finger, "are richening themselves in this war. Moneys are laid out from the royal treasury and they fatten upon it. They pocket their share. That's why our bobtails are still on this verminous plain. Because the generals and colonels and majors sent against us would rather fill their pockets than wipe us out. It's greed—damned slatternly hellish greed on both sides—that keeps this corpse alive on the one hand and makes it stink on the other. God in his mercy help us if this country ever comes to grapples with an enemy really bent on beating us."

The sneeze gathered finally, and expanded, and exploded.

"By the way, Billy Howe's resigned," he said.

They were on the parade ground, cleared of stumps during the winter by soldiers put to the clearing as punishment when they got drunk. The ground had been cleared fairly soon.

"Resigned? When?" said Washington, and a tightness bit at his stomach.

"Last autumn, after Saratoga. Common talk in New York. Billy's no dunce. He'll toddle home and leave this mess of porridge to Clinton."

Washington thought to ask what sort of porridgy mess Clinton could possibly be in worse than his own. But he decided not to. Lee would only have been caustic, difficult.

He said, "If you're right, General, perhaps we can lift our heads again, come summer."

"I'm always right," Lee said.

They cantered a little farther, to the redoubts designed by Du Portail, past companies marching and countermarching and debouching on the flank and spreading into front, learning the formations of the accepted warfare.

They reined on thick-burgeoning field grass, the staff at a proper distance. Behind them were the regimental huts, to the right and left, the defensive works, and ahead the long, leveling, fence-crossed plain. The day was sunny.

"Since you are back with us, General," Washington said, "and have seen us as we are—what would you say?"

Lee drew his shoulders so high that the epaulets over his bone-supported uniform brushed his ear lobes. He hunched. His tone was a spitting.

"Oh, God," he said. "Oh my sweet and wide-eyed arse."

John Laurens handed him the packet of instructions from the Congress. It had been opened and set in order for him, and he sensed from young Laurens' grinning excitement of eyes that there was something unusual in it.

Its import dawned on him slowly as he read the items. Ticonderoga to be destroyed and its garrison withdrawn, sealing the fate of any Canada expedition. Gates to continue at the head of the northern forces. He himself, Washington, reauthorized to seize property and persons as he saw fit for the good of the army. He, Washington, to call a council of war and form a plan for the over-all strategy and operations of the next campaign. The final item, the crisp concluding lines, summed the whole. They put the keystone in the arch: "Major Generals Gates and Mifflin, members of the Board of War, have leave to attend the said council."

Washington went over these lines again, carefully, and looked up from his chair at Laurens, whose excitement was spread on his face now as well as in his eyes.

"Do you take the meaning of this, Colonel?"

"Yes, sir. It means Gates and Mifflin must come to the council like the other officers, and sit under your orders. You're still their commander."

"Yes, I read it that way." He wanted to jump up and clap Laurens on the back. He wanted to let out his voice and bounce it against the walls of the room. But he compromised instead for a long, steadying breath. "Yes, Colonel, I read it that way, too."

Martha, when she heard, was not so restrained.

Though she took a different tack from what he had expected.

"I've been morally certain ever since the flubdubbery of that Canada thing. The Congress could hardly be blind to that. The Gateses over-stuffed their pillow and the feathers have all spilled out. I'd just like to see Mrs. Gates's face *now!*"

In the first week of May the Congress sent another packet from York. King Louis of France had approved a treaty of alliance with the United American States.

In the stunning suddenness jubilee ran like quicksilver.

Ultimately Washington found himself at his desk, his face still blush-ing from the kisses Lafayette had planted, weeping, on each cheek, and his voice shakily giving Hamilton the details for a General After Orders, 6 P.M., May 5, 1778: there would be a parade tomorrow of the brigades, a prayer by the chaplains and a sermon of thanksgiving; there would be a salute of thirteen guns, infantry volleys, and a show of maneuvers on the parade ground; tables spread under marquees where the ladies would look on, and as much feasting and wine as the camp provisions would allow.

"We'll open the celebration at nine in the morning and continue all day. Soldiers confined to the guardhouse will be given freedom for the day. You have those points in mind?"

"Yes, sir."

"One thing more. Each man in the army is to have a gill of rum. Each officer and soldier is to wear a nosegay in his hat."

It was a postscript, he knew, that would rejoice the companies.

Sitting in the bakehouse, with Martha beside him, he watched a per-formance of Addison's *Cato*. Theater plays had been forbidden to the army by the Congress, along with horse racing, any kind of gaming, cockfighting, and other expensive diversions. He himself wouldn't let his officers gamble at cards, for he'd learned from self-experience at Wil-liamsburg that this could lead to debts. But when it came to the Congress rule for plays at the Valley Forge he ignored the rule. A play, a theater piece, would be fun and good medicine for his officers, an outlet and a surcease that would cost them nothing.

The May night was comfortably mild. Mosquitoes were not yet out in force. His seat on the first bench left him room to stretch his legs. He pushed them to full length in front of him, crossed at the ankles.

His mind was comfortable as well, and mild. The French alliance could bring a quick end to the war. He looked for that, everyone looked for it; even, obviously, the ministry at London, for his spies in Phila-delphia were telling him that General Lee had turned out to be right.

Sir William Howe had resigned, and the London ministry had accepted the resignation. Sir William was going home, Sir Henry Clinton appointed in his place. And Sir Henry had orders to evacuate Philadelphia and concentrate in New York for defense. France, as ally, could furnish the sea power needed for victory, the men-of-war needed to keep Clinton from using the ocean as a highway for attack at any spot on the coast, any major city. Control of the sea was the key to his land-throttled problem. And France could send over a final and crushing weight of numbers, the weight he had never yet had. He could suppose, reasonably, that all this would come about in the next year. King Louis would live up to his treaty. The sight of Lafayette, absorbed in the play a few seats beyond, brought him assurance. King Louis had forgiven the marquis for running off to America, and the boy pulled strong strings at the French court.

He gave his attention to the stage. His mind had been occupied in the multiplicities it had to cope with. The scenery was in taste, the piece well done, the female parts taken by some of the younger officers. They were all very earnest, all the actors. An enjoyable, extemporized, makeshift illusion that allowed an hour or two of escape; along with the whiff of scented handkerchiefs and hair powder and a May night and tallow footlight candles.

> 'Tis not in mortals to command success,
> But we'll do more, Sempronius,—we'll
> deserve it.

He liked those lines. They expressed what he felt.

He shifted a little, easing his position on the wooden bench. Martha was at his right. At his left was Lee, windy in the stomach and mutteringly caustic.

To deserve success . . . It wasn't a pride in him, nor an ambition, that cast back an echo from the actor's mouthing. It was a memory, pulled dim and veiled from the past, when he and Sally Fairfax—and her husband—had sat in the parlor of Belvoir, and read *Cato*, and he had given a stripling's worship to Sally. . . .

Behind him were Laurens and Tilghman and Hamilton. Laurens' father was president of the Congress; Tilghman's father was a Tory, would probably be jailed when Sir Henry Clinton moved out of Philadelphia; Hamilton's father, in the West Indies, had begot a son without benefit of marriage. These were clashing and diverse elements. Clashing and diverse as the profiteering and power grasping and the meanness of man, the flourishing of evil like a green bay tree, that had starved him all winter at the Valley Forge.

He knew that the winter of Valley Forge needn't have happened if all men had been honest. If all men had put themselves, as he had done, to the task and the sacrifice.

He didn't revile these men. He detested them, would destroy them when he could, but wouldn't hate them. He had, by now, too much knowledge of human nature to permit himself hatred. A cold and implacable justice was the better way. It was the sure sword.

With such a sword, put to the root of the green bay tree, he had pledged himself to hew a nation.

He carried himself with more than his usual straightness when the play was done and he escorted Martha out past the applauding benches.

At long length, he came face to face again with Benedict Arnold. The general's appearance shocked him. Arnold's forehead and cheeks were heavily lined, his hair was graying, and he depended on the support of a soldier to give him walking aid for his shattered thigh. Washington saw, as Arnold came into his office leaning painfully on the soldier's shoulder, that it would be months before Arnold would be in the field.

The soldier lowered Arnold by slow inches into a chair and pulled up another to brace the stiffened leg. Arnold grunted, using curses to cover his agony. This second battle wound of his had left him baited and angry and suffering as an Elizabethan bear.

Washington welcomed him doubly. First because he was alive, second because he would add his fierce aggressiveness and proven military flair to headquarters.

"General Arnold, sir, I'm delighted you're here. Now for the first time you and I will be serving together in a campaign. It's what I've much wished for."

"Serve?" Arnold said wryly. He looked at his propped leg.

"In our councils. The active service will come later, I heartfully trust."

"The surgeons say I'll sit saddle again. But your counselings, General, are more likely to be French than mine."

The answer startled Washington. Then he remembered that the French Canadians had not rallied to Arnold outside of Quebec. The veteran of that fight would naturally feel sourly about Frenchmen. Briefly he wondered if Arnold had doubts about the French alliance. There were people who felt that way. They felt France might harness America to its own coach and take the reins. There were certain doggerels going the rounds of the camp. . . . As in the case of Mrs. Loring . . . But he couldn't debit Arnold with so narrow a view. Couldn't while Lafayette and the swarm of titled Frenchmen were so heart and soul in the cause. Arnold would see, as he came to know them. Arnold was an active and imperious man, chained. When he could lead troops in a charge and work off his spleen on a battleground his outlook would change.

It had been only a flicker of hesitation, not so much as would disturb two men who had the same forcefulness and energy, the same goals.

Arnold's gray-green eyes closed a moment, and then opened full. They had their old fighting look.

"With your indulgence, sir, I ask leave to go to the Congress at York."

"The Congress?"

"Those damned ledger-grubbing ninnies say I've played fast and loose with military funds. They want an accounting. So do I, by God! I've been plagued since the war began by bookkeepers and totters-up of pennies, men who sit in the seats of the mighty and aren't worthy to fart in them. They want an accounting. *I* want a court-martial, an investigation—anything! I want to clear my name. To go before the Congress and get justice."

Justice. Washington understood. He gave a sigh. Justice—or justification. Accusations by the Congress. Flare-ups from the generals. There had been so many courts-martial sitting for his officers that he sometimes felt he was leading a band of criminals.

"Perhaps you take this too seriously," he said.

All Arnold's touchiness spined at once. "Seriously? I can be serious, sir, when a sapping party digs under me to blow me up. The devil with 'em. They've got to be beat."

Washington could appreciate, there. He'd just escaped Gates's sapping, by way of circumstances and Gates's fumblings and a miracle he couldn't quite comprehend. His case hadn't been a matter of bookkeeping, of course—he was scrupulous in his accounts, being primarily a man of business—but to be haled in for the sake of pettifoggery would have put him to fury. Especially if he'd had Arnold's record of Champlain, and Danbury, and Saratoga.

"Very well," he said.

His words were a little resigned, a little gentle. He had built, by watching him from afar, a faith in Arnold. He knew Gates had consigned Arnold to his tent at Saratoga, and that Arnold had broken out of arrest to storm Burgoyne's lines. This quizzical look at Arnold's handling of money might stem from Gates. He was sure what Martha would think.

"Very well, General, to the Congress for you. But come back to us."

"When will you break camp?" Arnold said.

"That depends on Clinton in Philadelphia. He has orders to retire to New York."

"M'mm. Vague."

"Very."

"Well, if it will happen, it will happen this summer. But my leg, sir," Arnold said, and gave it another look, "is like to be more of a handicap at headquarters than a help. Particularly when you start maneuvering. I don't maneuver easily as yet."

Washington saw the fact and swallowed the disappointment. A crippled Arnold, unable to do for himself, would be a hindrance if the summer came to quick movements and forced marches. But the disappointment had its aftertaste, once swallowed. He had pinned considerable hopes on Arnold, his grasp of leadership and things military. He felt another prop knocked from under him. The war council he had summoned at the Congress' order had voted again to stay on the defensive this year. He didn't think Arnold would have voted so. He would have liked Arnold's voice with him, Arnold's sharp impetuousness. But that, apparently, was not to be.

"Then we must find a place for you, General. Until you are well."

Arnold said, "Clinton will be pulling out of Philadelphia."

"You've heard that?"

"I don't need to hear. The moves are plain. The French fleet—our august allies—will be operating offshore. You're here in front of him. Clinton has to scramble back to New York or risk being bottled up by the French on the sea and by you on the land."

"Provided the French can operate unhampered at sea."

"Yes. But they have a powerful navy."

"I've always thought the war would be won by sea power."

"With land troops co-operating."

"General," Washington said, "we've worn out so much shoe leather on land—"

"The French are strong at sea," Arnold said. "Strong enough to challenge." He tipped his body forward. "Your Excellency, someone must command in Philadelphia when Clinton moves out. I'd be glad to oblige you there. Until my leg heals."

Philadelphia.

A cauldron of Tories, like New York. Families like the Shippens and the Tilghmans and the Chews, openly or overtly enemies to the revolution. A city that had just given to Sir William Howe the most dazzling and romantic extravaganza ever seen on the continent, by way of farewell and acclaim. To put this treasured general, Benedict Arnold, into that seething and confused stewpot? To plump him down, like a bit of appetizing fat, into a broth long flavored by the enemy occupation and not to be too well trusted?

But there could hardly be a better man. Hardly one who merited it more. Arnold had proved himself, over and over. He couldn't do field service. But he might bring the socialites of that city back into line.

Washington saw Arnold's eyes on his, frank and burning, the unspoken bridging of soldier to soldier.

"So be it," he said. "When Clinton retreats, take command in Philadelphia."

XIII

"Sharp and Keen"

Already, by midmorning, the June day was so hot that Nat Greene had his wig off. He mopped his wet-daubed scalp with a handkerchief and fanned his face with his hat.

The rest of the officers did the same. Their wigs were on their laps, their handkerchiefs were salty wet crumples blotting at temples and beneath chins, and their tricornes waved without unison back and forth. The fluttered movement, frondlike, of the score of headpieces made the only stir of air in the room.

The heat stifled. It had been doing this for the past week. It lay like the cooking of a charcoal burner's furnace over the land, broken occasionally by drenching thunderstorms that pounded and blasted and swept on, bringing no relief but leaving the cook-oven coastal plain hotter than before. The officers' coats were unbuttoned. Their chests panted for breath. Any exertion, the shift of a leg or the twist of a body, brought an outbreak of more sweat. They gasped. As fish gasp, dying, stranded on sun-cracked mud, or as hard-run dogs in August.

Yet the day was not bright. Nor the room. A strange immensity of drabness pervaded and closed in, something of no color but swelled monstrous, a blanketing of luminosity, an absence—not a twilight, not a grayness of clouds, but the slow shutting of a door, on a star-feeble night, against shadowiness that cast no shadow. A formless hush. A limbo.

Nothing of the world reached in through the wide-flung windows. No voice nor clatter from the life outside. The birds had left off chirping, the dogs did not bark, the lieutenants' commands and the whistlings of the soldiers had fallen still.

All things seemed suspended in a kind of awe.

The sun was due to eclipse at ten.

Even so, here was another of the long train of war councils. For Sir Henry Clinton, leaving Philadelphia, was marching through the Jersey flatlands toward New York. Lee had been right again. New York would be the enemy headquarters. It stoppered the Hudson and had the best harbor on the coast.

Lee spoke. He sprawled by Washington's desk in virtue of his rank, and toyed with the muzzle of one of his dogs, which nestled on his lap. The weather didn't beat him down as it did the others, he being rail-thin with no fat to be cooked off.

"Thank God for civilization. We'll not have to throw cloaks over heads to act out an eclipse. We've advanced from the time of Pericles. Eh? No?"

And he darted a look at Washington and went smug. Washington said nothing, not knowing too well about Pericles.

But Knox, a rivulet of perspiration, flung back, "Pericles? Gave a practical demonstration to his naval pilot before a battle. Knew an eclipse was due, put his cloak over the man, and explained eclipse, and kept off panic. What's that to us?"

Knox was always blunt. Perhaps it was his fat.

"Nothing, nothing," Lee said. "But that was a sea battle. Forget the damned eclipse. We won't run from it. But remember we're on land."

"Against Clinton," Anthony Wayne said. Wayne had Arnold's love of a fight, and carried it into the councils. "Scrabble him," he said.

"Scrabble—or scrapple?" Lee said acidly. He knew Wayne was a Pennsylvanian.

"I said scrabble," Wayne said. He glowered at Lee. "By God, sir, if this day wasn't so hot—"

"We'd all be cooler," Lee said, unruffled.

Washington broke in before the day and the tempers grew hotter.

"Clinton's in open country," he said. "The problem is very simple. Do we attack him, or don't we?"

Answers piled in on him.

"No, no, we can't."

"Let him escape to New York."

"The safety of our army, sir."

"Clinton will dodge and vanish."

"It's suicide to attack him," said Lee. "Pee on the notion."

"I say attack," Wayne said.

"And I," Nat Greene said.

Washington looked slowly around the circle of officers, sweated and rubbed and for the moment baked. Some stood with him, some did not.

He turned a quill pen in his hands, and wished a soldier's cuffs weren't so stiff.

"It seems to me," he said, "the quarry is going to ground."

This was a figure of speech from his hunting days, and he put it forth and was glad to hear Wayne say, "So we sound the tallyho."

"I'd say so, Wayne," he said.

In his own mind he wasn't sure what Clinton might aim for. He had a new opponent, a new strategist. A new commander of the enemy forces, who might strike this way or that way, out from New York or seaward at the coastal cities, like Boston, or Charleston in the deep Carolinas. He knew, and it was a bored well dug in his heart, that the states of America couldn't win without help from the sea. Yet here was Clinton, crawling like a fat worm out of Philadelphia toward New York. Nowhere near the sea.

It was a tempting toward action, which he craved.

He said, "We have the choice—to attack or not. Which shall it be?"

And he said, "Your judgments, please . . . General Lee?"

"Oh, you've heard, by hell, sir. Nothing could be more damnably stupid than to attack. To plop this shotten army against disciplined troops. Rely on the French; they'll be with us shortly."

"You wouldn't go at Clinton, sir?"

"Rather build him a bridge of gold to carry him across to the Jerseys. Least done, soonest mended."

Washington swabbed his forehead. It was as wet as the others.

"General Greene?"

Greene's bald pate shone. "I'd be for attack. Conditions stand for us. Clinton has baggage and a long column. He could be cut down, supply-weak, like Burgoyne."

Lee snapped, "You're quartermaster, aren't you, Greene? What gives you privilege to advise the field?"

"Nothing," Greene said, his manner calm, "except His Excellency's question to me."

Washington felt this had gone far enough, this slapdash between his top officers. He intervened.

He said, "Knox, your notion? Stirling?"

The bookseller from Boston and the man who claimed a lordship in England traded looks. "I'd feel, sir, that General Lee's views make sense. Attack on Clinton would be risky."

This was not to his liking.

"General Stirling, sir?"

"I side with General Knox."

"General Wayne?"

"Attack."

"General von Steuben?"

A volley of German and French. Washington gathered that the stress of it was for bringing Clinton to battle. Young Laurens interpreted, roughly. The room darkened.

"Marquis?" This to Lafayette.

"*Mon Général.* Put a troop to come in against their baggage train. Harass them, nudge them. Eat at their hearts, bite at their heels. At least don't let them cross placid in front of our noses. Are we fearful to go against Clinton?"

Wayne laughed, and Greene, and von Steuben.

But they were the only ones. The upshot was a kind of cowardly decision to harry Clinton's flanks and rear.

He dissolved the meeting, and turned to face the eyes of Hamilton, who had been in the room as his aide and heard it all.

"Well—?" he said.

"Well, sir," Hamilton said, and stiffened himself to his small height, "this result would have done honor to the most honorable body of midwives. And to them only."

The sun, at the same moment, was obscured. A flaccid darkness, wan and eternal, fell on the New Jersey countryside and into the room. A darkness malevolent, as if it would lay waste the human spirit, as if it were an ultimate and insensate force from a nether cosmos, groping and exulting to blind and conquer.

He shut his eyes. He did not want to see the eclipse.

The more he thought about it, the more he was dissatisfied with the war council's verdict. Written reports from Greene and Wayne after the council meeting urged him to do something more than prod at Clinton. And when von Steuben, who'd been reconnoitering, came back with the news that Clinton was on the road to Monmouth Court House, he moved his army forward and sent for General Lee.

The general was in an amiable mood, having dominated the war council and won his point. He fed snuff to his nose without quite so much acerbity, and listened quietly.

Washington was a little dubious about putting the proposition to him, since Lee didn't believe in an attack; but Lee was second in command and had the right of place. Washington tried to be conciliatory.

"General," he said, "I want to send a strong detachment against Clinton, against his left flank and rear. I have thoughts of putting Lafayette in charge of it because he is for vigorous action. But you are entitled by rank to have the refusal of the leadership. What are your sentiments?"

Lee crossed his skinny knees and looked down at them. His face, his expression, the vulture beak of his nose were almost soft. "Such a duty," he said, "could be performed with more suitableness by a young and volunteering general like the marquis than by the next in command of the American Army. It will be brush fighting, mock warfare. I want no part of it."

"Thank you," Washington said, and signaled to Hamilton, and saw Lee rise to leave the room, and began to dictate. "From headquarters, Colonel: General the Marquis de Lafayette is to take twenty-five hundred to three thousand of the rank and file and make tentative contact with the enemy columns with a view to bringing them to a possible engagement. . . ."

As Lee went out the door, while he specified the number of men to be involved, he noticed Lee's swift, backward glance.

Lafayette, of course, jumped at the assignment when he heard.

"We'll do it, *mon Général,* we'll ride their backsides and goad them and goad them. When?"

"Tomorrow," Washington said.

But on that tomorrow Lee was back again, his manner superb, his voice dry in the pervading heat.

"Your Excellency, I had not realized the detachment sent against Clinton would be so large. Might it not seem odd if I failed to command it? My position with the army—Your Excellency knows—"

Jealousies, ambitions, school-child egotisms. Whether a man would lead five hundred troops or five thousand. The continual scramble for fame, and place, and public acclamation. Washington was sick of it.

He said, "The orders have gone out, General."

"There never was an order that could not be rescinded," Lee said tartly. "God damme, Your Excellency, am I to be superseded in the eyes of the American people by a boy from France?"

"It was your own decision, General."

"Before I knew the size of the maneuver."

Washington had never enjoyed backing down. That had always seemed to him a sign of weakness. Yet he was coming to learn that in melding divergent elements, cross-cut elements, elements acquisitive and bullying and sentimental and amoral, a certain flexibility was the philosopher's stone. Out of the fire of human weakness, burned and smelted, would come the human gold. It was a matter of persuading men to work together.

He said, "If you wish to lead the detachment, General, I'll do what I can."

So he asked for Lafayette. And when Lafayette had presented himself, shining in uniform and epaulets, he said, speaking like a father to a son, "Marquis, General Lee thinks the thrust against Clinton is important enough to warrant his command. You know the general's position with the army."

He saw Lafayette's face droop and go blank.

"*Oui, mon Général.*"

"Militarily, he is correct. But I believe he'll be willing to let you lead the first contact with the enemy and carry it through if fighting has begun when he comes up to your support. Afterward, or if fighting has not begun when he joins you, he will take charge as senior. Is that satisfactory, Marquis?"

Lafayette had an instant reply: "Completely, sir."

When the youngster had left, Washington thanked his fortune that all men were not childish-minded, or as hungry for the center of the stage as jealous actresses, or as slavering for public notice as politicians at a poll. The marquis was capable of unselfishness and an adult view.

With Lee suavely agreeable to the arrangement, he saw Lafayette march off that afternoon with sweat-soaked companies to worry Clinton's flank, and, later, tried out the mettle of his new war horse. It was a large, strong, handsome animal, pure white, a present from Jersey's Governor Livingston.

He rode by himself, only Billy Lee trailing him, testing the horse's paces and obedience with the instinct of old skill, unconsciously. For he was thinking as he rode—putting the clutter of office papers from his mind, weighing the views of his war council and the numbers of his troops, and reaching for his own conclusion from the maps of the neighborhood, which were still as clear to his memory, from his surveyor's training, as if they had been laid in front of him there across the horse's mane. They told him what he already knew in his heart: that this would be his great chance to smash Clinton.

He hardly needed, returning to headquarters, to have Greene and Wayne come at him again with appeals to push in and force a battle. The majority of his generals might be against this, but his mind was made up. He had decided alone. He wanted a victory.

That night he moved his army forward again.

By early afternoon his plans were ready—as ready as ever they could be in that new, unscouted region, checkered by roads and blistering in the sun. He laid the plans before his officers.

"Clinton has stayed two days at Monmouth, gentlemen, either to provoke us to action or to rest his troops. It's not likely he'll attack. But I wish to make an attack ourselves as soon as he stirs. I wish to catch him in motion. We will close up our columns today and be prepared to advance on immediate notice. General Dickinson and a thousand Jersey militia are on Clinton's flank. Colonel Moylan is at his front with our troop of horse—too few for anything but intelligence work. Lafayette's advance force is probing for a weak spot, and the marquis may be rash.

"I am going to strengthen that force to five thousand men and direct General Lee to command it." He paused and looked.

"Indeed, sir," Lee said.

"You will confer with your staff, design a method of attack, and strike as soon as Clinton marches from Monmouth."

"Indeed, sir."

"We will push the main army nearer and stand to support you. General Greene will have the right wing, Lord Stirling the left."

"Do I understand, sir," Lee said, speaking more slowly than he usually did, "that you order me to attack?"

"I can't do that, General. I'll not be on the ground with you and can't foresee the conditions. But I'm very anxious to attack unless there are heavy reasons against it."

"I'm to act at my discretion, then," Lee said.

"Any commander must do that, General."

"From what I know of the opposing officers, sir, they'll turn about and strike back."

"That," Washington said, "is what I intend." He paused again. "If there are more questions, gentlemen, bring them to me individually. General Lee will want to make his start. Tomorrow's countersign will be 'Sharp and Keen.'"

He slept little during the night. Before he went to bed he called Hamilton in and had him draw up a message to Lee urging the general, once more, to attack before the enemy could get out of reach. It seemed to him he had never wanted anything so much. It seemed to him the whole justification of his leadership hung on it, the proof to the Congress and the people and to his own self-respect that he could fight on the offensive after the years of defense and delay and retreat, that he could provide another Trenton, another Princeton, on a larger, crushing, decisive scale; the proof that the suffering, hardening, sinewing winter of the Valley Forge had not been in vain.

There was a vicious thunderstorm at midnight. The storm lashed down, and thunder shook, and the steamy darkness sizzled with lightning. He tossed and twisted on his solitary bed, for Martha had gone back to Mt. Vernon with the coming of summer and its evident battles, shifting the positions of his arms and legs, stifled, wakeful, his mind and body wrought up for tomorrow's unfoldment, trying to rest.

At five in the morning he was up and dressed, in time to read a dispatch from General Dickinson. The enemy were moving; Dickinson was sending men to scout and annoy them.

Dickinson had been prompt. This was good. The day was beginning as he had outlined it in his mind. His main army was turned out and waiting for him in marching column, blankets and packs discarded because this morning would be as hot as the ones before it.

The aide on duty looked to him for orders. He gave them. "Colonel Meade, ride to General Lee. Tell the general to have his men leave off their packs, follow the enemy, and bring on an attack."

"Yes, sir. But if the general thinks an attack improper . . . ?"

"There might be circumstances, but I very much want an attack."

The noise of the dispatch rider, and of Meade galloping off, brought his aides tumbling into the office, owl-eyed after the haggard night—Tilghman, Laurens, Harrison.

Laurens asked to scout ahead toward Monmouth. So did McHenry, a new aide who'd joined him at the Valley Forge. He sent them on. He had no intention of marching blind to a battle.

Outside, when he stepped from his headquarters, the sun was already blazing, a hot weight that pushed heavy at his neck and shoulders. He stood a moment, surveying the standing columns clustered along the road, muskets sloped, faces sweaty, faces turning to him with a kind of dogged, heat-drained expectancy, faces that showed they knew as well as he what might be in store for them, how a single error, a single misjudged order, could bring a horror of steel and cannon ripping through them. Standing, he figured the outlines again to himself: Dickinson and the thousand militia, Lee with five thousand troops and a dozen cannon, Morgan on the right flank of the enemy with six hundred riflemen and orders through Lee to attack, his main army of nearly eight thousand marching to support Lee. And Clinton crawling out of Monmouth with a lumbering train of baggage wagons. The net was closing.

Billy Lee held the stirrup of the big white charger for him. Behind, on a leading rein from Billy's mount, he saw his own Betsy, the chestnut mare with the long mane and tail.

"What's this, Billy?" he said. "It's the white today."

"Yes, suh, Gen'ral, excuse me, suh—but I like Betsy along. We know how far she'll do."

Washington laughed, and didn't stop to argue. He threw a leg over the great white animal's saddle and gave the command to go forward.

Dust choked them before they had gone a mile. Dry, sandy dust shuffled up by thousands of dragging feet, to swirl and clog in an air that had no wind. Before they had gone two miles, men began to drop out. Silently, suddenly, they tottered to the side of the road and collapsed from heat and stroke. After a week of searing inferno and night marches they were done.

Englishtown, the next hamlet, was only three miles farther. They might be able to break their march there for a little, Washington thought.

Lafayette had been at Englishtown the night before. He was not there now, but out with the advance. Instead there was von Steuben, his round face pinched, his lids reddened, to say the enemy were making a quick pace and he doubted about catching them. This meant no halt for the army here, and Washington ordered it to keep marching, shambling and panting through sand and the fiery morning that shimmered the landscape like a picture seen across hot coals.

"Go into a house and find some rest, General," he said, and answered the salute as von Steuben reined around weakly. Von Steuben had been all night on horseback, scouting.

He had not yet had breakfast himself. His aides knocked at the home of Dr. English, and the doctor took him in, and he sat in a small dining room and ate in hurried bites—it didn't matter to him what he ate—and wrote the forereport of battle to the Congress, which would be expecting it from him, and all the while in the background, through the wideflung windows, was the dry, persistent sibilance of plodding feet.

By noon he was mounted again. The doctor rode with him, and the staff, at a gallop past the columns in a spur for Monmouth.

The country was a burned green, flecked with unmoving leaves and the darts of hot, spice-needled scrub pines. Out of the stillness over the fields rolled the boom of a cannon. A second boom. Four or five in all. Then nothing. Slowly, he angled his head in the direction of the sound, listening for the rattle of musketry in reply. He could hear only silence. But down the road from Monmouth he saw a horseman coming full tilt. An American officer, evidently. Washington pulled to a stop. The horseman reined up sharp in a sprawl of dust. It was his aide McHenry.

"I've just left General Lee, Your Excellency. He wants me to tell Your Excellency that the rear of the enemy is made up of fifteen hundred or two thousand, that he expects to fall in with them and has a great certainty of cutting them off."

"Fine news. Splendid news." Here was the kind of grapple he'd dreamed of. The enemy on the run and his own troops thrusting in. The day would go well. He felt its promise.

His eye caught another officer: Meade, back again with the staff.

"Colonel, ride forward and see what's afoot."

Meade spurred and was away.

Washington lingered briefly. There was still no sound of definite fighting. From places he couldn't see, from problems he couldn't gauge, he had to piece the scattered patterns and bring them to a whole, give them drive, and direction, and weight. But if Lee was attacking, the largest pattern was certainly clear.

Another officer drew up beside him, the horse as foamed as McHenry's. Major Clark, who'd been his confidential secret agent once.

"I'm on my way to the front, sir. Can I take any message to General Lee?"

"You may inform the general that it's my order he annoy the enemy as much as he can, but at the same time be careful the enemy don't draw him into a scrape. Tell him I'm marching to reinforce him."

"Yes, sir."

And Clark was gone, too.

"We'll ride along, gentlemen." He spoke elatedly, for elation was growing in him. Lee had his orders, would execute them. Would stab at that rear guard, and badger it, and hold it, until the main army would be on it like last night's storm. This time, this nick of time, there would be no failure.

He settled into an easy canter, to spare his horse and those of his aides; they'd soon have work enough. There was still no sound of guns. Ahead of him, through snake-fenced fields that seemed flattened by the heat, the bare yellow road rose and dipped over short, tumbled hills and into shallow ravines. Beyond one of those hills—the next, or the next—the forces of battle were shaping themselves, winding through tree copses and past scattered hedges and muddy bogs, drawing in like iron filings to a magnet. At any instant they would clamp and mass. At any instant he would sight them. Behind him the dust of his army was a portentous cloud.

He seemed to be cantering through blank space toward a mute horizon that teased him on.

It must have been well after midday, as he was near the Monmouth Meeting House, when Hamilton rode to him. Hamilton had been out with the advance. He said Lee was about to commence the fight. He added, before Washington could speak:

"Your Excellency, might I advise you to throw the right wing under General Greene well around to the right? They could flank the enemy in case Lee's pushed back."

Pushed back. He had expected Lee to hold; if once he engaged, with his numbers, Lee could certainly hold. Hamilton was dripping hot, of course, and keyed up, but Washington thought he caught a disturbed note in Hamilton's voice.

He halted while he pondered this over. Hamilton knew the terrain, and he did not. And yet, to split the right wing from his army—he looked at Greene, who drew closer, as if for orders. He looked at Stirling.

Knox came careening in from the direction of Monmouth. He was sweating lard and angry.

"Damnit!" he said, "Damnit!" and puffed for breath.

"Knox, Hamilton says to throw our right wing wide to the flank. Would you say so?"

"Damnit, yes! Lee's dillydallying. There's confusion in his troops. Put Greene on the flank as a safety measure. Believe me, as God's my judge. I've seen!"

And Hamilton said, "I don't like Lee's tactics. Don't think he has a purpose."

For all the blistering heat Washington felt a chill go through him. But he said, "Very well," and signaled Tilghman to bring his maps. Greene's knee was by his, horses side by side.

"You will turn off to the right, General, by Tennent's Church, and march to the south. There's a road there that parallels this. Do you mark it? Follow the road and you'll be in flank position to cover us."

He watched Greene spur away with some misgivings. But he was not granted much time for those; his aide, Harrison, was saluting.

"A man, sir. To speak with you. The officers took him for a farmer, but I questioned him. He's a Colonel Henderson, sir, of these parts. Had his house burned by the enemy yesterday."

"You did sensibly," Washington said to Harrison.

"He says Lee's falling back, sir."

The man was wearing countryman's clothes. Washington said to him, "Where have you come from, Colonel?"

"From near Monmouth, sir."

"Where did you get this story?"

"From a fifer, Your Excellency. He's standing on the road, yonder."

Washington swung an arm and they brought the fifer to him. The fellow looked frightened.

Washington snapped at him. "Do you belong to the army?"

"Yes, Your Excellency. Musician and soldier."

"Why have you come back here? Deserted? Run away?"

"No, Your Excellency. The Continental troops are retreating."

His answer was so sure that Washington's temper flared. "That's not true," he said, and his voice rose higher, as it always did under stress. "It can't be true! If you mention any more of that, you'll be whipped. Tilghman, put a light horseman over him, keep him from spreading the rumor. Ride ahead, gentlemen."

The ride wasn't long. He'd hardly got into a gallop before the road around him began to trickle with men, scurrying the opposite way, like trickles from a crumbling dike. He stopped again, questioned again. They were soldiers, they were retreating. Everyone was retreating.

Rather than chill, Washington felt complete bewilderment now. Without notice from Lee of any difficulties, of any withdrawal, he was advancing to Lee's support to be faced by a retreat. And with no sound of firing since midday.

Dimly he heard Harrison and Fitzgerald offering to ride ahead and bring him clear reports. Dimly he was conscious of waving them on. Dimly he realized he was leaving the road and galloping beside it up a long ridge topped by a woods, taking instinctively to the high ground where he could discover things for himself.

What he saw was a slope that fell gradually away in front of him, a boggy, pale ravine threaded by a thin brook, and beyond the ravine a shorter slope leading up to a hedgerow, and orchard, and an old barn. The road crossed the middle of the ravine, going on through fields and scattered woods toward Monmouth.

What he also discovered were men. The road was full of them. They poured slowly, wearily, down the far slope, and over the ravine, and up the slope where he watched. Other men dragged themselves through the fields.

Two regiments wove toward him. Once more the questions, once more the answers. Officers' answers.

"We're much fatigued, sir."

"Yes, sir, ordered off to refresh ourselves."

He blurted, "With a battle in prospect?"

Two colonels blinking, stuttering.

"To tell true, sir—"

"It's like this, sir—"

"We're sent to look for a pair of cannon left on the field somewhere—"

He could only think heat and fright had crazied them. That they weren't responsible for their actions under the brassy sky overhead. "Take your men into woods," he said, "to recover themselves. And draw some rum for them and keep them from straggling."

He still would not believe that from this last hill's rim he was seeing, not the beckoning horizon, but the slow seep of decay. He could not believe it.

He glimpsed epaulets climbing the ridge, and galloped toward them. The officer stiffened. "Colonel Shreve, Your Excellency; Second New Jersey."

"What is the meaning of this retreat, sir?"

"I don't know, Your Excellency."

"Have you been in action?"

"No, Your Excellency. Not fired a shot."

"How far have you come?"

"Two miles or more, sir."

"Why?"

"I've retreated by orders, sir." The colonel put on a significant look. "I don't say by whose order."

"Halt your men on the hill and refresh them," Washington said. He looked about him for someone who could tell him something more definite. He was dazed. Five thousand men were falling back on his main army just when he was poised to surge forward.

Then, as he looked, his eye lit on General Lee. The general and his staff were on the road, falling back, too, at pace with the troops.

He put his charger over the little roadside ditch at a single leap, and bore down on Lee.

"What is the meaning of all this?" he said, and felt the blast in his voice and saw the staff gaping.

"Sir? Sir?" Lee seemed not to understand.

"What's all this confusion for, and retreat?"

He used no formality; he gave no ceremony to Lee. He was too angry for that. Lee had let him march to the front in ignorance that Lee was marching to the rear. Lee had missed the perfect opportunity. Lee had—

Lee thrust his hand in his pocket for snuff, took it out again empty. His flat cough was disconcerted, and he mumbled his words.

"I see no confusion, sir, except from damned contradictory intelligence —orders not being obeyed—impertinence of persons intruding themselves in matters out of their sphere. . . . Things thrown into a whoreson state —didn't choose to beard the king's army in such a situation." Then the beaked nose came up sharply. "Besides, I'll remind Your Excellency this whole bastardly affair was done against my opinion and my advice in council. I didn't think it proper to risk so much."

"Whatever your opinions are," Washington flung at him, "if you didn't think it proper you shouldn't have undertaken it."

Then, afraid of his self-control, he wheeled his horse. Lee's staff were like numbed statues. Lee's voice trailed after him, "—can obey orders— am a soldier—but major engagement contrary to my judgment—" and died away.

"Go to the rear. Come up when you're refreshed."

He started for the front, wherever that might be now, breasting his horse past the regiments shuffling rearward. His staff jangled after him. None of them spoke to him. He didn't want them to. He was grim. His face forbade speech. All plans, all direction, all organization, were being undermined by this backwash and collapsing at his feet. Somewhere, somehow, he must find a point to make a stand, put heart into these drooping men to turn and defend themselves.

He found no front—only a thicker, viscous tide of confusion. Out of it bolted his aide Harrison.

"No farther, Your Excellency; the enemy are pressing. Their weight will be on us in fifteen minutes!"

This was the first news, the only news, he'd had of the enemy. It paralyzed him. He sat stricken in his saddle. With this jumble around him, how could he hope to hold off Clinton, so close? Before his eyes, in the waves of heat over the fields, danced the phantasm of retreat—full Continental retreat. Rout, perhaps; pandemonium; slaughter. He gnawed his lip, and tried to shake his mind free.

Tench Tilghman touched his elbow.

"Your Excellency—"

"Well?" His voice shrilled.

"A Jersey colonel, sir, a moment ago. Colonel Rhea. He knows the ground. It's favorable. The colonel will guide, if you wish."

His shock fell from Washington like a clay cast. He could feel its fall, feel the blood run in him again.

"Fetch him to the command post. On the ridge."

Tilghman vanished. Washington rose in his stirrups. He swung his sword, pointing, and shouted to the men in the road.

"There! Behind the hedgerow! Stand there!"

One colonel was already doing that—Livingston, he thought. He saw two others he knew, called for them.

"Colonel Ramsey, Colonel Stewart," he said. "Gentlemen, I'll depend on you with your regiments to check the advance of the enemy until I can form the main army."

"We'll check them, sir."

He took Ramsey by the hand, left him, and spun, leading the gallop back to the long ridge, pausing to shout other regiments into line and order as he rode.

Colonel Rhea was on the ridge with Tilghman. The colonel was brief.

"This is the best spot, sir, in the immediate area. High ground, in a half circle. You can see. The length protected by the swamp—she's dried now, but makes an obstacle. On the left a strong height. Excellent for cannon. Another on the right, with woods to protect more cannon and cover reserves."

"Thank you, Colonel. I'm indebted to you."

Now the details were less smudged. He had a good position; he knew what he could do.

"Colonel Harrison, I want guns. Colonel Oswald's are near, I noted them on the road. Have them set in place, to open when the enemy fires. Colonel McHenry, find General Wayne. He was with the advance, can't be far off. Tell him to reinforce the regiment behind the hedgerow with his and Varnum's brigades."

Without waiting for answer he galloped for the road again, to the rear. Detachments from Lee's troops were still threading back. Let them go, let them go, he thought; they're sapped, worn down; bring 'em up for reinforcements later. He passed the colonels of the main army's regiments, coming forward—hurried them along—looked for General Stirling and found him.

"We'll engage shortly," he said. "Take post to the left of the road, General, along the ridge. Knox will be with you, for artillery. You've two regiments in front of you, in a holding action."

How long this occupied him he didn't know. Time was a blank quantity. But when he galloped up the ridge again the forward elements of the main army were forming along its slope, facing the swamp and the slope on the other side.

His aides had been watching for him.

"Colonel Oswald's got four guns on our right, sir," Harrison said.

And McHenry said, "General Wayne's moving into position now, sir."

From where he sat in the saddle he could see Wayne's men footing it across the swamp and scrambling to the shelter of the hedgerow that bordered the orchard, and a few barricading themselves in the old barn. They had rolled up their sleeves, their bayonets glinted.

Knox joined the group. He'd been out keeping track of his precious cannon. His brigade major, the Chevalier de Mauduit du Plessis, was with him.

"Your place will be at the left, Knox. I'm told the highest ground is there."

The two officers made off.

By now it was midafternoon. The sun was unbearable, the heat a torture. At the distant parsonage of a church, almost on the spot where the battle would be joined, a line of men had already formed at the parsonage well, craving water. In the church graveyard, villagers were clambering on top of the tombstones to see the fight.

Very well, they'd see one.

He stayed where he was until movement and clatter beyond the orchard opposite, beyond the hedgerow sheltering Wayne's bayonets, told him the enemy were massing. They would use artillery first, of course. He waited for the crash of it, his aides waiting too, tense on either side of him. And when it came, the flame and bark and spit of guns, and the thud of cannon ball against sod, he waited longer and heard his own guns blast.

Their sound had a sting in it. They were being served well, by men who were not beaten or afraid. His ears said so.

Five, ten minutes more. He satisfied himself that the guns on the right would give the enemy pause. But on the left—?

"Colonel Hamilton, you will accompany me."

He set off at gallop again, Hamilton after him. This was action, desperation, energy, the thing his nature was made for, the same lift and pound of hoofs, the same smoke and powder stench, the same physical exultancy in danger he'd known with Braddock. From the edge of his eye he saw Billy Lee, glued to a gallop too, but hampered by the lead mare. What was a mare? He had a battle on his hands.

On the left wing he ran into Knox.

"There's a headland here, Your Excellency. A damned fine site. General Lee's helping with the disposition of the guns."

He turned to find Lee confronting him. The thin general had at last begun to sweat. There was no trace of snuff on his neckcloth. He seemed to have full possession of himself.

But Washington was still angry.

"One or the other of us must take charge, General," he said. "If you wish to stay here, I'll go back and rally the center."

The beak nose was not so high. It was almost subservient. "I'll do all in my power. Your Excellency may rely that I'll be the last man off the field."

With this, Hamilton came thundering in. He looked as if he had heard what Lee had said. He pulled out his sword and jumped to the ground. "We're betrayed, Your Excellency! It's the time when every friend of America must die in her defense! We'll all die here on the spot!"

They both looked at him. He was young, and overwrought, and keyed to the breaking point.

Lee said, "Colonel Hamilton, look at me. Am I the master of my faculties?"

"Yes, sir. I should judge so."

"And I am responsible to His Excellency for the troops under my command. When I've got them in a good position, I'll gladly die with you on this spot, if you wish."

Washington wasn't quite sure how to take that. It might have been sarcasm, it might have been genuineness. But he couldn't allow the scene to go on. He said, "Colonel Hamilton, you will mount your horse."

He was getting out of his depth here. He was too open and plain for these vagaries of temperament and recrimination. It was a relief to hear von Steuben's voice.

"I've slept, Your Excellency. I report to you."

"Help to form the left," Washington said. He raced for the height where Knox was jockeying cannon; spurred again, and took off at flat gallop for the command post on the ridge.

The cannonading was vigorous now. Enemy infantry were assaulting Wayne at the hedgerow. Smoke from their volleys curled and hung. Wayne was holding steadfast. To Wayne's left, Ramsey's and Stewart's regiments were being overwhelmed. Knots of men went down under steel. Colonel Ramsey was off his horse, surrounded by royal dragoons, fighting them sword to sword; blades flashed at his chest and belly, plunged. Knox's guns began to hammer at the enemy support.

More guns loosed bellowings on his right. Far to the right, dominating the swamp.

He raced over there. These were Greene's men, filing into battle line. An aide said to him, "General Greene heard the noise of fighting, and ordered to march to it."

So that was secure. He could depend on Greene. The Rhode Islander was not one to fight battles by the book; he fought with his head and his native skill. Greene was firming himself on the right wing, planting himself, with a sure grasp of tactics, where he would be most useful.

"My compliments to General Greene, and hold them off," he told the aide.

Then spurs again. He hadn't figured how long he had ridden, the number of hours he had spent in dashing about the field. But all at once the white charger stumbled and fell. He pulled boots from the stirrups, rolled clear. Not like that time with Braddock, when his horse was shot under him, and he had lain tangled beneath it, weak with fever and ripe for Indian tomahawks if old Bishop hadn't gotten him loose. This was different. He vaulted clear as the animal went down, and stood swaying, the heat and the surge of his blood addling him, giving him a drunkenness.

A soldier ran by.

"Why aren't you on the ridge?" he grated. "Go back there."

The man opened his mouth, showing his tongue and pointing to it with a blunt forefinger. It was swollen beyond power to speak; he manifestly was in torment, parched and squeezed juiceless, and on the edge of madness. There would be hundreds like him, Washington thought. Heat would kill more men than bullets today.

Suddenly came Billy Lee. The white charger was dead, its heart burst. Billy had Betsy mare.

"Can't keep up to you, Gen'ral, suh. You too fast for me. Here's our Betsy, scurce breathed yet."

Billy got him on the mare, and his knees felt familiar ribs.

"Thank you, Billy."

"She'll carry you, suh."

He'd left his aides behind. His gallopings had passed everyone.

But he spurred to the command post, and they gathered in on him. They were all safe except Hamilton, who was half-doubled in his saddle. His horse had been hit and had fallen on him, and he was hurt. Washington motioned him to retire.

The noise of the guns reached a climax and stayed constant. Knox on the left, Greene on the right were answering the enemy fire shot for shot. Washington believed they could hold. They had already held for longer than he remembered during other battles of the war. At the hedgerow, Wayne was beating off another assault. But the defense was weaker; splashes of red showed along the hedgerow, enemy coats at Wayne's line like spray at a sea wall. And on the left Stirling seemed to be in trouble. Stewart's and Ramsey's regiments had been slashed to pieces. The remnants of them were scattering back to the ridge, and the main army's left wasn't yet in position. There was milling there, a dangerous delay in forming. Washington caught the uncertainty. He lifted his reins.

"I may be needed there," he said, and put his spurs ready at Betsy's flanks. But he waited for a moment or so, trying to look calm. He had set his battle order, and it was his duty now to keep his post, to supervise the whole, not a segment of it. Unless those half-muddled men broke and ran.

Then he saw von Steuben. They all saw. The baron had pushed his horse to a small knoll, and sat conspicuous in his epaulets and his heavy solidity. He was roaring at full lungs. They couldn't hear the roars. But they could see the wagging of his head, his vehemence, see the tattered, raveled lines wheel in drill-ground obedience, fix bayonets, and deploy precisely. As if they were back at the Valley Forge again, going through parade. By the time the enemy assault on the left got under way they were poised to meet it.

"By God, sir," Tilghman said, low, "I never knew till now what discipline would do."

Washington didn't think a reply was called for; von Steuben's training results spoke for themselves.

He was watching Knox's guns riddling the enemy infantry trying to charge across the swamp. Riddling it and halting it, plunging it back to regroup. He was watching Wayne being smothered by a final wave of red over the hedgerows and on the flank.

[187]

"Wayne will have to fall back to this side," he said. "Have the main body cover him, let him through to the rear and close ranks."

He followed the maneuver while Wayne gave ground at the hedgerow, and crossed the morass, still fighting, and got to the protection of the lines on the slope, and the lines blazed and beat off his pursuers.

Another attack on the left, and another blasting from Knox's guns. The red-coated wave spent itself and retreated. Washington had a quick glimpse of Clinton riding out to it, trying to stem it and sweep it forward. Cornwallis stormed at the right wing. Greene did not yield a foot, and the Chevalier du Plessis tore Cornwallis' guards and grenadiers with shot, enfilading shot that mowed down the packed ranks.

Clinton brought up his cavalry. Washington had feared this, and he left his post and galloped down the slope, swinging along behind the lines of the grimy, cursing, exhausted men. "Fight them off, boys! Fight them off!" They raised him a ragged cheer.

Clinton's horsemen charged over the morass, yelling. Volleys met them, musket balls, cannon. The Continental fire did not slacken, did not waver. Washington's heart pounded in him. These bitten and sinewy troops were standing up to the best in the royal army.

The yelling horsemen were only forty paces away when they were stopped. But they were stopped. Like the infantry, they faltered and lost momentum and then went struggling back, to the safety of the far slope, out of reach of the American guns.

A long, peculiar quiet spread over the battlefield.

With the sound and the fury gone, the absence of noise was ponderous.

Washington's watch told him the time of day was after five o'clock. His neck and shoulders told him the sun's knifing was duller. It seemed almost possible to breathe again without a shrivel of lungs. He knew Clinton's troops must have been weather-seared as his had been, the grenadiers in their tight neckcloths, the Hessians with their heavy uniforms and monstrous boots. The two forces measured each other warily, dry and hot and cooked as bricks in a kiln.

Wayne moved his Pennsylvanians out, and the infantry firing started again. With ball, and bayonet, and a wild rush, the Pennsylvanians drove the last of the enemy from the swamp and up the other slope, and dodged back, whooping, to the American lines.

Washington sang praises to Wayne in his heart. He recognized his advantage and took it.

"Get word to Baron von Steuben to bring up the men that have been loitering on the Englishtown road. Send General Poor and the Carolina brigade against the enemy right, General Woodford against the left. Station artillery to pound at the center. We'll counterattack."

Out of the threat and dismay of five hours ago he had wrenched his army into order and planted it unshaken. Now the initiative was his again. He could still smell triumph.

But the brigades' movements were slow. The men's feet dragged, their shoulders hung limp. No enemy volleys challenged them; Clinton made no resistance. The sun had set before they had hauled themselves into position, flies wading through molasses. Human stamina was gone out of them.

"They are, *mon Général*—as one might say—beat out," Lafayette said. In the lull of the fighting he had sought Washington. He had been all day without command, serving where he could, but Washington knew he bore no grudge. "Give them till tomorrow."

There was no choice. The battlefield was theirs, their flanks were advanced, but bone and muscle and will could take no more. The two armies stayed looking at each other through the twilight, and when darkness came down the men dropped to the ground and slept where they fell.

Billy Lee spread a mantle for him under a tree, and he stretched stiffly out on it.

Lafayette stretched beside him.

Last night's thunderstorm had cleared the sky, and the stars were very bright. He stared up at them, lying on his back, hands locked under his head. Their brightness, and the calm, brought him calm too, utterly weary, as though his body were a substance apart from him, floating in motionless water, as though his mind were a slate wiped by a sponge.

For the first time in the war he was camping on a field he had defended and held, and that realization was enough for the moment; to lie there and feel the strain of the day relax, and know he had not failed.

Lafayette twisted restively.

"*Mon Général—*"

"Yes, Marquis?"

"I cannot close my eyes."

"You're tired," he said. "Like the rest of us."

"No. I think of General Lee."

"What do you think?"

"I try to think why did he do it. The retreat."

"It was a strange thing."

"He could have tangled Clinton among the baggage for you to crush."

"Better, Marquis, he could have opened a chance to end the war."

There was a reflective silence.

"I cannot think why," Lafayette said.

"Nor I. But I wasn't with him in the advance."

"But I was. And we moved out against Clinton's rear guard and he said to me, 'My dear Marquis, I think these people are ours.' Those words were in my ears, and my ears do not lie. Wayne is ready to attack, the guns are placed. Then without notice, without the pull of a musket trigger, he changes his mind."

"His privilege, Marquis. And Lee has a fickle mind."

"He might also have a purpose."

Washington continued to stare at the stars. Somewhere beyond a horse cropped grass, snuffing contentedly, and the tree above his head was tall and black against the night. "A military one," he said.

"No. Jealousy."

Washington made no reply. He waited a little. He could hardly credit that. Yet there had been Gates—

Of the two officers nearest him in command, the two whose high rank he had helped them to, were they both connivers?

Lafayette spoke again. In the drowse and quietude around them his voice made a lulled murmur. "He might have built the confusion for you so he would shine by contrast."

"A general who retreats does not shine, Marquis," Washington said, and did not add that he knew this from experience. Lafayette was well aware of that.

"I saw him on the rearward road once, in the afternoon," Lafayette said, slower. "He was sitting his horse, quite still, looking dazed, as if he did not believe what you were achieving."

"But he fought well. And gave good aid to Knox in setting the guns."

"Then why did he at first fall back? Was it a mistake, or not? Or some ugly reason?"

"I don't know, and I don't propose to ask," Washington said shortly. "He'll give me his own explanation."

He was still angry with Lee. Lee's conduct had thorned him; not in his pride—he'd known Lee long enough, the egotism, the unstable superciliousness—but in his concept of duty, in the law on which he based his life, that there are things a sure man will not stoop to, times when he will refuse to falter or stumble. There must be dependence on each man, faith in his words and reliance on his motives, to create any foundation, any mutual trust. If not—anarchy or another king.

Lafayette had said nothing. It occurred to him the boy might have been hurt by the sharpness in his tone. He'd not meant a rebuke. He cleared his throat apologetically.

"I'm sorry to have sounded abrupt," he said.

He heard a soft, immature snore.

Lafayette had fallen asleep.

And in the morning the place where Clinton had camped was deserted.

XIV

Jack and a Sip of Sherry

House Alice had seen to it that the candles were lighted in the glass lantern of the central hall at Mt. Vernon, and candles in the music room and parlor and library, and was upstairs now, helping Martha to dress. Martha was in a state of nervousness. But House Alice possessed the soothing calm of her race, the calm and the inbred sense of philosophic humor that made so many Negro women such exceptional nurses and protectors and guardians of the white children of plantation families, where they were a trusted and essential part of the family life. Martha found House Alice indispensable. As she'd often said, she didn't know what she would do without her.

House Alice's husband was the chief gardener. The two of them had special quarters of their own, and House Alice's husband knew almost as much of soils and mulchings and tree grafts and fertilizers as the general. Under his hand the Mt. Vernon grounds had continued to bloom while the general had been away. He was especially good with the herb garden. Martha liked to have a flavor of herbs in the cookery; it counteracted the salting and pickling and brining that was necessary for preserving meats and fish for the table.

House Alice dropped to one knee, smoothing the ruffles of petticoats.

"Now then, Miz' Washington, no case to hurry. No case at all."

"But I'm late, Alice—such a lot to do. Which shall I wear, the yellow or the purple? Oh, dear, I hear carriages."

"The purple is the elegantest."

"I'll wear the purple, then. Who's in the carriages?"

"Can't say, Miz' Washington, 'thout I look from the window. And you'd not want my face bobbin' and pryin' upwards of the doorway. But

Master Jacky and Miz' Nellie are down there below. Now you try to stand still."

"Is the purple the best?"

"You says so. Lemme put it on. Huh-huh, you're thickenin' around the hips. These fastenin's."

"Do hurry, Alice."

"Yes'm, all in good time. And Mr. Lund wants to know if outbuildings will be ree-quired to sleep coachmen and such. So's he can ready 'em."

"No—no, there won't be that many. Just a small gathering. I've told him. He can put the coachmen up with the Mt. Vernon people. Are the musicians here?"

"Yes'm. You saw 'em yourself."

"Oh, to be sure. No, no, the hem, Alice—pull it farther down. That's it. Is my hair suitable?"

"Wasn't never more so."

"A touch of powder, don't you think?"

"Well, yes'm."

There came the powder, dusted on with a large puff. There came the subsequent prickle of nostril and the blowing of nose.

"Remember, Alice. The collation at eleven o'clock."

"Yes'm. Us folks all got word of that."

"Oh! . . . Fowl. Have the kitchens enough fowl? I counted the joints and the fish, but I forgot the fowl."

"No worry, ma'am. A chicken is easy wrung by the neck and plucked and spitted. If y'all has appetites, they'll be filled." Alice cackled like a chicken herself.

"This means so much to me, Alice."

"We all know, ma'am."

"It must go properly."

"Ain't any jubilification here ain't gone properly, long's I can remember. Now you best stop frettin'. There—you meet yourself. See?" A swift black hand, a small mirror. "That's Lady Washington, ma'am, and we all ain't failed you yet. Now you best go down. Ain't any more I can do. You're like a belle, Miz' Washington."

Martha went down. She descended the landing-leveled stairs, sure in the knowledge that she had been a belle once, but surer, now, in the knowledge that she was chiefly a mother. She wanted, tonight, simply that things should go smoothly. Her days as a belle were past. Her days were being lived for Jacky.

He and Nellie were at the foot of the staircase, greeting the guests as they came in. She kissed him lovingly. "I want you to have a wonderful evening, dear," she said.

A tuning of fiddles came from one of the rooms. Guests clustered at her—the Bassetts and Lewises and Dr. Craik and her brother-in-law John, and Mr. Mason. Formal coats and formal dresses, wigs and silk stockings, and wafting scents of perfume and powders, and murmured voices, and a great gentility of manners and attire.

For she was having, tonight, a triumph of her own. Jacky had been elected an assemblyman of Virginia.

She watched with pride-dewed eyes while Jacky, smiling, wearing his new dignity with a becoming gallantry, led Nellie to the center of the floor for the opening minuet, then accepted for herself the arm of Burwell Bassett. Burwell was married to her sister, and it was correct that he should proffer his arm, though his nature was somewhat retiring. He and her sister lived very quietly, farther south toward Williamsburg, at a distance that made visits between their home and Mt. Vernon infrequent. He didn't dance too well, but Martha knew that she would have to overlook that. Being her sister's husband, he was closest kin, and the first measure must be his.

She noted from the corner of her eye that House Alice had two small boys in tow and was setting up the punch bowl in the room across the hall.

The beginning strains of the music—the bowing—the circling elegance, hand in hand.

"Since I saw him last," Burwell murmured to her, "Jacky seems to have matured."

"Of course," she said. "The father of two children." But she was pleased that Burwell had observed. She had observed, too. Jacky was growing, was less scatterbrained than he had been. The horses he rode didn't so often come into the stables smeared with foam and nearly broken-winded. He paid more heed to George's letters to him, reading them over a second or third time instead of cramming them into his pockets.

"This election to the Assembly should be the making of him," she said.

She enjoyed a minuet because it gave chances for snatched talk. The moments when the hands met and arced, and the dancers were face to face. Earlier, as a girl, she had found those moments useful for flirtation. She found them useful now for the joy of discussing Jacky.

The candles were bright. She curtsied and moved forward in a stately billow of skirt. "What does George think of these politics?" Burwell said.

She'd known he would ask that. Everyone would ask it, of course. She had her answer ready. "George thinks Jacky inexperienced," she said. "But I can understand his concern."

"Jacky in the Assembly might involve him somehow?"

"Oh, no, Burwell—not at all. He's not thinking of himself."

A figure of the dance took them apart, a tread which must be daintiness and grace, and then brought them together again.

"No, Burwell, he's thinking of Jacky. George loves Jacky like a son. He doesn't show it as much as he used to when Jacky was younger, but I know."

"Agreed. His little jaunts with Jacky to Williamsburg. Beaming all over when they stopped by our home."

"Sometimes he's too severe. Sometimes too soft. But—"

"Too soft? This from you?"

"Oh, I'm too soft always," she admitted happily. "But George always has Jacky's best welfare at heart."

The minuet's gentle tide flowed back and forth, washing intermittently between their brief undertones.

"We'll hope George's heart can keep Jack's head for him," Burwell said. "He doesn't look brash at the instant."

Martha, turning her head a little at the next circling measure, found Jacky quickly with her eyes. He was squiring Nellie faultlessly, and looked as if he had one foot in paradise.

"George is merely anxious that Jacky shouldn't plunge into anything that might be beyond him, and so be hurt," she said. "He would like him to go slowly—for Jacky's own sake—until he has proved himself. But with this election, I'm sure he has."

Burwell sensed her finality, and tactfully shifted ground.

"Do I hear that Queen Marie Antoinette has sent you a magnificent gift?" he said.

"Rumor, I'm afraid. If she has, I've not seen it."

"Oh. A pity."

"I'm just as glad. I shouldn't know what to give her in return. She probably considers us as half savages. They say Dr. Franklin is quite a curiosity at Versailles."

"In that case, send the perfect gift."

"What?"

"Scalps."

"Burwell, that is scarcely funny."

"I beg your pardon," he said.

She forgave him at once, but they finished the dance in a tacit silence.

In the intervals between dances there were polite forays around the punch bowl, where men spoke of crops, and the loss of the British tobacco market, and whether Empress Catherine of Russia would come in against King George as the Hollanders had done, and the rising costs of living and the falling off of the Continental paper money.

This last was the item that hit most strenuously home.

"Someone has remarked," Fielding Lewis said, "that inflation is now at such a pace that a trotting horse can just about keep up with it."

He grimaced at Jack, who was standing beside him at the punch bowl, and Jack laughed. It was a laugh of courtesy to his Uncle Fielding, who was trying to make light of something that was not light. He guessed, from the wry inflection, that Uncle Fielding was trying to keep up courage; he'd loaned upward of thirty thousand dollars to Virginia, dollars he wasn't likely to get back; and the works he'd built for manufacturing army muskets were draining his money away like blood from an open wound. But Jack respected him as the husband of Papa's sister, and as a man who acted on his convictions. He was polished and had cultured tastes, but was not especially well. Financial strains might have something to do with that. Yet he kept turning out the muskets.

"Yes, sir," Jack said, "that about says it. We've had to give up our privateer, Papa and I. Can't afford to build her."

Another of Jack's uncles had been listening. John Augustine Washington. He lived near Fredericksburg, across the river from the Lewises, on the old family farm. A slow-spoken, smiling, congenial relative, but rather ineffectual. "Money's dropping two or three per cent a day," he said. "Well, privateering isn't what it was, Jack, as an investment."

"Papa says land is better."

"I shouldn't wonder. When will you be moving to your new house, Jack?"

"Oh, several years maybe. We've started on redoing it, but it's hard to get workers and materials. We want to keep near Mama, besides, while Papa is away."

"Speaking of lands," Fielding Lewis said, "you'll be in the middle of them in the Assembly."

Jack nodded quickly. "The western lands."

Uncle Fielding shot him an approving squint. The boy was far from stupid. "Yes."

"Papa's talked to me about those. In his letters, too."

"Your papa," Uncle John said, "is almost fanatic about the western lands. My God, the land grants we handed out to soldiers after the French and Indian War. Your papa about pushed the governor into that. But people didn't want to move out beyond the mountains just then. Too risky."

"They'll move in due course," Fielding Lewis said. "The question is which state has the best claim to issue grants—Virginia or Pennsylvania?"

"Virginia," Jack said.

"The Pennsylvanians are arguing that," Fielding said.

"Virginia," Jack said. "It's our right. Damn it, Papa tracked those lands before Pennsylvania knew they were there. He surveyed most of 'em himself."

"And you propose to say that in the Assembly?"

"If I have to, Uncle Fielding."

"I don't object. The record is clear. But be careful of saying more. Differences between states are better settled, just now, by cool voices than hot heads. The Ohio country has had enough bloodshed already."

"Uncle," Jack grinned, "I'll make you a promise. I'll never speak in the Assembly while closed windows heat me up."

"Scalawag," Fielding said.

George Mason drifted by. He took a glass of punch from the Negro boy who was serving at the punch bowl, sipped politely, and wiped his lips with a snowy cambric handkerchief.

"Well, Jack," he said, "we've known one another for a long time."

"Yes, sir."

"I'm delighted with your new stature. You'll soon be learning what it is to be a legislator."

"I'm getting the feel of it already," Jack said. "I've just been called a scalawag."

Mason laughed and said he'd be lucky if he was never called anything worse. "Remind me, Jack, before I leave tonight. I've brought you some reading you might like to dip into. As a neophyte in the Assembly, you'll want a smattering of political theory."

"Oh, Lord, I hadn't bargained on that," Jack said in mock dismay. But he saw Mason was serious, and put on another tone. "You're very kind, sir. What reading?"

"Rousseau, for one."

Jack wrinkled his forehead. "French, isn't he?"

"Yes, but I have him in English. You'll find him instructive. We have shaped much of our independency around his ideas."

"The 'natural man,'" Uncle Fielding struck in, a bit dryly, perhaps. "He believes in the perfect goodness of man's nature."

"Then he's never met *me*," Jack said.

Mr. Mason suffered this to pass without comment. "He also believes in the rights of man," he said. "As does Voltaire. I've brought him too. Together with some of the speeches of Mr. Burke in the British Parliament. The speeches are rather garbled gazette versions, but they carry Mr. Burke's governing philosophy."

Jack swallowed, and tried to look grateful. His effort at it, he could see, amused his uncles. He could only say, "I'll do what I can with them, sir. I'm afraid I've never been a great reader."

"Shovel into 'em, shovel into 'em, Jack," Uncle John said, and laughed. Uncle John wasn't bookish himself.

"Oh, I know I'm putting you to a chore, Jack," Mason said, unruffled. "But I shouldn't wonder if you're capable of it. It will cost you some head scratching and searching of mind, I don't doubt. Yet since you are to sit in the councils of state, the councils of freedom, the cost will be cheap in the end. For you will remember that a decent freedom has always to be paid for."

"For God's sake, Mason," Uncle Fielding struck in again, putting a congenial arm around Jack's shoulder, "don't speak of payments. They make me think of my debts. This is supposed to be a merry evening."

"Quite," Mason said, with a sly pull of humor at his lip corners. "I was about to propose another glass of punch all around."

". . . and he's fetched all these books and speeches," Jack said dramatically, while the musicians tuned up once more. "And he expects me to read 'em. What am I to do, Nell?"

"Read them, silly," Nellie said. "Now go dance with Mama. I'm promised to Uncle Burwell."

Nellie thought that if the life spirit rose any higher in her she would burst. She could vision her two daughters at home in their beds, baby girls, sweet dears, little nestlings to be cozened and wrapped in security and love. (She and Jacky were trying for a boy, now, and she had a suspicion that she might be pregnant again—a week or so would tell.) And she could vision Jacky in the Virginia Assembly, taking his place as a man in the world, with decisions to make and votes to cast, and possibly speeches like those of Patrick Henry's in the years gone by. She looked for Jacky in the gold glow of the candles, and saw him across the room, laughing with Mama and Auntie Bassett, and knew from the toss of his head that the laugh was genuine and all was well.

It was long past ten now, and the supper would be served shortly, and they would dance until the early hours, and she would adore it.

She was still enough of a girl to realize that she was lovely in a paneled gown of sienna-and-white satin, with topazes at her neck and ears. There were not too many young people tonight, but she gave that no mind. Plantations in Virginia didn't provide young people now, what with the war, but her uncles had been joyfully attentive.

She found herself, during this break in the dance, seated alongside Aunt Betty Lewis. Aunt Betty had some of Papa's frame and much of his character. Conversation must be made, though light conversation was always hard with the Washingtons: they were sincere and affectionate, but words didn't come easily to them.

Aunt Betty had asked after the children, and congratulated her on Jacky's election, and then fallen silent. Nellie felt it her duty to make talk.

"How is your mother, Aunt Betty?" she said.

"As well as she imagines herself to be," Aunt Betty said. "Which isn't of the best."

"Oh, I'm sorry."

"No need," Aunt Betty said. "Mother takes sorrow to herself. I think she enjoys it."

There was a rawness there, as of flesh cut open, that gave Nellie pause. She could only think of saying, "Of course, I've never met her."

"And probably never will. She's not sympathetic with your papa, Nellie—your papa George. She thinks she's ailing, and she complains. Oh, look, there's Martha with a cluster of men around her. Isn't that nice?"

"Mama is a beautiful woman," Nellie said.

"You should have seen her when she married your papa. Oh, well, the calendar creeps up on us."

Nellie set herself against this woefulness. She didn't feel woeful. This was a festive and glittering night for her.

She said, "Mama dances divinely. Why wouldn't the men cluster? Men are so simply the same."

Aunt Betty darted her a look. "Discover that, my dear, and you discover the secret. I'll tell you something. Never let Jacky out of your sight."

"Because of women?" Nellie said. "I don't think Jacky—"

"Because of mothers," Betty said, and her ample bones seemed to spread. "Because of one mother who'll spoil and another who'll alienate. Fielding and I live a biscuit throw from Mother Washington, and I can tell you my life is fiendish. Mothers never let go, even when they pretend to let go the most. Why are the men clustering around Sister just now? Because she's motherly."

"She might also be—ah—attractive," Nellie said.

"Sex, my dear?" Betty said, with a lift of eyes.

"Well—" Nellie said.

"Sex is merely mother love in another channel. For men, let's say. For women, it's an impulse—a home building. Do I bore you?"

"No," Nellie said faintly. "Not at all."

"George and I," Betty said, "with brothers John Augustine and Samuel—when they can—and Sam's now on his third wife, and drunk, and in debt, keep Mother in comfort. George has written to me, I've wrote to him, that Mother should be looked for. But yet, Nellie, she doesn't appreciate. She doesn't. She wants more. What more? No one can say. I certainly can't."

Nellie felt a flood of embarrassment. She had had inklings of this, that the Washington family was less than harmonious, and had seen signs of it, in intimate times, from Jacky's father. But she had not known the gulf went so deep. She stuttered for words.

"But your mother," she said, "certainly likes Papa's victories? as Monmouth?"

"Pays no heed to them," Betty said. "Thinks George should stay at home and tend his fields."

Nellie could think of no reply to that.

The music tuned up again, and Betty rose and laid her hand in the crook of Mr. Mason's elbow, and Jacky's bowing handsomeness was in front of Nellie and she practically flung herself at it. She needed him. He was her husband, and young and forthright, and the clouds Betty Lewis had pulled down on her mustn't be. She told herself they wouldn't be. Stepping to the dancing floor with Jack, she promised herself that hers would be the best kind of motherhood. With Jack beside her. The best, the best . . .

The candles had burned almost to the sockets. But they could be renewed.

Nellie dallied her body close to Jacky during the dance. She felt his throbbing response.

During the next weeks Nellie gave a good deal of thought to what Aunt Betty had said. Not so much the actual saying of it as the reflections from it that played around her. She was maturing, as Jacky was, and could see more clearly now, with larger perspective, the contrasts of life and people, and the mingling pressures on human nature. The way people affected one another, and bent and formed each other's characters. She had been murmurously aware of this, as of someone standing outside a locked door and hearing voices, muffled, within an inner room. Aunt Betty had turned a key and flung the door open.

Little pieces that had been scattered before in her mind, hardly impinging on her consciousness, began to harden now into bits of mosaic and fall into place.

She had never felt her father-in-law was stern. He had never been stern with her. He had always paid her affection and deference and an unstrained easiness of relationship, looking to her often to make some spry remark in answer to one of his, and then both of them laughing. And she could remember, at Mt. Vernon, in the short time after her marriage, before the war, his sitting at the table for a pair of hours after the meal was eaten, breaking almonds in his thick-knuckled fingers and joking and smiling and keeping the table merry. Even at Cambridge, at the Boston siege, he'd been like that. Drawing the whole company to him, winning, lovable. Yet she knew he could be cold as rock. She knew he had an awesome temper. She knew he lived by inflexible rules. Now Aunt Betty had told her why.

He's had no warmth from his mother, she thought, nothing but being thwarted as a boy and nagged as a man. And she thought immediately afterward, but I know his mother was convinced she was a good mother. No mother really wants to be a bad one.

And then her mind came to Jacky, for here was the contrast Aunt Betty had, wittingly or unwittingly, sketched for her. Jacky had never been thwarted. He wasn't rock-cold, and he never lost his temper. He'd been coddled like a precious cockerel. He'd never had to kick against the pricks, batter his head against the wall of Virginia society, and hope for a royal commission from London. Jacky had been protected, adored, guarded, all his life. She had no quarrel with her mother-in-law. She had married Jacky, knowing these facts and overlooking them because she and Jack loved each other so much. Her mother-in-law didn't interfere with their lives nor their household nor their children; she only wanted to know that Jacky was somewhere in the offing, somewhere where she could put a hand on him and pour out her worship for him.

That was the contrast. What had her father-in-law, what had her husband had from each of their mothers? From one, too much severity; from the other, too much sentiment.

It's almost dangerous to be a mother. It's frightening. But to see the dangers is the most important. We have to steer, and steer, and understand. Thank you, Aunt Betty, thank you.

And Jack, taking more after his father now and shucking off some of his indolence, got out of bed in the early mornings and rode around his lands, playing the part of a supervisor and master. He'd not have admitted he was playing a part, but Nellie and the field hands knew better. Master Jack would throw himself into anything that took his imagination. Yet he gave an impression of sincerity. And when he had come back to the plantation house, and had had his breakfast, he bored into his accounts and into the books Mr. Mason had lent him.

Nellie observed this from a soft distance.

She said one day, at last, "Jacky, are you learning anything?"

He took the book he was reading and slapped it shut and spun it across the desk top. "You can't tell me," he said, "that the county men who go to the Virginia Assembly know this stuff."

"I wouldn't be sure they do," she said.

"Then why should I? I can vote on roads and funds and army quotas and raising militia companies and such without all this."

"Mr. Mason may think you'd vote better if you read it."

"Nell," he said, and was all unaffectedness now, "I don't read properly —this philosophy jaggle. I keep thinking that here's Papa out in the country with an army, and here's this Frenchman Rousseau doesn't know a haw from a hackle about our country, and here's Patrick Henry and Jefferson with so damned many words but never saw a battle, and—oh, the devil with it!"

The great gap between the idealistic and the actual was just commencing to open at Jack's feet.

Nellie had a sense of this. She said, "But, Jacky, these men have to point the way for us. We have to know what we're fighting for, don't we? I mean it's a mental thing—it's a—"

Jack got slowly to his feet. In his riding boots, his coat, the crop that he gripped from the table, he was suddenly, in his youthful way, impressive.

"Papa knows what he's fighting for," he said. "He doesn't need the others. He knows. He knows."

Nellie repressed a giggle. It was rather a delighted one. This was what she had been hoping for from Jacky.

Martha sat on the Mt. Vernon terrace, in the shade of the columned portico, and read a letter from her friend Mrs. Bache, of Philadelphia, who was Dr. Benjamin Franklin's daughter.

> *Everything seems at stagnation here* [wrote Mrs. Bache] *except society. There is nothing done in the war. Your dear general is face to face with Clinton across the Hudson, and both seem afraid to move.*
>
> *Have you heard of General Lee? You know he demanded an inquiry after Monmouth, saying the general had insulted him—and the inquiry—a court-martial—came down on him hard for disobedience and unnecessary retreat and arrogance in his demand to the commander in chief. He's been dismissed from the army for a year and is not like to return, and has fought two duels in his spite, one with that exquisite John Laurens, and is wounded, and now gives it out to the gazettes that General Washington seeks his assassination. I think the man's mad. But isn't Laurens a hero?*
>
> *For the rest, quiet, except—oh, I must tell you. General Arnold cutting a most elegant figure in the city. Drives with carriage and*

four, dines at the best houses. And is squiring Peggy Shippen about. What she sees in him, I don't know, still crippled as he is. Yet he does have a fire. I admit to it. I've met and spoke with him. A most engaging man, really. But the Shippens, as you know, are Tories. The battle for liberty makes strange bedfellows, does it not?

You may be passing through this city to join the general for the winter, as no one can think the war will be concluded this winter, and I should be more than happy to have you here for as long as—

A step on the flagstones was an interruption. Martha creased the letter and put it on her lap, her hands covering it.

"Yes?" she said.

It was Lund Washington. Near kin to the general, modestly, neatly dressed. He supervised the additions to the house, managed the plantations, the hands, and the business of the estate. His face held a look between that of a bookkeeper and a farmer. An ingenious earnestness. A face to be trusted.

Because Lund so seldom intruded on her, Martha felt a trifle startled. "Yes, Lund?"

"I beg your pardon, ma'am."

"Not at all, Lund. Sit down."

He pulled a chair under him, sat awkwardly.

"What is it, Lund?"

"I—I opine it's money, ma'am."

"Oh?"

"You know money's been falling."

"Yes, I've heard."

"We've done what we can. Barter—oh, the general suggested that, long since—calling in loans. I think your son, Mr. Custis—Jack—will be better at calling loans. The general's loans have been mostly so personal that he's not likely to get much from them. Unless he wants to press at law, and I doubt if he will. He's too kind at heart."

Martha sniffed something in the wind. "Very well, Lund," she said. "What do you have to tell me?"

"We're going to have to sell, ma'am."

"Sell?" This was all new to Martha. Mt. Vernon had always sold: tobacco, wheat, fish, whatever the plantations produced. "We live by selling, don't we?"

"Not this kind," Lund said.

"Lund," Martha said, with a flurry of impatience, "will you please stop being cryptic? When must we sell, and what, and how, and why?"

House Alice and her two boy shadows appeared on the terrace and brought gingerbread and decanters and glasses—sherry for Martha, Madeira for Lund, and disappeared. Martha and Lund tasted. The Potomac flowed beneath them.

She said, "Well, Lund?"

He said, "The old ways that prospered us have been breaking down. Confidence has been breaking down."

"I know that," she said. She could have fallen back, for confidence, to the Monmouth battle which had elated her so, but the doldrums that had persisted since rather prevented. Small use for her to talk of her private trust when the public one was being sapped away. She signed to Lund to go on.

"In short, ma'am, if we're going to live we've got to sell."

"You've said that already, Lund. Sell, sell, sell. What must we sell?"

"It's desperate because of the inflation, ma'am."

"Very well. But what?"

He screwed himself to the sticking point. "Slaves, ma'am."

For a moment she could not comprehend. "Slaves?" she said.

"Ours, ma'am."

She stared at him, feeling her spine go rigid. "Our Mt. Vernon folk?"

He tried to soften the blow. "Not many of them, ma'am. Only a few."

"No," she said, and her voice thinned and grew hard. "No. No, never." The rigidity of her whole body prickled with horror.

"I fear it's got to be," Lund said, gently as possible, suffering from the suffering he had to inflict on her. "The sale of a half dozen would bring in cash money."

"Do we require cash money?"

"Yes, ma'am. No one will stir foot any more without cash."

"Our folks can make most of the things we need."

"Most, but not all. And for the others—it's cash. Hard money. The Continental paper is so low it's hardly worth a—" he brought himself up in time. "You could almost paper a barbershop with it and be no worse off," he said.

"Lund," she said, and lifted one of her hands from her lap and steadied herself by it on the table that held the wines and gingerbread. "Lund, you cannot do this. You must not. Write to the general."

"I've written, ma'am. And he's answered. He's agreed we must sell slaves if we have to. There's no other course."

"Sell off Mt. Vernon folks—"

There wheeled through her mind the swift images of Mt. Vernon and its people, a succession of images in which she saw herself giving medicine dosings in the field hands' quarters or standing by Dr. Craik over fevered black-skinned moanings on a cot, or helping at a childbirth that had come on unexpectedly in the middle of a hapless night. Images of dark, sweet familiar faces, strong backs and adept hands, loyalty and a taking part and a rootedness. She thought she was going to be ill.

In spite of her hand clutching at the table, she swayed in her chair. Lund was on his feet. His arm was by her.

She grasped at it. "Sell—oh, Lund—"

"Try to think of it as a kind of condition of the times, ma'am."

"But I can't think—thank you, Lund, the queasiness will pass. A sip of sherry—"

He handed her the glass. She took a very small swallow. Her throat wouldn't accommodate anything more.

She put the glass from her. Lund took it and set it on the table.

The grass beyond the portico was smooth emerald. The trees cast lazy shadows that bulked insolent on complaisant green. The wide Potomac was as it had been yesterday, and was now, and would be forever in the years to come. A pale-sifted clatter of mules' hoofs on the houseway's gravel, and muted Negro shouts, and the breaking of laughs told that the harvest was being gathered in to the home buildings and storehouses.

The air had the smell of cut wheat and animals and the tidal sludge and working men and the lazy tang of wood smoke from the kitchen chimneys, and all should have been or seemed so well.

X V

Spring-Summer, 1780

Nellie sometimes wondered if the war would ever be won.

Or lost.

The thought of losing made her shiver. Her father-in-law either dead on a battlefield or hanged if he were captured, and maybe Jack in prison as his stepson, and her own father likely, and for herself and her mother and her mother-in-law, who could predict, unless the families could escape over the mountains and into the west. A losing would snap all threads.

Then she would know that she was having moods because of her pregnancy.

She would know her moods and thoughts were evoked by the kicking form inside her. The small and enlarging life she felt there would go on, by God's mercy, long when she was laid in coffin; and the structure of her mind and body now were given to create and preserve, not destroy. Blind destruction, the clash and clangor of the essentially unessential, of men, woman-born, who ranted like veriest children and like children tore and clawed each other in a stupidity of senseless folly, nagged and confused her. To love, to give birth, to set the feet of an offspring, be it boy or girl, honorably to the upward, eternal road—wasn't this the ultimate, the mortal touch toward the hem of immortality's garment? The law and the prophets for the puniest tribe of nature? "Be ye fruitful, and multiply." . . .

But you gave birth to a child brought forth in the fogs of war and destined for something no one could foretell, no one could forestall by shout or the fling of an arm in a half night. You launched a child as a ship is launched, and the winds and the seas snatched it from you.

That your heart might be involved, might be happied or crushed, was beyond your power to govern.

Yet every cradle was a seed pod of the human race, and each woman who had known a man was an Astarte.

A memory dashed over her—for she had read her *Hamlet* under her father's eye—"These are but wild and whirling words, my lord."

She knew they were. And realized, of course, that she must be a little out of her head. People from day to day, not pregnant, didn't think that way. When her baby was born things would turn clearer, simpler. She would have only the plainness of her love and motherhood then.

Meanwhile she could read by the signs in Jack that he was as perplexed, as rudderless and uncompassed, as she.

The war was drabbling out, taffy running slick from a spoon, to the cold platter of another winter. Mother Washington had left for Philadelphia, to go on from there to the army encampment at some place called Middlebrook, in the Jerseys. As Mrs. Bache in her letter had predicted.

"It sounds drear, Mama," Jack had said.

"Well, we can dance to keep warm," Martha had said. "It might seem frivolous, but we'll dance."

She had had the bristle of an old campaigner, and was there now, and sending letters home. The letters did not say a great deal, and Nellie concluded there was not much to say. The snow months would pass. They would have to be lived through.

She and Jack had a quiet Christmas. The snow was kind to them, and they drove to communion service at the Pohick church, where Jack's stepfather was a vestryman, and Jack loitered on the church path afterward and talked politics and crops and the money collapse and she loved him and felt he was really in the way of carving a future.

If only he could slough off the last bits of his spoiledness, of wanting something because he wanted it as a right and not as anything to be earned, and of that temptation to larking that led her to suspect that on his trips to the Assembly his hours were as many with cards and companions around a tavern table as in his seat as a delegate. If only he could take on the bodied vintage quality that one could savor occasionally even among the younger men.

But Jack was not vintaged. Though she found again, as her time came on her, that he was devoted and affectionate and concerned over her.

It was all too complex for her to grasp just now. She shut her eyes and felt the first familiar spasm of the labor pains and hoped things would all come for the best.

The baby was another girl. They'd been hoping boy, and Nellie lifted a pallored look to Jack and said, "I'm sorry, Jacky."

Dr. Craik was with them, giving instructions in a low voice to a servant at the door. He'd attended at the birth, as he'd done for the second daughter. For the first, Nellie had gone to her parents' home in Baltimore.

"Sorry?" he said crustily. He was a man angular and strong-boned, as if he had been put together with adzed beams, wearing a coat the color of slate, with no wig and dark brown hair whitening at the temples. He'd pulled Jack's papa through a touch-and-go bout of fever on Braddock's march a quarter century ago, and was physician to Mt. Vernon and most of the county families. "Sorry? What for? Women, ma'am, are the earth's salt. Take 'em, take 'em."

"There's no other choice, is there," she whispered, "when they're here?"

Jack said, but she saw him hazily, "Nell, it's all right. Now we have one we can name for you. The other two for our mothers, this for you."

She was wrenched and weak and agonized with the curse of Eve, but she managed a smile, clasping to herself the wonder and mystery of the womb and lighting her face for the lover who had been in her arms.

"We'll call her Eleanor, honey," Jack said.

"Show her to me," Nellie said, and they put the baby beside her and she snuggled it. "She looks like you, I think," she said to Jack.

"That could be," Jack said, and he chuckled. "I had something to do with her being here."

"But men want men-children," Nellie said, and the tears came silently because she still hurt so.

"Balderdash," Dr. Craik said gently. "Masculine ego riding on an outmoded theory of virility. Takes just as much virility to produce a female as a male. Your little bundle there is no slur on Jack's maleness. She just proves his potency."

"He wanted a boy," she said. "And Jack's always gotten what he wanted." It took them some time to comfort her.

Mr. Mason came to pay his respects. Mr. George Mason, of Gunston Hall. There was a soft electricity among the servants, and a flutter by Nellie, and Jack selected a suit of maroon velvet, and silk stockings and the shoes with the rectangles of brilliants, and a starched and ruffled neckcloth of sunned whiteness, with lace edges, and a flowered waistcoat and the handkerchief drooping elegantly from the pocket and the cuffs of his shirt also of lace, and went to meet him.

Nellie joined him at the top of the stairs. She was wearing yellow, in brocade, and had at her ears the topazes he liked, and nothing at her throat, which left it so clean and virginal that he could have nipped his teeth to it. But he didn't, since eyes were watching him.

"You'll be for dinner, Mr. Mason?"

"With apologies."

"Nellie, dear—"

She was out of the room after that, mapping what was to be done in the household, returning shortly.

The two men had Madeira.

"Mr. Custis, sir, your health."

"Yours, sir."

Jack drank rather deferentially, this being the man who had inked the document of rights that Virginia now stood on, and who hobnobbed with Henry and Jefferson.

"To your success as an assemblyman, sir."

"To yours as—as Mr. Mason, sir."

The preliminaries, the accustomed graciousness, Tidewater style.

They sat, and Mr. Mason asked after the children's health, and theirs —"though that becomes a mere courtesy question as I look at your complexions"—and said it was too bad Mrs. Washington had to be shuttling out of Mt. Vernon once more, the war promising plainly to stretch itself into this coming winter, too.

"I hold her to be a plucky little woman," he said.

"Mama likes to be with Papa as much as she can," Nellie said. "He hasn't been home once since all this began." She stopped for the briefest of pauses, and said, "She feels so strongly that so many of his old friends aren't rallying to him as they did, and are letting him carry the whole load on his shoulders."

Her voice was sweet, but Jack held his breath. This was very close to accusing the early leaders of Virginia patriotism of staying snug by their fires while Washington fought their battles and camped in winter snows.

Mr. Mason, however, merely nodded gravely, as if understanding that Martha and Nellie couldn't know all that passed between headquarters and Virginia mansions.

"Some of us have no training in the military way, ma'am—and some of us no nature for it," he said. He followed this with a soft chuckle. "I can tell you in confidence that your papa was rather more than relieved when Patrick Henry gave up his colonelcy of a regiment and left the warrior's trade to others. But all of us are in continual correspondence with him."

"Oh, Lord, letter writing," said Jack. "That's worse than a dozen bullets."

"But just as effective at times, Jack." He resumed his gravity for a moment. "It often seems to me that our entire revolution is being nursed and kept alive by the pens of a dozen letter writers, your father included."

Then he changed the subject.

"Are the improvements to your new property progressing?"

"Progressing? Good God, no. They're at neap tide, standing still, like everything else. Except prices."

"We have to wait," Nellie said. "We can't afford the costs."

"I can sympathize," Mr. Mason said.

"But it's a beautiful spot," Nellie said, to keep the talk from turning gloomy. "Higher above the river, even, than Mt. Vernon or your lovely Gunston Hall, and on clear days I think you could see almost to Baltimore, and when we can build as we plan I'd like the house just to nestle on the hilltop like a sky bird settled there for a quiet rest, and it won't be as big as Mt. Vernon or the Hall, but big enough for Jacky and me and the family."

"And for a good wine cellar," Jack said.

"What's your acreage?" Mr. Mason said.

"Eleven hundred acres. And we were lucky to get 'em when we did. We couldn't begin to, now. Way over our heads. Lord, have you even bought a coat lately?"

"Near a thousand dollars," Mr. Mason said.

"Don't you men take on so," Nellie said. "I paid five hundred dollars last week for six yards of ordinary chintz."

"Mr. Mason, what's the answer to it?" Jack said.

"Perhaps for the Congress to stop its money-printing press and hand the quandary back to the states. Unless Lafayette can use his face-to-face persuasion on King Louis to grant us a loan. Though that could be little more than a drop in the bucket." He didn't emphasize Lafayette's mission to France. It was common knowledge. "You must have heard discussions of ways and means in the House of Delegates."

"Lord, yes," Jack said disgustedly. "Talk, talk, talk. Besides, I don't know much about money." He said, "Papa thinks *my* answer is more land."

"I should judge he would," Mr. Mason said with a trace of smile.

"He says—well, wait, sir, I've just had his letter—I'll read it to you."

The letter was on his desk. He jumped up and strode into the library and got it. When he returned Mr. Mason was walking easily up and down the room, his hands behind his back, and Nellie was thanking him for the books he'd lent to Jack, the Rousseau and Voltaire, and was saying that Jack was trying to make headway with them, and Mr. Mason wore a quietly quizzical look.

"Here it is, sir," Jack said, and they both took chairs, and Jack picked out the bit he wanted, and read.

"'A moment's reflection must convince you that lands are of permanent value; that there is scarce a possibility of their falling in price, but almost a moral certainty of their rising exceedingly in value. A pound may not, in the space of two years more, be worth a shilling, the difference of which becomes a clear loss to the possessor and evinces in a clear point of view the force and efficacy of my advice to you to pay debts and invest in something that will retain its intrinsic value.'"

Jack dropped the letter abruptly and slapped his velvet-covered thigh. He was more exasperated than really angry.

"Pay debts!" he said. "Good Lord, Mr. Mason, does Papa know what he's talking of? People don't *want* to be paid."

"Quite logical, with the money so diseased." Mr. Mason spoke equably but looked condolence.

"They run from being paid. They want to stay creditors. They know a thousand-dollar loan is only worth a hundred now in cash."

"And may be worth much less, as your father says. He's correct in his advice, Jack."

"But I can't follow it. I've been to three creditors of mine in the past three days. The first wouldn't let me repay him—said there was no need, he had no intention of calling in the loan. Damn it, I couldn't stuff the money down his throat, could I?"

"I doubt if he could have swallowed it all, and there would have been grounds for an assault action," Mr. Mason smiled.

"The other two must have gotten wind that I was paying," Jack said, "and they went into hiding—plain hiding—and pretended they weren't home. They were downright avoiding me."

"Clearly."

"Then what am I to do?" Not so much a question as a burst against the times. A burst against something to which Jack had been born and couldn't control.

"The best you can," Mr. Mason said, and his look was not only condolence now, it was compassion. "But your father is right on both counts, the debts and the land. And speaking of land," he went on, and made a parenthetical gesture of his arm toward Nellie, "Mrs. Custis twits us with inactivity, but you know of Colonel Clark."

"Clark?"

"George Rogers Clark. The Virginian."

"Oh—yes."

"Kaskaskia," Mr. Mason said. "Stormed and taken through waist-high frozen water. Then Vincennes. Our western fringes cleared. Come now, you've heard."

"Months ago," Jack said.

"Just so," Mr. Mason said, and he glanced at Nellie. "Possibly the most far-reaching action yet, the most significant. Mr. Jefferson and Governor Henry set it afoot. I had something to do with it. But that's of little consequence. It was a major stroke."

"Was Papa told?" Jack said. The question was rude, but Mr. Mason's suavity, his bland assurance of knowing what was best for everyone tended to rub Jack on the raw. "Papa's the commander, isn't he?"

"In his area," Mr. Mason said, judicially and with aplomb. "Which is the east. He can't cover both east and west."

"Oh?" said Jack. "He's sent General Sullivan to the west, hasn't he? To break the Indian nations and stop the frontier raids."

"But not Vincennes," Mr. Mason said, unruffled. "Jack, these things are for older heads than yours. So if there should be a bill presented to the Virginia House to make the Illinois region a Virginia claim, might I recommend that you favor it? Seeing that a Virginian drove out the enemy and freed the territory to us."

"Well, maybe, sir," Jack said, and couldn't define why he found himself aggressive. "But there are other states pushing west."

"As—?" Mr. Mason said.

"As Maryland," Nellie said sweetly.

"Oh, Maryland," Mr. Mason said. "A lot of damned rascals, trying to grab land."

"And the Virginians, Mr. Mason?" she said.

Jack guffawed. "Nellie's a Marylander, Mr. Mason," he said.

A bricky flush came to the cheeks of the politico-philosopher. "My humblest, ma'am, my humblest," he said. "I'd forgot."

"Not at all," she said. "Not at all, Mr. Mason—as long as Jack votes sensibly in the House."

"Well, I've voted for four geldings for Papa," Jack said. "That should be sensible. The rest is mostly lung breath."

"But this western push?"

"I'll vote for it if you ask, sir. But what will Maryland do?"

"Probably oppose us."

"And the states are supposed to be united," Jack said.

"It is a supposition," Mr. Mason said calmly, "but unfortunately not yet a reality."

A disturbance at the front door took Nellie from the room. She re-entered shortly, and whispered to Jack.

"Him?" said Jack. "Oh, Lord."

"He told Cully he'd come on business."

Jack half rose from his chair, looked at Mr. Mason, grinned slightly, and plumped down solid again. "Let Cully say I've a private visitor and mustn't be disturbed."

"Jack, if it's business," Mr. Mason said readily, "please disregard me. I don't want to be a hindrance."

Jack's grin widened to its fullest. "You're no hindrance, sir, you're my salvation. The man's only business here would be to pay me the debts he owes me." He broke into a laugh. "I can be as good at avoiding as the rest. Cully'll shoo him away."

Mr. Mason laughed, too. It was a matter of laughing or of letting go in a complete despondency.

Martha had tasted the cup of triumph and the cup of bitterness for five years, and was ready to taste them for another five, if needful. But, without being sacrilegious, she devoutly wished that her cup of bitterness didn't include Mrs. Gates.

For Mrs. Gates had descended again on Mt. Vernon. This time, ostensibly as the last, stopping in on her road from Philadelphia to the Gates plantation over the Blue Ridge. Knowing that the road leading to Mt. Vernon was hardly the shortest one between the city and the Gateses' home, Martha could only suppose that Mrs. Gates had brought something to crow over, though she couldn't guess what. From Philadelphia, where the Congress was re-established now, any important news would have to go to George, in the northern Jerseys with the army, and then delayingly south in his letters to her, before she heard it. Mrs. Gates, new-coached from Philadelphia, would undeniably have it first.

Since guessing was useless and Mrs. Gates effusive and inscrutable, she ordered dinner for them both and put aside rather testily House Alice's predictions of woe, and made conversation afterward, according to the best Virginia rules, under the Mt. Vernon portico, where both the Gateses had sat once in a year so swiftly bygone, and the summer sunset was tender on the Potomac.

Time had not changed Mrs. Gates, nor custom sweetened her intimate society.

She began with Peggy Shippen.

"Married to General Arnold. Do I say married?—I think she caught him. He's a prize catch, especially for a Tory family. You've met her, haven't you?"

"Once or twice, rather formally," Martha said.

"An engaging little baggage, but a schemer," Mrs. Gates said. "Oh, she was sweet as honey, hanging to her husband's arm at the reception they gave General Gates and me—for they did give a reception—Arnold is scattering money like fountain water—but I think she's play-acting. I also think she's with child."

"Then it might have been a marriage of love," Martha said. She masked in her voice any sentimentalism she might have felt, for Mrs. Gates would have taloned it like a hawk in a chicken yard.

"It might," Mrs. Gates said. "But it might have its overtones too. Don't you say it's odd, at least, that Judge Chew and Mr. Tilghman are under house arrest as Tories, while Peggy's father rambles around where he will? And Tory as the other two? Well, he's father-in-law to the military commandant of Philadelphia."

"I don't know," Martha said mildly, for mildness was on her that evening, the sky-arc like soft blue slate and the smells of earth from everywhere. "You see, Mrs. Gates, I think it best I should keep aloof."

"The last thing a woman should do," Mrs. Gates said.

"Oh, not entirely aloof. Next month I shall go to Philadelphia to be with Mrs. Bache, and we'll try to raise a subscription fund and stitch shirts for the army. But I don't like politickings."

That final sentence had a firmness that warned Mrs. Gates. She was a quick woman, far from being a fool. She said, "And your recent winter at Morristown, my dear. Was it very bad? Why, here in Virginia the Potomac froze. The coldest winter in years. You must have suffered."

The shift of tack was transparently obvious. Martha smiled to herself. She would give Mrs. Gates something to exclaim about, something to exercise her gift for insincerity. She would tell the truth.

"We were worse than at Valley Forge," she said factually. "More snow, more cold, and less food. And expecting a possible raid from New York any minute. There were nights when some officer lad would come back to the camp from sparking, and he would be a little drunk, and the sentry would shout, and all the regiments would turn out in alarm, and soldiers would pound into my bedroom, five to a window, and stand so as guards for an hour or more while the wind blew snow over my quilts and I shivered with my head under the covers."

"Private soldiers in your bedroom," Mrs. Gates said with a dry-skinned smile. "What an interesting situation."

"A shivery one," Martha said.

"But strange men in your room."

"George was always near. And the circumstances hardly made for familiarity."

She purred a little to herself. She had given Mrs. Gates a scent that would tantalize her, but would freeze Mrs. Gates's nose if she tried to cry havoc up *that* trail.

She asked herself, resting, her elbows comfortable on the chair arms, with remembrance of the starved, sleety nights at Morristown and the slow-spreading pale violet of the day's end creeping on her from the east, why Mrs. Gates was the woman she was.

Her only answer came from something she had overheard General Lee say, that first war winter in Cambridge—and she hadn't intended to hear it but had been passing the headquarters door where General Lee was holding forth to George—"A damned bitchy female."

Mrs. Gates had only one reason to be jealous: the fact that George was supreme commander. Or the fact that George had somehow, by his plain honesty and his supreme devotion, managed to catch the imagination of the public. This imagination was something Martha had not been prepared by birth nor training to recognize, her life not having been patterned toward public contacts, but she was slowly, through the war years and the encampment winters, coming to recognize it. It permeated and it fused, like the fusing of separate drops across a pane of glass, and it encompassed all kinds—farm folk and wharf folk and traders and mechanics and apprentices and members of the Congress and governors of states, and the aristocrats of a tradition and the up-thrusted who knew no tradition—and joined them in a strange, totally unexpected, common stream down the pane under the thunderstorm of war, while the future, like some giant eagle, perched drenched and waiting for the war's cessation with the folded wings of immense flight.

These were not, literally, her thinking words; they but carried the impression that misted around her. But she knew, better, that the public could huzzah Horatio Gates but that it trusted George. George had never made a spectacle of himself, ranting and shouting at the Congress, as Gates had done to get the post of northern command. Gates's head was too full of Gates. She would rather have enjoyed clouting that head.

Yet the faction for him was still alive. And the fribbling, relentless undercurrent against George was still running. General Lee, dismissed from service after the court-martial he had insolently demanded, was eddying the current with scabrous letters to Philadelphia editors. And she supposed Mrs. Gates had been dinning Horatio's praises into congressional ears. Poor George—he had to fight not only the soldiers of the English George, but the childish pettiness and scheming of the two men nearest him in authority, his two highest generals.

Well, Martha thought, maybe Gates will see one day who's putting the spurs to him, and maybe Lee will repay the money George lent him when they rode to Cambridge.

The sunset, which they could not see in the west, was in the east a glory. A huge castle of cloud, indolent, bulbous, with idle, somnolent changing of its shape and form in slurring quarter hours of time, raised lonely buttresses in the eastern sky, like the thick and languid smoke of an explosion, tinted now saffron, now shrimp-pink, now tired carmine and soft amethyst against sweeter turquoise. The Potomac, glimpsed below, was a widening of pewter.

"A hard winter," Mrs. Gates said. "And then Charleston lost. That nice General Lincoln. He's from Massachusetts, I recall."

"He is," Martha said.

"General Gates says that if he'd never listened to the Charleston families and their entrenched pride, he'd never have had to surrender," Mrs. Gates said. "He could have abandoned the city."

"I wouldn't know," Martha said.

"We're our own worst enemies," Mrs. Gates said. "We want to dance a new dance to the rhythms of the old. Those Charlestonians were plain, plain—oh, what?—Southern mules. They kicked General Lincoln in the face. . . . No wonder. Massachusetts man. But they're paying now."

"We may all pay," Martha said, who was a little awhirl at this point. Martha said, "With Clinton and Cornwallis marching through the southland."

"Clinton will go back to New York to face your husband," Mrs. Gates said, with a kind of authority, "and General Gates will stop Cornwallis in the south."

"Oh?" Martha said, not so much in a questioning as in the swift thought that she was plumped down before footlights to watch this formidable woman pulling strings to events like a puppeteer.

"Oh, yes," Mrs. Gates said. "The Congress voted just before I left Philadelphia. General Gates is to have full command in the south."

Martha murmured something at random. She wanted time to adjust herself to the jerked strings and Mrs. Gates's fillip of a smile.

"Which is quite logical, of course," Mrs. Gates said, "after Saratoga."

The logic was reasonable and unanswerable, though Martha wished Mrs. Gates might have omitted the "of course," which had an adder's sting. At Saratoga Horatio Gates had halted an invasion from the north. Now, with Lord Cornwallis holding Charleston as a strong base and assuredly bent on an invasion from the south by way of the Carolinas, Horatio Gates was also the man to halt that one. But she couldn't shake off the instant suspicion that here was another belittling of George, a sly whittling away at him, a disregarding of him, steered through the Congress by the Gates-Lee faction. For she was morally certain George had not been consulted. If he had been, she would have heard from him about it. He seldom included military fragments in his gossipy letters to her, but the fact of Gates being considered for full southern command was too large for him to have omitted it.

She returned Mrs. Gates's smile without the iciness she felt for the woman, and looked composedly toward the cloud-castle which was enriching itself in a deep royal purple moment by moment. "General Washington will be pleased," she said. "He's wanted to see General Gates in the field again." (She could have said "your husband," but the iciness prevailed in her.) "He wrote me he was sorry General Gates refused his offer of leadership in the expedition against the Indian nations who have been massacring in New York and Pennsylvania."

"To lead a mere expedition is hardly suited to Horatio's rank," Mrs. Gates said. She forgot in a little testy flurry to call him General Gates, and Martha guessed that George's effort at preserving the courtesies toward his second-in-command had been taken ill by the Gateses. "General Sullivan is more fitted for that style of thing," Mrs. Gates said.

"Well, I leave that to the military men," Martha said.

"Horatio will start south at once," Mrs. Gates said, "and we can expect the best of news very shortly thereafter. He is taking over the management of things from Baron de Kalb—I believe General Washington sent the baron there—and I made certain you'd be delighted."

"Oh, yes," Martha said. "Yes."

"For naturally, if the war is going to be carried southward, we on our plantations will have to tremble unless there is someone to defend us. You're nearer to danger than I, aren't you? But never fear, my dear, you can come to us over the Blue Ridge—though with Horatio in the Carolinas I cannot conceive that you would have to."

"I'm certain not," Martha said, to be polite.

"He's persuaded Daniel Morgan to come back into the army," Mrs. Gates went on, "and he'll have Baron de Kalb—though I can't think he needs propping by anyone. Horatio—General Gates—is quite able to stand on his own."

"I'm certain," Martha repeated, and by now had grasped explicitly the meaning of the puppet play, the hub of plot around which the spokes revolved. The new honors, the foreordained triumphs for Horatio Gates would wipe out, as a damp rag over a school child's slate, the bumblings and fiasco of the Canadian nonsense under his presidency of the Board of War, and would bring Horatio fresh-illumined to the footlights (the strings being invisible to the general eye) and clothe him in the garments of heroism, the gold and silver of adulation.

He had worn this garment before. He was now in a fair way to wear it again. The second wearing would shine with a double luster, and he would certainly try to topple George. Given the fortune of battle, he might almost certainly succeed.

She couldn't bring herself to believe this would happen. Her wifely instinct was repelled by it, and provoked a retaliatory thing in her.

"I think the evening will be slightly cool," she said. "Shall we move inside?"

She did not until later, when she was undressing in her bedroom, see that her remark might have been ironic.

When she saw, she laughed aloud.

In late August she learned from the gazettes that Horatio Gates had had his battle. At Camden, the gazettes said, in the region of the longleaf pines in South Carolina. Only it was not a battle. It was a holocaust. Gates had been ground to bits. A thousand of his army killed or wounded, a thousand taken prisoner (he'd had three thousand men to Cornwallis' two), de Kalb keeping the field to die there sieved by bullets, and Gates galloping off past running militia, surly whipped Continentals, and shrieking wives and camp women, scuttering a hundred and eighty miles before he drew final rein.

"Oh, mercy!" she said. "Oh, mercy!"

She was frightened for the country, for what would follow in the wake of such a blow. She was grievous over the death of de Kalb, for she had known and liked and joked with the hearty baron in the winter camps. But she couldn't keep herself from a private, deliciously wicked sense of exultation. The reports made the battle a tragedy. But they also made it, in Gates's flight, ludicrous and cruelly humiliating. Honors and a future had been canceled out, at one stroke, for Mrs. Gates's husband. If Martha had been the smirking sort of woman, she would have smirked.

Small stories of the battle drifted in, as they always did: tales and rumors and hearsay, eyewitness accounts repeated from mouth to mouth and swollen in the repetition. How Gates had found himself with three thousand troops instead of the seven thousand he thought he had; how he had said, "These are enough for our purposes." How he had waved aside the plan de Kalb and his staff had drawn up for him. How he would not wait for supplies, but flung himself at Cornwallis. How, the day before the battle, he had outmarched the wagons carting the army's rum and had ordered a gill of molasses to every man instead, so that half the army were breaking ranks all night to squat by the roadside in nature's answer to a cathartic, and half the army's bowels were watery defeat before guns flashed in the morning.

"Do you know, Doctor," Martha said, "it seems almost like a dispensation. An act of Providence toward George. Suppose Gates had won? I couldn't endure to think what George's fate might have been at the Congress' hands."

Dr. Craik was at Mt. Vernon to medicine a mild summer flux that had taken House Alice. Nothing serious, but Martha always called him in when she couldn't remedy a sickness herself.

He spoke like a kindly old prophet. "Providence, Martha, is a name not to be bandied about. General Gates has been eliminated from the colonel's life, true" (he persisted in referring to George as colonel, having first known and nursed him at that rank on Braddock's march), "but Providence needn't have overdone it. I frequently wonder about Shakespeare's letting Hamlet moralize over the fall of a sparrow. Or a Divinity that shapes our ends. Pah. By the way, Alice isn't in danger. She'll recover, and lace you up for years to come."

"Thank you, Doctor," Martha said. "I'm relieved. Alice is my mainstay."

"As you are hers."

They had come to the entrance hall of Mt. Vernon, and he had his medical bag on a table and was puttering with it, packing it to suit his taste. Martha said, knowing he wanted the question and feeling that she was somehow required, by her own curiosity and perhaps something beyond curiosity, "What do you mean by Providence overdoing it, Doctor? That's an odd figment."

"Not odd at all," Dr. Craik said snappishly. "A simple 'there it is.'"

"But you don't say what—"

Dr. Craik clamped his bag shut, and turned. He was not angry, nor scornful, nor argumentative. Merely the bearer of truth. "Providence," he said, "took the Gateses' boy to itself the day before his father lost a battle."

"Oh!" Martha said, and the word spilled from her lungs with a gasp that drained her breath. "Oh!" she said. "How horrible!"

"He was dead while his father fought Cornwallis," Dr. Craik said. "I've no love for Gates, but—" the shrug of his bony shoulders was eloquent as a speech. "Your Providence has smitten twofold its lightnings. Or is it Providence?"

"I don't know," she said weakly. "Doctor, I—I don't know."

"It's not my part to philosophize," Dr. Craik said. "I've not much use for that breed. But Providence—no. Such a buffet from the fist of Providence would be sheer malice. I—well, to be true—my heart goes out to the Gateses, Martha."

"So does mine," she said. "And you say General Gates didn't know his son had died when he fought the battle?"

"No. Mrs. Gates held the news from him. Didn't want to upset him. Kept it to herself."

Martha sought for a chair and found it and collapsed into it.

"Dr. Craik," she said, "God forgive me for ever having said anything unkind about Mrs. Gates. God help me never to say anything unkind about anybody again."

She broke into tears.

XVI

Treason at Summer's End

Hercules Mulligan had sent a warning from New York City.

Because of the warning, the little official party that had trotted to Hartford in Connecticut to meet the Comte de Rochambeau had taken another road than the one they'd planned, and still another coming back. So that, while he breakfasted near the protection of the American posts along the middle Hudson, Washington felt thankful to Mulligan. The token escort of the commander in chief, which had been only six staff members and twenty-two dragoons, had not been attacked. They had dodged the enemy neatly.

He'd had no doubt, when Mulligan's warning reached him, that Sir Henry Clinton had found out about the visit to Hartford and intended to capture him on the way. Hercules Mulligan had proved to be one of his most reliable spies. The man was a fashionable tailor in New York, cutting and fitting dandified uniforms for the king's officers stationed there, and by the same token able to sop up bits of useful information which he turned over regularly to American headquarters. Washington made a mental note that if the war ever came to a successful end it would be a pleasure and an honor to breakfast with Hercules Mulligan.

The man had possibly saved his life. He hoped that Mulligan would be clever enough to prolong his own until happier times.

Yet he wondered, even as his thought went out to Mulligan, how Sir Henry had learned the road they would take to Hartford. He couldn't remember that he had told anyone about it beyond his own aides, except Benedict Arnold. And for Arnold to have let any hint slip was impossible, of course. Arnold was in charge of West Point and would be the first to keep the plans of his commander secret.

He wiped his lips with his napkin. Odd, though, that that warrior of so many battles had wanted to be assigned to a half-finished fort garrisoned largely by invalids. There was no promise of action there, of perilous fields and desperate charges and guns smoking, the things Arnold loved, unless Sir Henry Clinton moved up the river in force, something Sir Henry seemed unlikely to do, being cosy in New York and making feints toward the Chesapeake. Yet Arnold had asked him twice for the West Point command, and he'd finally granted it, supposing Arnold's old Saratoga wound was still bothering him and keeping him from service in the field. Arnold had said it was.

He told himself he must ask Hercules Mulligan to trace the leak, if Mulligan could. It was dangerous to have his goings and comings known beforehand to the enemy.

He got up from the breakfast table in a glum frame of mind. The meeting with Rochambeau had not gone well. Oh, personally, well enough —yes. Rochambeau was amiable, patient, co-operative, and friendly. And Lafayette had translated. But Rochambeau was also an agate-eyed soldier, seeing at once that the Americans were much weaker than the French had expected them to be. Seeing at once that any offensive was impossible unless more men, money, and equipment were sent by King Louis of France; and admitting candidly that the French were locked up in Newport by a stronger fleet of King George of England, and not able to promise any grand designs.

So, he knew the French position as they knew his, but his was more humiliating. For he had gone to Hartford, he and his company, with no more than eight thousand paper dollars among them; and had wondered how they would even pay their expenses until Governor Trumbull had said that Connecticut would stand the cost. "Brother Jonathan" Trumbull was loyal and perceptive.

He thought of the glitter of Rochambeau's staff—the comtes and barons and chevaliers—the Duc de Lauzun with his own legion—Count Ferson and Count Ribbing from Sweden—and sighed, and faced once again into the long road, to helplessness and hope deferred.

"Billy, hand me my horse." The often-used words, the creak of the saddle's leather as he swung up, the barrel-chested feel of his steady gelding Nelson between his knees, a soft touch of the spur.

He had Lafayette beside him again, and this was some solace. The unquenchable marquis had been a good ambassador to the French court; his results were the General the Comte de Rochambeau, money, a strong French army and a small French fleet; but all these would still be not enough, for the Americans were so weak; and Rochambeau was under orders not to move unless he acted jointly with the fleet; and two French fleets were blockaded, one at Newport, the other in the French harbor of Brest. Not precisely, he told himself, the liveliest of prospects.

But Lafayette had returned now, and was doing his best to be optimistic. "France will send more men and ships, *mon Général,* as soon as she can break the blockade at Brest. You will see."

"I'd be glad to see, Marquis," he said.

Knox was riding on the other side of him. Knox, like a great faithful dog, never complaining, strict to his duty, and, like Lafayette, refusing to be doleful in the face of dreams sinking lower and lower, and he himself getting fatter, it seemed, every month. It was a frequent marvel to Washington's mind that such a tub of a man could be so energetic. Not to mention the maimed left hand. Knox had the bull-baiting tenaciousness of a tough breed. "The French officers were damned cordial, Marquis."

"They are gentlemen," Lafayette said blithely. "And they are—how does one say?—of your party. What is the difference of a ruffle or two, a title or two, when men look to each other as men?"

"Well put, boy. No difference at all, if you've read anywhere deeply in your books."

"I am not unacquainted with the writers."

"Those fellows around General Rochambeau, I could really get along with 'em. I wonder if they know Defoe."

"*Pardon?*"

"An English writer. Not too long ago. Had a tale of a man Crusoe, wrecked and alone on an island, and what happened to him. Preposterous, but somehow a figuring of man's spirit. I sold copies of the book in my store."

"Ah? With success, I hope."

"Tolerable. But it proclaims, in its bumped and old-fashioned way, the triumph of a man—a single man, mind you, Marquis, against whatever the world can throw at him. Perhaps Mr. Defoe didn't take it as such. But I take it as such. Would you agree?"

"I've not read the book," Lafayette said.

"Your French nobles understand a man's spirit," Knox said. "They are not overpractical, they are not in hysterics for liberality. They balance. They have humor. I like them."

The horses footed on, raising small dust along the highway and observed only by the low and confusing ridges spawned into New York by the Berkshires.

"I am rejoiced that you like them," Lafayette said. "And will you still like them when they give their thoughts about General Gates?"

"Oh, him," Knox said, with a hugeness of disgust.

"They do not think much of him," Lafayette said.

"Nor I," Knox said. "He's lost the whole south army. Always felt he would."

"That Gates. *Mon Dieu,* to run those many miles."

The two had been talking across Washington's saddlebow, or behind his shoulders, as the shift and flow of the horses took them forward or backward. Washington said, now, "Can we judge him, Marquis, not having been there?"

"To be sure we can. With mockery. You would not have run away so."

"Who can say? Gates had a rabble of militia in a scramble to the rear —any rear, as long as it would give them safety. The Continentals, thank God, held ranks and left the field whipped but unbroken. But the militia swept everything back." He was thinking—the thoughts were conscious and crystal-clear—of other panics he had seen: the blinded, stampeded, riddled soldiers of Braddock along the Monongahela; the fleeing soldiers on Manhattan through a cornfield, where his aides had kept him from throwing himself on the enemy in a rage of despair.

"Gates had to get far enough away to rebuild his army," he said.

But it sounded hollow. Lafayette's look told him so. So did Knox's.

"I've done too much of the same sort myself to feel like mocking at Gates," he said more firmly. He paused, and added, "Mrs. Washington writes me that his son died at home just in advance of the battle."

A lull in the talk held for several hundred yards.

Then Knox said, "What will happen to him? The usual court of inquiry?"

"It's most likely. And I mean to see that the court acts in the fairest way possible."

"Has he been fair to *you?*" Lafayette said with one of his incisive Gallic shrugs. "You could demolish him."

"That's beside the point, Marquis. I can't take joy in being vindictive. Besides, I don't think all the fault lies with him."

"But *mon Dieu*—where else?"

"With the militia, partly," he said. "They seldom fight well. You can't ask it of them, coming raw and shambling to a battlefield. Gates had chiefly militia troops, not used to being charged at. And the fault lies even more with the Congress, which is afraid of a large and regular army. It won't vote us the amount of long-term enlistments we need in the Continental line. It continues to depend on militia. No militia will ever acquire the habits necessary to resist a regular force, and I've not seen anything, ever, to justify a different opinion. The disaster to Gates comes from saying that men can take up arms overnight. Damned lie. Who's to train them overnight? Teach them to wheel and maneuver and obey orders? Who's to toughen them for battle overnight? Even Steuben couldn't accomplish that." His voice had been rising, like his temper, and although he heard Knox, by his other elbow, cluck approvingly, he realized he was being too loud in the quiet of the day. He modified his voice, and laughed apologetically, and said, "Well, Marquis, you've been getting part of the lecture I've read to the Congress. The lecture, sorry to say, had to go by letter. We have to shore up the southern states somehow, and I've not time for orating to the Congress. . . . Knox, what of Greene for the south?"

"Couldn't be better."

"And for quartermaster general? Pickering?"

"Not too much a friend of yours, but probably good."

He thought this over. The switch came about—or was it opportunity in disguise?—because the Congress had attacked Greene, accused him of making private profits as quartermaster general, and Greene had promptly and furiously resigned. This left the cleverest general in the army free to operate again in the field. And Pickering as quartermaster was a possibility, acceptable. The man was an administrator. Whether he might snipe at Washington was hardly a matter of consequence now. With Gates's fall, and Lee dismissed, the snipers had no rival to promote.

"I'll talk with both," he said to Knox.

Then he heard Lafayette, on his left, the boy's voice a music of harshness, an inharmony of young disillusionment.

"The Congress, the Congress, the Congress." Lafayette was brooding. "Always the Congress. And always the Congress is wrong—and must be pleaded with, or cajoled. We have the word in French, and now I know it in English. Must be cajoled. Or else scolded or frightened into being right. What is this Congress—a Moloch? A creature built of high priests? A something with fiery maw that demands sacrifice? . . . *Non, non, ce n'est pas juste.* I will speak more simply. It is a something that keeps itself in office not by thought and wisdom and a vision for the liberty, but renews itself by groveling to all who can get drunk at your elections and make a vote. I am dejected with this liberty. It is getting nowhere. Americans do not want it, and the Congress has the mind of a spitting infant."

Washington let the marquis' emotions boil, knowing they would cool eventually. He couldn't contradict them, in honesty, having felt the same emotions too often.

Lafayette's feelings were their own fuel. The disappointment of his French compatriots, of Rochambeau and the eager, crusading nobles at the tottering bones of American effort, seethed in him. Rochambeau and all the French had been won by the character and personal charm of his beloved general; but that couldn't lessen their doubts as to what was going to be accomplished in this new world. He fumed. He was responsible for their being here.

But he had wit enough to keep his anger from spilling entirely out of the kettle. That would produce nothing. His voice in his next pronouncement was less harsh, more insinuating.

"To win this war, *mon Général,* takes a single leader, I think. A one man to say 'Puff!' to the Congress and blow it away. Or knock the Congress heads together and say what shall be. Do you know the history of Rome?"

"Indifferently," Washington said.

"But you will have heard of the Rubicon."

"I have."

"The Rubicon was small," Lafayette said guilelessly, as if he were musing to himself, "but Julius Caesar was very great."

Washington drew rein. The little cavalcade stopped. The aides and a few junior officers and escorting dragoons took the opportunity to lift their hats and mop their foreheads. Some of them sneezed in the dust that spiraled lazily.

"What do you imply, Marquis?" Washington said, sitting his saddle at complete halt and boring his eyes into Lafayette's.

The youngster didn't flinch. "Exactly this, *mon Général.* It needs one mind, and one voice, to order affairs as they should be. All is now futility, a conflict of little men trying to make themselves big. That is not freedom, and freedom can't be won so. It becomes plucked at, and unweaved, and it falls apart—as when wives pull stitches from a stocking. To win this war there should be a single voice, a very loud voice that can be heard. Yours would be heard, *mon Général.* The war should have a Caesar, and not a Congress."

The boy was so patently sincere. And so patently wrong. Washington looked at him with a kind of compassion. The marquis saw freedom with European eyes, eyes that had never known a frontier. He'd never seen an American forest, or a river like the Ohio. Or owned slaves and wondered what to do about them. Or seen the whooping, fruitful, barrel-bunging nonsense of an American election.

He wished Martha were with him. She could put Lafayette straight.

Yet he'd caught mutters from his officers that ran along the same line: he should push the Congress off the driver's seat and take the reins himself. The mutters didn't appeal to him, repelled him. The fight was not being made to replace one autocrat with another. True, he could march his army into the Congress and dissolve it—as Cromwell had done—but that would be an evil thing. A betrayal of trust that went against all his nature. He was fighting against tyranny, not for it, and personal tyranny was an evil weapon he could never bring himself to use. He would as soon have hunted a fox with poisoned bait.

He was silent so long that Lafayette said, "Have I offended you, *mon Général?*"

"No," he said, and chose his answer with care. "No, Marquis. And it is far from my heart to give any offense to you. But I shall ask you not to bring up this subject again. I find it very distasteful."

Then, with Knox gaping in wide approval and the marquis blushing along the fair skin of his cheeks, he put the cavalcade forward again and took the talk to lighter matters.

They passed through Fishkill, drawing nearer the Hudson. And he had a mind to turn off and visit the invalid camp near there, where men were sent when shirts and stockings and breeches and under drawers were so ragged they would have been indecent in public. But he wanted very much to end his trip that night, and rode on.

He had only fifteen miles or so to go when he met the Chevalier Luzerne. That French officer was returning from a look at the American camp, with a report to Rochambeau. He was voluble and insistent. Such a happy chance! Would the general pass an evening with him at the nearest public house? They could trade news and ideas and explore deeper into ways of perhaps making some campaign. Washington didn't see that talking would do much, but he didn't want to seem brusque toward an ally.

They spent the night at an inn.

His aides looked grumpy the next morning, facing the fifteen-mile ride to Arnold's headquarters before breakfast. They thought that sort of thing a hardship. It didn't bother him.

"Colonel Hamilton, will you take the baggage and go forward? Tell General Arnold I'll have breakfast with him at the Robinson house."

"Yes, Your Excellency." Hamilton was owl-eyed, but prompt.

The rest of them mounted a little later. "And gentlemen," he said, "remember that you'll not only get a tasty meal, but a glimpse of General Arnold's wife. We're riding toward a reward—not only of the belly but the eyes."

He thought they perked up somewhat after that.

The miles were easy. Not far from the Robinson house a lane traced down toward the Hudson. He turned into it.

"*Mon Général,*" Lafayette said, "this is not the way to General Arnold."

"It's the way to some earthworks, Marquis," he said. "I'd like to look at them. You can come or not, as you choose. If all you young bloods are in love with Mrs. Arnold, go on ahead. I'll join you soon."

Lafayette laughed, and stayed with him. So did the others.

It was midmorning before they reached the Robinson house, a rambling wooden home belonging to a Tory who, Washington thought, should have been on the patriot side, being originally a Virginian. He and Washington had been casual friends before the war. Now Robinson was leading Tory troops against the Americans, and his Hudson River home was forfeit.

David Franks was waiting on the porch of the Robinson house. The David Franks he'd known in Philadelphia, with sister Rebecca and Peggy Shippen. Major Franks now, junior aide to Benedict Arnold. He'd seen David occasionally, while Arnold had been hovering around headquarters, asking for the West Point post.

"Well, David? It's good to see you. Will you tell General Arnold the landslide has descended on him?"

"General Arnold, sir," Franks said, his voice uncertain, "has asked me to make you his apologies. A message called him to West Point a short time ago. He should be back in an hour or so, I think."

"Very well. Why not?" Washington said. "Colonel Hamilton was to arrange for breakfast here."

"Yes, sir, he has, sir. And we'd want to put on our best performance. But Mrs. Arnold is ill, upstairs, and Colonel Varick, General Arnold's top aide, is felled by a—well, you know, sir—the seasonal complaint." He attempted a shy grin.

Washington met it square. "Nothing new to a man playing war, David. It happens to all. Just set out the food and everything's well."

It was a sturdy breakfast, though rather too much of the New England style to suit his taste, and he rowed up and across the river in a barge afterward to West Point.

A small tangle of officers received him at the landing stage. The tangle was predominated by John Lamb, colonel, one-eyed, an artilleryman who'd been a Son of Liberty in the riotous early days in New York City.

"We do our best, Your Excellency, with what we have. Come and look at us, sir."

But there was a gap among the welcomers. There was no Arnold.

Again, Knox was near, and Lafayette. He looked from one to the other. "Where is the general, Colonel?"

"Not on the post, sir. I've not set eye on him this morning."

"No?"

"No, sir."

Washington gave another look at Knox and Lafayette. They'd heard the oddly disturbed David Franks say Arnold had gone to West Point. He thought it strange that Colonel Lamb had not seen Arnold, stranger that Arnold was not at the landing stage to greet him. But it could very well be that Arnold might be involved in something that needed his attention along the outworks.

"Will you direct the inspection then, Colonel, if you please. We'll doubtless catch up with the general during the rounds."

He could not quite shake off the feeling of oddness, though, as he climbed the steeply jagged road to the rough heights where the forts squatted above the Hudson, to have Arnold missing from the reception at the river's edge. Beyond the qualities of dash and flair in battle, Arnold usually had a soldier's respect for military etiquette, and knew this visit was to take place today. Besides, Arnold was one of his favorite officers. He had to strengthen himself against a twinge of personal hurt.

But when he reached the scatter of buildings that made up the post, and began his tour, any feeling was smothered by numbness and any hurt by a blank horror. He forgot the neglect of etiquette at the river's edge. The neglect of care, above on the bouldered plateau, was too much worse. It leaped at him from the first fort he entered.

"We've named this Fort Arnold, sir," Colonel Lamb said.

He nodded shortly, puzzled that the place should be still not completed, and angry at a way of building that laughed at doom. What there was of walls, or bastions, had been woven together with wood, with dry fascines, planks and bundles of fagots where there should have been good stones topped by earth; this nest of jackstraws was no better than a ready bonfire; a few mortar shells would set it blazing.

The sight dismayed him. "We'll go on," he said.

They climbed high among rock outcrops and hacked tree stumps and came to Fort Putnam. As they got near he could see wide, toothless breaks in the line of *chevaux de frise* that was supposed to shred an enemy charge and keep the walls from being carried by assault. He walked silently through one of the breaks. The walls, it seemed, hardly called for protecting; the eastern wall, facing the river, had fallen down and lay haphazard where it fell. No one was doing anything about replacing it.

Rocky Hill overstrode this fort a few hundred yards away. Guns set there would be in a commanding position. The hill was an obvious prize for capture, and should be a strong point. Yet he found the ramparts there, when he ran his eye along them, were weak—so weak they could be taken in a matter of minutes.

He always tried to put the best face on things in front of his officers and men, but face or pretense were not possible here. Wherever he looked he saw rot, and lack, and disrepair. His officers saw, too. Their muteness said they did. The facts were too glaring for concealment.

One other thing he saw—the scarcity of men. There were curiously few of them. Arnold had eighteen thousand militia to repair and strengthen and defend West Point, but as the inspection moved from fort to fort, from barrack to redoubt to outer work, Washington could not reckon that number on the place.

"The garrisons seem thin, Colonel," he said to Lamb, "and I'd thought more masons and carpenters would have been busy."

"The masons and carpenters have no orders what they should do, sir," Lamb said. "As for the troops, many of them have been sent off on detachments."

"What detachments?"

Lamb's single eye met his. There was a chafed, disturbed glint in it. "I'm uncertain on that, Your Excellency. I wasn't told. Guard detachments, as a guess, to form scattered outposts. I do know that two hundred have gone as woodchoppers."

"Woodchoppers!" This burst from Knox.

"Yes, sir." Lamb stood stiffly.

A kind of throttled gasp ran through the group, quickly stilled as Washington said, "Keep on with the tour, gentlemen. I want to learn all the conditions at this post for myself. Keep on. We'll meet General Arnold somewhere about."

They did not meet him.

For two hours they walked and viewed and questioned, made their notes and compared their opinions. During the two hours they had no word from Arnold and no sight of him. No one at West Point had seen him that day.

It was with an empty feeling, one of clouded puzzling, that Washington stepped into the row-barge for the return trip across the Hudson. He sat immobile, his hands on his knees and his cloak loosened about his shoulders, while the oarsmen pulled against the upstream current of the tide. The westering sun slanted along his neck and cheek, and slicked the river surface into beauty.

The beauty held no comfort for him, nor the rising upswing of the hills ahead of him, hugely green in the afternoon, darkened here and there, in gullies and moist ravines, by heavier green wedges of spruce and juniper and pine. The hills lay like slumbering things, broad and inert. They did not menace, they were too old for that. They were rounded by ages, imponderable, indifferent to men who would never be able to tame them into farmlands or till their ancient soil. They took no part in comings and goings, in wars or revolutions or human scrambles.

The massive lift of Anthony's Nose, on the east bank, the heavy-lidded somnolence of Bear Hill and the Dunderberg on the west could have obliterated river, and barge, and men in a shrug. Behind him were the formidable heights in back of West Point, and beyond those to the north, the still-higher buttresses of Cro'-Nest and Butter Hill. The river cut deep and twisting past their feet.

He did not like these Hudson Highlands. Last winter, in headquarters at New Windsor, a few miles upriver from Butter Hill, he had thought the whole prospect very gloomy. He missed his Virginia fields, and detested the fogs that rolled on damp mornings like gray snakes reaching from the sea to blind and loop the river valley in their coils. Or, sometimes, fountained by a change of breeze, streaming up the sides of the hills like great inverted watercourses. It did not surprise him that the Dutch had made legends about these Highlands, nor that they had not been conquered. He knew, for he had been told by the Yorkers, that in occasional autumn sunsets the Highlands draped themselves in a purple not to be matched, an ineffable glory of color and tenderness and awful majesty. But he had not seen this himself. He had seen only the grisly winter, and the reluctant spring, and the hot, brilliant, humid summer. The mid-Hudson folk were accustomed to these as he was accustomed to the auburn-earthed tranquillity of his Virginia Tidewater. They were accustomed to the rearing, bearded hills, and to the fractious winds from the hills that held vessels for days on end at anchorage in Peekskill bay or off New Windsor, waiting for fair passage through the river gap; and they made allowances for the long roundabout roads they had to take through the narrow valley slits they called cloves when they skirted the Highlands by horse or wagon. They were accustomed, but he was not. He was new to this region, as the hills were old.

Yet he drew something from the motionless dignity, the immemorial grandeur, that surrounded him there on the Hudson. He could not be sure what it was. But he knew that his barge seemed an infinitesimal speck; and that its smallness, while it humbled him, brought him also to a kinship with all the small things that make the life of men: things propelled, as he was now, on a deep and fluctuating estuary whose beginning and whose end were far hidden from sight, the one in a common tiny source, the other in a wide, eternal sea: things only partly grasped, less partly understood—a clear day or a gentle rain, storms, or a snatch of loveliness, a child's laugh or the tears of a woman. And other things larger, more sharp, as hunger, and love, and ambition and guilt and cowardice, money for the pocket, and the nerved need merely to keep direction in the current. These were also the portion of all men. The hills proclaimed it, silently re-echoing Sinai and the mountains of wisdom. Men could be brothers if they but knew.

For some reason that evaded him he thought of Cain and Abel. They had been brothers. And there had been murder, and hate let loose in the world. Treachery and death. His mind was not in a state to ask why.

The hills set up a slow murmur of breeze, the first music of their longer shadows. There was no stirring among their trees, along their huge slopes. Only a faint soughing, and bright ripples on the water surface like the silvery backs of herring.

"This river here," Lafayette said. "She could growl, in growling weather."

"Yes," he said. He spoke rather curtly, and they left him alone.

His thoughts traveled to Arnold. They had been on Arnold all the time, actually, but he had been hiding the fact—or possibly trying to diminish it with the scene's immensity. As the shore inched closer, though, and the landing for the Robinson house, he knew that he was worried, unaccountably worried. He went over in his mind his recent talks with Arnold. He felt the general had come off poorly in his investigation by the Congress; but he also felt Arnold had been hounded too brutally, too vindictively, by the Pennsylvanians for his record as commander in Philadelphia. Then Arnold had asked him for a sea command. Remembering Arnold's hornet-like defense of Lake Champlain he would have granted it, except that he needed him more with the army. There was already a man, a John Paul Jones, who seemed capable of breasting a ship into some sort of guerrilla battle. And Arnold was too adept on land, where there were few enough adept generals, to be spared to the sea. So he had refused. And then Arnold had asked for West Point; the first time casually, in the Jerseys, the second time bluntly, while the army was crossing the Hudson at King's Ferry a few months ago. He had refused again, suggesting an active command, and he recalled, now, how Arnold's face had fallen and how Arnold had answered not a word.

Was there any clue in all this? Was there any indication before he had finally given in to Arnold's plea to take over West Point that anything might be wrong? He couldn't think so. Arnold had fought tenaciously for the revolution; he had been wounded twice in battle, heavily, and was still in the service when many officers had dropped out because of bad health, or discouragement, or their harassments by the Congress.

He went over again the conditions at West Point. They seemed to him slovenly, careless, suicidal. But with Arnold nowhere to be seen, nowhere to be questioned or brought into council to map his tactics and defend his planning, the conditions remained an enigma. He couldn't explain them.

He was impatient until the barge grated on the shore sand.

His horse was waiting for him, with Billy Lee, and he ripped a willow branch for a riding whip, and rode uphill at a smart pace for the headquarters.

Hamilton was at the headquarters, brisk and looking active.

"Any word from General Arnold, Colonel?"

"No, sir."

"Very well. The inspection took longer than I'd thought. Dinner will be late."

He went into the room that would be his office for the night. He wished Arnold had sent some message. He dropped his hat on a chair.

A knock at the door. It was Hamilton. He had a bundle of papers in his hand. "For you, sir. From Lieutenant Colonel Jameson, near Tarrytown."

"Thank you."

He opened the bundle. With a dark sense of impendingness his mind slowly took in what he read. . . . A man by the name of John Anderson seized on the road to New York . . . Papers found in his stockings, and the papers forwarded herewith.

He leafed them in his hands, studying them. A pass admitting this John Anderson through the American lines. A report of the troops stationed at West Point, and the strength of the place. An outline of artillery positions there and the number of guns. A copy of the minutes of his own last council of war, which had been sent to Arnold. . . . Two of these papers were in Arnold's own writing.

"Another letter, sir," Hamilton said.

He opened this, too, with fingers that shook a little. A note from Colonel Jameson, enclosing a written confession. He read the confession. John Anderson was not John Anderson but Major André, John André, adjutant general of His Majesty's forces in America. The major wrote with engaging frankness. He'd rowed ashore from the royal man-of-war *Vulture*, anchored near Peekskill, to meet someone who would give him information; had been led, unknowing, inside the American lines; had been given, or forced to put on, civilian clothes for his return to New York; and had been captured at Tarrytown on his way to the city. He asked for safe conduct because he had been betrayed—the words burned out at Washington—"into the vile condition of an enemy in disguise within your posts."

Washington's brain spun. Only one man could have given a pass to "John Anderson." Only one man could have arranged such a meeting with a high-ranking enemy officer.

He paced the length of the room. Came back again. The willow branch was still in his hand. He chewed at it. His world was crashing.

"Hamilton!" he said, and didn't recognize his own voice. "Harrison!"

Hamilton was there, Harrison burst in.

He said, "Arnold has been dealing with a king's officer. He seems to have met with him. Can you tell me anything more?"

The two aides stared at each other. Washington caught their stare. They didn't know, even as insecurely as he did, now, by a horrible instinct, what had happened.

Harrison, the older of the pair, calm-speaking, diligent, said, "Your Excellency, what can we tell?"

"More," Washington said thickly. "More. Anything!"

Hamilton gave a faint cough. He was sensitive, he had imagination. His mind was already working far ahead. "Sir, at breakfast—at General Arnold's breakfast—I was here—you recollect? I rode on in advance of you—"

"Yes? Well?"

"A paper was given him, some sort of note. From this Jameson at his command post. General Arnold read it and turned white. A minute later he excused himself and disappeared. I think he went to the river landing. He said he was called to West Point."

"Where he was never seen."

"Yes, sir. But the ship *Vulture* was in the river. The one that brought Major André up."

"Take saddle, Colonel," Washington said. "Take saddle, and try to cut Arnold off. He's a traitor, and fled to the enemy. I'm certain."

"Yes, sir." Hamilton wheeled, darted away.

Washington stood. "Oh, God," he said, "whom can we trust now?" He put the willow branch to his teeth again, unconsciously, gnawing and worrying it. He stalked the room, back and forth, back and forth, Harrison watching miserably. "Whom can we trust?"

He walked in an utter blackness, in a hot numbness that dried and scorched the last juices of his spirit.

"Arnold, of all! Arnold!"

A sweat dew beaded Harrison's forehead as he watched his chief.

There could be no consolation. No mutter of words. This was an agony that had to be suffered and endured.

"Can Hamilton catch him? I want Arnold fetched here—alive!"

"Ham may somehow intercept him, sir, but it's doubtful. Arnold's been gone since morning."

"I know, I know."

He felt strangled. "Thank you, Colonel Harrison—that's all." He was out of the room, plunging toward the porch. And suddenly Billy Lee was by him, announcing dinner, and he was trying to guide his voice as he said, "Very well, Billy. Call the staff." He tossed the willow branch away on the porch floor, and the sentry stopped mechanically and threw it on to the lawn. It had been gnawed to a pulpy frazzle. He didn't see, however.

Dinner was a charade, a play-act, and something without appetite. The staff forked dull at the food. Knox was a round giant felled, Lafayette a once-virgin who'd learned rape, Tench Tilghman and Harrison and the other aides grittingly somber. For him each mouthful was an indigestible lump. He couldn't bring himself to take many mouthfuls.

But the calm, the calm, the outward calm, he knew, had to be preserved. Lost now, the whole fabric would rip and shred. In calm he had to hold the threads, in this hour, as more than in all others; in calm he had to finger the pattern of another day, another weakness or another follied call to strength.

The dinner was miserable. Spiritually, not gustatorily. There was sturgeon from the river, and a saddle of lamb. But there was no heart for these. He didn't prolong the misery.

"David, may I speak with you?"

"Indeed, sir."

He and David walked on the grounds of the Robinson house, and went straight at the matter.

The young major was keyed to a strained pitch.

"Your Excellency has every excuse to arrest me—an aide to a traitor."

"Oh, no, David. Nothing of that sort. Unless you belong to a conspiracy."

"There's no conspiracy, sir. I'll give you the keys to all my chests and so will Colonel Varick. You can see all our papers. We had nothing to do with it. We only suspected."

"Suspected?"

"A good deal of correspondence to and from New York City, sir. And absences from post we couldn't account for. And that strange order for John Anderson's pass. Should we have come to you with this, sir?"

"It's very hard to bring charges against a ranking officer, David, without proof."

"So we thought, sir. It was so monstrous and incredible that Colonel Varick and I scarcely breathed it to each other."

"But you *did* have a guess?"

David widened his eyes, and batted his eyelids in fright. He was trapped in this business.

"And you could have come to me?"

"Yes, sir."

"But you didn't because you hadn't proof?"

"Yes, sir."

"You've observed things, though. What have you observed?"

"Well, for one, sir, General Arnold seemed to think nothing when the king's ship *Vulture* sailed up and dropped hook off Peekskill. But Colonel Livingston across river at a small redoubt thought something and asked Colonel Lamb for a gun to shell the *Vulture*. I don't think General Arnold knew about that. Colonel Lamb laughed at the notion as being a waste of powder and shot, but he sent the gun, and Colonel Livingston's pop fire drove the *Vulture* downstream." He halted, thought. "By God, that could have been why André started back for New York by land—because the *Vulture* was out of his reach."

"It could be. Did you see this Major André?"

"No, sir."

"Nor had dealings with him, or with this treason?"

"No, sir. On oath."

The smooth olive face was innocent and terribly troubled.

"Consider yourself in confinement until all this is cleared," Washington said, more gently. "But I don't doubt you, David."

"Oh, Your Excellency." The fine, somewhat lyric voice almost broke. They walked back to the porch in rather an awkwardness. But Washington had satisfied himself that Franks, nor Varick either, had had no part in the Arnold scheme.

For scheme it was. Pure treason, clear and sure. The bundled letters, the secrets headed for New York inside a stocking, the open invitation for attack at West Point, and the disappearance of Arnold painted the picture all too plain. The details of it, the workings and undercover prowlings, he didn't yet know. These would come in time, perhaps by any next express that might gallop in a foam to the Robinson house.

Meantime he must protect West Point, call in the scattered troops there, man its redoubts with a full roster, and make ready for a possible enemy onslaught up river.

He went back to his office, called his aides.

"Colonel Hamilton is returned from Peekskill. Arnold has escaped us. Write General Greene at Tappan to send troops here. Wayne and his division would be best. Ask General McDougall if he is well enough to take charge at West Point. Get those damned woodcutters back at once. And call in every outpost. Don't delay. Nor lose a moment."

There was a chorusing. "Yes, sir," and "Yes, sir," and the aides were gone. One stayed. Harrison, staring at him.

He spoke crossly. His nerves were jangled. "Well, sir—?"

"It's Mrs. Arnold, Your Excellency. She's very ill. Upstairs. She's been flighty in her head all day. She raves. She keeps calling for you." Harrison stopped like a man feeling his path. "Could you—would you see her, sir?"

Washington braced himself. Mrs. Arnold. Peggy Arnold. The bright star of Philadelphia memory.

He walked to his desk. He frowned. He pushed the papers aside with a resigned movement. All the hurts, all the bindings of this war's wounds, it seemed, fell on him.

"To be sure," he said. "Yes, I'll see her."

XVII

Tragedy Questioned, Tragedy Certain

He climbed the stairs to the second floor. Colonel Varick led the way; Lafayette and Hamilton trailed behind. He smiled. Lafayette was married, and a father; Hamilton was engaged to Schuyler's daughter; but the interest of both toward Peggy Arnold was plain. They were men.

He wondered what his own interest might have been. But he was twenty years older than Peggy. Let the young ones cavort.

The problem for the moment was that Arnold had made a dash for the enemy lines and left her behind.

Sweet as she was, winsome and laughing and fructible as she was, she was now in American hands and her husband a traitor to the British.

The climb of the stairs seemed very slow to him.

"She has a local doctor with her," Colonel Varick said. He was a grayish man, just up from a sickbed, nondescript, but with an aura of decency. "We took liberty to call him in."

"Quite right. Glad you did. Is Harrison correct? Is she touched in the head?"

"Afraid so, sir."

"H'mm."

"But she keeps asking for you, sir. Otherwise I'd not have troubled you."

"As well you did."

Peggy might have some hint of what had happened. She would have known her husband's mind. Maybe here was the solution—the why, the how of her condition.

Colonel Varick, not too steadily, knocked at the door.

The local doctor opened it. He looked not too prepossessing, but efficient enough. He had the countryman's build of jaw.

"Come in, come in, sirs," he said.

They went inside the room, and Colonel Varick said, "Mrs. Arnold, ma'am, here's General Washington."

Peggy was standing near the bed. Her back was to the door, her baby in her arms. She turned at Varick's words, and stared. Her loose hair trailed to her waist.

"General Washington, ma'am," Varick said again.

She looked, and faltered backward. "No, no. Oh, no."

"To see you, ma'am, as you asked," Varick said.

"Oh, no," she said, "that's not the general. He's come to kill me."

"Peggy," Washington said. "Ridiculous."

She didn't seem to know him. "Take away the irons," she said.

"The what, Peggy?"

"The irons in Benedict's head. And don't kill my baby!"

She retreated behind the baby's cradle, which stood between her bed and the window, and looked at the cradle and bundled the baby in her arms. "The sweet precious thing," she said. "They'll murder it."

"Peggy—" Washington said once more.

She turned on him. "You're one of the plot! Hot irons to Benedict's head. I can't endure. Take the irons away. And don't kill my baby! Burning, burning!"

"Peggy—Peggy, child," Washington said, and was wordless with the gape of Lafayette and Hamilton on him, and didn't know what to say nor how to soothe.

She laid the baby in the cradle, and rocked it. "Dear God," she said brokenly, "shall I know peace again?"

"Peggy," he said, "no one will harm you or the baby."

"Baby," Peggy whimpered. She snatched it up again and took it to the window, and held a pose there, and was all at once a saintliness in martyrdom, so lovely that Washington heard the breaths of Lafayette and Hamilton. "My baby."

"But can we help you, Mrs. Arnold?" He couldn't deal in sentiment. Sentiment confused him. Babies were not of his world. But he would help if he could—big and doglike and gawky-pawed. He felt possibly if he used more formality she might grow calmer. "Can we, Mrs. Arnold?"

Her sudden whirl broke from pathos to terror so swiftly that he was not prepared for it. "No, no, no! Keep away!" Her voice shrilled. The weight of the baby seemed to have tugged at her dress. It was rumpled now and had fallen free from one shoulder and hung askew. "Murderers!" she screamed.

The doctor went to her, took her arm. The others were glad for his gentle professionalism. "There is no murderer here, Mrs. Arnold. Try to listen to us."

"There is, there is!" Her cry was torn, a wrenching to hear.

The baby squalled.

With an unexpected sinuous movement she brushed past the doctor and began to pace, back and forth, back and forth, across the room.

And now there were tears on her cheeks.

"My precious one. Cry, my darling. They are torturing your father."

Not in his life, at home or in the field or even among the audiences at Williamsburg plays had Washington ever met a scene like this. Never had he seen this grief and madness, nor felt so inadequate, nor so much of a longing to stand as a rescuer.

"Peggy, my dear," he said, speaking slowly and as tenderly as he could, "believe me. We have not been near your husband."

She stopped pacing and stared at him, her eyes very wide, her voice making little sounds like the whimpering of a kitten.

"Her mind is too distraught," the doctor said. "She cannot believe."

"But *mon Général,* this is a torment," Lafayette said. "To stand here."

"We'll make one more effort," Washington said. He glanced at Colonel Varick, whom Peggy had been seeing and talking with every day all summer. The colonel returned the glance and stepped farther into the room.

"You wanted His Excellency to come to you, ma'am. Do you remember?"

The answer was another scream. "Don't come nearer! Don't! . . . Doctor, keep them from me!"

The doctor hurried over to her again. "There, there," he said. "There, there."

"Leave my baby alone!"

She gave way to choking sobs.

Lafayette and Hamilton shuffled their feet uncomfortably, susceptible and miserable young men. Varick, in the middle of the room, looked stranded and shamefaced, like an oarsman aground on a sand bar, unable to go forward or back.

Peggy lifted her eyes, gazing vacantly over the heads. "Another woman would know. Or friends. But there is no other woman here. No friends. I am alone."

More tears welled, and fell to the baby's dress.

Washington caught at this mood before it should pass. "We can send for another woman if you wish, Peggy."

But Peggy looked glazedly at him and did not see him. Presently she dried away the tears that had splashed down on her baby's face.

"It's useless," Hamilton said piteously.

"I'm afraid it is," Washington said.

"Then for God's sake, sir—"

"Yes. We'll go," Washington said. He motioned toward the door. Hamilton went out quickly. Lafayette followed, damp-eyed. Colonel Varick, bolting from the room, fumbled for a handkerchief.

"Your Excellency," the doctor said, "if there is any improvement shall I notify—?"

"Yes," Washington said. He made a final attempt. "Peggy, my dear, you can be with friends in a few days. When you are recovered enough to travel, you'll have a carriage and escort to your parents in Philadelphia."

Peggy didn't give him a reply. For an instant she seemed to turn rigid, sensate, as though his words, these words, had reached her consciousness; as if she indeed found a kind of triumph in them. But she said nothing. She only leaned closer over the baby.

On that day he had a letter from Benedict Arnold, written from on board the *Vulture*, the enemy ship that had brought Major André to his rendezvous and had been scared off downriver by Colonel Livingston's stubby cannon. The letter had been sent ashore under a truce flag. He opened it.

> *Sir: The heart which is conscious of its own rectitude cannot attempt to palliate a step which the world may censure as wrong; I have ever acted from a principle of love to my country, since the commencement of the present unhappy contest between Great Britain and the Colonies; the same principle of love to my country actuates my present conduct, however inconsistent it may appear to the world, who very seldom judge right of any man's actions.*
>
> *I have no favor to ask for myself. I have too often experienced the ingratitude of my country to attempt it; but from the known humanity of Your Excellency, I am induced to ask protection for Mrs. Arnold. . . .*

He laid the letter down.

This talk from Arnold. This talk of a heart that was sure it was right. This bitter comparison, this nasty contrast with his own heart, his own tenacious suffering.

"If I could have him here," he said to himself, "he'd hang."

Strangely, he didn't try to examine his anger against Arnold. He didn't try to excuse him, nor find reasonable cause for what the man had done. He couldn't be judgmatic here, tempering anger with policy and human feeling as in the cases of Lee and Gates. He didn't even think about the differences in the cases. Lee had been egotistic, unbalanced, an actor strutting; Gates had been envious. But with both those men the attack had been against him personally, aimed at him as the army's leader, and he could turn, and had turned, the weakness of each to its own defeat. Arnold, though, had struck a foundation, at the basis of all he was fighting to build. Arnold had wanted to undermine not a commander but an America. And America was bigger than men or commanders because it held the total of all men's parts—their hopes, skills, failures, promise—yes, use the word—their painful, slow, and greening promise, like buds in spring, of what a country of men could be. Arnold's treason could have blasted that promise as a late frost blasts the buds. Not that Arnold's treason would have killed him, but because it would have killed America, he hated Arnold. He had never hated Lee or Gates. Those nudgings, insinuatings, those cabals and political schemings from Lee and Gates he could fend off as a human being, as someone given a task to be met and a goal to be reached. And he could do it without rancor. But for Arnold to be willing to cut the whole cause from under him. His army and his country were in peril. And Arnold had put them there.

He knew, too, that the peril was not only physical. The threat was much greater. They could face the danger of attacks and bullets. He and his army could lay down their lives. But this threat was annihilation of the future, destruction of what he and his army were pledged to achieve. He framed the achievement in his mind, seeing its dim outlines: a land, simply and frankly, where men could live and move and have their beings unfettered and unafraid. This land, these men, could not be handed success or security; that was hardly a part of the promise—for who could promise success and security to everyone without being a liar?—but at least they would have freedom of will and of voice. Arnold, of course, had obviously wanted success, and the security the king's bribe would give him. But suppose Arnold's example should spread? Suppose West Point and the Hudson should be lost, and Arnold a conqueror? The war might not be lost. But other generals, or politicians, discouraged, rapacious, might turn to this devil's medicine and use it. They could all take bribes, or make blind and childish reasons for themselves. They could eat away, as with an acid, integrity and honor, and could bring America, even if it won freedom, to nothing but a dying stink.

This was the menace, this was the ugliness of Arnold's treason. It jeered at, it flouted, honesty and honest people. A cup of poison. It was man brought lower than the beasts. How far would the poison run? He beat his knuckles together.

He couldn't ride out and collar Arnold personally. He couldn't order that shrug of the Highlands that would have slid them into the river and blocked off Sir Henry Clinton. He had only his quill and his writing desk; his aides, and the officers he still had faith in.

He began a letter to the Congress. . . .

No. He pushed it aside. The lower reaches of the river had to be watched, protected if possible. He penned a note to Colonel Lamb to go down and take charge of Stony Point. Lamb might slow an enemy advance up the river. He wrote to Major Low, commander of the Massachusetts militia, to bring the militia to full strength at speed. Wrote to Colonel Jameson, at Tarrytown, to fetch Major André to headquarters and not let him escape.

Then he took up the Congress letter again, for the Congress had to be told. The letter ran on until nearly midnight, and when he had ended it he went to bed. The troops would be moving, the orders would be carried out, and he knew he needed sleep for what the morning might bring.

Morning brought a kind of relief, in a military way. The wind had swung to the north, blowing heavily downstream so as to slow, perhaps stop, enemy ships and transports. He might have time to muster his defenses. He stood on the porch of the Robinson house, watching the dawn and praising the wind. It seemed, in his worry and anxiousness, like a gift from heaven.

"Food and water at West Point, Tilghman," he said to his dark-haired aide, the first to be up and about. "Are they supplied?"

"Ample water, sir," Tilghman said, "and pickled fish to eat."

"We'll try to do them better. Set at it, Tench."

"Yes, sir."

"Pickled fish aren't a happy belly to fight on," he said.

"No, sir." Tilghman saluted and disappeared, and a small party of horses clopped into hearing and drew up by the porch.

He saw the man in the midst of them. Smith. Joshua Hett Smith. A landowner along the river below West Point. He knew him, had breakfasted with him once or twice, in the comings and goings of the army around the Hudson. Arnold had known him. In the fog of confusion and messages and galloping expresses his name had come to headquarters as being somehow implicated.

Washington didn't even try to be polite. He was too far gone for the civilities.

"Smith," he called out furiously, "if you were helping Arnold to sell his country you'll die on the nearest tree!"

"Your Excellency, Your Excellency!" Smith set up a wailing.

"Fetch him to my office," Washington said.

Smith was one of those gross, slippery men who seem to be neither here nor there in their dealings with people. He was, besides, very talkative. Washington wasn't sure he believed him, yet he told an open-enough story, orating as he went along.

He was loyal, he swore he was loyal. He'd thought he was doing his part to get information for the army. A few days ago Arnold had asked him to take a letter to the *Vulture*, at anchor above Peekskill, and fetch Colonel Beverly Robinson ashore. Instead of Robinson, a king's officer in uniform, a John Anderson, had climbed down the sloop's ladder into his boat. He'd rowed Anderson to the river's west bank and then led him to the Smith house, and General Arnold had talked to him there. The house was outside the American lines. Presently Arnold and the officer went away. The next night they came again, and he'd crossed the river with the officer on the Stony Point ferry, with orders to guide him to White Plains. But he'd been sick with a fever, and had left the officer alone on the east bank after giving him directions about the road.

"I believed I was aiding General Arnold to have news of the enemy, sir. I believed that, Your Excellency. I did!"

Knox and Lafayette and Hamilton were in the room. Lafayette said, "This officer you left—was he then in officer dress?"

"No, sir. No, Marquis. General Arnold told me he was not really an officer—"

"*Tiens!*"

"—that he had borrowed a military coat on the *Vulture* to make himself look more important. But he could not go back to the enemy lines as an officer. So I loaned him a coat of mine."

"Who suggested that?" Knox growled.

"General Arnold, sir. You see, the *Vulture* had been fired on by then, and she'd gone downriver. We couldn't get this Anderson back aboard her and had to send him off to New York by land. Or so they said, sir. I didn't know. They didn't speak much to me. Oh, gentlemen, whatever I could do for my country, whatever I could do for our cause, I was trying to do it! A noble cause, gentlemen, one that engages the heart and grasps the mind of every patriot, one that—"

Washington broke in. "Did you lend your coat willingly?"

"No, Your Excellency. For it was a good coat. And I thought maybe an American uniform would be safer for him in that neighborhood on the east shore, there being American patrols about."

"M'mm," Washington said.

"I knew a woman, a Mrs. Beekman," Smith said, "who had an American uniform in her care. I put the idea to her. But she wouldn't give the uniform up. I had to give my coat."

Washington breathed a silent thanks to Mrs. Beekman. If she had let André use the American uniform, the whole treachery might have succeeded. André would have reached New York with his papers, and West Point would have fallen.

It occurred to him, with a shudder, how events could hang on trivialities.

"How long did you stay with the Anderson man?" Knox asked.

"Well, General, when we got to the east bank of the river there was a militia officer there. I don't know his name. This Anderson had a pass from General Arnold, and the militia officer was ready to honor it. But he was so almighty curious about our riding south in the dark that we stayed overnight with him at a tavern to make ourselves look innocent."

Washington breathed another sigh of incredulity. Chance, fortune, two people unknown and unwitting, had possibly rescued the country by putting their small sticks into the wheel spokes of this plot. He was bewildered by the twists and turns, and the unexpected human elements involved.

He said to the others, "We have a great deal to thank Colonel Livingston for, with his cannonading of the *Vulture*. And Mrs. Beekman, and that militia officer."

He said to Smith, "And then, after that night, you didn't guide your Anderson any further."

"No, Your Excellency. I—I was sick. The fever."

"If you were fevered," Hamilton said coldly, "too fevered to row him downstream to the *Vulture*, why did you agree to lead him to White Plains? A much harder task for a fevered man, I'd say."

Smith was silent. He hung his head. Then he lifted it. "You will find Major André's own uniform coat in my house, if you wish it. There's been no concealment on my part." He wiped his forehead with a thick handkerchief. "I've told you all I can, sirs. I repeat my loyalty. I'm a plain, honorable man—"

"As Brutus was," Knox said.

"Your pardon, sir?"

"Never mind," Knox said.

"—an honorable man, with no blot of treason on my conscience. Give me the rights, gentlemen, give me the rights you are striving to win for all of us. Hear me under oath, and judge me honestly!"

"The man thinks he's a Cicero," said Knox.

"Or a Catiline," said Hamilton, and seemed pleased at topping Knox for once. They were both scholars.

"Or," Lafayette said in his most melodious voice, "a Juvenal. A true historian."

And the marquis smiled, not too pleasantly.

Washington scrubbed his face with his hands. He'd got what he wanted to know, some of the pieces and fragments of what had been going on. There was nothing else to be had from this Smith. Knox and Lafayette and Hamilton obviously distrusted him, but distrust was not the way to justice. Besides, Smith's papers would be seized and read.

He said, "You'll be tried by civil court, sir, as you're a civilian. That's all for the present."

All for Smith, he groaned to himself, but not all for him. Where were the reinforcements for West Point? Where was André? He got up and went out to the porch again. He couldn't hide his anxiety.

The sound of marching feet smothered it. He looked, and saw Anthony Wayne at the head of a company. The rest of the division would have stayed on the other side of the river, to enter West Point. Wayne had made a midnight race to his support.

He jumped down the porch steps and grasped for the general's hand. "Wayne! A fabulous march! All's safe now. I'm happy again."

Wayne's face—full, strong, a little cocky but entirely affectionate, bent toward his. "We're here, sir."

"Billy," he said, "breakfast for General Wayne and me."

They ate together, and Wayne told him how Hamilton had sent on an early warning, and how the camp at Tappan had been roused, and how quickly General Greene had started Wayne's division on its march.

"They won't take us blindfolded," Wayne said, wolfing food. "We're all on the alert."

"West Point's in sorry shape," he said.

"Clinton'll be in a damned sight sorrier one if he hits us," Wayne said.

Again Washington gave thanks.

Events tumbled, trailing each other end over end. After breakfast Hamilton came to tell him Mrs. Arnold was in a happier state of mind and was ready to start for Philadelphia.

He dismissed Hamilton and called in David Franks.

"Peggy Arnold appears to have recovered," he said to Franks, "and will take coach for Philadelphia. She will need protection along the way because she is Arnold's wife and the story of his treason will have spread. You will escort her, David, with leave to visit your family. I rely on your honor not to break your arrest."

"Yes, sir," Franks said.

"Carry a brace of pistols with you, and keep an eye for danger signs when you pass through towns. And David—"

"Sir?"

"Peggy was far from rational, yesterday."

"Yes, sir. I had it from Colonel Varick, sir."

"You may find yourself with a hysterical female on your hands."

"I don't think so, sir."

"No?"

"No, sir. Her yesterday's ranting doesn't surprise me, or her quick recovery today. Good Lord, sir, she and my sister Becky have played at passions and rantings and actings ever since I can remember. For the sport of it, to entertain themselves. Peggy, sir, is what one could call a gifted amateur of the drama."

Washington was nonplused. "David," he said, "what are you suggesting?"

"Nothing at all, General."

"Very well. The coach will be ready some time this morning. See Harrison or Tilghman."

"Yes, sir."

"My compliments to your family, of course."

"Of course, sir."

And Franks was gone, and Washington threshed in the shallows of doubt. Peggy had seemed true, yesterday. Now, by Franks's hint, she was not true, was deceitful and wool-pulling and deep in treason as her husband. Had used her dramatics to get herself pitied and safely away from American headquarters.

He decided to let the comedy-tragedy run its course. If it had not already done so. Peggy Arnold might possibly be covering guilt. But he was not making war on women.

She came down from her bedroom, and Hamilton and Lafayette were solicitous beside her, and he held her fingers for a moment and would have stripped the husk of their parting to the honest and genuine core, but she stopped him with a fashionable simper. "You and all the officers have been so sweet, General." And then her coach flung a spatter of fine pebbles in the noon drizzle.

And he went back to his office, and tried to smooth the wrinkles in his thinking. Peggy Arnold, he thought. Women like that, he thought. Either she had made a fool of him, or had been a female in great distress.

He would write to Martha about that tonight. Martha would judge more acutely.

With Martha as the focal point, his thoughts spread to include all Mt. Vernon. He wondered if the kitchen wall was finished. And knew he should raise the wage of Lund Washington as manager, inflation was galloping so.

And didn't know how he could afford it. And was twisted and pulled by a succession of home images, and Jack and Nellie near at hand, and his step-granddaughters, and nothing of the war anywhere near at all, or jealousy, or ambition, or treason, and the broad sun spreading beyond the shade of the portico, and his life as he longed for it to be.

So from Peggy Arnold his mind had turned, for curative, to Mt. Vernon. Mt. Vernon was sanctuary for him, even in imagination. Martha's letters said things were going smoothly.

But Peggy Arnold could have been acting. . . .

He came to the conclusion that she must have been acting. But he kept the conclusion to himself. It was not a crisis. The bared treachery was the crisis.

Rain had begun to fall, faintly. Through the rain came a little cavalcade, a squadron of dragoons, along the telltale south road. He'd been lingering on the porch of the house, rather waiting for it. He peered intensely toward it, to recognize. To his relief, he knew the leader well. Benjamin Tallmadge, major, a smart and fearless man in the work of counterspying and intelligence; no better an officer in that service. With Tallmadge here, things would be less misted. He'd get sharper news.

With the squadron he saw, riding in the midst of it, the stranger. A young man, a very young man, like Lafayette and Hamilton; darkhaired, dark-eyed, his clothes messed and his cheeks carrying the fretted soft velvet of a few days' beard; not tall, as he sat his saddle, but handsome in a gallantry way, and handling his horse with an accustomed skill. There was a proud, gentle lift to the manner in which he held his head. In an easier situation the delicate cock of it could have been called gay. He cantered up the road with the dragoons, looking around him interestedly as he came on. A nearer sight showed his features to be as delicate, as alertly poised, as the cock of his head. His face was finehoned, a frank portrait of his character, which he had obviously never tried to conceal from the world—a sketcher, a poet, and a dabbler in pretty drama; a youth who would have friends everywhere because he could be friends with everyone; a masculine granite behind the lacy posturings of the times; a war man, after the wine and port at the mess table; a blade, tempered; a born and well-trained gentleman. He wore a faded red civilian coat, nankeen breeches and waistcoat, and elegant white-topped boots. Washington guessed that the boots, which never would have hugged calf of average traveler on the Tarrytown road, had given him away. . . . Conspiracy was never infallible. It left glaring loopholes.

The young man bore himself with unquestionable breeding and courage. He seemed not at all afraid.

It must be André.

Washington retreated into his office.

Major Tallmadge came in promptly. He might have been a few years older than André—not many—and his face was more weather-burned and had a stronger outline. A saber slapped at his calf.

"Major André is outside, Your Excellency. Would you care to interview him?"

Washington shook his head. "No. He is involved in treason. His statements should be made to the court-martial, not to me. I want to be scrupulous, carry everything in legal fashion."

"Yes, sir." Tallmadge relaxed his stance for a moment, taking a tone that was confidential without impinging on dignity. "I think you're right, sir," he added, "for other reasons."

"Other reasons?"

"May we let those wait, sir?"

"If you wish. Give me your story."

"I judge you're much in the dark, sir."

"Very much. I only know that Arnold has escaped to the enemy, and that he had offered to sell West Point to Clinton. And I know Major André was taken near Tarrytown with compromising papers. I know that I have his letter confessing that he was plotting with Arnold. But I must get the rest from you."

"Simple, sir. André was in the clothes you saw just now. He'd been inside our lines below West Point—Arnold's fault, not his, I think, for he says Arnold led him there. The *Vulture* had dropped downstream, the man Smith was to fetch him to White Plains. They stopped overnight at a tavern—"

"I understand that. A militia officer was suspicious."

"Yes, sir. Next morning Smith rode with the major to about fifteen miles from White Plains and left him. There's a tangle of roads there, sir, unmarked; the country's full of turns and little hills, confusing."

"I've been there." Washington kept his voice impassive, but he was thinking of the duty Tallmadge had done among those same hills, ferreting out enemy agents and the numberless probings from New York. And he could picture the fix in which Major André had found himself.

"The major rode for two hours. In a circle. Then he was back where he had started. By this time three militiamen were watching the road. They'd gotten permission to go out and hunt cowboys."

Washington nodded. Cowboys were ruffians who stole cattle and herded them to New York and sold them to the enemy provisioners in the city. They operated on both sides of the river. They were the usual brand of ugly moneygrubbers he and his army had to contend with. No one ever quite knew whether militiamen who hunted them did the hunting because of patriotism or out of chance of having the cowboys bribe them off. But that was no matter now.

"And they found Major André instead," he said.

"Not exactly 'found,' sir. I'd rather say Major André found *them*. When he met them he thought he was safe with Tory lookouts, and he talked so openly that it came over them they'd netted something interesting, and they made him strip, and searched him."

"And found papers inside his stockings. Colonel Jameson sent them to me."

"And sent André back to Arnold, as a prisoner."

"What?"

"Yes, sir. And sent a rider to you with a full report. The rider missed you."

"I came back from Hartford by a different road. Mulligan had sent word from New York. Clinton had too precise news of me."

"So Jameson's rider missed you. If he hadn't, you'd have pinned General Arnold."

"Arnold," Washington said. "He's no longer general."

"Yes, sir . . . But you'd have pinned him. Or even if you'd come in the night before. Damn it, Arnold walks under a lucky star."

"You say Jameson sent André to Arnold as a prisoner. That's turning over the burglar to his fellow burglar. What prevented it?"

"I'm afraid it was me, sir. I picked up the capture story, and set out for Colonel Jameson's post. I smelled something—can't say why, except I've operated so long in the Neutral Ground. And I argued with the colonel to send and fetch André back, before he reached Arnold. I persuaded the colonel, but I couldn't stop him from getting off a report to Arnold." Tallmadge shrugged. "He outranks me."

Washington began to see now the blind inversions of chance in all this involvement. Suppose Tallmadge hadn't argued and André had been safely returned to Arnold; suppose his route from Hartford hadn't been changed because of Mulligan's warning, and Jameson's rider had reached him; suppose he hadn't met Luzerne on the road and wasted a night in futile talk; suppose a fantastic number of things that would have let him catch this treason in the cradle and smother it. But none of them had happened.

With the best of intentions from local officers, and his spies, and his intelligence service, chances had turned the other way and Arnold had escaped.

"Well, we have André. God wish we could have Arnold." The rungs of his chair protested under the twist of his body. "What do you make of him, Major?"

"Frank, charming, lively. And quite free-spoken. He says if Arnold had opened West Point he'd have landed with a select body of men. He described the spot, the path to Fort Putnam, better than I could have done. He's very damn genuine, sir. Too much for his own good."

"Does he understand what he faces?"

"Well, sir, yes and no. He's his worst enemy. Things he's confided to me are enough to convict him."

"Why would he do that?"

"I don't know, sir. But the only time I've seen him flinch was when I told him Nathan Hale was my classmate at Yale College."

"Very well." Emotions must be shut off. He said, "The major is to be treated considerately, please."

"You can make certain of that, sir. I've taken a great liking to him. Everyone who talks to him does."

"I see. And now your own reasons for my being right in not interviewing him?"

"What I've just said, sir, in the main. You spare yourself a doubled anguish, if the court-martial goes against him, by not having known him and lost a piece of your heart to him."

Now, almost overnight it seemed but in point of time somewhat more than that, his gratitude was doubled, trebled, that he had never talked with Major André face to face.

This was the army's camp at Tappan, and this was his headquarters workroom, and this was a hutch table at which he was sitting, and this was a letter he had begun to Martha. He had begun it as a drowning swimmer snatching at some last straw of rescue, floundering toward some haven from a sea-vast turbulence of spirit. He had begun it as by instinct, as a man attacked flings an arm in front of him for protection; or as a soldier, riddled with wounds, will call out to his dearest name.

"My sweet Patsy—"

He had got only so far when he heard the distant fifers playing "The Blue Bird." Coming nearer. Nearer still.

Thoughts of the recent past jumbled across his mind, as they say the life thoughts of that drowning swimmer do, and kept him from Martha, and isolated and battered him.

André imprisoned—as to be expected. How else?

Sir Henry Clinton, in New York, confidently asking for André's return, since André had gone ashore under a flag of truce. The young major's honest answer that there had been no flag of truce, that he had been led unknowing, by Arnold, to within the American lines.

He, Washington, bargaining with Clinton for André's life. "Send me Arnold and I'll send you André"—that had been the gist of it.

And the impossibility of that, while there was a code of honor. Arnold would live, and fatten on the ten thousand pounds of his bribe, and André would—

Shut off the now, he gritted to himself; shut off this hour.

The court-martial, six major generals and eight brigadiers, with Anthony Wayne left out because André had once written a sarcastic ballad about him. Every fairness, every scrupulousness.

But the verdict foreordained. Tallmadge had prophesied it. Von Steuben said, "It is not possible to save him. He put us to no proof, but in an open, manly manner, confessed everything but a premeditated design to deceive. Would to God the wretch who drew him to his death could suffer in his place."

Rack and thumbscrew for the whole camp, André being so open and courteous and so friendly to everyone. Wet-eyed, the generals of the court-martial signing the verdict, "A spy from the enemy . . . he ought to suffer death," and General Greene bending his head while he wrote his name, bending it to hide the tears.

His own hand shaking until the quill gibbered as, commander in chief, he approved the verdict.

Then André's letter to him asking to be shot instead of the disgrace of hanging, and Hamilton's angry, broken plea for shooting, and Tallmadge's plea, and the wild, unbelieving eyes of his staff. And his refusal.

"The Blue Bird" on fifes had come to its nearest.

He remembered that André, as prisoner, had been fed with food from his own table, the general's table. And how André, on trial for his life, had conquered not only pieces of hearts; he had taken them whole.

He could have pardoned André. He had no anger against him, only against Arnold. He was at the moment working on a plot to kidnap Arnold and drag him back to his deserts. But André was more than a frank, luckless human being, engaged to a girl in England and engaging in everything he said and did. André was a symbol. Symbol of that penetrating evil of treason which could spread wide and far, the country's independency being in the state it was, unless punished to the letter of the law. The court-martial had found him a spy, and spies were hanged.

The fifes had fallen quiet.

He could call an aide—he could lift a hand—and it would be stopped.

Stopped . . . A weakness in the eyes of Europe, perhaps; a faltering, a fear of reprisals, a softening of will. Europe's chancellories too often took humanity as a sign of timidity. And the French, the allies. They had a heavy stake in America. The treason had been against them, too. Law, politics, military pressures kept him from lifting his hand. His stomach knotted, and sweat poured from his armpits, and down his back and forehead. But his hand did not lift. He would carry this day to his dying one. It would be forever with him. But he could not lift his hand. In the matter of law he had always been inflexible. It was his nature, it had been born in him. He groaned with the pain in his mind and belly.

A thousand people swarmed outside, around the gibbet.

He sat immobile, stonelike. The quill that should have been on his letter, that should have been tying him in this awful instant to Patsy, racing with its cry, had dropped to the table top, mutely angled in its slight arc across the paper.

He put his fists on his thighs and stiffened his body, as if in a brace. "I can't help myself," he whispered. "I can't help it. An evil is an evil, and a principle is a principle. Oh, God . . ."

This was the poacher at Mt. Vernon again. This was Jack's signature demanded for bearing money to Lund. This was his living by his rules. But all swollen now—gross, expanded into monstrosity and inexorably fatal . . . "Oh, God—" But he had to abide by them. No quirk, no fault in the slow-built granite of his being, opened at a miraculous last moment.

He jammed his fists heavier to his thighs, and suffered.

He did not stir.

Borne to him on the air, from beyond the window, came the sigh of a thousand throats, wavering, penetrating, infinitely sad and muted by a thousand infinite shocks.

He did not stir.

"Oh, God . . ."

After eternity, Tallmadge was reporting. Tallmadge had had the guarding of the prisoner and would have to report, in formality, the carrying out of the court-martial's order. Washington didn't raise his eyes, at first. But, as Tallmadge stood at attention and waited, he at last did.

"It's done, sir. It's over."

"Yes," he said dully. "Yes."

He saw the major's face streaked where he had been crying.

"Yes, Major," he said.

"When I saw him swinging in the noose, sir, I couldn't endure it."

"Your sentiments, Major, are a credit to—"

"While he walked to his hanging a little girl gave him a peach," Tallmadge said.

"Major," Washington said. "Major, I beg you—"

"A little girl gave him a peach," Tallmadge said, and blubbered outright.

Washington rose from his chair unsteadily, like a man about to vomit, and made for his bedroom, which adjoined.

"That will be all, Tallmadge. Thank you."

The bedroom door slammed. The chair in which he had been seated tottered from the push of his legs; and, tottering, fell with a noisy clatter, backward, to the floor.

The quill for the letter to Martha stayed where it was, faintly outlined in the moonlight that rose over Tappan.

XVIII

Red Sky in the Night

Nellie Custis, being frightened, as she had reason to be, nearly able to smell the aroma of burning tobacco leaves, dried, and the hot ashes of burned tobacco warehouses, and hearing the clatter of violence so near, and uncertain and yet sure with a woman's sureness, broke through the web of tradition for Southern gentlewomen. She spoke her mind.

"Jack, you're only sulking," she said.

"I am not."

"But you are."

"I know when I'm sulking and when I'm not."

"You can know it, but that doesn't mean you admit it."

"Why must I admit anything?"

"Besides, you're making yourself ridiculous."

"What's the harm in that?"

"I don't like to see my husband looking ridiculous."

"Nobody says I'm looking ridiculous."

"But they will," she said.

"Let 'em," he said. "Will you please be quiet?"

"You're acting like a child," she said.

"So are they," he said. "A parcel of children."

"Well, then, how to deal with a parcel of children. Turn your back on them?"

"Or birch them."

"M'mm. You've never been birched, have you, dear?"

"No."

"I could say 'a pity,' but I won't. But you couldn't birch the members of the Virginia Assembly."

"Hardly."

"So you came home instead."

"Why not? Most reasonable move a man can make."

"Yes," she said, and took a little time for the rest of her sentence. "Yes, dear. But who is to define what is reasonable?"

"Now see here, Nell—"

"Jack, I love you. And maybe this next one—" she moved her hand lightly across her protruding abdomen—"will be the boy you want. I love you. But I don't like to sit by and watch you crumple. I want your feet iron, Jack—not clay."

"Very well. Granted. Granted and acknowledged." They were at the dinner table in their home, and Jack had had his wine and was inclined to be slightly redundant. "Iron feet, not clay. But what are those feet to stand on, hey? If iron feet stand on clay soil, and the soil gives way, what use the iron?"

"To stay firm."

"Firm on what?"

Jack's question had the snap of a slingshot. His face was the face of a David. But his Goliath was not there.

"They're no support," he said, with a jerk of his head in the direction he had traveled from the Assembly. "Precious Virginia House. Soft as a bog. And don't know what they're doing. And stupid, besides. Nobody could stay firm on them."

"You could at least stay, then."

"And listen to 'em quarrel and bicker with Baron von Steuben when Papa's sent the baron here to protect the state? Good Lord, I'd like to have *you* try it a few times. No, thank you."

"But Jack, if you—I mean—a little more patience—"

"They're dragging at von Steuben like a coach brake. They don't like him."

"I don't have the pleasure of the baron's acquaintance. Perhaps they find him difficult."

"Of course they do. He gets angry at delays and questions, and swears in German and wants his orders carried out. What of it? He's a major general and a drillmaster, and he's here for our own help. But no—no—they get their dander up, and balk. Could anything be stupider?"

Well, possibly. Or so Nellie thought. She could sympathize with the Virginia lawmakers for not wanting a military man from outside the state to come in and tell them what to do. That had only happened once before in Virginia's generations, when General Braddock had sailed over from England to lead the forest march against the French at Fort Duquesne. And they hadn't loved General Braddock too well, to judge by the tales that had sifted down through a quarter century. But her main thought was not on the Assembly or von Steuben but on Jack. She waited only very briefly, for emphasis, before she answered.

"Yes," she said. "It would be stupider to turn your back on something that wants tending to."

His eyes widened. "Will you please to explain that?"

"It doesn't need explaining. From what you say, the baron and the Assembly are at loggerheads and nothing is being done."

"Nothing, my sweet, is a feeble word. My God, I think they'd almost rather invite Arnold back again than give in to von Steuben. Mules," he said. He gave a quick laugh, and his face took on the engaging smile it had when he was pleased with himself. " 'Mules' is the right word. Plain stubborn, and unable to produce a thing."

Nellie kept herself from giggling because she knew this trick of Jacky's, to divert criticism or unpleasant subjects by pulling out the red herring of some joke or other. She didn't intend to be diverted. Within herself she felt to a certainty that in this running away from the Assembly, Jack's character was involved.

"But something *must* be done. And someone should say it."

"He'd not be heeded."

"Say it again and again, heeded or not."

"Wasted breath."

"When something requires saying, Jacky, which is stupider then?—waste of breath or waste of conscience?"

"Damn it, Nell, you always crowd me into a corner," he said.

"You picked the corner yourself," she said.

"How?" he said.

"By walking out of the Assembly and coming home to sulk," she said.

"I'm not sulking," he said. "And now you're just back where you started."

"Where I meant to be," she said matter-of-factly. She let him dangle a moment while she spooned into her warm custard, a dessert that fitted well into the latter months of winter. "Jacky," she said then, "look into your heart and be honest. Didn't you leave the Assembly simply because people disagreed with you and you couldn't have your own way?"

His eyes flickered, startled. But he said, "Pouf."

"This story of Baron von Steuben. You're not exaggerating?"

"No. It's true."

"Then you should have stayed there and worked for understanding. Or voted, at least."

He shrugged. "Governor Jefferson has the majority on a leading string. No use."

"Why should the governor dislike Baron von Steuben?"

"Don't know that he does. He wouldn't say in so many words, naturally, and it's pretty much hard to tell what he really thinks about anybody. But he isn't exactly raising a big hand to build up von Steuben. Maybe he has to build himself up first, again, for the public, after what happened to him. I don't know. But the Assembly's yipping after von Steuben like a hound pack. Like dogs. And damned unmannered ones at that."

It was not odd to Nellie to hear Jack complain of ill manners. Even when his jibes and irreverent remarks were at their worst he had never overstepped the bounds of good social usage.

"Let 'em walk to a mirror and look at themselves," he said. "What have they done to get Virginia ready for these raids? We all knew we were like to be hit sooner or later, and what have they done? Not a damned thing. There wasn't even a decent defense of Richmond. Now they yipe at von Steuben. Good God!"

Nellie hadn't intended to go this far. But it was true that Virginia was a sad and riddled state. Those to the south, the Carolinas, had General Greene, who was throwing his strategy against Lord Cornwallis. Virginia had no one. Benedict Arnold, in an enemy coat and a slash of triumph, had only recently chased Governor Jefferson hotfoot out of Richmond, and another raid had routed the governor from his Monticello home, and nobody knew how many hogsheads of tobacco, how many warehouses had been burned before the raiders swung back to their camps, and not a hand laid on them. She expected, almost any day, to see enemy cavalry gallop onto their plantation. Jack, in his way, was right. The talkers, the political philosophers, the Henrys and Jeffersons, fell solemnly (and sometimes a little ridiculously) apart when confronted with actuality. They could trigger independence with a smooth squeeze of finger, but could also lack the powder to blast the ball to its target. Her stepfather-in-law had to pierce the target, he was the one left to do that. She had always felt he was a giant in the land. Most likely the only one.

"That's neither here nor there," she said, "as it touches on your own part."

"All right, all right," Jack said. "But study the thing sometime. Women don't study things. Too bad. And they don't understand their husbands."

"Do their husbands try to understand *them?*"

Jack slopped some wine into his glass. "That is a notion," he said. "You know, Nell, that's a notion."

"Are you finished dinner?" she said.

"I'd as soon sit here," he said.

"Very well." She took a quarter of a glass of wine, and sipped at it.

"It comes into my head," she said presently, "that you may not have been studying your lessons."

"My what?"

"Mr. Mason loaned you those writings of Rousseau."

"Oh, those." He turned suspicious. "What have they to do with it?"

"The natural man is a pure animal, neither good nor bad. Mr. Mason said Rousseau believed that. Perhaps Mr. Mason wanted you to see it in the Assembly."

He blinked at her for a minute as if trying to make out whether she were serious or joking. In either case he was in no frame of mind for it.

"Natural man. Ho!" he said. "If Rousseau found anything pure in the animal, he was dreaming. I'll gamble he never sat in an elected assembly in his life. The natural man *there* is for more votes and higher office, and the devil with good or bad."

"You can't accept Rousseau? Oh, dear, I thought he might have persuaded you to more tolerant views."

"Why should *I* be tolerant? *They're* not. Anyway, your Rousseau's out of his head."

"Yes," she said, nodding, and surveying him a little sidewise. "My papa says he died mad."

She could see that he still was not sure if she were joking with him, trying to lead them both out of this tangle before the quarrel might turn more serious and they might really set about hurting each other with words and coldness. And a certain prescience told her there was something more on Jack's mind. He wasn't following his usual pattern. He was shifting and sputtering too much, and some of his phrases were too bitter. She concluded that somewhere, in some way, he had been wounded. In pride, or in place, or in prestige. Jack reveled in them all.

So she said, after another sipping of her wine, and the napkin to her lips, and avoiding archness across the candelabra on the table, with the candles not yet lit because the days were lengthening, for she knew he detested archness, "Jacky—what is it?"

He must have been waiting for her to say that, must have been knowing that she could peer so deep into him that the question would ultimately have to come, knowing that the binding of their passions and their bodies had also bound their spirits, the delicate sensate antennae of them, until one could hardly start a sentence without the other knowing how it would end. Until thoughts and moods and blends of feeling lost entities in a one and desirous mingling.

And of a sudden he threw off his truculence.

"Nell, honey, it's mostly because I'm ashamed. Papa's mother."

"Oh?"

She was puzzled. This was a different horse. Papa's mother lived at Fredericksburg, in a small comfortable house near Aunt Betty and Uncle Fielding Lewis. Papa had bought her the place, and was paying rent on her slaves. Nellie had only seen Papa's mother once or twice, and didn't particularly care to see her again. She was a complaining, domineering woman who felt she had been put-upon by the world and fate.

"What about Papa's mother?"

"She applied to the Assembly for a pension."

"She what?"

"Applied for a pension. Said she was—well, what are the words? Destitute? Starving? Neglected? Oh, God, it was horrible."

"Jack—you hadn't told me."

"You can see how *I* felt."

"But she doesn't need a pension. There's Papa, and Uncle John, and Uncle Fielding, and—"

"God knows why she did it. God knows Papa's sold slaves off Mt. Vernon to be able to send money to her. But here I was—in the Assembly —and this comes up. Well, not exactly comes up, because Mr. Harrison, and may he be blest, sends the appeal to Papa first, and Papa says to squash it flat. But everybody knew about it. Good God, Nell, the way the old girl wrote you'd think our family were all a lot of starvers of helpless old women. I guess—I guess maybe I didn't want to show my face in the Assembly for a while." He propped his elbows on the table and leaned his forehead on his palms. "Women," he said. "Women. Mothers."

"All except yours," she said.

He raised his head and looked at her. "That's right," he said. "That's very right. All except mine."

Jack had written to his father, who in any case would have heard about his leaving the Assembly. His father's reply came a few days later.

He took it to Nellie, finding her on the path to the box garden, looking for the quick green spears of daffodil sprouts and first starrings of crocus. He was beginning, after their argument and now that he had had more time to think, to be a little ashamed of himself, and to see how she could be ashamed too, and the letter would be a convenient excuse for broaching the subject (she'd not brought it up again, neither had he) and the easiest way of telling her so.

They stopped on the path together and she put her hand on his arm while he unfolded the sheet and read:

I do not suppose that so young a senator as you are, little versed in political disquisitions, can have much influence in a populous assembly composed of gentlemen of various talents and of different views. But it is in your power to be punctual in your attendance (and duty to the trust reposed in you exacts it of you), to hear dispassionately and determine coolly all great questions. To be disgusted at the decision of questions because they are not consonant to our own ideas, and to withdraw ourselves from public assemblies or to neglect our attendance at them upon suspicion that there is a party formed who are inimical to our cause and to the true interest of our country, is wrong, because these things may originate in a difference of opinion; but, supposing the fact is otherwise, and that our suspicions are well founded, it is the indispensable duty of every patriot to counteract them by the most steady and uniform opposition.

He refolded the paper and slipped it into his coat pocket.

Her hand on his arm had tightened gently while he read. Now it tightened slightly more. She looked at him.

"Why did you read it to me?"

"Because it's so close to what you said. So near to how you feel."

She did not shift her look. Her eyes were still at his.

"How do you mean to answer it?"

"I'll go back to the Assembly."

She kissed him. "You'll be happier. We'll both be."

They moved toward the box garden, slowly, for her time was only three weeks away.

After a few steps he threw back his head and laughed his old teasing, irreverent, careless laugh. "Papa can run you through so sharp you almost admire him for it," he said.

It was a boy.

He was strong, a well-formed mite, and the beaming family Negress who helped Dr. Craik at the birth said he was going to be handsome, and Jack and Nellie took her word for it happily, even though not having seen any babies grow to adulthood, they weren't quite sure how she could tell.

They named him George Washington—"Naturally," as Nellie said; "what else?"—and added the ancestral name of Parke.

Martha came coaching down from New Windsor on the Hudson, the month now being May and the perennial summer campaign beginning to stir (the French had broken out of their blockades and could move freer now, and the general and Rochambeau had their eyes on New York City); and Martha stood over her grandson's cradle, and she and Nellie grew dew-eyed unabashed, as women will do at the frail yet inexplicably tensile innermost moments of life, and Jack blew his nose on his handkerchief. Which is also what men will do. The baby George stared unseeing at them, and bubbled at his mouth and paddled the air with his hands.

So Jack had a son, and Martha dabbed hemmed linen to her eyes contentedly, and doted on Jack and on the baby; and Nellie, when she could be up and about again, raised herself and threw up a few defenses. The boy was not to be doted on as his father had been. He would be not smotheringly adored, but loved; not left to his every whim, but disciplined. She would see to that.

She was surprised to hear Martha say, "Bring him along better than I've done with Jacky, dear. Put your foot down and put mettle in your soul. If I'd had this advice twenty-five years ago there could have been differences today. Not that I think advice worth much, it's so seldom listened to. But sometimes it strikes a chord."

Nellie lowered her eyes, thinking impulsively. "Mama"—she couldn't picture her as Lady Washington, a term that was in vogue, and obviously silly, and a too frequent sycophancy—"Mama, isn't the main thing to keep them from growing spoiled?"

And Martha looked at her, with the full acknowledgment of having spoiled Jacky, and the full acknowledgment of having enjoyed doing so; with the maternalism of a fond hen and the deft bathos of the mother of the Gracchi. "The more you spoil them the better they like it," she said, "and the farther, eventually, they must fall. Every mother should know that, but we prefer to hide it from ourselves. . . . I gather from the sounds, dear, that Baby George could do with a change."

"Mammy Jenny will tend to that," Nellie said.

The family Negress, big-bosomed as some old earth goddess, moved with clucks and suppleness toward the cradle.

The farther, eventually, they must fall.

Nellie lay in bed, wakeful, her eyes open unseeingly, staring upward at the pitch-black tester canopy of their fourposter. Beside her Jack had fallen asleep, bunched on his hip, his knees tucked toward his chin and his back toward her. He didn't snore but breathed rustlingly, like the swish of a soft brush across a fly screen.

The farther, eventually . . . How to bring up young? Indulge them, pamper them, praise them always, and you led them to the precipice.

Be indifferent to them and you were sheer criminal. How to guide them, train them, deny their whims and ignore their tantrums, and force them to the truths that the world does not center around them; that the only center is the vast lump sum of all mankind; and that the world will be deaf to their whines and their puerile braggadocio and quite prepared to drop them into the pit? The three girls—Elizabeth and Martha and little Nellie—were angels. But a boy, but Baby George, might be different. Or, with boys, was it the mothers who were different? There were two sorts of defenses to be prepared, she thought—one sort for Baby George, the other against herself.

She was trying to cope with all these problems, and something seemed to be distracting her.

She could not, at first, quite make out what it was. There was no strange sound, no wayward smell except for the faintly and not unpleasantly pungent waft of skunk from a yonder field, and the sheet that pulled across Jack's shoulder and folded under her chin had the same feel to her touch as always. She stared less absently at the bed canopy, steadying her mind's wandered compass to the present of time and place. What was there in the room that was changed—changing more even as she sought for it—what was there that was not as it should be?

And, staring, she grew gradually aware, as in a kind of disbelieved mystery. As in a kind of inexplicable magic-lantern show. The canopy of the bed was tinged with the faintest, palest light. Yet hardly so much light as ghostly luminosity, if one took stock in ghosts. The canopy had been ink-black a few moments before.

She knew there was no moon. But her first thought was to sit up in bed and look to the window. She saw no moon, of course. But the panes of the window were suffused with the same luminous touch, frail pink like the most delicate of shore shells. And the night beyond the window was filled with the silent lessening of dark, as in the half hour before a harvest moonrise. The angle from bed to window was too great to show her anything else.

But for some reason her heart began to pound. "Jack," she said. "Jacky?"

He twitched a leg.

She shook him. "Jacky."

"Ugh," he said. "Go 'sleep."

"Jack, wake up."

"Whaffor?"

"I think there's trouble."

"Wha' trouble?" He grunted, and sat up beside her. "Women always on the watch for trouble."

"I didn't watch for it, it simply came. Look at the window."

Jack looked. But his eyes were too new from the pillow. He shook his head.

Then men shouted, voices yelled, and in the haze of noise it seemed as if the plantation were exploding.

Nellie scurried out of bed and fumbled her way into a nightgown, and Jack did the same, and suddenly they were gaping, past an alarm of candles, at Cully from Mt. Vernon. Cully had galloped over, sweat-haste, with things to say.

"Mass' Jack—ma'am—they's a raid. King's navy ships comin' up the Potomac. We ain't learned but just now. But Miz' Washington, she won't leave Mt. Vernon, suh. Y'all come over and fetch her up here. She don't belong to be near the river for no raid."

"Raid?" Jack said. "Is it serious?"

He knew he looked silly in the glow of the bedside taper Nellie had managed to light, his bare calves spraddled blond-hairy beneath the hem of his nightshirt and gown.

"Plenty serious. They's burnin', suh."

"Don't you go about to spread panic."

"No, suh."

"You'll be sorry."

"Yassuh."

"Where's the burning? Have you seen it? How do you know?"

The sweep of the Negro's arm, the gesture of undisputed fact, was too honest to be resisted. Jack went where Cully waved him—to the window. And with eyes clearer from sleep now, and with an open view, he looked once more. Down away, on the horizon, there was a burdock bur of red, spiny and clinging.

"Burning," he said.

"Yassuh."

"Whose home?"

"Cain't say, suh. We dunno. Might's be anyone 'long the river."

"You think the raid's heading upstream?"

"We thinks so, suh."

"All right, Cully. I'll come see Mama."

"Yassuh."

"Go tell old Nemmy in the stables to saddle a horse."

Cully left, and the other Negroes with him, with their candles. Jacky closed the door and began to pull on his clothes.

"You must order the coach, Jacky," Nellie said.

"Coach is too slow."

"But I'm going with you."

Jack halted in his dressing, one leg in his breeches, the other out. Nellie had slipped into pantalettes and was giving her petticoat a determined shake.

"No, Nell," he said.

"I'll not let you go into this danger alone."

"Oh, for Lord's sake, Nell," he laughed. "Don't let's have a theater play. I'll fetch Mama here, that's all. There's no danger."

"But you don't know what they're doing down there, under that red sky."

"I won't be down there, sweet. I'll be at Mt. Vernon."

"It might even be Benedict Arnold."

"Arnold is with the king's army. Cully says this raid's navy."

"Cully could be wrong."

"Arnold's never come this far north in the state. He stays nearer his base. And he's no grudge against civilians. Philadelphia shipped his wife off to him in New York. Untrustworthy woman, etc., etc. He's got what he wanted."

"But suppose you get to Mt. Vernon and you find the raiders there, and—Jack, I *will* go with you."

"They won't be there." He had his coat on now, and his cravat, and took no time with his hair except to tie it in a queue with a quick ribbon and slick it with the palms of his hands. "They'll not move at night on a river they don't know. Tomorrow morning, maybe. By then I'll have Mama here."

"I *will* go."

"You will not."

The finality put a kind of stature into Jack that she had never encountered before. She drew back, a little aghast, a little uncertain, but not entirely hating the strength of his tone. The moment of hardness between them was very fleet, and then he laughed again and shrugged. "Oh, Lord, Nell, no heroics. The whole business is absurd enough as it is."

"Absurd?" she said. "When friends' homes are being burned?"

But he only shrugged again, and went out into the hall, and she heard his boots go clattering down the stairs.

Jack heard the clattering, too, perhaps because he was older now, the father of a son, and faintly, reluctantly aware that there might be a dramatic of undramatics, a posture against posturings; which might be the most insipid posture of all. For all men posture, and who has better right? And all men puff themselves, and who can do more than pity them? It is not decided—it surely could not be decided in Jack's mind as he coursed toward Mt. Vernon—whether puff or pity is the final lot of man. Neither seemed to him particularly enviable.

Mt. Vernon sat tense as a nesting bird when a blacksnake nears the foot of her bush. The first rush of hysteria had passed, and Lund Washington had sent the Negroes to their quarters, and no one moved among the outbuildings or along the paths or the drive; but it was a hair-trigger immobility, cocked, the flint ready to spark. Cully took the two horses, to walk them till they cooled. They were well sweated, not to be stalled yet.

Lund was in the main hall, brought there by the horses' noise. So was his mother. So, too, was old Bishop. The old veteran was more a skeleton now than a ramrod, but he had a musket and he leaned on it belligerently, defying anyone to make him discard it.

Martha kissed Jack. She was perfectly calm. "I didn't go to send for you here, dear," she said. "I only wanted Cully to tell you what's happening. So you could prepare."

"Cully has notions of his own," he said.

"That Cully," she said.

"They're raiding up the Potomac," Lund said, "and burning in some places. That's all we know."

Jack glanced into the dining room, to the elegant mahogany buffet backed against one wall. "Shouldn't you hide the silver?"

"It's a provision raid, not a plunder," Lund said. "As we hear."

"Hide the provisions, then," Jack said.

Lund rather mumbled an answer and said he must be making his rounds. He went outside.

"Nellie and I think you ought to come to us tonight, Mama," Jack said.

"Is that why you're here?"

"Yes, Mama."

"That's sweet of you, dear—it's sweet of you both. But of course I can't."

"But you must."

And then he knew in a flash that because he was tired, and worried, and hot from his hard ride, he had blundered pathetically. No one had ever said "must" to his mother successfully.

He tried to retract. "That is, Mama, I mean—for your safety—"

"I prefer to stay here."

"With the king's sailors all over the place?"

"They won't see me. I can stay indoors. And their officers, being officers, will be gentlemen."

"But they're sure to burn the house."

"Then I shall ask permission to leave."

"Hold the fort," old Bishop cackled suddenly. "Hold the fort. March out with flying colors. No white feather."

Jack gave a start. He had forgotten the old man. "Bishop," he said, "go to bed." And then, seeing the hurt, pouting thrust of the almost bloodless lower lip, he softened the order. "To be ready for tomorrow's work," he said.

Bishop gave him a joint-stiffened salute, like a bugle call from a bygone past that once had been a present, and strong, and pulsing with life's juices—and wheeled about, and retired out of sight. And again Jack had that odd sensation, that wonderment of being pushed in spite of himself into heroics, or half heroics, which he didn't want and couldn't stomach, for he would rather laugh at the whole lot. But so many, like the Assembly members, like Bishop now, seemed to dote on the heroics. The big gestures, to truckle to the crowds. To make themselves important. Yet Bishop wasn't making himself important. Bishop believed in what he was doing, believed to the bottom of his soul. Bishop had a musket, and had his duty. It struck Jack as funny, and yet he couldn't bring himself to laugh after all.

Some men's roads went one way, he supposed, some the other. And some were hypocrites, and some were not.

"Please, Mama, leave Mt. Vernon to Lund."

"No, dear."

"Mama, you're the wife of the commander in chief. They could take you hostage."

"Pooh," she said. "They wouldn't harm me, and they know I'd be more trouble than I'm worth."

He laughed. "I'll grant you that," he said. "Mama, you've spunk."

"Then go home," she said.

"No, I'll stay tonight."

She looked pleased. "Nellie will worry."

"Lund can send someone to tell her."

"Yes. Yes, he should."

She looked at him, so abrupt and adult and so absorbed in her welfare, and she spread her arms and flung them around him and buried her face in the shoulder of his coat because he was taller than she was now, and was her comfort and her rock and her beacon.

"Oh, Jacky, my darling, my darling, you do love me, don't you? You do love me—and I love you too, so much, dear, so very much. . . ."

The morning was a delayed thing. It was a letter overdue by post, it was a public coach behind schedule. It was a useless, vapid, blank stretch of time in which the life of Mt. Vernon rolled backward and forward in a muddied inconsistency.

Lund felt that, since the raid was for provisions, the pigs should be driven to the farthest fields. The stables were safe. There'd likely be no taking of horseflesh. Nor of hounds.

"And the wheat?" Jack said. "What's left of the vegetables? The barreled fish?"

"Where would we take it?" Lund said. "They'd pounce on any fresh-dug earth. We can't bury it. We haven't enough carts to spirit it away."

The climax grew almost softly, almost sweetly. A call from a Negro throat, rich-timbered and tinglingly melodious: "Sloops in the river!"

The sun by now was high. And the sloops wore upstream. Three war vessels running with an incoming tide, and dropping anchor opposite the Mt. Vernon fishing wharf, and putting a gig out, and a row galley with marines. Their musket barrels were plain in the overhead sun, and with the proper display of fuss and feathers but with the reality of powder and shot behind him, an officer trampled the lawn to the Mt. Vernon portico.

Lund was there, as steward of the place. Jack lounged in the doorway. Martha, as she had promised, stayed out of sight upstairs in her bedroom, peering from behind curtains at as much as she was able to see, House Alice crouched beside her. The other house servants were clustered panicky in a knot under the portico.

"What wouldn't I give to have the Marquis de Lafayette march in with his troops just now," Lund said, low.

"There's no chance," Jack said.

Washington had sent Lafayette to aid von Steuben, and the marquis had won over the Virginia Assembly and got a flow of supplies and was thrusting and parrying farther to the south, where the heavier raids were. In the Carolinas, Nathanael Greene had outmaneuvered Cornwallis and whittled deeply at his army, and it was rumored Cornwallis would give up the Carolinas and come into Virginia, too. Lafayette would be busy enough without sidetrack marches to Mt. Vernon.

"No," Lund said, "but wishing is enjoyable. My soul, is this a hard-ened sea dog?"

The question was appropriate. The man had more the look of what was beginning to be known in the jargon of the fops as an Exquisite. He was precisely, faultlessly, painstakingly dressed—or, rather, over-dressed. His lace cuffs were unnecessarily long, almost hiding his hands, from one of which drooped a dainty handkerchief; his neckcloth rose almost to his ears, his lace-and-ruffle shirt front swelled like a pouter pigeon; his breeches were satin, his boots high and skintight and gleam-ing as with lacquer. He wore a small curled wig, heavily powdered, and a monocle, and the artificial queue behind his wig was tied with a broad ribbon of purple velvet and it bobbed as he walked in the manner of a struck daffodil stalk.

His expression, as he reached the portico, was one of profound distaste, though whether for the work he had been ordered to do or for the two country bumpkins who stepped out to meet him neither Jack nor Lund could guess.

"You come uninvited, sir," Lund said. "But not unheralded."

"God demme, I should think not," the officer said. He had a nasal, affected accent. "And we will have no churlishness, please. We scarcely require the amenities of social invitation, do we? Hah."

Lund said nothing, nor Jack.

The officer took off his monocle, wiped it with the handkerchief, screwed it back into his eye again, and said, "We're given to understand this—ah—" he waved a hand as though the house and its outer offices and quarters and dependencies were so many ramshackle huts—"this place is the home of Mr. Washington."

"It is the home of General Washington," Lund said.

"Mr. Washington. But he is not in residence at the moment."

"No."

"And you are—"

"His steward. The estate manager."

"Ah. Good fellow. We shall deal together. Amicably, I trust. . . . And this?" He looped a forefinger at Jack.

"I'm part of the family," Jack said.

The officer closed his free eye and squinted the monocle at him. "H'mm, demned int'restin'. Thought you'd have been in uniform. Family, you know. All that."

Jack reddened and put his fists in his pockets.

"Where are your slaves?" the officer said to Lund.

"In their quarters."

"H'mm, ah. Please be so good as to conduct me. By the way, your name?"

"Washington. Lund Washington."

"Most int'restin'. Family, too?"

"Distant kin."

The officer gave a laugh. It was surprisingly wholesome. "Oh, all you rebels are kin. Might as well try to uproot wild grapes."

"You know wild grapes then, sir."

"I've met 'em," the officer said shortly. "Served in this demned war five years. Mostly playing mother hen to the demned army. Where're your slaves?"

Lund led him around to the west front, where the entrance driveway was, and then farther toward the huts and outbuildings of the Negroes.

The officer didn't go to the huts, but stopped on the higher ground of the driveway and called in a loud voice.

"All you black folk who want your freedom, you have it now. Go down to the wharf. Go down to the wharf. We are your friends. We set you free. Go down to the wharf. You'll be taken aboard our ships."

Jack was stunned. Lund's jaw fell open. It was a gambit they hadn't foreseen. It could strip the plantation of labor; it could ruin Mt. Vernon. But they stood motionless in shock. This was too sudden.

Forms emerged from the huts. Black figures, wondering, suspecting, but lured by the call to the wharf, lured by the knowing that the master was powerless, with those warships in the river and this shouting man taking charge over Mass' Lund.

"Hey-ya," they said. "Hey-ya."

Around a corner from somewhere came old Bishop. He still had his musket. He put down his head and rushed at the officer with a kind of prance and presented the musket with a banging efficiency and said, "Sir, I rode beside Braddock. You can't play this game with me. Fight like a man. I fought in a British coat."

"Demned pity you ever changed it," the officer said.

"You whoring spawn of Satan," Bishop said, and in the next minute was down and trampled by the blacks making for the fishing wharf.

Two or more dozen of them went, pouring over Bishop's doubled-up body and shoving it aside with their feet. They spilled down the path at the lawn corner to the fishing wharf, a stampede of waved arms and rolling eyes, like some bewildered, blind-led herd. The officer watched them equably. "Well-fed lot," he said. "Healthy. Should fetch nice prices in Jamaica."

Jack ran over to Bishop. The old man was conscious, moaning. The Negroes hadn't intended hurt to him. He'd simply been in their way. Jack wondered if any bones were broken.

"Bishop," Jack said, kneeling by him. "Can you hear me? Can you talk?" He signaled two men from the Negroes who'd remained, standing and gaping, and said, "Carry him to his bed and send for Dr. Craik."

Bishop opened his eyes and said, "Don't give up, Mr. Jack. Don't give up," and closed his eyes again and fainted. Jack thought this pummeling would be the old man's last. He felt an unbearable wave of grief. Bishop had so often trotted him on his back and told him forest tales of the Braddock march.

"I presume," he said, as bitingly as he knew how, rising and striding toward the officer, "you will allow us to take away our wounded?"

"Dem fine man," the officer said. "We don't breed 'em like that any more. We're too dem elegant. Hope he doesn't come to danger."

"Small thanks to you," Jack said.

The officer shrugged. "Mr.—ah—Washington-kin, you've no doubt heard. The purpose of our little fleet here is to gather fodder and food-stuffs. We ask that you supply them. Compliance will be met with courtesy. Refusal with the torch."

"That's the barbaric way of putting it," Lund said, white to the lips, and his lips trembling thin over his teeth. "Are you fighting a war against armies or against homes?"

"I do not take your meaning, sir."

"You've burned homes along the Potomac. I judge because they wouldn't hand their granaries and livestock over to you. What sort of war is that? Defenseless householders. Very brave on your part, sir, very brave."

Jack was afraid for a minute that Lund had gone too far. The officer stiffened in anger. Yet Lund, with his years of plantation management, had gained a certain insight into personalities. He had read his man correctly.

"God dem, sir, we're not quite barbarians. And a burned house won't win a war. But one has orders and one must see them through, whether or not one approves. I merely repeat you my orders."

There was a quiet exchange of looks between the two that made Jack breathe easier. He saw a common ground of meeting: Lund devoted to saving Mt. Vernon, the officer detesting the orders that set him to prey on helpless plantations.

"May I have time to consider?"

"Until midafternoon, sir."

"Then we understand each other, sir."

"We do."

And the officer went down to his gig, and was rowed with suitable pipings and splashings of oars to the sloops in midstream, and Martha came down from upstairs and questioned Jack, and they both questioned Lund.

"Will he really burn us if we don't provide him?"

"I think so. He's burned other plantations that stood up to him."

"But for the general's plantation to provide him," Martha said.

"Lund, it wouldn't look right," Jack said.

"Do you want to lose Mt. Vernon or don't you?" Lund said. "That's what it comes to."

"I know what George would say," Martha said tartly.

"Perhaps I do, too. But I prefer to save Mt. Vernon. It's in my charge;

I am responsible for it, I'll not throw it away in a patriotic furor. It's a small matter if a few sheep and hogs are spread on an enemy deck, but it would be a great and discouraging matter to the nation if the general's home was burned to the ground."

So, because Martha did not feel she had the political or military authority, and the matter was both political and military; and because Jack couldn't outargue Lund; Lund went aboard the enemy sloops and took provisions with him, and made a social time of it, and asked to have his Negroes back. He didn't get the Negroes, but he got a stay of the torch at Mt. Vernon. And the enemy sloops dropped downriver the next day.

But it was not yet done with. Lafayette heard of the thrust, and the giving way, and wrote to Washington. And Washington wrote to Lund. And Lund's skin reddened along his jaws, and up his cheeks, and over his forehead when he read what Washington had to say. "It would have been a less painful circumstance to me to have heard . . . they had burnt my house and laid the plantation in ruins."

"That's the thanks I get, Master Jack," Lund said. "That's the thanks."

"Oh, swing easy, Lund," Jack said carelessly. "We've both had our ears pinned back. It's bound to work out someday."

XIX

"We Have a Chance"

Betsy mare's hoofs galloping through the night made the best sound, Washington thought, that he had ever heard. In the plain way he'd have given it no thought at all, a gallop being chiefly the speediest method of covering grounds. But in the present state of his mind and body his imagination played tricks of sentiment on him.

The pounding of Betsy's gallop became a music, rhythmic and beckoning. The quick air on his cheeks was wonderfully soft in the dark. The night had a honeyed smell. The hidden, widespread, well-remembered countryside beyond the veining hedgerows lay stretched in a shyness of late summer already sweetly pregnant with winter's sleep. There were stars, but no moon. No stir but the hoofs' tattoo. No swirl or emotion but the lift of his own heart.

Though he did not put it into so many thoughts, he could afford himself a little sentiment, a little touch of the lyric wand. Five years and four months ago he had left Mt. Vernon. He had not seen it since. Now he was coming home.

Betsy kept on without slacking. Flecks of foam from her bridle spattered against his thighs.

He began to sense, through the darkness, the near and familiar landmarks.

He sensed also, as a horseman, that the roads were very bad. They were torn, dilapidated; sad proof of Virginia's collapse. If the coming campaign dragged into the winter they'd have to be repaired or the army's transport would be crippled. But the campaign must not go into the winter. One more winter would be sure ruin. He had until the middle of October to play his trumps. A month.

Of the last five days he'd spent two in the saddle, directing his army's line of march, and the French, down from the Hudson; ridden, written, and given orders incessantly; lived in excitement, suspense, and churning eagerness.

The army was left behind him, the Americans and the French, transferring to boats that would float them down the Chesapeake to the York River, saving legs, time, and shoe leather. Rochambeau was behind him and the French staff. They hadn't been able to match his headlong rush toward home. Only his new aide, David Humphreys, was with him, and that clinging shadow Billy Lee.

He tingled to the drum of Betsy's thuddings.

Billy rode almost abreast of him. He shouted, "That lane, Billy. You know it?"

"Yes, suh."

"Seems the honeysuckle's thicker. Or it may be the dark."

"Seems."

"And there're the smells of the tidelands. Sniff 'em. The tide's down. Breathe 'em in, Billy."

"M'mmm, *m'mmm!*"

"Good, Billy?"

"Yes, *suh.*"

His hand went to his hat, tightening it. Sweat and the wind of the gallop were working it loose. "Another quarter hour, Humphreys. Can you hold out?"

"I'll manage, sir."

"Pull to a trot."

The young aide's voice had had a clenched tone. A stitch in the side, likely, from the long run. He himself had never felt better. The full use of his body and energies always exhilarated him, put him on his mettle. But he slowed for Humphreys' sake.

They trotted. Humphreys' breath came sharp and rasping. His own was easy. He could have galloped all night.

He said, "Billy, first thing tomorrow send over to tell Master Jack and Miss Nellie I'm here."

"Yes, suh." Billy chuckled. He prodded his horse closer, almost head to head. "Will all the farm folks see you, suh, 'fore y're off again? They'd admire to see you."

"You fetch them to the house."

"Yes, suh, truly."

And they rode a few more yards, and then a kind of wail broke from Billy, an almost voiceless moan as of a man threshing incredulous in a glorious dream. "Oh, Lawd," he said. "Oh, Lawd, we're gettin' home!"

"Yes, Billy. Now pray God we don't wake up and find ourselves at Morristown."

"Oh, dear Jesus," Billy said.

"Amen," he said.

He heard the Negro's half sob beside him. He would have said more, words that would have framed clumsily the mutuality of their feelings, but Billy would not have wanted that, nor did he. But he tapped Billy's saddled knee with his riding whip.

They passed between gate posts, timber sentinels. "The Muddy Hole Farm, Humphreys. Mt. Vernon."

And his spurs bit compulsively into Betsy's flanks and he was at a gallop again, leaving Humphreys and Billy with flung sand in their faces; at a gallop over the loved road through fields and orchards until he came to the smoother, upward level of the House Farm and to the house itself.

He was alone. The house was dark. He pitched from the saddle, leaving the reins on Betsy's neck. She would stand. After that ride she could hardly walk.

He had to fuss with the latch. It was new to him—one of Lund's improvements. But he got it open.

He shouldered into the hall.

"Martha! Patsy darling!" His voice echoed and echoed again, through the house and out past the open door.

He wasn't quite prepared for what happened. Dogs barked. There was a yell somewhere in the house. He heard windows flung up. From the direction of the field hands' quarters a woman's throat squealed high, shrilled with fear. Figures, lights bobbed around the outbuildings, and running feet bit on gravel.

"Who's there?"

He recognized Lund's voice. "It's me, Lund. George Washington."

"Oh, good God!"

Lund burst in. He held a lantern and a musket. He stopped inside the door, in the hall, and swung the lantern toward Washington's face, and turned to shout. "No raid, no raid! Keep to your quarters! It's Mr. Washington!"

A kind of moan, like Billy's, a kind of relief or cheer, a sigh and a waiting prayer, went up from the paths among the outbuildings.

"Go sleep!" Lund shouted, and waved his lantern. "Go sleep, all you! The general's here, that's all!"

He swung back to Washington, his lantern ready. "What's wrong, sir? Is the army broke? Is it all over?"

"No," Washington heard himself saying gaily. "No, Lund, it's just beginning."

He had caught the nervousness, the long, tensed alertness of a house living day to day on the brink of fear. Of raidings, and plunderings, and flames. It was like the tension of a blockhouse in the scalping days of the frontier—a house, a home, a family, laid bare and exposed to whatever might strike it. He was joyed to bring it to calm at last.

"Nothing disastrous, Lund," he said.

And then Humphreys and Billy Lee were at the door, and Lund went out to them. The house servants were lighting candles in the hall, and Martha called, "George?" from the top of the stairs and everything was as it should be.

He was really home.

She came down from above, and hesitated on the stair landing, at the turn, and looked at him, and saw him, and pattered down the rest of the steps. She'd pulled a dressing gown around her. She was in his arms.

"George! My dearest!"

His lips drove to hers. There was silence in the hallway. The house servants disappeared, understanding.

After a little she pulled away, gently.

"George—at Mt. Vernon?"

"Because I've the time. I've made the time."

"But no word from you. I couldn't guess you were near Virginia."

"It's not been a space for writing letters, Patsy. My dear, I'm sorry."

"You startled me."

"Late in the night. I know. But I couldn't wait to get to you."

"From New York?"

That was where they had parted—at New Windsor on the Hudson in New York, after another drear, grinding winter; and she had traveled off to Mt. Vernon, and he had gone on to hope for an attack against New York City with the French. Her eyes showed a moment of panic. Showed that if he were here, so far from New York, something must have miscarried, something collapsed.

He read her eyes.

"Tell me, George," she said.

He kept his arms around her and laughed a loud laugh of comfort and enthusiasm. Lund Washington, coming back into the hallway, and Humphreys, and Billy Lee heard it. It broke through the rooms of Mt. Vernon and stopped the servants in their tracks. It was an utterly happy laugh, one that seemed to set the candles in their sconces to a brighter flame.

"Oh, Martha—what news! The Comte de Grasse is in the Chesapeake with twenty-eight ships of war and three thousand more French fighting men. And Lafayette's pinned Cornwallis at Yorktown. We have our chance at last!"

His arms were so tight about her ribs that she couldn't take a breath. "Martha, we have a chance!"

The next morning was beautiful, the Virginia beauty he had dreamed so long in absence. The sky was blue, the earth red. The crops were heavily green, the trees heavily pendant. A freshness from the night-cooled river was like a slowly-lifting coverlet over the fields.

He rode another horse this morning, to let Betsy mare rest in the stables, and threw questions at Lund. How many crops would there be, and what quality? Had the field hands kept well? Were the brood mares in good condition? How long would the carpenters need to finish the work on the house?—and nodded briskly at Lund's answers. Mt. Vernon was poorer than at the start of the war—slaves sold, and those who'd run off in the raid, and lands sold to meet expenses—but it was sound at the core. The inflation would be slacking; the Congress had stopped printing its worthless paper money.

When he had asked enough farm questions he put a different one, something he was trying to puzzle out.

"Awhile ago, Lund, as the field hands gathered in at the house to see me, they looked sober. Almost sad. The house servants the same. Why?"

Lund gave him an odd glance, as if the explanation were too simple, as if wondering how little it was possible for a man to be conscious of himself.

"They saw your grayed hairs," Lund said, "and six years of war on your face. It took them with a shock."

"Oh." He could imagine that was so. The idea had not entered his head. He said, "And you?"

"I expected a change. I've had your letters."

He let the horse take its own gait, an ambling walk, while he sat musing, digesting the slight shock that had come to him too.

But only slight. Of course there would be a change in him. He felt more apologetic than startled, sorry he hadn't realized before embarrassing Lund.

"A man fighting a war with a noose around his neck," he said, smiling, "forgets to count mortality and time."

"I should think so," Lund said.

"But you know, Lund, I don't feel quite decrepit yet."

"Good God, no!"

"Thank you." Washington laughed. "Hold to that vote for some years to come. Is the lane to the fish wharf still fit for a canter?"

They spent several hours on the farms. He needn't have spent so many, he knew, but the old sights and sounds, the smooth green pastures and cultivated fields and mistily distant wood lots put such a joy in him that he couldn't tear himself away. He felt like a schoolboy on holiday. Tomorrow General Rochambeau and the French staff would be at Mt. Vernon, and there would be the war pressing in on him again, but today was his.

Lund said the Mt. Vernon cellars were stocked and that there should be enough to feed the company, but that he would have more food sent to the house to be on the safe side. Washington said the safe side was the best, for he wanted to invite his neighbors to a celebration dinner while the French were there.

The sun was reaching high in the sky. They took the way to the house. Lund needed to get at his ordering, and Washington wanted to go over the account books.

Now that the subject of the French had come up, Lund had questions of his own.

He said, "We never looked for the French here. We thought they were helping you against New York."

"The French army, not the navy." Washington spoke a bit curtly. The New York campaign had not gone well. The usual disappointment. His ranks had been too thin.

"Why not the navy?"

"They give several reasons. I think the first in their minds is the sand bar at the harbor. They failed to get across it once, remember. The second is that they would have to batter into New York harbor against enemy ships. But the Chesapeake is open to them."

"Why come to the Chesapeake, though? Cornwallis?"

"Yes."

Lund thought a moment, and said, "We've sat at Mt. Vernon and watched his lordship, never knowing when he'd start for us. We followed how General Greene nipped and smarted him until he fell back to the North Carolina coast and let Greene slip in behind him into South Carolina. He should have gone after Greene; Greene will clear out the king's posts in that state too. But he moved up into Virginia instead. Why Virginia?"

"I'd say Cornwallis had had a bellyful of Greene and thought Lafayette would be easier swallowing—certainly by joining forces with Arnold."

Washington made an impatient noise in his throat as he spoke. Any mention of Arnold's name rubbed him wrong. He thought of the Virginia homes burned, the thousands of hogsheads of tobacco and the warehouses of supplies gone up in smoke. One of his strongest hopes on this southward and forcing march had been to catch Arnold in the same net with Cornwallis. But the man seemed to live a devil-charmed life. Arnold had fallen sick and been recalled, and was back in New York now. And Washington was braced to hear news of Arnold's fire and sword in New England towns.

Lund was waiting for his answer. He smiled and said, "But you see, Cornwallis didn't have Arnold."

"No. And Lafayette didn't have anything but his courage."

"I couldn't reinforce Lafayette. I sent him all I could spare."

There was a shortness of tone that made Lund think the questions might have overreached themselves and fallen into criticism. He hurried to say, "Well, Clinton couldn't reinforce Cornwallis either."

Washington was already sorry that he'd been short with Lund. His long negotiations and conferences and schemes with the French, and the Frenchmen's long deferrals, had left the nap of his sensitivity worn. He tried to suit the color of his answer to the Virginia sun and landscape.

"He didn't dare, Lund. Which was the point I always held in mounting an attack against New York, that by threatening that city we'd force Clinton to draw in his troops and weaken other danger spots."

"Such as Cornwallis?"

"Such as Cornwallis. He wanted reinforcements, but hasn't had them. Clinton has kept the regiments in New York. So that Cornwallis has gone to ground in Yorktown, looking for aid he won't get. Because the amazing marquis is still alive and fighting, and because de Grasse has stolen a month from the West Indies to set in at our seacoast for what good it may do."

"Then, sir"—Lund's pitch of voice was even, that of a manager of farms—"then, sir, between you and de Grasse you'll take Cornwallis?"

Washington's voice had gaiety. He felt the gaiety, and let it sweep him. "It's almost certain, Lund." He said, "There are two main enemy armies on the continent—Clinton and Cornwallis. If we can't pepper the one we can bag the other, hey?"

"I'd say so."

"I'd laid my heart on New York, Lund. But if de Grasse settles on the Chesapeake"—he shrugged—"the Chesapeake it is. And for once the French navy is stronger on our coast than King George's. Cornwallis is trapped, unless Lafayette lets him claw his way out."

"Hardly likely."

"No, it isn't; Cornwallis has entrenched himself and is looking to Clinton to strengthen him."

"Which can't be done now. Unless Sir Henry moves faster than you have."

"We've moved," Washington said, and recalled a phrase from one of his letters to Lafayette, and quoted it, "on the spur of speed. Besides, there's de Grasse's fleet. Sea power, for once."

The sea power, he knew, was the solution. That, and Robert Morris' borrowing of hard cash from Rochambeau, repaid with King Louis' livres; and the quick readiness of the teamsters and workmen that the hard cash brought; and the swelling of volunteers at the rumor of success. The volunteers had always swelled at success, shrunk away at failure. But he was too happy now, too sure and content, to turn sour or to begrudge. Maybe that was the way they always had been and always would be—the people who mouthed freedom and called for it, but who would not put themselves out, or sacrifice themselves. So they had come to nothing, a nothing less than nothing, a shrunk pride, a tatterdemalion army, a scooped-out treasury, and were having to depend on the charity and self-interest of a foreign power. He would have thought, if he had not been generous, if he had not had faith, that the people had got in these years exactly what they deserved.

He had led them, at their own calling, through the war. And most of them had neglected him, or turned their backs. Most of them had been busy haggling over their own woes or their own profits. Very seldom had the people, as a mass, listened to him or rallied to him. There had been something bestial, animal, dog-eat-dog in their response. Something selfish and tragically greedy, in the old Greek meaning of tragedy, where a man or a nation fell to the sword of an enemy because of a fatal flaw, a creeping, cancerous, diseased weakness within. What he had studied of history convinced him that powers and civilizations did not go under the ax of conquerors for physical weaknesses, but for spiritual, moral ones. The thirteen American states, whose commander he was, did not have, any longer, much spirit or much morale. They had childishly given up the fight. Yet like all children, they could be roused again. The French were in the Chesapeake, with a power that could top King George's. At least until the middle of October, when they would turn to the battle seas of the West Indies.

He had a month. And he had Rochambeau, and the French army, and the added men de Grasse was bringing, and his own troops. And Cornwallis was like a rabbit in a covert at Yorktown.

He forgot any gloomy thoughts. He was in Virginia, and the sun was overhead.

"We hold sea and land both," he said. "Only for a moment—but we hold them," and trotted his horse quietly and happily, searching ahead for the sight of his home's great brick chimneys.

That afternoon he sat with Martha and Jack and Nellie and his three step-granddaughters.

Tomorrow Mt. Vernon would be a maelstrom of hospitality for the French, and his neighbors, and his staff, and it would be crowded and clattering as the horse races at Williamsburg or the card tables in the Williamsburg taverns, but this afternoon it was peaceful and his own.

He looked curiously at the girls. Eliza was nearly five years now, and little Martha just enough younger to spill gingerbread crumbs, and a toddling Eleanor, whom Nellie shooed away from tables and delicious breakables. They had come into life while he was far away facing death, and he knew no more about them than they about him. Yet they were part of his family, or—the ugly pain again—Martha's family. He liked children. He leaned forward in his chair and spread out his arms.

Eliza and Martha came in to him doubtfully, encouraged by Nellie. He knew he must seem very huge to them, a very different person from anything they were used to. But his own Martha was beaming and nodding, and he contrived to keep from a frigid attitude, a frosty shyness.

"Well, now, Eliza," he said. "Well, now, Martha. And what do we do now—sit on a knee, hey?"

And he took them up and bounced them, and they squealed.

"Oh, George, this is such a joy," Martha said.

"Wait till after Yorktown, Patsy," he said.

"Are you so certain of Yorktown?" she said.

"As if I'd tree'd a 'coon," he said. "Nellie, who does your baby George look like?"

"Well, you know," Nellie said, "babies look like everybody in the family for the first few months. Then they take on their own."

"I'd like to have seen the boy."

"He's only barely above four months, Papa. We didn't feel we could bring him. Especially as you'll be so crowded."

"I'll see him afterward."

"How many are coming, George?" Martha said. "All these Frenchmen."

"Yes, well, you've met them mostly, Patsy. And they'll sleep anywhere —on floors, on chairs." He laughed. "Rochambeau and I shared a hedge once, in Westchester."

"But I want it to be right, George. And proper."

"It will be. I don't worry about you, Patsy."

He was too exalted to worry about anything. Mt. Vernon would take care of them all—somehow, anyhow—the generals and the counts and the staff, and the white breeches and the thorough politeness; and he would be able to repay Rochambeau some of the geniality and comradeship the French count and general had spread to him, and show him a bit of the way of life along the Potomac in Virginia, not quite frontier yet not quite Versailles-style either, and pleased that maybe Virginians had found a good compromise path for what man should be and what he should attain to.

"Have we enough food, Lund, after the raid?" he said.

For he had seen Lund at the door. He had forgiven Lund for turning provisions over to the enemy. He could forgive anyone in the present welling of his spirit.

"Have we enough food?"

"Yes, General. Except—"

"Except what?"

"Frogs' legs. I understand the French like frogs."

Washington roared. "Fold your umbrella, Lund. Draw in. Frenchmen don't live on frogs. I campaigned with Rochambeau for weeks north of New York, and frogs sang from every swamp, and he never put up a craving for one. If we don't have frogs' legs at Mt. Vernon, no one's going to die."

"Yes, sir. I only thought of pleasing."

"Pleasing is sometimes the worst enemy, Lund."

"Yes, sir." Lund couldn't match his kinsman in drink nor in philosophy.

"Never mind the frogs. Just have plenty to eat."

"Yes, sir."

Then Lund was gone, but Jack was still there. Jack said, standing by Nellie—the babies were left to Martha, who gathered them up and collected them and huddled them into a baby corral that somehow made amusement and sensibility—Jack said, "I'd like to go to Yorktown with you, Papa."

There are records of silences.

There is no record of this.

But it can be assumed it was deep.

And then, after a wait, "I'd like to go, Papa."

Another wait. And, "Why?"

"Oh, I don't know. The sport, I suppose. All the Frenchmen. It'll be on the upturn, won't it? So many French. And throwing Cornwallis out of Yorktown as you threw Howe out of Boston. Such fun. And Papa—they were going to burn your home."

"I know."

"For that, Papa, I think for that I'd like to rattle at 'em."

"Would you?"

"Yes, sir."

A trying pause, not written except in the hearts of the men who knew it.

Then Martha said, "George, I didn't know he wanted to, but let him go with you."

"How, Patsy?"

"Well—as an aide."

"All my aides are colonels. I can't appoint Jack a colonel overnight. With no service record whatever."

"No, but you could—"

"No, Martha."

"I wouldn't have to be official," Jack said. "Just part of your office family, maybe?"

"George dear, don't you see? Jacky wants to be at Yorktown," Martha said.

He could have said, "For what reason?" He could have said, "For what nonsense?" But he didn't. Martha was speaking.

"As long as Jack keeps out of the way of bullets and can help you with messages and such, why should you begrudge him, George?"

"I don't begrudge him."

"Then let him go with you."

"I don't know in what capacity." He swung to his daughter-in-law. "Nellie?"

"He's set on going, Papa. Can't you make room for him somewhere?"

"Both women, eh?" He brushed his fingers over his chin. "Nellie, you haven't the slightest conception of a 'somewhere,' have you?"

"No, Papa."

"Then why throw it at me?"

"Because," Martha said stoutly, "if any but your own kin wanted to join with you, you'd find excuse fast enough. If Jack wants to go to Yorktown, George, you should let him. And be grateful that he wants to go."

He gave in, in face of the two of them, and of Jack. There were, besides, larger things for his attention. Rochambeau would be at Mt. Vernon tomorrow, and a staff that ran like a vein of gold with French aristocracy. If Jack wanted to go junketing, this was no time for him to stop it. No time for a family squabble. "Very well," he said. "Jack can come with me. Informally. He won't have an official post; I can't give him one. But he'll see Yorktown, if that's what he wants."

The women gushed, of course, and Jack said, without his immature laugh, "That's what I want, Papa."

He left the details to Martha—not as a coward, but as a man whose masculine comprehension was unequal to grappling with such things —and marveled at the way she rode smoothly over the torrents of French staff and American staff, and French counts and American colonels, and the dinner for the neighbors and the joint staffs in a magnificance of mutual worship and comradeship. Triumph lurked in the corners of the dining room like a sweet perfume, and the silvery flakings of Versailles and the tobacco dusting of Virginia mingled bouncily. Happiness sat everywhere. He forgot how many toasts there were. For Cornwallis was bottled up, and de Grasse was in the Chesapeake, and there was something in the wind that could be as good and as fatal as Saratoga. (And he thought of Gates, and the crush of Gates's southern defeat, and the death of his son, and passed by the next few toasts.) For men were subject to Fate, were they not? Or to their own weaknesses. And whether the weaknesses were really Fate or were their own vapidity and foolishness, who could say? Some seemed to be born to weakness; some accumulated it; and some merely watched the fireworks, content with noise and pictures. Which was the sorriest weakness of all, and he prayed it would not spread in the country he was trying to make free. For if it did, there would be no more freedom. Men would live as if drugged, mere community insects, if there were nothing but noise and pictures, nothing but political yells and bought hallucinations. Which is to say that he wondered, that night at Mt. Vernon, with Rochambeau on one hand and Knox on the other, with the sophistication of Europe and the innocence of America combined to form a doctrine new to the sight of Europe and the West, whether the doctrine really had validity. Whether democracy was democracy, or mere anarchy. And how much depended on self-control. A great deal depended on self-control. Good God, hadn't he learned that, through the five years? He didn't know if anyone else had learned it. Learning was a one-man process. Not to be confused with the Indians' tossing out of dead fish and each fish snatched up and buried in a corn hill. That was practicality. Learning, the look and feel of mankind for two thousand years, was something more.

He felt all this only vaguely, for he bustled with the rub-a-dub of Rochambeau's getting off, and his kiss for Martha, and his signal to Jack to fall in behind him, and the leaving of Mt. Vernon while he rode south toward Williamsburg.

Rochambeau was at his side, Jack at his flank. There was a continent's difference, but a heart's sameness. The three made talk as they rode.

Jack dropped off for a day or two at Uncle and Aunt Bassett's on the road to Williamsburg—and because he wasn't in an official capacity he took the whole lark unofficially, and who could blame him—but Washington pressed on. He had his aides, Humphreys, and Tench Tilghman, and Jonathan Trumbull, Jr., and the movement of the horses and the crisp autumn air and the jokes from Rochambeau's staff, mostly from two brothers called Deux-Ponts. The two were lively and very friendly.

Eventually they came to Williamsburg.

Lafayette met them there, and Virginia's new governor, Nelson; for Jefferson had resigned and gone home. And Lafayette kissed Washington from ear to ear, and was not a boy any more, as Cornwallis had called him, but a fighter who had outplayed Cornwallis, and had kept his small remnant intact and constantly threatening; and whether he had driven Cornwallis to ground in Yorktown or Cornwallis had been ordered there by Sir Henry Clinton, Lafayette still carried away the palm.

Washington, for once, let his emotions show that he felt so.

"My dear Marquis."

"Ah, Your Excellency!"

"Marquis—to see you again. Governor Nelson, sir, delighted."

"And I, General."

"Marquis, this time—surely this time—hey?"

"It's to be prayed for, *mon Général.*"

"You're well, Marquis, you're successful. I'm joyed to know it. And what do you mean by 'prayed for'? With all of us on one side of Cornwallis and de Grasse's warships on the other, the thing is certain."

And then a silence, which took him suddenly like a plunging sword. And in the silence, perceiving something, a sense of gap, he commenced to hunt with his eyes for a man who should have been there, scanning over the ranks of the officers and not finding him.

"Where is the uniform of your navy, Marquis? I see no one from de Grasse."

Lafayette's reply came honestly, with a cleanliness of report and no pretense at hiding its chill.

"The comte, *mon Général,* has sailed out to sea to meet an enemy fleet that challenged him off the coast. That was several days ago. We've had no news since."

Washington slumped in the saddle, his heart sinking in him and his mind and body feeling old. Without the fleet to block Cornwallis' rescue by water this whole push might well be hopeless.

Lafayette saw, and gave Rochambeau a warning look and put on a briskness like an actor rising to his cue.

"Our regiments are lined up, ready for your inspection, *mon Général.* We should be honored to have you review them."

X X

October, 1781: Yorktown

Ever since Boston, the mockery had remained the same. It had never really changed. It sang a dry, dispiriting, leaching tune, and the tune was hope deferred.

His feeling, at the moment, was too big for talk. He stared at Lafayette a little stupidly. Then the marquis's smile and small half gesture reminded him—or rather nudged him into consciousness of the fact—that the oft-worn mask must be worn again and the play must proceed. He was the center of eyes in Williamsburg. He couldn't afford the luxury, the release, of tears over disappointment or spilt milk. The good face must be adjusted for the public. Though he had done it so often. And now this. At the curtain fall of his greatest suspense.

But he controlled his voice to answer, after a moment or so.

"Thank you, Marquis, the review of course. Please to lead the way."

Oddly enough, while he rode along the ranks of stiff-attentioned troops and remembered the other Williamsburg of card playings and theaters and horse bettings, there drifted over him the legend of Sisyphus, once heard from the Reverend Boucher tutoring a bored and heedless Jacky, at the age of twelve; how Sisyphus, condemned by Olympus, rolled a huge stone eternally up a mountain; and how always, as he neared the top, it escaped him and plunged to the bottom; and how he must begin the task again; and how this was his punishment and his hell.

He was undecided whether he were a Sisyphus or merely an actor in a wild and scrambling play.

They saluted him with twenty-one guns at the review, and tendered him a dinner that night at the inn.

Sitting in the inn he looked around him. Faces and names and persons had changed with the years, with time. Putnam crippled with rheumatism, out of service; Ward gone long since, from age; Gates, Lee, Arnold, the pangs and the thorns. Stark, of Trenton and Bennington, resigned in a fit of anger. Daniel Morgan the same, from a quarrel with Greene, pulling out of the fight with his woodsman's turkey gobble, and the second time he'd quit in a huff. But Knox was still at hand, and Greene—not precisely at hand but beating up enemy posts in South Carolina—and Lincoln, exchanged after his defeat at Charleston, and Anthony Wayne, not mad except toward women, and a good soldier.

And the French. There had come so many French to the camps that he couldn't count them. And there would be more.

So he gave a toast to the French. And they responded with a toast to the thirteen states, and to General Sullivan, who had scoured the Indian lands on the Mohawk and the higher Susquehanna, and laid them waste, and lifted from the settlers beyond the mountains the hood of fear.

And he toasted Greene, and Rochambeau matched him, and the glasses of wine overspilled, for Rochambeau knew Greene's skill at battle as well as he, and all was mellow and comradely.

"And now, *mon Général*," Lafayette said, "for the tactics."

"I want only one tactic," he said. "Cornwallis bagged."

"You shall have it, *mon Général*. But look. Here is de Grasse, ready, in the mouth of the Chesapeake. And at once, down the sea, come a fleet of King George. Under one Admiral Graves. So what for de Grasse? To be trapped in the bay, dawdle at anchor like a child sitting on hands? No. He has wind at his back, and cannon, and the lurch for battle."

"And used them, I gather."

"*Oui, M'sieu*. And used also energy. He cut cables and stood to sea. As swift and sure as ever sailor or admiral has been. He flung himself from the bay to make an answering to this threat. And how has the answering fared? We cannot tell. So we sit with our patience."

Washington couldn't help a smile. Lafayette's enthusiasm for anyone who showed energy, initiative, was still refreshing. He said, though, "The admiral wrote he would be here to co-operate with us."

"He is," Lafayette said. "He is! Only—"

"Only he's not."

"Then," Lafayette said, his lips happy above his white teeth, "then let us think him here." He flicked a hand. "De Grasse could have been by now—*comment dit-on?*—caged. Caught in the landward waters and no space for stirring. But he has the will to fight, thanks to God. De Grasse is one for action. Is bold. . . . He put to sea. He will rout the enemy ships. You will hear."

And Lafayette smiled a bright smile, and hacked at his serving of the roast with a hungry knife.

With that, Washington had no choice. He was pulled to Lafayette all the more for the youngster's buoyancy and optimism.

Without those, Lafayette would have been laid low, long before, here in Virginia, by Cornwallis' venomed slashes. For Cornwallis, beginning to feel on the defensive in Virginia as he had been in the Carolinas with Greene, had stormed into the state with the sworn purpose of obliterating the French boy.

So far he had not obliterated him. And that "so far" sat content between Washington and the marquis.

But one thought occurred. Or, rather, it was the thought perpetual. "Marquis," Washington said, as he ate his dinner, "if de Grasse should be beaten?"

Lafayette's fork was halfway to his mouth. He had no prophecy, no explanation. He merely looked at Washington and shrugged.

The shrug said a great deal.

The ground under his feet changed from mire to gold, as on that night of the miracle frost before the Princeton battle, and he was raised from dumps to heights. For while de Grasse was at his sea fight, a squadron of French from Newport, flagged by the Comte de Barras, slid into the roadstead untouched, and gave the final power over salt wave and tide. And within not too many days de Grasse was back at anchorage himself, having mauled his enemy in a length of sea fight. So the sea was shut against Cornwallis, and the land also.

Washington went to council with de Grasse aboard the admiral's flagship. De Grasse, who topped him by an inch, embraced him French fashion and laughed then, and said, "My dear little General!"

De Grasse could linger, would linger, till mid-October in the Chesapeake. Would set ashore several thousand sailors from his ships. The meeting ran swimmingly. The admiral was gracious, eager to be of service. He had heard of Mr. Washington, was delighted to be at his military side. . . . And if Washington felt like a poor relation in the face of all this French wealth, well, he'd known poor relationship before, and knew how to be humble toward it.

His only troublement was a tempest on the Chesapeake which raged for two days, and battered and hampered the sloop which should have brought him to land.

He rode the storm out until the second day and then set out, like a cork, in a small boat, for he'd never been afraid of water, and splashed ashore and got horses for Williamsburg.

He was intent on getting the siege started.

It would not be a siege in the color of chivalry and the Middle Ages. No forays in full strength, no grisly battlings under the loom of parapets, not even a siege of the Dutch towns in the jockeying murders of Queen Elizabeth and the splayed victories of Marlborough. This would be a foredoomed siege with sand ramparts and a river village and an openness of approaches, and an absoluteness that the village under the river bluffs and the enemy garrison would fall.

They'd all ridden over from Williamsburg now, the officers and the staff, and he'd slept on the ground for a night and then moved to a house where he could quarter. And Jack had joined him, trotting down from Eltham, the Bassett place. He thought Jack looked tired, possibly from a night of casual prodding in Williamsburg; but seemed well enough; and asked if there would be any leave for aides or subalterns. He said no, and that sex wolves would be court-martialed. And then he realized that Jack had been laughing.

"I don't sleep reckless, Papa," he said, "and you've the clamps on Cornwallis. Everybody says."

But excitement ran a little too high in his cheeks.

"Get your sleep, Jack," Washington said. He had an urge to look, to peer more closely, and yet he didn't want to humiliate the boy.

"Get your sleep," he said. "And fight off the charms of Williamsburg for a few weeks. The women like you?"

"Yes, they do."

"Get your sleep."

He wished he hadn't this responsibility on his hands while he had the greater responsibility of subduing Cornwallis. But Martha and Nellie had laid it on him.

In the scour of Yorktown he would not forget Jack.

Siege guns were needed, and Knox was slapping them into position. The going was slow, for the sandy soil and the heat and the shot from Cornwallis. But Knox contrived special carriages, and picked out judicious spots for his roarers, to cover sappers and diggers and slam at Cornwallis' embrasures. The first cannon, by right and by sentiment of Knox, was fired by Washington.

He was, by now, alert to sentiments. He was also alert to results. Knox was, in a way, going maudlin as well as partaking of formalism by asking him to fire the first gun at Yorktown. But from the viewpoint of the public and the states, that, he supposed, was what Knox should have done. He was beginning to realize the value of a gesture, the swept assertion. Yet at the same time he saw the hollowness of it. Could any man, granting he would want to make himself big in the public eye, so caper and mouth in front of a footlight? The audience would know the play-acting and reject him. His shyness, his reasoned modesty told him so.

But he put fire to the touchhole of Knox's gun, and the fieldpiece boomed.

"The work is done," he said to Knox, "and well done."

The replies from Cornwallis were weak. His lordship hadn't the number of guns Knox had. He could do hardly more than pepper the flat, sandy plain with cannon balls that were a larger nuisance than a danger. If a man kept his eyes and ears about him he could fairly guess, as on the bumpy fields outside Boston, where a ball would hit. It was just a matter of dodging. The whole camp heard, and hugged the tale, of von Steuben and Wayne, and a roundshot whistling at them. And von Steuben, active for all his hulk, tumbling into a trench. And Wayne on top of him. And von Steuben, growling over his shoulder, "I always knew you were brave, Wayne, but I didn't know you were so perfect. You cover your general's retreat in the best possible manner."

Von Steuben's trench was one of many, for the siege was a matter of digging and digging. Of shoveling nearer to the two covering redoubts and to the main walls. The light, easy-spaded soil made the digging possible, and the French engineers with Rochambeau had skill in such matters. The guns boomed incessantly, and men dug and scooped out parallels, and nosed like moles toward Cornwallis' parapets.

And the parapets, being formed of the same soil, began to be knocked about. Is there ever a child who, at the seashore, hasn't heaped up a sand castle against the advancing sea tide? And failed? Been driven out because the sand insisted on crumbling? Lord Cornwallis was in something of the same position.

It was, in a way, not so much a siege as the painful playing out of a foregone conclusion.

But Cornwallis struck for time. Even, perhaps, for escape.

He held Yorktown, and the village of Gloucester, a mile away across the York River. If he could reach Gloucester with his army the whole Maryland shore would be open to him. He was too clever a general to let that pass. He threw out his best cavalry raider, a man better than Arnold and more ruthless, Banastre Tarleton. Tarleton probed out of Gloucester toward that saving Maryland shore, and was trampled by the Duc de Lauzun. Literally trampled, as the news screamed back from the affray. Tarleton had been unhorsed, and the duke had pushed at him and borne him to the ground. Cornwallis' thrust had been cut off.

There came another gambit. Cornwallis had ships and longboats, enough to make him water-borne if he wished. So he embarked his troops in the boats, and keeled them off for the other shore, to Gloucester village and perhaps his saving. But that same night the wind blew and the sea rose (the thought of Scripture may not be amiss here), and the boats faltered in the tossing space of storm, and pulled back to Yorktown for their shelter.

From then, it was inevitable.

And, because of that, Washington turned impatient. He had a boy's eagerness to see for himself how fast the trenches were burrowed forward each day. The inspections he made took him closer and closer to the enemy guns, far from the American and French tents, that quiet, imponderable half moon on the Yorktown sands. Once he invited a local parson to ride with him, and a ball fell at their feet, and there was a spray of sand and dirt. The parson got up from his face, where he had flung himself, and would have dusted off his hat, but Washington said, "Mr. Evans, you'd better carry that home and show it to your wife and children."

He pushed and pushed to slice the trenched parallels nearer to the enemy works. He wanted the thing over with soon. He wanted for the states their right of freedom, nothing more. He wanted a stalemate, a chance for the diplomats, so that he could go home.

Of course there was no stalemate. Not until Cornwallis was taken.

He was eager for that. An aide, Colonel Cobb, tried to urge him away from enemy shot, for he rode out reckless.

"You are too much exposed here, Your Excellency. Hadn't you best step back a little?"

But his answer was, "Colonel, if you are afraid you have liberty to step back."

This was said with a laugh, of course, the recognition of the colonel as no coward but as a man of precautions for his general.

Precautions led him to think of Jack. He sent for the boy.

Jack presented himself. He looked thinned, and his color was still not good.

"Papa—sir?"

"Jack, are you well?"

"Tolerably, sir."

"But not entirely."

"No. It'll pass, though."

"See a doctor, Jack. Go to a doctor. I can have Dr. Craik down."

"Oh, Lord, Papa, it's not that heavy."

"You get your rest. You're not used to camp life. What do you do at night, Jack? Make for Williamsburg?"

There were, naturally, whorehouses at Williamsburg.

"Oh, Papa," Jack said, "I couldn't ride that far."

Washington scanted the reluctance in the boy's tone. He said, "What symptoms, Jack?"

"Bowels, Papa." He looked ashamed. "I seem to have come all apart."

"That's not good. I'll send for Dr. Craik."

"Oh, don't, Papa, please. I mean until—"

"Until what?"

"Until Yorktown, sir. The surrender. It's bound to come. I've got to see it."

"You can see it. But, Jack—"

"Sir?"

"You'll go to Aunt Bassett's afterward."

"Yes, sir."

"And I'll send a surgeon to look to you."

"Yes, sir."

"And the symptoms?"

"I've told you, Papa."

"We'll have Dr. Craik."

And Jack was gone. Washington sat for a time, considering. Why did this boy—well, young man now, grant him that—want to see Lord Cornwallis surrender? Could it be a personal feeling, after all the laughter and disrespect? But that was something he could not fathom.

Then, having put a surgeon to watch, he let Jack be smothered in military actions. For they took the two outer redoubts, as his French had told him they would. Hamilton, for action now, and given a colonelcy of the line, and Guillaume Deux-Ponts for the French. And with only nine dead, and few wounded, they carried the redoubts, and brought the noose tighter around Cornwallis' neck.

He became happier and happier. There were three times as many French as Americans. Thirty-one thousand French. But they subdued themselves to the Americans, humbly and with the line of helpfulness, as the Comte de Rochambeau did with him. And they plainly knew how to fight, how to besiege.

And all the time, day upon day, the sanded piles of Cornwallis' works crumbled and sagged.

At last, as they had all foreguessed, there was a white flag.

Cornwallis was forming his ranks to march out. Not with shot and bayonets, but with muskets empty and flags cased, surrendering with the honors of war.

It had come at last—a few dickerings over this and that, Cornwallis trying to get the same privileges Gates had given Burgoyne on almost the same date four years ago, but finding that Washington was not a Gates, and then capitulating entirely, there being nothing else to be done.

It had come. And Washington sat astride his Nelson horse—picked because the horse was steady in the face of noise and because of the honor to Virginia's governor—and looked over the sand-blunt plain, and the wagons and carts and local folk come to see the show, and on and on, past the yards and the rods, along the armies.

They were lined up on parade, stiffly, self-conscious under the eyes of top commanders, self-conscious after conquest a basketful of their fellow men. Or perhaps they exulted over a beaten army. No one knows the thoughts of the common soldier, for each is different. But the generality can be sensed by someone alert to those minds, who can draw them out to him. Washington could do that, and that had been his secret with them. That, and his honesty. The honesty he didn't take as a virtue. It was his by nature. A contrived honesty, of course, would be a warped thing.

There flittered over the plain the beat of Cornwallis' drums.

Washington had often thought of himself as a player pushed reluctant to the footlights. He thought of himself, now, as horribly on a great stage. He thought of the news that would go, up and down, up and down, all along the Atlantic coast, from state to state, of how General Washington had sat his horse, and so-and-so and so-and-so, and what he had said, and which arm he had moved, and whether he had had to scratch his nose. And he felt more clamped than ever Cornwallis had been.

With the drum beats, as the distance shorted, came the sound of bands. Well, naturally, Cornwallis would come out with music.

His own bands played well, too. With more enthusiasm than skill. The French had overdone them, being gay and precise. The French were also white-gaitered, reminding him of dogwood in a Virginia spring. They were sprightly and practised.

Rochambeau sat his saddle, opposite, across the road.

Behind, Jack was getting his view of the surrender. Though Jack had to be braced by riders on each side of him. The boy was really ill. He shouldn't have stayed. As it was, Washington had sent for Dr. Craik. And Martha and Nellie should come down from Mt. Vernon, and Jack would go prompt to Aunt Bassett after this play was over.

Its formality had been planned. He only had to take his part in it. His aide John Laurens, and the Vicomte de Noailles, had scrubbed it out with Lord Cornwallis. A formality, a pageant, a saving of face. He was particularly glad that John Laurens had a hand in this. Laurens' father, who had been president of the Congress, was now a prisoner in the Tower of London, and Lord Cornwallis, by force of his title, was commander of that tower. This created a fillip that Washington enjoyed.

Dust formed itself into a cloud, earth-hugging, over the Yorktown breastworks.

Humphreys said in his ear, "They're approaching, sir. But slow."

"I wouldn't think they'd run to it," he said.

Humphreys laughed and reined back.

Washington was left alone, conspicuous in front of everyone. His shyness came on him again. All these people, all the thoughts, all this showiness centered on him. He didn't want it that way. If Cornwallis was beaten, he was beaten. Why the pride and the fulsomeness? He rubbed the rocks of his mind against each other, and in the slow wear of the grinding found the answer. Cornwallis was a shibboleth. A password. As was he. And as he would be. A figure of success for time to point at. This meeting, now, between him and Cornwallis, would go for painters' canvases and writers' wordings. Only that. No one, at any day to come, would read or picture exactly what he felt.

And with that, he knew the sharp and minored chord in life that sets each man to asking, "Why?" And knew too well the pain of an asking. Inscrutability.

He ran his tongue over the iron wires that held his teeth.

"Colonel Cobb," he said.

Cobb was by him at once. "Sir?"

"Ah," he said. "I'm sorry—ah—nothing, Colonel."

"Yes, sir." Cobb reined back, as Humphreys had done. The two traded looks.

"It's been so long for him."

"Very long. And he's not one for fanfare."

"No. He's uneasy in this performance."

"Wouldn't you be?"

"Yes."

"Then grant it him."

"I'll do. And you could never guess from his public manner."

So the aides talked low, with sly breath, unheard. And the drums and music from Yorktown thrummed nearer, and Washington looked at the stiff lines of troops on either side of him, and himself in their center, and the audience of civilians crowding the background, and all the French in their lines across the road, taking their mark from him. He was, at that moment, the first man of the continent. And was the last man to wish it.

In his shyness he motioned Knox toward him. He needed talk.

"His lordship is surrendering in good faith, Knox, and with my promise of his safety. But the Congress may order me to hang him."

"Hang Cornwallis?"

"I've had report of some such."

"It'll never be brought to debate," Knox said.

"But if it is?"

"Then hell take the Congress."

He sucked his lip. "You may have a point there, Knox. You may have a point."

"You'd not obey that order."

"For the first time in my life, no. I'm not a barbarian."

"The Congress has a few hotheads," Knox said, in his deep-piled, resonant voice, "but it has heads with sense in 'em. Sullivan, for example. Or New York's Duane. Or Virginia's Harrison. They know something of the world. It's those who don't know the world who are dangerous. But I'd say a motion to hang Cornwallis won't reach the floor, and couldn't pass."

"I hope so. Because of my word."

"I think they'll recognize that," Knox said.

He reined a little to the rear, like the others, for the surrender column was in sight now, and Washington must be left the dominant figure, the leader in the drama.

Of course, victory was a sweet taste to him. But as with every sweetness, disturbed and contrary thoughts wafted at him. He couldn't be sure this surrender would end the war. Cornwallis' army was smallish, hemmed in, battered by an unexpected gathering of forces. Clinton in New York had another army, larger than this one plodding toward him. Fighting could still drag on. He put that thought frankly to himself. Burgoyne had been stopped at Saratoga, and all the troops of that invasion, but the war hadn't stopped.

Strange he should think of Saratoga, waiting here in the middle of this expanse of sand and sun and men and trappings. Cornwallis' flag of truce had come to him on its anniversary. Some of the officers who'd been at that battle had planned a celebration dinner in the camp, until the bigger news had burst. He was not superstitious, didn't believe in omens and portents, and the coincidence came only from the fact that summer campaigns reached a climax one way or the other in the autumn —but it *was* a close coincidence.

With Saratoga, he thought of Gates. Of the contrast between him and Gates since the day they had sat on the portico of Mt. Vernon and Gates had asked his help for getting a command in the Congress army. Gates was at home now, the disgrace of Camden clouding his Saratoga glory. While he—Washington? There was a twist in it, more than a touch of the fickleness of things, the unforeseeable win-or-lose that might come with the next flip of the card. He knew Gates as a good organizer who'd served well. If he'd schemed, insinuated, whispered behind backs, that was the result, most likely, of Mrs. Gates's nagging. Mrs. Gates wasn't a Martha. And he himself had been genuine in offering Gates the command of the right wing of the army against Yorktown. But Gates had refused.

From Gates his thoughts went to Greene. Greene was still fighting in South Carolina. Recently there had been word of him, cheery word. A spot with the name of Eutaw Springs. And Greene had neatly, with exquisite tactics, slipped another dagger under the ribs of the London ministry's plan to beat the South to earth. The South refused to be beaten to earth. He'd heard the doings of Sumter—Marion—and Greene's precise battles wore down his opponents' strength.

He wished Greene were with him.

But Greene wasn't, and time was on him full.

Past the double line of his troops—Continentals in front, militia in rear—past the neighborhood gapers and the officers on horseback, the column on the Yorktown Road thumped closer.

Drums there were. Foot beats, foot beats. Drums.

He could see the officer from Yorktown who rode ahead of the first troops.

He could hear the music of the surrendering soldiers—well played, persuasive, acidly martial—and recognized the tune, "The World Turned Upside Down." Apt, he thought; very apt, from their view. They were having to humble themselves, which was hard on them.

And then he saw the leading officer more clearly.

The officer was swarthy, weather-burned. He wore few decorations. Certainly not Lord Cornwallis. He wore a loosed sword.

With quiet dignity, a balance between superciliousness and an amazed respect, the officer reached the spot between Washington and Rochambeau, the one on one side of the road, the other on the other. He hesitated, spoke to Rochambeau.

"Your Excellency—"

Rochambeau could have taken the surrender, but no trace of such an idea showed in his face.

"To your right, sir. General Washington is on your right."

The officer bowed in the saddle and turned. He put his horse toward Washington, unsheathed his sword and offered it.

"I am," he said. "Brigadier General O'Hara, the only general his lordship has with him. And I have the honor to be in his lordship's stead, since his lordship the Earl Cornwallis is unfortunately indisposed. But if His Excellency General Washington will be pleased to accept my sword—"

Washington interrupted. Cornwallis was too proud—too flustered at his situation—perhaps too snobbish—to surrender in person to a backwoods leader of a pack of colonials. Or he may have been definitely ill. His lordship had had a difficult row to hoe in the Virginia campaign. This surrender could not be altogether laid on his shoulders. His spirit must revolt at it.

All this went through Washington's mind in the space of a second or two.

He saw O'Hara's proffered sword.

"Never from such a good hand," he said, and signaled O'Hara to General Lincoln, on his right. "Pass on," he said, knowing his military etiquette, and that Lincoln was his second in command, as O'Hara was Cornwallis'.

Lincoln received O'Hara's sword, returned it at once. The exchange was a gesture, and Lincoln was too kindly to prolong it. A person civilized, a person who sought the amenities, did not twist knives in the wounds of the fallen. "The surrender ground is yonder, General O'Hara. Will you direct your troops?"

They were directed. They stacked their arms. They behaved perfectly and abjectly. Some of them were fairly well drunk.

That night Washington gave a dinner for O'Hara.

That night he sent his report to the Congress. Humphreys wrote it out for him. It was as plain and simple as possible, for he was weary of flourishes after these hours of them.

Tench Tilghman would carry the report. He added a recommendation that Tilghman might be promoted, in the Congress' generosity, to brigadier.

Then his day was over.

Or not quite. Because he went to see Jack. Jack lay in a tent not far from headquarters, on a kind of cot like the one Washington carried with him and which could be rolled up and slung into a wagon, and Jack threshed around considerably, his arms over the covers and his legs under them, and the surgeon attending said, "Camp fever, sir."

"Dysentery."

"Yes, Your Excellency."

Washington spun on the heels of his boots. "Tench!"

Tilghman was never out of call. "Sir?"

"Make arrangements to have Jack taken at once to his aunt's plantation. He mustn't stay here a day. Get him there as fast as possible—by coach or carriage—but don't tire him by the ride. Do that, Tench."

"I will, sir."

To Jack, Washington said, "You're going to Aunt Bassett's. The quicker the better. I should not have let you stay."

"I'll be all right, Papa. It's just that I shake so."

"And pass your inwards out."

"Yes."

"Well, Jack, I've given orders. Aunt Bassett's it will be. But you mustn't race there, you mustn't be worn by the trip. Do you understand? Will you abide by that?"

"Yes, Papa," Jack said. Then, as if correcting himself in front of Tilghman and the surgeon, he gave a fluttering wink and a try at a grin. "Yes, General."

XXI

"Where Else Would I Be?"

He wanted to follow Jack to Eltham, the Bassett plantation, as soon as he could. From there he would go on to Mt. Vernon and beyond that to Philadelphia, for the Congress would wish to have the account of Yorktown from his own lips. But he was a prisoner to the niceties, the actions and courteousness expected of him, and to the smooth unraveling of the great land-and-sea fabric he had woven together hardly more than a month ago.

Tilghman went off the day after the surrender, with the Congress message, and riding guard for Jack, who was lifted into a light coach and managed a wave of hand as the little group pulled out.

"For the expenses of your trip, Tench," Washington said, "you'll have to apply to the Congress."

"Yes, sir." Tench knew that cash was at rock bottom again. The members of the Congress would probably have to dig into their own breeches to find money for Tench's victory trip.

Humphreys would go a few days later, with stands of the captured regimental banners to offer to the Congress.

Lafayette's troops had to be shifted to another command, for there would unlikely be any more action this year and Lafayette was champing to get to his wife and family in France. "But I'll come back, I promise," he said.

"I hope you will, Marquis," Washington said.

"To sit with you and your amiable lady at Mt. Vernon would be a joy," the youngster said. "But *que voulez-vous?*—I also have a lady."

"You should go and comfort her," Washington said.

The marquis laughed, grew serious. "We should also comfort France,"

[299]

he said. "We must carry liberty. I will fetch you news of that when I come back."

"There, Marquis, I can't speak honestly. I don't know the French people. But avoid rashness. Our own liberty might have a different complexion if King George were in this country instead of beyond an ocean."

"What are you thinking of, sir?" Lafayette said, not entirely bristling, but on the defensive.

"Perhaps of the Boston mobs before the spark at Lexington," Washington said. "The street gangs in New York. Colonel Lynch hanging Tories in Virginia. Ugly things. They might have been uglier, Marquis, if there'd been a royal scapegoat at hand, a monarch's palace to be stormed instead of a mere governor's mansion. I wonder if you understand our independency. It is something withdrawn to itself. It is being won from the top, not from below. This war is not a clawing, a tearing down, an overturning. It is only a separation. But if you throw independency into closer quarters, where hate can boil and passions can be squeezed to eruption—" he looked at Lafayette and shrugged.

"You won't strip me of my ideals, *mon Général?*"

"No, Marquis, by no means. Go to France, and hold your ideals, and convey my gallantest wishes to your lady, the marquise. And come to us again when you can." The eyes of both said they thought that would be soon. And so there was no impossible sorrow in their parting.

There was then the dinner to Cornwallis. Custom prescribed it, as he'd had the Hessian officers to dine after Trenton. His lordship was eliminated from the fight now, on his parole not to act again against America, and could be accorded a gentleman's tribute.

The earl was very civil, though eating gall and wormwood, and made no display of sulk or pettiness. He seemed to have rallied from the first damnation of his fate, and to be determined to push through the genteel ceremonies in good order. He appeared to be astonished, chiefly, that Washington made so little of his own standing. "Your Excellency's name," he said, "is on the lips of every American, every European. The stare of the world is on you, sir. But you worry whether or not my hat is on my head, lest I come to a rheum."

"And I worry," Washington said, "if the world will approve my clothes. If I'm to be stared at."

"You have little to reproach yourself for in the way of dress, Your Excellency."

Which was pleasant, but not quite true. Clothes had never been his best point. He was in a way fastidious, but very plain in dress. He'd been taught by the frontier.

Then, at the dinner, of course the toasts.

Rochambeau gave the first. "To the United States."

Washington gave the second. "To the King of France."

Cornwallis gave the third. "The king."

Washington laughed, and sent his voice out higher. "Of England," he said. "Keep him there and I'll drink his health in a bumper." And he reached for the decanter and filled his glass till the wine spilled over.

So it made a convivial evening, an evening pleasantly remote, as such evenings are meant to be, with wine-drooped eyelids against the cares that, life being life and humanity humanity, were irremediably to come. It crayoned a parenthesis in the patriotism and the partition of the times. Men, gentlemen, who forty-eight hours ago would have gutted one another with cannon balls, sat and dined and wined in—well, if not amity, certainly in etiquette and the lace of polite phrases.

It did not occur to them that their century was unusual. It did not occur to them that in the advance of cultures and manner and gentility anything could possibly be otherwise. There was a chivalry there, a long-pulled but rooted chivalry from the Middle Ages, when baron against baron could spraddle the fall of one or the other, but when all was said and done, the overthrown, the ransomed one, was still a baron. It was a game played by the rules, and the rules had existed for a thousand years. Ever since King John of France had been captured with his young son at Poitiers, and neither had been drawn and quartered. One dined the loser, and went on to win more dazzlingly, if possible.

Time passed while Washington tried to argue de Grasse into staying in American waters, into helping Greene to retake Charleston. But the admiral answered from his flagship that he had stayed too long already. His main goal was the West Indies. He was hurried more by sighting, off Yorktown, an enemy fleet out of New York under Admiral Graves, bringing Sir Henry Clinton and thousands of troops to relieve Cornwallis. It was too late for relief, the surrender was already done. Yet Graves could choose to smash his way into the roadstead and possibly catch de Grasse at moorings and certainly with no room for maneuver, and for some hours there was a strong tugging of anxiousness to know if he might. Graves, however, did not risk a tangle with de Grasse and sailed north again; and very soon afterward de Grasse's sails melted into the haze of the southern horizon—rather, Washington judged from the speed, to de Grasse's own relief. It had been a brave and dangerous thing for him to do, to anchor for weeks in the unprotected and confining York waters. Washington granted that the French admiral's stanchness had given even more than he had promised.

Finally the last scrapings and bowings were ended, the last papers written out for moving the army to the Hudson again, the last good-bys wined and spoken between him and Rochambeau, who would be going back to France now, a victory achieved. And he could leave the York-town plain.

He kept his travel party small. One or two aides, a light escort. Humphreys with the battle standards for the Congress. The morning, as they picked toward the road for Eltham, was bright and warmish; and they took their own of it, threading at relaxed walk and trot against the russet-golden curtain of early November in the Virginia peninsula.

He stopped at Williamsburg to make a tour of the hospital there. To talk with the wounded men and the sick ones. They weren't having the care they should have. He knew that. The army's hospitals had been horror holes for all these years, and more patriots had died of sickness and cold and under-nourishment and no medicines and no nursing than had ever been riddled by hot lead or cold steel. It had been no one's fault—Dr. Shippen, Dr. Thacher, those who headed the medical branch, had worked to the bone, were devoted. The country, the states, the people were simply unprepared, unequipped to deal with military hospitals. When you throw yourself against an enemy in a spate of fury, you don't think of your wounded. The country hadn't anyway. Could hardly have been expected to. But at least he could show his gratefulness to these cripples. They had kept his army in one piece. He could show his immense indebtedness, and his sympathy.

They seemed to look at him with new eyes. And he thought, leaving the hospital, that since Yorktown so many men and women had seemed to look at him with new eyes, as if he had all at once grown larger and larger in their sight until they were dwarfed, and willing to be dwarfed as long as they could admire.

He doubted if the victory at Yorktown—now the thrill of it was over, the turn in the road of hope-deferred put behind him—he doubted, and pendulumed in his mind from jubilation to sober accounting. The victory might not be as much as it seemed. Nothing was changed, basically, except that the thorn of Cornwallis had been dug out with a sharp penknife.

Outside the military frame, the scene was still a fighting. He would be fighting the Congress, a ramshackle association of thirteen states, each squalling its own destiny and its own interests; would be fighting the merchants and profiteers and ghouls, who would as well sell to an enemy as to the country that gave them nourishment and protection, digging under their own ramparts like rats, and the first to scream for help when the ramparts fell; would be fighting for a justice for those who had borne the burden of the war, the plain soldiers, the troops, the starved and frozen and trudged, with swelled tongues like heat-crazed dogs at Monmouth, with stink-sweat and bleeding feet at Valley Forge, while the nice ones and the neat merchants sat at home.

No, it was not done yet.

He had grown in this war. Had set his hand to a small plough and turned a furrow, surprisingly, for a nation. He had not meant this. And hoped he would not have to track that furrow much longer. But feared he would. For who else was there? Who was to walk the furrow of the future? He thought he would leave it to Jefferson. To Adams. To the Congress, in its wisdom. For he had walked for many years, and was like to walk for years more. He was longing for Mt. Vernon.

He could give only one advice to those who might make a nation afterward. And the advice was simple. Destroy the rats, poison them out, exterminate them. And if a man were only half-educated, or had only a half stake in the sweep and surge of his country, he would recognize the rats as well as the next. And perhaps, just perhaps, those who might make the nation might remember that it was not made by gifts of gold and silver, but by sacrifice. And they might turn on the rats and trample them, and bring all that had led to Yorktown to a fruition.

Cha . . . It was too good to be true. Decency couldn't be accomplished. Too many men were flagrantly dirty—selfish, criminal, gone for the main chance. Too many were naked of ethics, stripped bare of any sense of what made a wholesome people. And too stripped to have any conscience when their nakedness was exposed. Men who would take the altars of Valley Forge and eat the sacrificial meat of them. Men who didn't deserve, by any judgment, to be a part of the nation he had wrought. Men whose only battle cry was Self, and Self, and Self.

It would depend—and he thought now with that long-foreseeing thought that is given to those who love a land and strive for it—it would depend on whether the land would win, or the crawling lice. The people who had been freed, or the maggots. In the years to come, that would be the choice of Americans.

He didn't know why he puzzled at these things, except that the stenches of the hospital had given his stomach a queasiness, and the sights had sharpened his disgust for less devoted men.

He ate a moderate meal at Williamsburg and started for Eltham.

The message met him while he was on the way.

He and his aides had stopped at the tavern, Bird's Ordinary, and were eating late dinner when the rider pulled up at the door.

There was a note for him, which he read.

"It's Jack," he said. A hollowness in his voice kept his aides silent.

The message said that he should hurry.

He did. Eltham wasn't far, not as reckoned distance in a lathering run.

They galloped. The night was fine—clear, with innumerable stars. The road unfolded before them, a grayish ribbon. He didn't speak.

Presently, for their horses, they had to come to a walk. He felt Humphreys draw alongside him. His aides wanted to protect him. He sensed that. They wanted to hearten him.

"Worry won't help, sir," Humphreys said, "about Jack." His calling him "Jack" seemed somehow not disrespectful in the way he said it, for the two had begun to be friends. "Thinking of him won't help—until we get there."

"Have you thought of General Gates?"

Humphreys jerked his breath in, an involuntary sound, said, "Well, sir—" and dropped back to the flank. They all remembered that Gates had lost his son after Camden. After a field of war. No one spoke for the rest of the ride. Camden, of course, had been a loss; and Yorktown was a gain. But still this could be another coincidence—and, like it or not, fair or not, Jack's report was critical.

They galloped again, slacked for a mile or so, went into the gallop. Through a breathing pearl of dawn they reached Eltham.

The Bassetts were at the door. The noise of the coming had run ahead. Negroes stood for the horses' bridles, ready to stable them. The front hall was lighted.

Washington scanted the introductions. They would have wasted time. "Gentlemen, Mr. and Mrs. Bassett," he said, and went upstairs to where Jack was.

A Negress showed him to the room. She'd been crying.

Martha was in the room, and Nellie, and little Eliza. Dr. Craik. There was a stillness of candles in the room, and a curious hush. Martha came to him, her face drawn. All their faces were the same, drawn and muted. He touched Martha's hand and went over to the bed.

Jack lay on the bed as pale as paper. His arms were under the body-raised sheet and quilt. They didn't move. Jack's eyes were shut and he breathed shallowly.

A pang smote into Washington, pronged and anguished. There was no evading it. He wasn't the old fox, in the face of this. No evasion here, no tactic or strategy, no council of war, no leap to the saddle or chatter of guns. Here was the absolute. The unavoidable. Here was death.

Jack was beyond speech. He didn't try him. He leaned and set a father's kiss on the young father's cheek.

He straightened then, lumped in his throat, and looked for Dr. Craik. This loyal man had been his friend and surgeon for so many years.

"Well, Doctor?"

"I can't give any hope, General. Only a few hours left."

Washington swept eyes around the room. He had a moment of panic, of more than panic, as of a dropping of the road into an unforeseen pit, as of a proud-built structure brought to rubble by a shift of the earth.

"Only hours?"

"Or less." The doctor's voice was modulated to a death room.

"Has everything been done?"

"Everything."

He knew Craik would have done everything. Craik had hauled him, by sheer will power he often thought, through his own fevers. Craik had delivered most of Jack's and Nellie's children. Craik had watched over the family and dosed them and scolded them and cured them. Craik had—

It was too much for him. He looked at Martha, at Nellie, at Eliza, at the doctor's grave eyes, and at Jack's closed ones, and went from the room.

The next room had a sofa in it. He dropped full length. It did not surprise him to be hearing himself sob, or to be tasting the salt of tears that ran from his cheeks onto his lips.

It was Dr. Craik who told him Jack was dead.

"He never regained consciousness," the doctor said.

"I'll go to Martha," Washington said.

"She's with him, with Jack," the doctor said in a quiet authoritative voice, choosing this way of saying that she needed to be by herself at the side of Jack's bed for a few moments. "But Nellie's here."

Washington stood up and Nellie came in.

The first agony of loss had wept itself out, but her eyes were rimmed with red.

"Papa—" she said.

She half stumbled toward him, and there was nothing to say, nothing to do, but to put his arm about her shoulders and smother her against his great height and try to comfort.

"Nellie—" he said heavily. "Nellie, Nellie."

"Papa, it's so past remedy."

"Yes."

"While he was alive, I could still hope for remedy. Oh, Papa, I dearly loved him."

"He never doubted it, my dear. And I loved him, too."

"I know. I know what he meant to you and how much you did for him. He was like your own son. And even if he was headstrong sometimes and didn't like to be kept from what he wanted—oh, Papa, why didn't I keep him from going to Yorktown?"

"You couldn't have guessed he'd take the fever, dear. You might better ask why I didn't order him away sooner, instead of letting him stay on. I'm more at fault than you."

"I think there should be no more of that," Dr. Craik broke in. "If you commence reproaching yourselves I shall have to be harsh on both of you." He kept on talking with the same quiet authority, easing the tenseness of emotion, as a violinist stills the quivering strings of his instrument with a smoothing palm. "You'll fetch this nonsense to his mother's ears, and she'll feel that she shares the guilt and she'll suffer double. Jack could as well have come safe through Yorktown as not. In five years no other aide of yours has died of the fever, General, and you had no reason to think Jack would. Just as Nellie had no reason to think of fever at all. These are chances everyone must take with life, all through life. Blaming yourselves about Jack and Yorktown is like blaming yourselves for having stairs in your house when someone tumbles down them. Forgive me for playing schoolmaster, but you are also my patients as Jack was, and it is my concern to keep your minds from brooding, which leads to morbidity, which leads to a pit of dark. Nellie, my dear, unless you feel you can sleep—and I shouldn't wonder at you if you didn't— you'd do best to keep yourself occupied. Grief is a toothed saw that requires dulling by activity."

"Yes. Yes," Nellie said. "The beds and meals for Papa's staff to be seen to. And Eliza. I must go to her. Aunt Bassett took her across the hall just before—before—" She left the final words unsaid. "Thank you, Doctor. Thank you, Papa," she said, and went out.

"The girl has spirit," Dr. Craik said.

"I've always said so," Washington said.

"She'll bear up," the doctor said.

"And Jack's mother?" he said.

The doctor frowned. He delayed his answer for a little, and for once seemed unsure of his ground. "I'd say that lies between you and Mrs. Washington," he said finally. And he added, in a low urging that was not authoritative but gently human, "She has had her moments with him now. I think she would want you to see him."

Washington stepped to the room where Jack lay. Jack's face had not yet been covered, but the quilt had been straightened and made orderly. Martha was on her knees beside the bed. Her head was bent. She did not look up, but she heard him come in, and stretched one of her hands to him along the quilt. He took it in his, and put his other hand against her cheek in a soft, steadying pressure, and stood behind her, wordlessly.

On the next day there were the preparations for the funeral. He sent his staff on ahead of him, for there was no purpose to keeping them there in a house of mourning, and made plans for the burial with his brother-in-law Bassett. They walked together on the terrace, and when the plans were settled, they talked on for a bit.

"How will Martha endure this?" Bassett asked. "In the long term, that is. Her last child, her only son."

"I don't know," he said. "Jack was her life."

He was conscious that Bassett gave him a curious look, as if to say he was right—that they all understood, subtly, that Martha had always appeared to be more wrapped in Jack than she was in anyone else.

"The question as we find it—her sister and I—is whether she'll bury herself with him."

Bassett called this a question. But to Washington it was a nightmare. It was the long riddle woven through his married life with Martha. He had so often wondered, when she gave Jack everything, sided with Jack in everything, if Jack had the most of her heart. He wondered stabbingly now if Jack, dead, would have more of her heart than ever. And now he must tug the riddle out of the marriage cloth, and hold it to the light, and know the answer. It would be a withdrawing from the world and her husband in her greater longing for Jack, or it would be turning to George, her husband, as the source of her solace and future happiness.

He could see, from Bassett's look and words, that the Bassetts realized the riddle and had probably been discussing it. But he had too much reserve to want to explore it aloud any further, even with a brother-in-law.

So he made an excuse about letter writing and went upstairs.

Martha was at the stair head, waiting for him. She led the way into their bedroom. "I've been spying on you," she said, "from the window. I didn't want to miss you. I've something to tell you."

She had brought no black dress with her, but she wore a dark shawl over her shoulders and a black velvet ribbon at her throat. Her eyes were dry, but had a numbed, stunned pain sunk deep in them, and she carried a handkerchief clenched in her hand in case she should begin to cry again.

"Yes, Patsy," he said.

She took his arm. "Ever since we married, George, I've felt your thoughts for him, your kindness. I've seen you care for his education and upbringing and morals, the companionship you gave him when he was younger, and your handling of the money he had from his father. I've felt these and seen them. He was dear to you."

She paused a little. He placed a hand over hers, where it held to his arm. She went on.

"You were the same to him," she said. "Call him spoiled, call him anything you will, you were dear to him. I've felt that too, and I must believe you have."

"I always wanted it so," he said. "There were never any words of it, but naturally there wouldn't have been."

"There are words now, George. He spoke to me yesterday—while he could still speak. He kept asking if you had reached Eltham yet, and when you hadn't, and when he must have guessed he wouldn't be speaking much longer, he told me that he had had sport at Yorktown, and was proud of you, and had a feeling of nearness to you, a—well, you're a man, George, and so was Jacky, and it's difficult to give shape to the feelings between man and man. A woman can't do it, I would think. Perhaps it is something that shouldn't be shaped. But the feeling was there, with him. He made me know it."

She turned her face to him in a smile which couldn't be a smile because of the body, sheeted now, in the next room, and then said, "I'm glad he did."

"So am I, Patsy," he said. A tightness rose in his throat and made him sound thick. He kissed her.

"Tomorrow is the funeral," she said.

"Yes," he said.

The look in her eyes had shifted from pain to the look of a traveler driven into the unknown. Emptiness was in them.

He felt at such loss. He wished with all his soul he could fill that emptiness.

He said, to take her mind from it, "And afterward, Patsy—Nellie and the children."

She said, "The children, poor sweets. Dear Eliza is crushed. The others will be too young to know tragedy, thank God. But something must be done for them."

"Something will," he said.

"They're adrift," she said. "I know that sensation. A young widow and fatherless mites."

"No, Nellie can't manage her plantation and four children."

"She could manage the eldest two. They'll be less care."

"Then we'll find someone suitable to give a home to the two youngest."

"That may not be easy, George. The war and the money troubles have set so many good Virginia families to scrimping."

"If we can't, I'll adopt little Nellie and Baby George as my own."

"Oh!" she said. "Oh, my dearest!" And her breath caught quick, and she put her arms to his neck and kissed him full and long.

"Though I may be overold to start being the father of toddlers," he said, and smiled at her, for he thought she might cry, and they had had enough of weeping and torn hearts in a day and a night.

"You're not, of course you're not," she contradicted. She took a minute to dab at her eyes with her handkerchief and then put it resolutely down. "And, George—there'd be children in the house again, and someone to come home to, and—"

"Someone to come home to?"

"Yes, surely."

"You mean you are intending to be away?" He put the question rather slowly, for the way the talk was trending it might be that this was the time to tug the riddle loose and hold it to the light.

"The war isn't over, is it?" she said, doubling a question back at him.

He looked at her eyes, and the emptiness in them seemed not so great as it had been, as though there were a path, a guide, a landmark for her through the place of shadows. His heart set to a faster beat.

"No," he said, "not until we have a treaty from the king's ministry. Whether they'll fight longer or confer for peace you can guess as well as I, Patsy."

"Then *you'll* be away," she said.

"I'll go to the Hudson again, above the Highlands. I'll watch Clinton in New York and protect West Point. But I may be there all winter." He stopped, and by dint of taking a firm breath effected to keep his voice at a level pitch before he continued. "I thought you might be tired of trailing up and down the land. I thought, considering the change in things, you might want to stay at Mt. Vernon."

She needed only an instant or two to catch his implication. Only another instant to look at him gratefully for his courage, for his bringing the long riddle into the clear, at this bridge of their lives, once for all. Then, neither hurriedly nor deliberately, but as though the riddle had never really been a riddle to her, she shook her head.

"I shan't tuck myself into Mt. Vernon alone with my memories," she said. "Besides, George, where would I ever expect to be, but with you?"

So that was how it was.

He stopped overnight at Fredericksburg on his way north. He'd grown into middle boyhood and adolescence at Fredericksburg, or near it, and his mother and sister lived in the town. He had old friends and acquaintances there and roundabout, both sides of the indolent, shallow-flowing Rappahannock.

But he was surprised at the number of people on the streets as he cantered in. And more surprised at the expressions on their faces and how they behaved. They didn't cheer too loudly for him, they didn't huzzah and toss their hands up for him as the New York crowds had done when he had first ridden from Cambridge. They seemed more to set their eyes on him in a kind of feast, a kind of reverent worship that went below the surface of noisy demonstration, and were content merely to look at him and have him in their midst, the same expressions he had met at Williamsburg and on the roads out of the Yorktown camp.

His mother wasn't in the town. She wasn't at home. She'd gone over the mountains to the mineral springs, for her health. She'd left no message about Yorktown, and it seemed she'd taken no notice of it.

But his sister Betty was at home, in the square-built, red-brick, airy Lewis home of Kenmore, flanked by its neat-proportioned kitchen and outbuildings, with a trimmed garden of box hedge and bedded flowers that ran down in autumn colors to his mother's place. And Fielding Lewis was there, who'd been ruining himself manufacturing muskets for the army. Washington was alarmed at the clamminess of his handclasp and said so.

"Have an eye for his health, Betty," he said. "We don't want another case like Jack's."

"I do what I can," Betty said. "But the cost of patriotism comes high, George."

"His muskets won the Yorktown fight," he said.

It was an exaggeration he felt indebted to make, yet not too far from the truth, and he knew it would please her. It did, and she saw the exaggeration, and thanked him for it with a frank smile.

"You needn't fret for us. I've my two boys, we can hold up our heads. . . . You'll want to rest, George. Any room."

"Yes, Betty."

He climbed the graceful, delicate-balustraded staircase, found a room, tumbled himself to the bed, and stretched to sleep with his boots on.

It seemed weeks later, though it may have been only half a day, that Betty waked him by pulling at his shoulder.

"You've always been so hard to rouse," she said. "Suppose I were Indians? Hey?"

"If you were Indians, Betty," he said, sitting up and scrubbing his eyes, "I wouldn't have slept. I was owing that sleep. What's to do now?"

"A ball," she said.

"A what?"

"A ball and supper tonight. A gala. A rout. A what-you-will. But General Washington is among us and we will make merry."

"Oh, Betty," he groaned.

"Make up your mind to it," she said. "It's an honored night, and you're the honored guest."

"What I ask, what I wish," he said, "is to go to the Congress and make my report. I don't wish galas and adulations."

"M'mm," Betty said. When it came to the rub, her character was the equal of his. She was the type of woman who is called stanch. She was also fearless, and had her brother's innate sense of how to handle people. "I think you'll have no choice, George."

"Please explain yourself."

"Certainly. You've been five years in the field. Your dealings have been with military men or political men. You haven't touched the common men, have you? Like the shopkeepers and apprentices and chemists and small merchants and traders of Fredericksburg. Like the men in hope all through the states. The men in faith. You haven't been able to touch them, see them. The war has kept you from them."

"Betty," he said, "I'm not a toucher or a seer. It's the last thing I want to be. I only want to go home to Mt. Vernon and to my fields. Once this is over."

She paid no attention. "So you don't know the American man, beyond what you know of him as soldier. But he knows you. He's talked of you, praised you, prayed for you, for five years. And he puts his trust in you. Because, I think, George—because of that in you that this man of trust sees might also be in him, that he might like to have."

"You're getting beyond me, Betty."

"Do you think so? Do you think so, George? Very well—make your toilet—you could do with a bit of primping here and there. You're to take me to the ball within an hour. Fielding won't be able."

And there were the same faces, the same awed starings, the ladies curtseying under the candled chandeliers of silver and crystal, and men bowing low, and the same great respectful air, when Washington entered the Fredericksburg ballroom, majestic in buff and blue, his commander's ribbon across his chest and Betty on his arm. He felt the tremor that ran through the room, that set him so much apart from them and yet so strong in their hearts. He would have faltered.

But Betty's arm was firm, lying within his. She steered him forward. "If Martha were here," she said, under her breath, "she could do it better than I. You need women to look after you, George. Every man does."

Though when the music started and the dances commenced, he outdid Betty. He delighted in dancing, and he delighted in that night at Fredericksburg. He was in every set, before going on north to a wintered Hudson again.

On the morning after, he stood on the great square step at the Kenmore door, and kissed Betty on the cheek, and raised his hat, and went down the brick path that opened on the road. With the great arching trees around, and the great staring crowds around—their faith in him, their wonder in him, their hope.

Always that same expression. That reverence. That look that said that even if a man might not be too worth saving, there was still chance for him.

And he thought, as he had said to her before leaving the house, when he had seen them there, "Haven't I done enough for them, Betty? Haven't I done enough?"

And she had said, answering, "They'll never let go of you, George, as long as you're alive."

Then he opened the gate, and tipped his hat again to Betty, and went out toward the road. And the gaping, murmurous crowd nudged itself back.

"Billy, hand me my horse."

And he passed out of their sight, dusty on the road to Mt. Vernon.

Born in St. Louis, Mo., Burke Boyce lived there only long enough to attend kindergarten. His parents took him on a brief tour of Mexico and then moved east, where he received his early education at both private and public schools in Newark, N.J.

After high-school graduation, and before entering Harvard, he did a summer stretch with the Merchant Marine during World War I, making the Atlantic crossing to France. He was awarded his A.B. degree (magna cum laude with honors in English) from Harvard in 1922; his M.A. in 1923, while he was instructing in English at his alma mater. Later he joined his parents in New York City, to write short stories and verse, to make two cycle trips to England and Europe, and finally to sign as editor of a ship's paper on a round-the-world cruise. Following his marriage in 1927, he worked for public relations firms in New York, headed for nine years the Continuity (writing) Department of the National Broadcasting Company, taught radio writing for two winters in the Adult Education Department of N.Y.U. More recently he served as trustee, and then headmaster (four years), of a boys' college-preparatory school, from which he resigned in order to continue his writing.

Having captained the Harvard Fencing Team, and placed twice in the finals of the National Championships, he was selected as a member of the American Olympic Fencing Team which went to Paris in 1924. In 1927, just before his marriage, a taste for dramatics led to the Broadway stage, to a part as one of the principals in a musical revue, The Manhatters.

Burke Boyce's first novel was a story of the American Revolution, The Perilous Night. *In addition to this and* Man from Mt. Vernon, *he has written two other novels,* Miss Mallett *and* Cloak of Folly. *The New*

Yorker *magazine carried two long series of his light verse about New York City, and his short stories have appeared in various magazines.*

His home since the mid-thirties has been at Vail's Gate, N.Y., near the Hudson about ten miles north of West Point, in country made historic by Washington. By appointment of Governor Harriman he is a trustee of Washington's Headquarters at Newburgh.

Since the death of his wife six years ago he lives alone with his three dogs. He has a grown son working for a Ph.D. in astronomy, and a younger daughter who is majoring in sociology at college.

He is perhaps as proud of anything as of the fact that his son, whom he taught, also captained the Harvard Fencing Team.